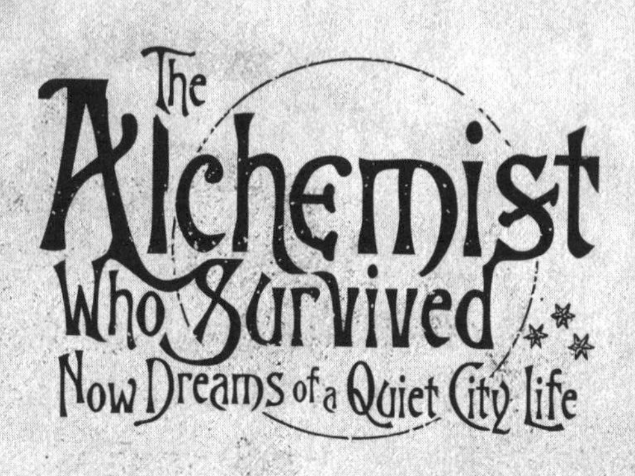

Usata Nonohara

Illustration by OX

06

New York

The Alchemist Who Survived Now Dreams of a Quiet City Life 06

Usata Nonohara

Cover art by **OX** Translation by Erin Husson

IKINOKORI RENKINJUTSUSHI HA MACHI DE SHIZUKANI KURASHITAI
Volume 6

First published in Japan in 2019 by KADOKAWA CORPORATION, Tokyo.
English translation rights arranged with KADOKAWA CORPORATION, Tokyo through TUTTLE-MORI AGENCY, INC., Tokyo.

Yen On
150 West 30th Street, 19th Floor
New York, NY 10001

Visit us at yenpress.com
facebook.com/yenpress
twitter.com/yenpress
yenpress.tumblr.com
instagram.com/yenpress

First Yen On Edition: April 2021

Library of Congress Cataloging-in-Publication Data
Names: Nonohara, Usata, author. | ox (Illustrator), illustrator. | Husson, Erin, translator.
Title: The alchemist who survived now dreams of a quiet city life / Usata Nonohara ; illustration by ox ; translation by Erin Husson.
Other titles: Ikinokori renkinjutsushi ha machi de shizukani kurashitai. English
Description: First Yen On edition. | New York : Yen On, 2019
Identifiers: LCCN 2019020720 | ISBN 9781975385514 (v. 1 : pbk.) | ISBN 9781975331610 (v. 2 : pbk.) | ISBN 9781975331634 (v. 3 : pbk.) | ISBN 9781975331658 (v. 4 : pbk.) | ISBN 9781975310455 (v. 5 : pbk.) | ISBN 9781975314798 (v. 6 : pbk.)
Subjects: | CYAC: Fantasy. | Magic—Fiction. | Alchemists—Fiction.
Classification: LCC PZ7.1.N639 Al 2019 | DDC [Fic]—dc23
LC record available at https://lccn.loc.gov/2019020720

ISBNs: 978-1-9753-1479-8 (paperback)
978-1-9753-1480-4 (ebook)

10 9 8 7 6 5 4 3 2 1

LSC-C

Printed in the United States of America

The Alchemist Who Survived Now Dreams of a Quiet City Life

06

Hey! The Japanese edition of this novel begins with a manga section. To preserve the right-to-left reading orientation of the material, we've moved that section to the back of the book, so flip to the end, read that first, then come back here to enjoy the rest of the story!

The Alchemist Who Survived Now Dreams of a Quiet City Life

06 Contents

PROLOGUE

The Abyss in the Fell Forest

01

"Master, I'm scaaared. The monsters are gonna get me."

"It's all right, Mariela. Daigis covers this house and conceals your magical power, and the bromominthra planted around it has a smell the monsters hate and keeps them away. The monsters won't come all the way here."

"But, Master, the monsters hate people, right?"

"No, Mariela, they actually don't. Dark, evil things collect inside them that cause them to get agitated when they spot humans. Even you don't want to be near people you don't like, right? It's not all that different. Just by keeping a safe distance, even people can live near monsters."

Mariela remembered that conversation taking place right around the time when her master had adopted her.

Every time the still-young Mariela cried about being scared of spending the night in their cottage in the Fell Forest, her master would tell her this and stay in bed with Mariela until she fell asleep.

Every day when the sun rose, Mariela's master would take her on a walk through the Fell Forest. The woods were a treasure trove of alchemy materials. Some days, the two searched for medicinal herbs to plant in the garden around their cottage. Other times, they gathered mushrooms for use in poisons and medicine.

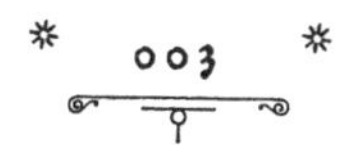

The Fell Forest was thick with trees and very gloomy, but there were occasional gaps in the dense canopy that beckoned shafts of light down from above. The places where the sun peeked through and rained down sparkling particles were safe and suitable resting spots for Mariela, who was young and weak. Sacred tree shoots sprouted in such places, and according to Mariela's master, they would protect everyone "when they grew up." When the pair left, they gave the tree shoots water infused with magical power in gratitude. Curiously, they often found something of use after doing so.

Thanks to monster-warding potions and magic circles that concealed their presence, they never encountered monsters, but sometimes Mariela's master would hunt them, saying, "This'll be tonight's dinner." Although the Fell Forest was a frightening place where fearsome creatures ran rampant, it was also an abundant woodland that provided Mariela and her master with seasonal produce, from fruit and mushrooms to tubers and wild grains.

The pair would hide behind a tree with pounding hearts as they watched the burning of strange chestnuts, which, on rare occasions, exploded with enough force to make trees collapse when they were tossed on a fire. There were other times when Mariela would pick a fruit that stained your mouth and fingers red with its juice when you ate it and used it to pretend to wear makeup, while her master would use it to pretend as though she were covered in blood.

One time, when they approached a fluffy furball that had fallen on the ground, they discovered it was a bird monster's chick, and it almost pecked them. That incident imprinted on Mariela's young mind that she wouldn't survive if she wasn't careful. Letting yourself be fooled by appearances was a mistake. When the chick's mother came looking for it, her master turned both mother and chick into "fire-roasted bird," which then became part of their dinner. As Mariela ate that evening, she felt she'd learned a valuable lesson about the survival of the fittest.

While the Fell Forest was home to many perils, Mariela's time living with her master revealed to her that there were many delicious and fun things to be found in those woods as well.

The forest had an abundance of gifts, but every once in a while, there would be a day when Mariela and her master couldn't harvest anything. During such times, Mariela's master would kick a sacred tree growing in the forest repeatedly while muttering something to it. Strangely, when she did, a bird flying nearby would drop prey it had caught next to her, or a sudden gust would blow and immediately knock down rare fruits from the nearby trees.

When Mariela imitated her master and drove her foot into the sacred tree, a gargantuan hairy caterpillar fell on her instead of food, and her master burst out laughing. "It's making fun of you." Mariela apologized and gave the sacred tree water to make amends. After that, a leaf lightly landed on the top of her head, giving her the impression she'd reconciled with the great plant.

In hindsight, Mariela realized the Fell Forest was filled with far more than monsters. It was also where the breath of the spirits could be found in the vegetation and even the light that slipped through the canopy.

That reminds me, I think there was a small spring in the garden of that cottage in the Fell Forest...

Mariela had possessed hardly any magical power when her master first took her in. She couldn't cast *Water* enough to handle the cooking, washing, bathing, and medicinal herb garden watering.

Seeing this, her master went out on a night of a full moon and sang and danced around as she steadily tapped a rhythm with the heels of her shoes, and the next morning, a small spring had appeared there. Mariela remembered how every time her master turned, her red hair and fluttering clothes billowed out, and the glittering decorations at her waist rustled and sparkled in the light of the moon. It was all lovely.

Perhaps due to the abundantly gushing fountain, the garden's medicinal herbs grew lush even without being watered. The spring water was cool even in summer, and fruits and vegetables soaked and cooled in it were extraordinarily delicious. Admittedly, drawing up the liquid was a bit of a pain, but it was thanks to that mysterious fountain that Mariela and her master were never in want of water in their cottage in the Fell Forest with no nearby lakes or ponds.

As Mariela's magical power increased, she quit the chore of fetching pails from the spring and instead began to use magic to supply water. Before she knew it, the small spring in the garden became hidden by the medicinal herbs' dense foliage. It wasn't long after that the little fountain vanished entirely, as though it had sensed that its job was done.

By then, Mariela could use enough lifestyle magic to manage the garden, and she could also cool ingredients quite quickly by using alchemy skills, so she'd forgotten for a long time that there had ever been a spring.

"That's the way I lived in the Fell Forest, so I'm not really scared of it," Mariela stated matter-of-factly as she swayed on the back of Koo the raptor.

The troupe was proceeding in a straight line through the Fell Forest, with Edgan in the lead. Behind him were Yuric and Franz of the Black Iron Freight Corps, and Mariela, who rode between Donnino and Grandel. Nick and Newie, two slaves who possessed low combat capabilities, had been left to house-sit back in the Labyrinth City.

Since the entire party was riding raptors, they progressed unhindered through the untamed foliage of the Fell Forest. Between Mariela's handmade monster-warding potions and a set of three magic circles—Forest's Welcome, Obfuscation, and Delusion—the plants moved aside to open the way as if to invite them in, and their presence and magical power were concealed from monsters. Even on the rare occasion that a monster sensitive to sound noticed the group, it couldn't overtake them due to the effects of the Magic Circle of Delusion, so it was a surprisingly smooth journey even to the Black Iron Freight Corps, who had traveled the main road of the Fell Forest many times over.

As you might expect, Edgan and the others held Mariela in high esteem because she'd been taught by *the* Freyja and had lived in the Fell Forest.

Mariela had shoddy riding skills—she could barely have the raptor walk—but she traveled through the obstacle-ridden Fell Forest like the open plains. No matter how exceptional the troupe's pursuer, they likely wouldn't be able to catch up easily.

Yes, even if that person was Siegmund, the A-Ranker who bore the Spirit Eye.

02

"Sieg's such an *idiot*! I can't believe this. I never thought he was that kind of person..." Mariela's muttering was frightening.

Little wonder. Her eyebrows were curved upward in anger because Sieg had thrown away Slaken without her permission.

"Yeah. Throwing away a living thing is unthinkable," Yuric added.

It's never right to throw away another person's belongings, no matter how long you've lived together. Sieg diligently stashed away items Mariela only saw as trash, but she didn't toss them. Above all, Slaken was alive. Moreover, due to its nature as a Slime-in-a-Vial, it would weaken and die in a few days if it didn't regularly receive magical power from Mariela. It was understandable that Yuric, an animal tamer who loved raptors above all else, would support Mariela 100 percent in this matter.

In general, Mariela's peers were too indulgent with Sieg. Illuminaria, the spirit of the sacred tree connected to Sunlight's Canopy, showed preference to him over Mariela, her own friend. Once in a while when he used his Spirit Eye, spirits of all shapes and sizes were drawn to him. Even the salamander Mariela summoned would turn toward Sieg and wag its tail.

The raptor Koo liked Mariela more than Sieg, but its favorite person was Yuric, so the only pet who favored Mariela had been Slaken.

Coupled with her daily jealousy—"No fair it's always Sieg"—his

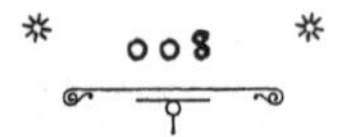

returning home yesterday carrying the empty slime-rearing vessel caused Mariela to explode in anger.

Sieg desperately attempted to explain, but Mariela didn't want to hear his excuses. She flew off the handle at him and then fled Sunlight's Canopy.

She was a runaway. "I'm going back to my *real* home."

Except Sunlight's Canopy was Mariela's only home, and she and Sieg weren't even married.

A year had passed since the Labyrinth's subjugation. Still, the relationship between Mariela, who happily made potions every day, and the good-for-nothing Sieg had hardly progressed at all, so you could say this huge fight was a significant change. Despite removing all obstacles in his way, Sieg was still unable to advance on the fortress that was Mariela.

However, it wasn't fair to make light of this battle as if it were some small trifle.

Mariela usually had terrible luck. But she'd survived the Stampede two hundred years ago, made potions with reckless abandon in the Labyrinth City after she awoke, significantly contributed to the Labyrinth's subjugation, and eventually even made the Elixir. She was someone who could do anything if she tried.

Of course, she'd received rewards worthy of her achievements, so she had excellent economic power. Thinking that now was the time to spend some of her tremendous fortune, Mariela had hired the Black Iron Freight Corps, led by Edgan, as her escorts to "go back to her real home." That was how she and the others had wound up riding through the Fell Forest.

Except her cottage in the Fell Forest, which you could call her real home, had been destroyed in the Stampede and no longer existed.

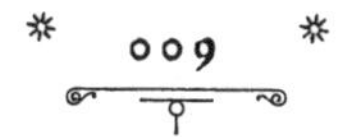

"When I say 'my *real* home,' I mean where my parents are. And an alchemist's parent is their master, right? My salamander says he knows where my master is."

Although the salamander liked Sieg, it also favored Freyja, perhaps because of how many times she'd summoned it while she was in the Labyrinth City. What a fickle lizard.

Speaking of fickle, Edgan… No, Erotigan…er, which one was it? Anyway, ever since the Labyrinth subjugation, he'd developed a reputation for himself in the Labyrinth City as a massive flirt. After his spike in popularity, scores of women had claimed compensation and child support from him, and he was now broke.

According to the Black Iron Freight Corps members, he rose to fame around a year ago, yet women with two- or three-year-olds and ones who had never even held hands with him had come to collect. Evidently, poor Edgan had been duped. The man himself believed he was popular and didn't doubt the many women, even after being stripped of most of his things.

As you would expect, the Black Iron Freight Corps found this problematic and discussed it. They agreed they would accept gold coins and blood relation potions, which reveal any familial linkage between two people, as compensation for Mariela's job. That way, they could sort out the whole Edgan situation.

Mariela had agreed, and thus she, Edgan, Yuric, Franz, Grandel, and Donnino were following a salamander riding atop a raptor's head down a trackless path. Since it was an animal trail, the iron carriages couldn't get through, so Grandel, who found even armor too heavy to wear, let alone a shield, served as the rear guard, riding on a raptor and sitting inside armor resembling an iron box. He was more luggage than man.

"Say, salamander. Do you think we'll reach my master's place soon?"

Yesterday the group had departed around noon and camped for the night in a less dense part of the Fell Forest. And now the sun was sinking again. They were far deeper in the woods than they had been the previous day, so the thought of setting up camp now was a little scary.

"Ar? Rawr!"

The salamander looked puzzled as it indicated the direction they should travel.

"Oh yeah, the Fell Forest is the monsters' territory, so we can't communicate..."

Mariela could speak with the salamander in the Labyrinth City, and when she'd told it her goal, "I want to go to my master," it answered, —Rawr, I know where she is. This way.— However, after they entered the Fell Forest, it became as though the two no longer spoke the same language. All the fire spirit could do was indicate which way to move. Mariela thought they were in a very deep part of the forest already, so how much longer would it take to reach their destination?

We haven't crossed onto another ley line. It's still the same one as in the city, so why can't we talk?

Mariela pondered these things while mounted on her raptor when suddenly, the salamander began to noisily shriek, "Rawrawr!"

"I wonder if that means we've arrived?"

The place they reached shortly thereafter was a gloomy marshland that abruptly cut the thickly grown trees short like it had swallowed them up.

Although it wasn't raining, the surrounding air was damp and heavy.

Perhaps because the sun was setting, the trees of the Fell Forest blocked the light, and the group couldn't see below the water's surface. Trees and tall grass grew all the way to the edge of the bog filled with black water, which resembled a gaping hole in the middle of the forest.

Monsters needed water, so this was probably an important place for them, but the surroundings were eerily silent; Mariela couldn't even hear the howls of rampaging beasts. When she happened to glance at the opposite shore, she saw an imposing monster with four horns emerge from the trees. She couldn't see details at this distance, but it appeared to be an extremely powerful creature with an enormous body and sharp claws and fangs.

"Get back..."

Sword at the ready, Edgan instructed Mariela and the others to retreat.

However, the monster drank water from the bog, then glanced their way before quietly going back into the forest.

"Maybe this is some sort of sanctuary."

"The air is rather stagnant for a consecrated locale."

"At any rate, it's fine if the monsters don't attack us, right?"

Franz muttered as he gazed in the direction the monster went, and Grandel answered from within his armor. Meanwhile, Edgan looked around and offered his usual half-hearted assessment.

This water gives me a real bad feeling...

The monster drank it, so the liquid held neither poison nor any other kind of harmful substance. The air around the marshland was damp and heavy like rain had just fallen, but Mariela detected no rotten smell or other foul odors. Even so, she had a feeling this bog was wholly corrupted. If monsters didn't attack, then the spot was a safe zone, but even so, Mariela didn't want to stay here longer than necessary.

Why would my master be here?

Wanting to start looking for Freyja right away, Mariela looked at the salamander, who stared at a particular spot on the bank of the mire and cooed as if to urge the group onward.

"Over there? Is that...a roadside shrine?"

Crumbled boulders lay in a heap, covered in moss that made the structure blend into the surrounding greenery from a distance.

As Mariela and the others approached, they saw traces of human influence—the ruins of a shrine from an ancient era. There was an opening under the heap of stone that was big enough to enter. The base was probably also made of rock, but given the distance and all the moss covering the shrine, it was difficult to tell. Upon closer inspection, they saw the floor was made from a large boulder. Under the light of illumination magic, they discovered the shrine had a stone door that led underground.

"Rawr!"

"So my master's here!"

When Freyja left, she'd had a Magic Circle of Suspended Animation, so she probably went to sleep in the cellar under this shrine. Since the magic circle would spontaneously resuscitate you when danger had passed, there was no doubt Freyja would awaken if the door was opened and fresh air let in.

"Master! Rise and shiiine!"

Mariela's master was resting down below. Just that thought alone somehow put a spring back in Mariela's step, and she pulled on the stone door with a grunt.

"Rrrrr, it's stuck."

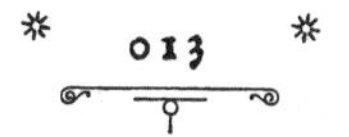

Although she pulled and tugged until she was red in the face, the door didn't give an inch.

"Want help?"

"Let's help."

"I shall assist."

"Leave it to me."

"Then I'll help, too."

"Rar!"

Yuric, Franz, Grandel, Donnino, Edgan, and even Koo the raptor tried to lend a hand. They tied a rope around one side of the barricade and pulled hard on it.

"Rgh, even with all this, it won't open...?!"

Try though they all did, the door remained stationary. Mariela gave up attempting to wrench it free, and she leaned on it to catch her breath. That's when...

Clunk.

The stone door opened inward, and Mariela tumbled down into the dark.

Apparently, it was a door you had to push, not pull. As Mariela was busy thinking *Dang iiit* at this clichéd development...

Plop.

The shrine had been on the bank of a bog, yet Mariela was now sitting in a deep pool of water for some reason.

No, that wasn't entirely accurate. Mariela's excess flesh would probably have given her the buoyancy to rise to the water's surface if it had been normal water.

"Glub, glub, cough."

Mariela uttered horrid sounds as she sank.

Deeper and deeper, as though the mire was bottomless.

She looked up toward the place she'd fallen from and saw from very far away a tiny sparkle resembling moonlight. It seemed to be sinking in the sky as the real moon would have. When Mariela looked around, she saw others descending with her in the gloom. Could everyone else have fallen, too, even though she'd been the only one to lean on the door? Maybe they had come down to help her?

The one demonstrating proper technique as he paddled to escape was undoubtedly Edgan. But although he swam his best, it seemed to have the opposite effect, as he was drawn farther and farther below.

Master... It's so cold. I'm freezing...

Although the mysterious place didn't seem grounded in reality at all, the chill of the water cut through Mariela's body like a knife. She managed to bend her frozen limbs and curl up into a ball before losing consciousness.

CHAPTER 1

The World of Water

01

"Nn... Ugh..."

Cold, icy, and hard.

Mariela had a memory of these sensations permeating her clothes.

Sometimes she woke up feeling like this. Could she have fallen out of her bed again today? The human survival instinct was nothing to sneeze at; when someone toppled off their bed and slept on the cold floor, they unconsciously drew their blanket to them and curled into the fetal position. Yet, today, the ground was chillier than usual and suspiciously more uncomfortable. The fabric she pulled toward herself clung to her and stole her body heat.

Ugh, blanket... Er, huh?

At last, Mariela's eyes opened wide.

"Um...I was looking for Master and came to a shrine near a bog... I fell into some water when I opened a door."

Mariela searched her memories, but she still didn't know what was going on at all. She understood that she'd fallen underground, yet couldn't comprehend how she'd wound up sinking in a deep pool of water. Could the basement be flooded? If so, where was Mariela now?

"I guess...no one helped me?"

The alchemist was lying facedown on stone paving that was flatter and firmer than her chest.

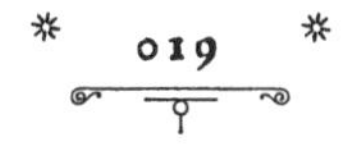

Both her clothes and her hair were sopping wet, so it didn't seem like anyone had taken her in or looked after her. She got off the ground, dragging her clinging clothes, which were heavy from the water they'd absorbed. When Mariela used the *Dehydrate* spell to dry herself, she felt the warm light of the sun, and with a sigh of relief, she loosened her curled body.

"Doesn't seem like much time has passed."

Considering Mariela had woken up on a frigid stone floor, her body wasn't especially cold. It was likely that hardly any time had passed since her fall.

"...But where am I?"

As Mariela warmed herself in the sunlight, she checked to make sure she didn't have any injuries. Some sort of silhouette passed in front of her.

"A bird...? Wha...?"

The place Mariela found herself in was a spacious circular room made of stones more than twenty paces wide. Overhead was a dome-shaped ceiling, and the walls had large, tall windows facing in eight directions. The apertures rose so high that Mariela couldn't reach the top of them even if she stood on her toes, and they were wide enough to match the span of her outstretched arms. They had no lattices, curtains, or any such decoration.

The warm sunlight filling the room was shining in through the windows, but the weather outside was misty and murky. Since Mariela was preoccupied with whether this place was safe, she paid no heed to the overcast weather. Another shadow crossed past one of the windows. This time, Mariela saw that it wasn't a bird, but a fish.

"A fish?!"

When she rushed up to the pane, she saw that it was not

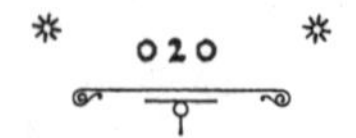

churning fog beyond the room, but water. Giant humanoid-looking fish were leisurely swimming through it. Mariela looked up through the window and saw this place was so deep, she couldn't spy the surface. Something must have been scattering the light, as the veritable ocean beyond the window was so bright that it seemed like either morning or dusk.

"Whaaa? So I did fall into water..."

It was incomprehensible. Mariela's best guess was that she'd somehow drifted to this place.

For some reason, she stretched her hand toward the water-filled window.

"Ack, there really is water!"

When she stretched her hand toward the pane separating the room from the sea outside and touched it, she found not glass, but liquid. The vertical surface of the water rippled where she'd felt it, as if a stone had been dropped there.

"Huh? This...isn't a dream; the water feels cold. Umm, some kinda strange world?"

With a *splish-splash*, Mariela plunged her hand into the bottom of the window and pulled it back again. If she violently struck the water, spray would come flying out, but mysteriously, the liquid didn't flood the room.

"This is bad. I can't swim."

That was the least of her troubles, though.

Mariela was the only one in this room, so no one was around to voice a sensible opinion like "Even if you could swim, could you escape this strange place?"

Splash-splash-splash.

It was funny how the spray that flew into the room moved horizontally and returned to the vertical surface of the water.

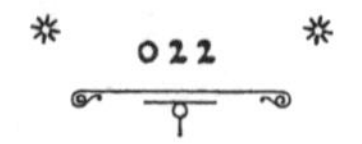

When she spontaneously started playing with the water, a fish approached.

Could it have thought the wriggling surface meant food?

"Whoa, it's huuuge!"

As Mariela jumped back in a fluster, the fish grazed the spot where her hand had been. It was so big it covered the window, and it swam shockingly fast as it left. It was most likely some type of monster.

"Scary. Even if I could swim, I dunno if I'd be able to reach the surface..."

To the very end, Mariela was fixated on the swimming part.

Although her point of consternation was a bit off, her conclusion that she couldn't escape through the windows was correct.

After the titanic fish swam away, Mariela turned to look around the room and made a guess that this was the top floor of a tall tower.

Underwater, the light shone in one direction only. If hardly any time had passed since Mariela had come here, wouldn't that make it the illumination of the setting sun? In that case, this was probably the southeast tower of an enormous structure. The seawater made it tough to see, but Mariela was just barely able to make out the surrounding forest greenery and two other towers at a right angle from each other.

Taking a deep breath, Mariela tried to sort out her thoughts.

The unusually humid air here had a damp smell that carried the scent of the forest near the shrine. Mariela felt this odd place was definitely linked to that bog.

"If I just sit here, all that'll happen is an empty stomach."

No one was here but Mariela, nor could she sense any other presence nearby. The place was probably safe, but she'd seen

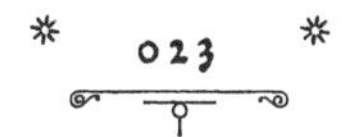

Edgan and the other members of the Black Iron Freight Corps falling into the water, too. It would be wise to hurry and join up with them.

"There's only one staircase, huh? It would've been so much easier if I'd washed up farther down."

The circular room had a single set of stairs, which led down. The spiraling steps built to run along the wall of the tower were wider than Mariela's arm spread, but the center of the tower was an atrium that allowed her to peer down toward the bottom. Torches lining the tower's walls illuminated Mariela's feet at regular intervals. Still, whatever awaited at the bottom of the winding path was too distant to be seen, which made the whole thing a little frightening.

Mariela didn't even have the materials for a monster-warding potion since the supplies had been stored on the raptors' saddlebags.

However, Mariela was not without an ally.

"Come forth, salamander, spirit of flames!"

Mariela charged the ring she wore on the middle finger of her right hand with magical power. If the salamander was with her, the surroundings would be lit even without the torches, and the spirit also seemed stronger than her.

Mariela called to the salamander, but...

"...It's not coming."

It didn't appear.

"Huuuh. Maybe it's still incarnated somewhere else?"

In return for leading Mariela to her master, she had used a large quantity of magical power to give the fire spirit its salamander form. It had seemed happy to appear even in the body of a small lizard, and it scampered around as it guided Mariela and

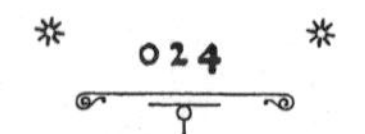

the others toward that marshland. Mariela would've thought it had exhausted the energy she'd given to it by now, but it didn't seem too unbelievable that it hadn't.

Although temporary, as long as it was in a body, the spirit couldn't readily pop up somewhere or disappear. Like any other corporeal being, it would have to walk to reach Mariela. That, or wait to be summoned again after its magical power ran out and it went home.

"I-it's fine! I'll be okay by myself. The stairs only go one way, and if I head down, I'll meet up with everyone! ...But preparation is important. For now, I'm gonna look for things that seem useful and then take the stairs."

It was easy to tell Mariela was just doing her best to put on a brave face. She sighed at the endless spiral staircase and searched around the room for anything helpful.

Trudge, trudge, round and round. Trudge, trudge, round and round.

How much time had Mariela spent walking down the winding steps?

"Maybe it'd be better not to get dizzy when I'm hungry."

Mariela spoke to herself as she held her empty stomach and sank to the floor in a room at the middle of the tower. The top

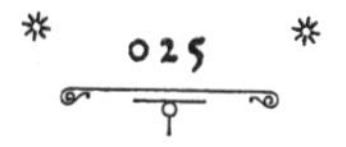

level had provided nothing but moss and ivy growing on the wall inside and aquatic plants flourishing outside. All Mariela had managed to collect was aquatic vegetation, not familiar medicinal herbs like daigis or bromominthra. Worst of all, the plants tasted a little too strong for her liking, so they weren't suitable as ingredients for food.

"I'm only eating these as a last resort..."

What Mariela had harvested as a last resort were the seeds of an aquatic plant called *gepla*. The small, tuft-like seeds resembling foxtail millet contained a lot of oil and were highly nutritious, but they weren't good to eat because of their foul, fishy smell. It was the kind of thing frog monsters preferred to eat. Perhaps because the plants grew on shallow watersides, there had been many around the water windows' borders.

Mariela fastened the gepla seeds to her waist with thin fibers wrapped together from a strong, soft plant known as *rope ivy*. Since rope ivy could be used in place of a standard cord, she'd twined a large quantity around her waist with the thought that it would probably come in handy in one way or another. She also put its leaves around her waist while she was at it. If you dried the fleshy leaves of rope ivy, they would become porous like a sponge. This gave them many uses, such as soaking up water or helping to start a fire. But at the end of the day, Mariela just looked like she was wearing a grass skirt. Déjà vu. It was a little nostalgic.

Although she'd been working her way down the spiral staircase in this completely unfashionable garb for a few hours now, she still couldn't see where the steps ended. When this middle room had come into view, Mariela had been overjoyed, thinking she'd finally reached the base of the tower. That excitement had been short-lived, however. The dismay brought on by the realization that she was nowhere near the bottom had caused Mariela to sink to the floor.

This new area resembled the room on the top floor, but the eight windows were long narrow slits vertically divided into threes that Mariela's head wouldn't be able to fit through. If the sun were still up, she'd be able to discern direction, but it had set at some point unnoticed. The room was bright thanks to the torches on both sides of the apertures, but the outside was pitch-dark in contrast, and Mariela couldn't see anything.

"It's like I'm looking at a pot of ink..."

Chilly air streamed in from the glassless windows.

"Huh? Wind?"

Strange. There should've been water outside. How was air blowing in? Mariela stretched her hand through the window into the darkness, but her fingertips didn't touch any liquid, instead grasping nothing.

"There's no water?!"

When had it receded? When Mariela stretched her hand to touch the tower's outer wall, it brushed against damp aquatic plants. They'd clearly been submerged until a short while ago.

"What's going on...?"

Even if Mariela wanted to figure that out for herself, the narrow windows prevented her from sticking her head out and looking around, and the outside was dark and inky. She felt like she'd be far safer underwater with good visibility. Somewhat frightened of the black unknown, Mariela uprooted the plants her hand could reach through the empty window, and she retracted her arm.

"This is harnonius. If it's growing here, I wonder if that means the inside of the tower is safe?"

Harnonius was also known as the Guardian of Waterholes.

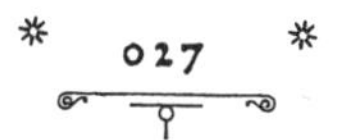

Like evergreen trees on land, it had relatively tough leaves for an aquatic plant, and its roots inhabited rocky areas and the like. It got the name Guardian of Waterholes because aquatic monsters stayed away from it.

Fish monsters had been swimming outside the room above, but this space was probably safe if harnonius was growing here. Of course, now there was no water, so the fish wouldn't be able to approach in the first place.

Incidentally, harnonius was also inedible. It wasn't poisonous, but it didn't possess any nutrients. Despite this room being secure, Mariela knew she had to keep moving while she still had the strength to do so. Rousing herself with a "Hup!" Mariela resumed the trudge, trudge down the staircase.

At last, when Mariela finally began to approach a third room, she caught the sound of a raptor going "Rar, rar!"

"Is that Koo?!"

Mariela hurried down.

This new enclosure, which Mariela burst into, was identical to the others—a dreary place with torches burning bright red next to long and narrow windows—but in addition to the stairs continuing down, it also had a pair of doors.

They were at right angles to each other, so if Mariela's reasoning on the top floor had been correct, they were on the north and west sides. The north door's top was rotting and damaged, and it was slightly ajar, perhaps because it couldn't be adequately shut anymore. The west door was fully closed, but Mariela could hear Koo, who had saved her many times over in the past, from just beyond it. A bright light shone from the stairs leading farther down, so maybe there was another chamber a short way below it.

"Rar, rar, raaar!"

Koo's voice wasn't desperate, but it sounded like he was asking for help. Mariela could also hear the sound of a tail violently striking something. Perhaps the raptor was fighting something?

A...an enemy?! If I had a vial or some other kinda container...

If Mariela only had a flask, she could use the medicinal herbs around her waist to make a potion that could help. This chamber provided nothing the alchemist could use, but it was difficult to imagine there being no vials or vases anywhere in this giant building.

Hang in there, Koo. I'll be right back.

Mariela practically tumbled down the stairs as she ran.

Just as she'd thought, a room lay just below, and as a further bit of luck, it appeared to be a storage space with items scattered around. Nearly broken shelves and boxes cluttered the place. Just like the floor above, there were doors on the north and west, but both were surrounded by baggage, and she couldn't even get near them, let alone open them.

"Vials, vials... Aha!"

A significant number of empty alcohol bottles lay messily in a box that had been casually left by the stairs.

After choosing two that were on the small side, Mariela expanded a Transmutation Vessel. What she was about to make weren't potions for healing people, so she didn't need to wash the bottles.

She produced the harnonius she'd plucked from the outside wall of the tower a short while ago.

This plant, which warded against aquatic monsters, didn't emit a smell that monsters hated like bromominthra. Rather, it absorbed the corrupted magical power of monsters. This made it a somewhat valuable plant that could turn a perilous stream into a pleasant spot for shrimp and fish.

"Pulverize, Water, Drops of Life, Extract, Condense, Anchor Essence."

Mariela nimbly made the concoction. The process was the same as crafting a low-grade potion. Usually, she would separate the dregs, but time was precious right now, so she skipped that step and filled the bottles.

"One more... Just to be on the safe side..."

Mariela took the gepla seeds hanging from her waist and pulverized them in the Transmutation Vessel.

"Drops of Life, Extract, Separate."

This process used neither water nor oil as a solvent. You abruptly dissolved the oil from the pulverized gepla seeds into Drops of Life and separated the remaining dregs. When the extract was transferred from the Transmutation Vessel to the container, only the Drops of Life would come out before vanishing instantly. Gepla oil didn't possess much of the quality necessary to store Drops of Life, so even when it was dissolved in a Transmutation Vessel, it separated from the Drops of Life as soon as it was removed. This left behind only the oil.

There might be too little of it. I'll infuse it with magical power.

Gepla oil was also highly sensitive to magical power. The frog monsters that liked gepla seeds were very active, emitting a fair amount of magic energy. In order to ensure its seeds would be eaten and carried far by these creatures, the gepla plant absorbed magical power to swell for a short time. This also caused its effects to strengthen.

When Mariela channeled her magical power into the gepla oil, which there was only a finger's width of in the bottom of the vial, it expanded as air bubbles formed. Once it had enlarged enough to fill seven-tenths of the vial, Mariela stopped it briefly. After adding the remaining material—the rope ivy—into the vial with the end dangling outside it, she packed dried rope ivy leaves tightly into the container as a lid.

"All right, it's complete!"

The whole process had only taken a few minutes. Mariela grabbed the two completed concoctions and hurried back up the stairs.

"Raaar, raaar!"

"Thank goodness, he's still okay."

Mariela could hear Koo's voice from the other side of the west door. It seemed like he might be saying something like "Get awaaay!" He sounded really annoyed, but not exactly afraid.

Just to be safe, Mariela discreetly opened the door and peeked beyond.

It was pitch-dark, and she couldn't even see stars in the night sky when she looked up, let alone water. There was no light other than that escaping through the door Mariela had opened, and it wasn't enough to see very far. However, a stone passage barely spacious enough for a carriage to pass through continued past the door. The place seemed like the topmost part of the outer wall, with a barricade as high as Mariela's waist flanking either side. This walkway likely connected multiple towers. If Mariela let Koo into the chamber she was in and closed the door, maybe she'd be able to keep out whatever Koo was fighting.

"Koo, over here!"

"Grah? Raaar!" Koo called out after noticing Mariela.

He began to move in her direction, though seemingly dragging something along behind him.

Koo's silhouette was just barely visible in the light from the door, and Mariela couldn't identify what was wrapped around him. He was violently thrashing his tail around, stomping at the thing, and trying to tear it off, but whatever it was sinuously stretched and altered its form in an attempt to swallow the raptor.

"Hiii-yah!"

Mariela hurled the potion made from harnonius, vial and all, at the creature. Since it only contained harnonius, it wasn't liable to be very potent, but it was enough to make most monsters flinch and back off for an instant. Any spot the concoction touched would leech corrupted magical power out of the monster. It wasn't fatal, but apparently, it was incredibly unpleasant.

Shudder.

When the thing clinging to Koo recoiled, he took the opportunity to shake it off and rushed toward Mariela.

"In here, Koo. Hurry!" Mariela called to him as she opened the door so the raptor could fit through.

As Koo's shape became more distinct, the light from the room also illuminated the monster chasing him, and its form became apparent. The viscous mass, reminiscent of a slime, was a deep, ebon shade—black as night. It slithered along the floor as it chased the raptor, its bottom edge fluttering while it gave pursuit.

"Eek!"

"Raaar!"

The shape definitely resembled a slime. However, it wasn't transparent at all, and Mariela couldn't tell if there was a nucleus in the pitch-black mass. The bottom of the mass, about the size of a large dog, wriggled every time it moved, like it was pulsating. On a second look, it acted as though it were a horde of small insects, and if a little bit of it was torn off, the bottom edge would immediately enfold and reabsorb it.

Since Koo had been able to fight back, the monster probably wasn't powerful, but this wasn't a gentle creature like a slime. It was most likely a very nasty sort of being.

Koo twisted his body as he leaped through the door, which was only big enough for a single person to get through at a time. At that moment, when his speed slowed, the black monster sprang at his tail.

"Grr, raaah!!!"

"Hey, Koo, calm down!"

Because the raptor was thrashing around in repulsion, Mariela couldn't close the door, and even the black monster clinging to his tail like mud ended up inside the tower chamber.

"Rarar!"

Koo's tail whipped around so violently it was like he was saying, "Get off me already!" The recoil from his thrashing sent the ebon monster flying into the wall above the door. However, this didn't seem to hurt it in the slightest, and it immediately began to wriggle and sidle toward Mariela and Koo again. Its movements were sluggish, though, so maybe it was weak in the light or hated fire.

"Gaaah, it's coming!"

"Graaah, raraaar!"

A person who opened her big mouth and let out an awkward scream, and a raptor. Although they were human and beast, they looked and acted as one. Maybe they had overcome the barrier between species, and their feelings were now united.

Mariela's plan to close the door and keep out the monster had been a failure. She was hesitant to use her one remaining potion here, so all she and Koo could do was escape before their opponent moved in. The tower had dead ends above and below them, and the black monster was crawling above the door on the west side where Koo had come through, so their only option for escape was the nearly broken northern door.

"Koo, over here!"

After throwing open the northern door and grabbing a torch next to it, Mariela rushed out into the dark, open air. Koo followed her and slammed the door shut with his tail.

Unfortunately, the strange monster simply slinked through the fracture in the broken door and gave chase.

"Pant, pant, pant."

Mariela was out of breath as she ran. She'd seen another tower to the north at the top of the one she'd awoken in. If they took refuge there, maybe this time they could shut out the black creature.

Although Mariela ran at full speed, the monster was clearly getting closer. Apparently, it did move faster in darkness after all. Mariela took out her one remaining vial packed with gepla oil, lit the string dangling from the opening, and threw it at the monster.

Crash.

The instant the vial broke, a blaze erupted with a fiery sound.

Mariela had strengthened the concoction with magical power and created a towering pillar of flame.

It seemed like she'd skillfully ignited her pursuer. After wriggling and twisting, it melted like coal tar, and in the next instant, it violently burst into flame.

"We made it, I think...?"

The burning column blocked Mariela and Koo's way, but its light allowed Mariela to inspect the surrounding environs.

They were currently on the outer wall, right about halfway

between the two towers. The one they'd come from and the one they were heading for, about the same distance away, were both visible. And, perhaps it had climbed the wall, but a black monster twice the size of the one Mariela had just defeated was in the passage leading into the tower and heading for Mariela and Koo.

"What should I do...? I don't have any more fire bottles..."

Maybe it was cautious due to the blaze behind them, as the creature appeared to be looking for an opportunity to spring at Mariela and Koo. Mariela tried to make some kind of feint by thrusting out the torch in her hand, but it didn't seem like that kind of thing would do any good. When the pillar of fire behind them went out, they might be attacked and swallowed immediately.

"Grar..."

Koo turned his back toward Mariela. He was probably telling her to get on. Mariela used the torch to keep the monster in check as she tried to get on Koo's back. But Mariela had always been clumsy. There was no way the creature would overlook her many openings. The monster spread its body like a cloth billowing out in the wind and sprang at the pair to swallow them both at once.

"Eek!"

Mariela reflexively threw the torch she was holding. As if in response to her unusually girlish scream, the burning stick burst into powerful flames for a moment and took the form of a lizard.

"Grrrr!!!"

Blinding white light and hot flames surged from the salamander and assaulted the black monster. It was so dazzling that Mariela closed her eyes. When she opened them again, nothing remained of the viscous mass, and the salamander burped a bit of smoke with a "Rawr."

"Salamander, you came to save us!"

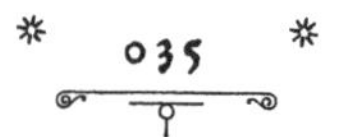

"Raaar!"

What a fantastic lizard the spirit was for gallantly appearing in Mariela's time of need. Where in the world could that Spirit Eye owner be loitering around at a time like this? And here Mariela might have even forgiven him if he'd appeared during this kind of crisis.

As if striking that person from her memory, Mariela lifted up the salamander, who could fit in her palms, thanked it, and put it on her shoulder.

"I'm so relieved you're here, Salamander!"

"Rar, rar."

Koo agreed with Mariela's sentiment. The salamander licked Mariela's cheek and flopped down on her shoulder. Apparently, it was going to stay with them.

The torch had gone out when the salamander had manifested, and when Mariela turned toward the pillar of flames behind them to light it again, she saw that it, too, had been extinguished. As Mariela approached the black monster's embers to relight her torch, she saw a small stone on the ground with a speckled pattern of scarlet on white.

"Pretty... That's not a magical gem, is it? Maybe it's that monster's nucleus. I'm not getting any bad vibes from it, but..."

Mariela retrieved the mottled stone with the torch's tip, and after waiting for it to cool, she gently stowed it away in a pocket.

No more black monsters appeared, and the group quickly made it to the next tower.

Braziers burned inside this tower as well, and when Mariela pressed on the door to the tower where light was spilling from, it offered no resistance. She'd thought it was the northeast tower, but the same type of door was on the opposite side of the one they had just come through, so it was likely the east one. The structure of this one was almost identical to the southeast tower. In addition to a door to the north, it had a spiral staircase going up and down.

"There aren't any more of those things, right?"

Neither of the exits in this chamber were broken. After locking the bolts on both, Mariela breathed a sigh of relief. The ebon-colored creature seemed fearful of fire, and since this room had torches burning next to the windows and entrances, those monsters probably wouldn't enter.

Unfortunately, Mariela realized they could slither down from whatever room lay above or up from the staircase below, so she couldn't afford to take a break.

"I'd better pick some harnonius."

The harnonius had worked against that black monster. The plant seemed to be growing at the top of this tower as well, so Mariela decided to head up with Koo.

It took Koo less than ten minutes to run up a distance that would have taken Mariela almost an hour to cover. When the light from a room around the middle of the tower came into view, Koo suddenly went "Rar, rar!" and broke into a dash.

"H-hey, wait! Koo?!"

Mariela desperately clung to the raptor so she wouldn't be thrown off. The salamander riding on her shoulder placidly enjoyed the little rodeo. From above, Mariela heard a familiar voice call, "Koo! And Mariela?"

"Yuric! You're okay!"

"Raaar!"

Koo and Mariela were about to leap at Yuric, but he warded the pair off with a "Whoa, whoa there!" and sidestepped. That was an animal tamer for you.

"Mariela, where are we? What were those black things?" Yuric asked after calming Mariela and Koo, who were overjoyed at the reunion.

"I don't know… But I think my master is here somewhere," Mariela answered as she hung her head. The salamander had indeed directed them here from that bog shrine. Since this strange structure was linked to that place, it probably held some relation to Mariela's master.

If so, what were those viscous entities? Something about them gave Mariela an ominous feeling.

The alchemist didn't quite understand why her master hadn't shown up, despite the dangers that prowled this place.

"I wonder if Master's in some kind of trouble…?"

As though to comfort Mariela, who was at a loss for words, the salamander on her shoulder rubbed its cheek against hers.

"At any rate, this place seems safe, so how about we have somethin' to eat and turn in for the night?"

After finishing their simple meal from ingredients Koo was carrying, Mariela and Yuric decided to get some much-needed rest.

03

The sky stretched on forever, as did the earth.

Mountains and sparsely growing shrubs were visible in the distance.

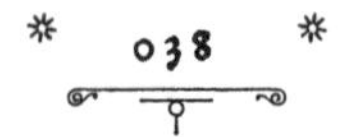

This seemingly infinite world was filled with a vivid, peaceful atmosphere and pale light.

The sky was brightening bit by bit, a signal that dawn was approaching.

The instant a giant bird pecking at the ground somewhere far off lifted its head, light rapidly filled the world.

As the color red came into being, she quietly watched the transformation from the back of her mother, who rode a raptor.

When the woman lightly kicked the stirrups, the raptor began running like the wind.

Steadily, steadily, toward the morning sun.

No matter how long they ran, they couldn't see the edge of the world, and it felt as though this scenery would stretch on forever, just like the sky.

This endless wilderness where water was scarce proved harsh and merciless, but the wind that brushed her cheeks was calm and clear.

It was her earliest childhood memory. The place she should return to.

If she closed her eyes, she could recall it, even now.

The sky's filthy...

The air above the rural settlement supposedly on the edge of the Empire always looked dull and stagnant. It was as though the sky were grimacing at the ugliness of people.

She followed a path through the forest, carrying baggage too heavy for her small body. She had to hurry back. She couldn't bear to be beaten again.

Evading detection, she progressed along the woodland path and returned to a house on the village's outskirts.

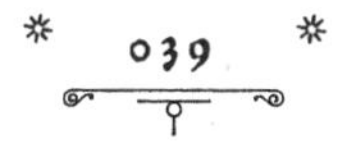

"What're you slacking off for?! No food for a blockhead like you!"

Although she'd returned in a great hurry, the mistress of the abode shouted that she would go without a meal.

"Hey, now. Let her eat. We'll be in trouble if she doesn't grow up fast and start being useful."

"Tch, I've looked after both of you part-beasts, parent and child. Be sure to show the gratitude your dead mother no longer can before you eat!"

The one who had intervened was the woman's husband, the head of this household that got by on animal husbandry. The husband eyed the girl nastily, as if he was appraising livestock. The girl wolfed down the bread and soup tossed her way, then ran to the animal enclosure.

"Rar, grar."

"Thanks. Are ya doin' all right?"

When she entered the room, where only one raptor was kept, she crawled into the straw. She felt at ease here. It was because of her that this raptor was stabled here. So she could train it.

Instructing ferocious raptors was difficult on account of their wild temperaments. People said it was impossible without particular skills. The creatures were daring enough to press forward through groups of monsters, however, so a trained raptor fetched a high price.

This raptor was partly trained and still only listened to the girl. It was hardly any different from a wild animal to the married couple, so she could sleep here safely.

She removed her holey shoes and transferred the copper coins hidden in the heels to a pouch concealed in the straw. Little by little, the girl was saving the money she obtained by picking it off the ground or haggling for a lower price on goods on days like today when she went out shopping.

"Let's run away after I've saved up a bit more."

"Rar."

She didn't remember how exactly she'd wound up here.

What she did recall was the sky and earth stretching on forever and the gentle voice of her mother.

Perhaps they thought a child from a foreign country couldn't understand their language, as this married couple had spoken freely in front of the child after her mother had died of illness.

"We hired that woman because she said she had animal taming skills, but all that's left now is this useless brat."

"Wait a minute. This kid is a female part-beast, after all. Once she's able to use her skills, she can pay us back for all our efforts, and breeding her could be profitable, too."

After that, the husband and wife not only started pushing her around, but they also took every opportunity to tell her to hurry up and remunerate them for raising her. Even though they looked down on the child, a member of an animal tamer family, as a "part-beast," the couple held her hostage with some sort of fabricated debt they felt she owed.

Back then, the girl had been too young to do anything on her own, but she'd saved up some money for traveling expenses, and above all, she had a raptor now.

"Wait for me, Mother. I promise I'll bring ya home."

Even if it was just a keepsake—a lock of her mother's hair—tucked away in her pocket, surely she would bring her back to the land under that sky.

Unfortunately, the girl didn't know where that place was.

She remembered her mother's final words even now.

* * *

"Yuric, you are free. You can go anywhere."

Surely she'd be able to find her way to that landscape.

04

"Graraaar, grararaaar."

Koo stuck his tail through a window in the topmost floor of the east tower.

Splish-splash, shake-shake. He cheerfully dangled his tail in the water. He'd been in rather high spirits since first thing this morning. Koo apparently enjoyed provoking monsters, since he used his tail as bait to entice fish monsters as he shook his body, too.

"One's comin'. Now, Koo!"

"Rar!"

At Yuric's signal, the raptor pulled his tail into the room and jumped to the side of the window.

Spuh-laaash.

Enticed by Koo's provocation, the fish monster that swam straight at the window plunged into the tower with an open mouth full of sharp fangs.

"Gah!"

Mariela, who was spacing out in the corner of the room she'd taken refuge in, let out a scream at the giant creature that flew in

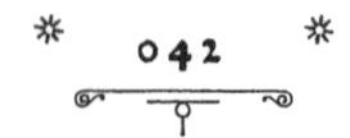

through the window. A massive fish monster's jump was a little too exciting at a time when she was lost in her thoughts.

Unsurprisingly, the outside was filled with water when they got up this morning, and Koo had started to fish for monsters to procure food for himself, as well as for Mariela and Yuric while he was at it. However, Mariela was curious about the dream she'd had last night, and it was distracting her.

That dream was about when Yuric was a kid, huh…?

Why did she dream about something like that?

As Mariela thought it over, a pair of bulging eyes caught her attention, and she reflexively staggered back and fell on her backside.

Owww, I squashed the materials in my pocket… Huh?

The scarlet-on-white speckled stone that should have been tucked away in her pocket wasn't there. Could she have dropped it somewhere?

"Hyaaah!"

Before the fish monster that plunged into the room could jump out of the opposite window, Yuric's whip cut apart its head and torso. The sharp sound it made likewise sliced through Mariela's thoughts.

"Wow, Yuric, you're so strong!"

The fish monster still splashed around despite losing its head, and Mariela approached Yuric while observing the creature from a safe distance.

"Fighting underwater's different, but I gotta be able to do this at least. I'd say it was actually unusual for someone settin' out for the Fell Forest to be as weak as ya."

"Ugh… That's…probably true."

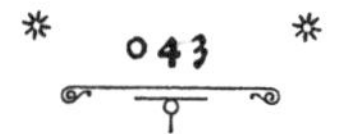

"But ya can make potions and cook, though. D'ya want to prepare this fish?"

"Yeah, leave it to me!"

Whether Mariela was used to Yuric's direct speech or whether she knew she meant no ill will, Mariela began to prepare the fish monster with no regard to the abusive language.

The now-headless aquatic creature was about the size of a human child. Mariela and Yuric, who were both around the same height, finished butchering the fish, and after they confirmed its liver wasn't poisonous, they let Koo eat it. Although it didn't suit Mariela's tastes, the liver was quite the delicacy—one a drinker would've been delighted to eat. The salamander, who had transformed into a scarf for Mariela, also began munching on the liver along with Koo.

As for the fish meat that Mariela and Yuric cut up, they only ate the exterior today. They thoroughly froze a portion for tomorrow, and after drying the rest, they decided to sprinkle today's breakfast with herbs and roast it.

Thankfully, there was plenty of rope ivy growing here as well, and by drying the leaves and using them as fuel, Mariela could create heat roughly equivalent to a straw-fueled fire and make a delicious roast. The oily abdomen flesh of the fish proved a little greasy to eat for breakfast. So Mariela sprinkled plenty of herbs on a portion of the back near the monster's tail to give it a light flavor. Quite a luxury this early in the day.

After Mariela threw hard bread into a Transmutation Vessel and soaked it in plenty of Drops of Life, she lightly grilled it to turn it fluffy again. Mariela had lived in poverty two hundred years ago, and this was a technique she'd worked out to make cheap, hard, stale bread tasty again. Drops of Life makes bread on the verge of being thrown out more delicious than the freshly-baked stuff. Sadly, the cheaper variety Mariela ate two centuries ago wasn't very tasty even when fresh due to its near-total lack of any butter or eggs.

But what Mariela had now was grain baked as a preserved food, which was made from plenty of butter and eggs, so when she softened it, it turned into bread as delicious as if she'd bought it from the most popular bakery in the Labyrinth City.

Mariela made sandwiches using the herb-roasted fish and added a few medicinal herbs with a good texture and hardly any bitter flavor. It was a good meal, considering the meager seasoning. The salamander, who had been chowing down on the fish monster's liver until a short while ago, opened its big mouth and looked up at Mariela to ask for a bite.

Perhaps Koo was happy to be able to share a meal with Yuric and Mariela, as he cheerfully stuffed his cheeks with the dead creature's innards. It was quite endearing.

"...I'm glad we were able to meet up, Mariela."

Moreover, Mariela seemed to have reached Yuric's heart through her stomach. Although it was merely an altered version of an existing recipe Mariela had learned from the Library, she was no less pleased.

"We have a lot to do today. Let's eat up and give it all we've got."

In response to Mariela, Yuric and the two creatures nodded, their cheeks filled with food.

"I wonder if that building's a temple of some sort. Maybe that's where my master is."

"Definitely suspicious. Bet you're right."

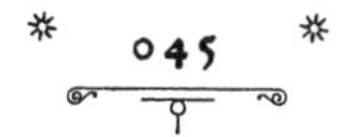

Mariela and Yuric were gazing at a courtyard structure from the third floor of the east tower. It had white walls and a jade roof. The complex, dome-shaped ceiling had a great many semicircles piled on each other, and it was the first time Mariela had seen this pattern. Since they were viewing it through the water, the details were blurry, but in contrast to the outer walls and towers that were covered with aquatic plants, the whiteness of the building's walls probably meant there weren't any growing on it.

It was an extremely conspicuous building that clearly housed something important.

Towers surrounded the temple, and a three-story outer wall likely connected them.

The passage Mariela had moved through to reach the east tower last night was at the roof level of the outer wall, and they were currently one floor down from there on the tower's third floor. This room had no stairs going down to the second floor, and the doors on the north and south side led to hallways.

The torches next to the hallways' windows kept things bright. This particular corridor resembled an archive in some respects, with paintings depicting everyday life and adventurers fighting monsters. The passages were also decorated with common furnishings that seemed affordable for even an average household.

Though the group explored to the ends of the hallways, the third floor of the southeast tower Mariela had first woken up in was packed with baggage and wouldn't open, and the northeast tower seemed to be flooded, if the sound that knocking on its door produced was anything to go on. Apparently, Mariela and the others wouldn't be able to leave the east tower until nighttime when the water receded.

Just as with the southeast tower, the third floor of the east tower had tableware and other miscellaneous items. But unlike the somewhat nostalgic feeling of the southeast tower, this place provided more unusual odds and ends such as perfume bottles with faint scents, classy-looking alcohol bottles that seemed to be filled with cheap booze, and silverware that was worn out despite being thoroughly cared for. Who on earth did all this stuff belong to?

It's like I'm looking at someone's past...

Mariela, feeling a little guilty, gathered up only the containers needed to replenish her supply of fire bottles and monster-warding potions. Their next goal was the northeast tower. If they waited in the third-floor hallway, they could probably enter it right after sunset.

The outside scenery grew clearer as the sun went down, and the color of the sky changed.

When Mariela stared fixedly at the landscape becoming less discernable as the light dimmed, she found the ocean outside didn't sink like the water in a bathtub flowing out after someone removed the plug; instead, it vanished along with the sun. They were able to turn the doorknob, and they opened the door to the northeast tower before the sun had set entirely. The strange sea was still visible but was more like a thick mist now.

"There are...no stairs going down."

"The door to the west passage is broken."

This chamber had several shelves and boxes as well, and women's clothes and decorations in brilliant colors peeked out from broken crates. There seemed to be letters and cosmetics, too, but all of them were wet and unusable.

"Mariela, stay there. I'll be right back."

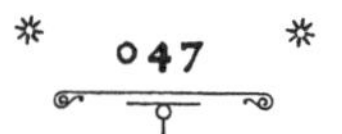

The door on the west side had come off, and Yuric quickly ran toward it to check what lay beyond. When Mariela and Koo peeked through, they saw the setting sun shining at the end of the misty corridor.

I can't see it very well, but is the hallway cut off? ...Huh? Where are the torches?

Up until they'd arrived at the northeast tower, there'd been lit braziers in the corridors, yet any in this room or the passage ahead had all been extinguished. Water had flooded the place, after all. It was natural for the fire to have gone out, but the torches in the rooms up to this point had burned constantly despite lacking fuel. So it wouldn't have been strange for those here to be lit despite any deluge.

Mariela felt uncomfortable that neither this chamber nor the western hallway had lit torches.

Boom.

As if to blow away Mariela's unease, a blaze erupted at the end of the passage. Yuric had probably used a fire bottle. The last hints of the strange ocean vanished, and things outside went wholly dark.

Mariela had no doubt a black monster had appeared.

She climbed onto Koo's back so she could be ready to escape at any time. The salamander, who migrated to the top of the raptor's head, illuminated the room for them.

"The hallway's useless. It's collapsed halfway through. And there's a ton of black monsters!"

Yuric returned and swiftly mounted Koo. The raptor began to run up the stairs as though he'd been waiting for the two of them to get on, and they went up to the fourth floor, where there was an outer wall passage.

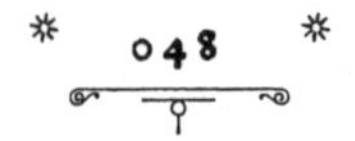

"Whoa! Here, too!"

The room connected to the outer walls on the fourth floor had no lit torches, either. The door on the west side had come off, and more of those strange, obsidian creatures packed the hallway beyond it as Mariela's group approached. Since these monsters' entire bodies were dark and soft, Mariela couldn't tell whether there were many small ones or one gigantic one, but in any case, they were closing in like a shadowy flood, and it seemed like the little band would be swallowed in an instant if they didn't make an escape immediately.

"Yuric, should we go up?!"

"We can't! At this rate, we dunno if up is any safer!"

"B-but there are monsters to the south, too...!"

A number of the black things were in the outer wall passage beyond the door Koo had skillfully opened with his forelegs, which led back to the east tower. Perhaps they'd climbed up along the wall, and just like on the west side, their numbers were steadily increasing, although not yet enough to fill the passage.

Should Mariela and Yuric escape to the upper floor or go back to the east tower? There were monsters along the path they'd taken here, and the upper floor was a dead end. It was hard to imagine any of Mariela and Yuric's companions being holed up in a place like this.

"Damn it, I didn't think there'd be this many. None of the idiots in the Black Iron Freight Corps would laze around in a place like this! Let's use a fire bottle and run through!"

"Got it! I'm gonna throw one, so we'll rush out the second the fire goes up!"

Mariela took out a fire bottle, used the salamander to light it, and then flung it toward the passage with a "Hii-yah!" Considering

Mariela had been the one to toss it, the container was well aimed, and it landed several steps past the door and created a low but wide conflagration. Some of the inky monsters recoiled from the sudden blaze, and an evident opening for egress presented itself.

Yuric took that opening to urge Koo forward. The raptor ducked under the door, and with this low profile, he flew into the passage like a bullet. With his first step outside, he put strength into his legs to make a running approach and leap over the blaze. Just then…

"! Above us?!"

It must have gone up the tower wall and avoided the flames. A black monster dropped down from overhead. Yuric snapped it with her whip and the salamander burned it, causing it to fall below the outer wall, but the raptor stopped on the spot, and in that opening, another monster dropped down from above.

"Wah, nooo!"

"Hey, Mariela, calm down!"

Yuric tried to knock down the new creature with her lash, but she couldn't move well because Mariela was brandishing a fire bottle behind her and getting in the way. Although the salamander had the power to burn the inky monster, it couldn't blow it away, so a blazing lump fell toward Mariela's group.

If Mariela and Yuric hadn't been on his back, Koo probably could have flicked away the strange creature with his tail, but if he made a complete turn with Mariela on him, she'd be tossed off with the monster.

There was nothing they could do.

Just when the burning black monster was about to fall on their heads…

"**Wind Edge** marks the entrance of: Magnificent Me! What-ho!"

Conveniently appearing in Mariela's time of need was the special right of someone worthy to be called a hero. Yet for some reason, the one who blew away the black monster with a blade of air and jumped down from a slightly higher part of the tower to land in front of Mariela's group was Edgan the dual wielder.

"Edgan?! Where'd you come from?"

"So an idiot *was* lazin' around in a place like this."

"Whoa, Yuric, don't you think that's a bit harsh?!"

Yuric's cold reception after Edgan had saved her and Mariela from peril pierced Edgan's broken heart.

"And here I'd come down the tower to save you guys. Geez, you're gonna make me cry."

Evidently, Edgan had somehow run down the wall from a window at the top of the tower.

There were protrusions, windows, and aquatic plants he could hang on to, but it was almost like a straight drop. Edgan sure could be nimble. Was this what you could expect from an A-Ranker? Or was he just a monkey?

As he said things like "You're gonna make me cry," Edgan cut the falling black monster in two with a wind blade he sent out from his dual swords and then dropped to the bottom of the wall.

"At least you saved us. You comin' with us, Edgan?"

Feeling it would be reassuring to have Edgan with them, Mariela nodded firmly at Yuric's suggestion, but…

"Uhhh, I can't? Y'see, things are gonna start getting crazy soon. So do you wanna try getting crazy with me here?"

"Wait a minute, I don't understand what you're sayin'."

"Don't worry, Yuric. I don't get it, either."

Edgan was talking nonsense. Given the mystery of their surroundings, it was hardly appreciated, and even Mariela shot Edgan a stern look. Edgan turned his ever-smiling face toward Mariela and Yuric, pointed his swords northwest, and declared, "You'll understand what I mean once you see for yourselves."

There was moonless, starless darkness. The tower lights had gone out, and the faint glow from the hallways leading to the north and south towers didn't reach the north wall. Mariela couldn't see anything but the heavy shadows stretching out before her. However, Yuric, whose eyesight was strengthened by magic, spotted a mass of black monsters gathering around the northern wall, which had collapsed in such a way that it looked like it had been gouged out.

And something formless and darker than night, more ebon than darkness itself, was about to close in on the interior of the excised outer wall from its opposite side.

"Uh...what? That's...?"

"Don't know."

Yet another sort of unknown being was advancing toward Mariela's group.

Yuric shuddered, her instincts telling her that whatever this creature was, it wasn't good. Edgan watched the entity with a tense expression. Perhaps because of how he usually conducted himself, he appeared composed and not particularly serious. He didn't convey a sense of danger at all to Mariela, who could only see darkness.

"That murky thing with the bad vibes is gonna rush in here any minute, and when those black slime-looking things slurp it up, a ton more of the slime things'll be generated in a big rush. I'm telling you, it's totally nuts."

"...What I got from that is you're a moron, Edgan. So why are we sticking around for this slime madness, exactly?"

Edgan's explanation had not a hint of urgency to it, but he understood the situation. In response to Yuric's question, Edgan gave a light laugh and a reply.

"Well, if we don't hold 'em back here, the slime-looking things'll probably get to be too much and enter the building. That's why I'll lure 'em over here so you guys can enter the temple and find a way for us to get out of this place."

"Edgan, that's..."

"Ya really are a moron..."

Could it be that Mariela's group had only been able to escape to a safe tower and sleep through the night unharmed because Edgan had lured the black monsters here and fought them?

Without breathing a word of confirmation, Edgan turned his back toward Mariela and Yuric before saying, "Well then, I'm counting on you," with an air like he was heading out to a shop where a young lady was working. Was he actually an unexpected hero?

"Take this! Those things seem weak to fire!"

"Ooh, thanks!"

After receiving the fire bottles, the harnonius monster-warding potions, and the bag of emergency rations Yuric tossed to him, Edgan ran toward the western corridor where the black monsters were crowded together.

"Let's go, Mariela!"

"Okay! ...Wait. This is..."

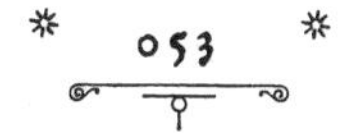

Mariela jumped down from Koo's back and picked up the small stones that had tumbled to his feet. There were some with a speckled green-and-bluish-purple pattern on golden brown, and one with scarlet speckles on white, like the one she'd had before. They were such perfect spheres that they looked like candy, not like a type of rock you would find scattered around at all. After Mariela stowed them away in her pouch, she got back onto Koo.

"Mind usin' one more fire bottle?"

"All right, here I go!"

"Rar!"

Mariela threw a fire bottle as hard as she could, and the raptor leaped over the blaze that came from it.

Perhaps the salamander was protecting its friends from the flames, as the path of fire that held the inky creatures at bay didn't feel all that hot to Mariela's group.

"Let's get to the southeast tower!"

"Yeah! Maybe it'll have stairs leading down!"

Edgan may have been luring the monsters, as there were fewer of them the farther south they went.

When Mariela looked toward the northeast tower where Edgan was, she sometimes spotted a light burning in the darkness.

"He's using the fire bottles..."

"...Edgan's stubborn."

That was Edgan for you. If it got truly perilous, he'd probably run away, but they couldn't waste the time he was giving them. Mariela's group passed through the east tower and returned to the southeast one just as Mariela used the last fire bottle.

05

"Hmm, the stairs down are suuuper conspicuous."

"That's random."

The third floor of the southeast tower, where Mariela had woken up, was a place that perfectly matched the name *storage room*. It was packed with boxes, shelves, and other things in a variety of sizes.

Mariela had missed it the first time she'd entered the room because she'd been frantically helping Koo, but the steps down to the second floor in this room were hidden under an enormous box.

The chamber had several crates that were taller than Mariela and Yuric, and there were others of a size for storing wine piled up in the vicinity. There was so much stuff, it left hardly any place to stand. Even if Mariela and Yuric tried to push boxes to move them, there was nowhere for them to go. And even if they wanted to break them, Yuric's whip would get entangled with the other baggage when she raised it.

Moreover, the hallways leading north and west were similarly stuffed with miscellany.

"There are empty alcohol bottles in them? And, huh, there's potion vials. Are these old clothes?"

Unlike in the east tower, this place had many goods that ordinary people used, particularly the poor. Looking over the objects, Mariela had the distinct feeling she'd seen them before.

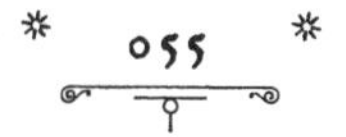

Since she'd used their last fire bottle, she was grateful for the empty alcohol bottles, which enabled her to make new ones. With just these, it seemed she could Fire to her heart's content.

"What's in this huge box? If Donnino was here, he could destroy it, but the best the two of us can do is remove the things blocking the north side."

It didn't seem like Mariela and Yuric could get to the floor below, and they had no choice but to head to the west side to look for other stairs and defeat monsters as they went through the fourth-floor passage. If they hadn't replenished their fire bottles, it doubtlessly would've been an impossible trek.

"Let's hurry and go collect medicinal herbs. Hold on tight, Mariela."

"Okay, I got iiiiiiiiiiiiiiit!"

Although she'd replied "I got it," Mariela had just a slight feeling of regret—"I didn't get it at all"—as she swayed violently on the raptor's back. It was all she could do to close her mouth as she bounced about so she wouldn't bite her tongue.

Although Yuric had regarded Edgan rather frigidly, it seemed she might be more worried about him than was first apparent. Or perhaps she was concerned about their other comrades, who surely had to be somewhere on the west side of this gigantic citadel.

By the time they reached the floor where the gepla fruit grew, Mariela was completely exhausted and not at all in a condition to harvest it.

Yuric had a slender build not much different from Mariela's, and she didn't appear to have much in the way of muscle, so what in the world was the difference between them? Yuric's animal taming skills? She wasn't a member of the Black Iron Freight Corps for nothing.

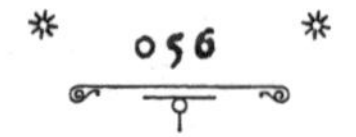

"Mariela, ya should rest a bit."

Yuric built up a pile of aquatic plants in front of Mariela, who had collapsed on the floor.

Yuric gathered up everything growing in the vicinity of the gepla fruit on the outer wall of the tower. This provided Mariela with far more weeds than anything else, though there were a few edible greens mixed in. Hopefully, Mariela could use them as soup ingredients after they had been dried.

Was there a point to me coming here?

As Mariela pondered this, the mountain of aquatic plants continued growing. Apparently, Yuric used her whip to grab the ones beyond her reach. Aquatic plants probably all looked the same to her.

"Hey, Mariela. Hurry and make some more of those fire bottles," Yuric instructed with a sidelong glance at the mountain of aquatic plants. It seemed like it would be an enormous task just to sort them all out.

Yuric was tough. This was good training for Mariela, who had grown lazy from Sieg spoiling her.

"Rawr har."

Something appeared to have pleased the salamander, as it was happily shaking its tail back and forth.

"Ugh, fiiine..."

Resigning herself, Mariela set about sorting the aquatic plants and making fire bottles while rubbing her behind, sore from riding on the wild raptor.

Yuric had plucked an unthinkable quantity of vegetation, but it took hardly any time for Mariela to complete as many fire bottles as they could load onto Koo.

Since the explosive concoctions were between low-grade and

mid-grade, Mariela could make them in the blink of an eye. Even when the time it took to sift through the stack of herbs was factored in, the entire process took less than two hours.

It was very easy to first *Crystallize* and remove the medicinal herbs, then dry the remaining aquatic plants and the gepla seeds and stir them with wind power while sorting them all at once.

No more than a few hours could have passed since reaching this southeast tower, collecting the gepla seeds, making fire bottles, and returning to the fourth floor. Yet…

"Huh…? It's already dawning!"

Could the flow of time be distorted here? It had remained dark for a standard period last night, so it should still be nighttime now, yet it was clearly lightening outside, and the water was already returning.

"Is there some kinda condition that makes morning come?" Yuric pondered.

"If we're talking about something that was different today… Edgan?"

"Yeah. Somethin' about him using a Fire Dance to handle all the monsters?"

Had Edgan gained a means to manipulate time?

This is where one would usually say something like "That's an A-Ranker for you," but…

"No way Edgan actually did somethin'."

"Yeah. But the black monsters disappear in the morning, so Edgan gets to rest, too."

"!!! That's it!" Yuric exclaimed after Mariela's offhand comment. "The black monsters didn't disappear when morning came; morning comes early like this when they're defeated!"

This world's nights and the ebon creatures were connected.

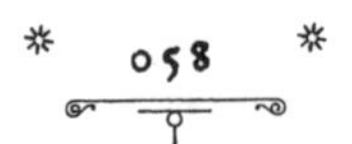

If the monsters weren't all slain, the day wouldn't come until it did under normal circumstances, and when morning arrived and water filled the place, the inky things vanished.

On the first day, they hadn't known the black monsters' weakness, so Edgan had probably battled them all night, but today, Yuric informed him of their vulnerability and gave him fire bottles. Edgan could put magical elements in his swords, but he didn't have a lot of magical power, since he wasn't a mage. However, if he made liberal use of the fire bottles, it was possible to quickly take out those black monsters.

That's what Yuric reasoned, anyway.

"Yeah, this world's so weird, it wouldn't be strange for something like that to happen. But if so… That means Edgan actually made the night end after all?"

"Ugh… When ya put it like that, it makes it sound like he did it intentionally, and that kinda irritates me."

"He definitely seems like he'd go 'Mwa-ha-ha, I'm the king of the night!'"

Edgan, king of the night. Mariela felt like that title was appropriate for a different sort of reason, but considering he'd traveled with Mariela to escape his women troubles, it might've been more apt to call him a slave of the night.

"If we said somethin' like that to Edgan, he'd call himself a god of the night, never mind a king. Since he's always playin' women, I think *fraud* of the night would be more fittin'. It'd be nice if he played with fire instead and burned himself out."

Edgan might have been in perfect form last night, but Yuric still had quite the wicked tongue when it came to that man. Although Mariela twitched just a little, all she could do was respond with a fake smile.

"Ha, ha-ha-ha-ha-ha. Well, I'm certain the fire was really effective. Oh..."

"What is it?"

The word *fire* made Mariela recall something: Neither the third nor the fourth floor of the tower where Edgan was had any lit torches.

"Say, Yuric. Torches are lit at regular spots along the wall in this room, right? I wonder if they create a barrier that repels those black creatures. One that was stuck to Koo got in here, so it's probably not totally safe, but..."

Mariela recalled the monster that had burst into this room clinging to Koo clearly moved more sluggishly in here.

"I see... So we can judge what places are safe by the torches?"

"Yeah, probably."

"Fire, huh...?"

Mariela likely wasn't the only one who felt like the blazes were some kind of symbol.

"Right now, we should do what we can. Let's clear a path in the passage leadin' north on the third floor." As though her mood had shifted entirely, Yuric laid out a plan.

If they tidied up the baggage on the third level of the southeast tower, they'd secure a pathway through the east tower to the northeast one where Edgan was. Since this passage had torches lit at fixed intervals, Mariela and Yuric wanted to secure it as a safe route. While they were at it, it seemed prudent to leave more fire bottles and food for Edgan.

"Leavin' stuff's a good idea. If we put the grub by a window in the hallway, I think the smell will draw him over."

"...Is he an animal or something?"

Strange days and environs, but Yuric was still the same.

After preparing fire bottles and food for Edgan, it was time for Mariela's group to have dinner, too.

Since they'd collected a subspecies of gepla seeds in the east tower that could be used as cooking oil, they had fried fish-monster sandwiches and soup made from dried fish and the aquatic plants they'd collected not long ago.

"I get the feelin' those black monsters are absorbin' somethin' when they stick to you."

Yuric clenched and unclenched her hand as she noisily chewed on her sandwich. Apparently, she'd fought a black monster that had clung to her before she met up with Mariela.

"Absorbing...blood? Or magical power?"

"Neither. I dunno what, but I feel like it was somethin' important."

Come to think of it, a black monster had been stuck to Koo, too. They appeared to do that to living creatures and suck something out of them.

"Grar." Whether or not he understood, Koo made a sound like he agreed.

The way he did made it seem like he was saying, "It got meee," which was adorable. It made Mariela want to comfort him, so she said, "Just a little bit, okay?" and gave him a piece of dried fish.

"Rar!" Koo immediately brightened. As far as Mariela could tell, it didn't look like anything substantial had been taken from the raptor, but it was probably better to proactively burn the inky creatures.

"I'm kinda sleepy now..."

Mariela's eyelids grew heavy soon after she filled her stomach.

"Your internal clock probably thinks it's the middle of the night. We should sleep a bit."

The night had shortened, but would the day become proportionately longer?

Not knowing what time it really was made Mariela feel restless.

The third floor of the southeast tower was a mess of many boxes, and the cluttered, cramped feeling was a bit nostalgic. Mariela curled up in a gap within the chaos, and the salamander, who had come to her unnoticed, nestled up to her stomach and made it feel nice and warm.

Mariela fell asleep the moment she closed her eyes.

06

The sky stretched on forever, as did the earth.

Mountains and sparsely growing shrubs were visible in the distance.

Things seemed to continue to infinity.

A single herbivore, perhaps one that had lost its herd, was devoured by several carnivores, and an underfed bird fluttered through the air in search of scraps.

That unbound place was undoubtedly challenging and cruel, but free at the same time.

She'd seen a place like that when she was very young.

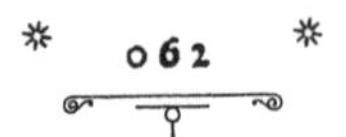

She had made her escape to find her way back to that place she saw whenever she closed her eyes, but...

"The sky's so cramped."

"Rar."

When she looked up from the slums of the imperial capital where buildings crowded together, things seemed narrow. It made Yuric sad to think this place couldn't completely satisfy even the sky.

Growl.

"I'm hungry... Wanna go catch some rats?"

"Rar..."

Before she arrived at the imperial capital with the first raptor she'd ever trained, Yuric had believed she could find that place from her childhood as long as she had a raptor. Yet she didn't even know where it was.

Yuric had come to the imperial capital to get information on its whereabouts, but her meager traveling money had dried up. The young Yuric didn't know whether or not she could get work training raptors, and she had limited combat abilities. Even with her raptor, finding work was going to be tough.

The only adults Yuric had encountered were those who had pressed her to sell the raptor, or worse, ones who either tried to take the raptor by force or trick Yuric.

If this had been a village close to a forest rather than the imperial capital, she probably could have caught forest animals to satisfy her hunger. That's why she and the raptor had been able to eat their fill before they arrived at the capital.

However, the imperial capital simply had a great many people, and even if she went out to the forest about a day's journey away, it didn't have decent game. Perhaps the humans had hunted any easily caught prey to extinction, as the rest had fled to a faraway forest.

The only option for hunting in the imperial capital was the unsanitary rats that crawled through the slums. Yuric aside, the raptor had a big body, and the rats didn't sate its hunger at all.

"Rar, rar."

The raptor nuzzled its face against Yuric. It seemed to be saying, "I'm hungry. Let's go to the forest. There's nothing but bad humans here."

Yuric hugged the creature tight. "That's right, this isn't the place we're lookin' for."

But where should they go?

The weather was still warm, and if they went to the forest, they would have no trouble getting food in a day or two. But the woods had no eaves to keep out the rain and no walls to protect from monsters.

Besides, what about when winter arrived?

Hunger, and the uneasy feeling of an uncertain tomorrow. The only thing the young Yuric could do was nestle close to the raptor and curl up in a nook in the slums.

She must have fallen asleep at some point.

"Rarar."

After the raptor shook her awake, Yuric opened her eyes in response to its cry and saw the creature with a delighted expression and a chubby, dead chicken on the ground.

This plumpness meant it wasn't wild. It had clearly been raised to be eaten.

"How did you...?"

When Yuric used her taming skills to feel around for the

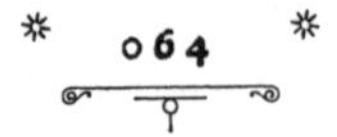

raptor's thoughts, she discovered it had apparently attacked a village on the outskirts of the imperial capital before dawn and stolen the chicken from there. Most likely, its hunger had led it to eat many more, as the raptor's mouth was wet with blood, and Yuric could sense the creature's full stomach.

"Rar!"

"It's tasty! Eat! I caught and brought it for you."

This animal, which didn't know it had done something improper, gazed innocently at Yuric as if it wanted praise for bringing meat to its hungry master.

"What...? You... It's because I'm inexperienced..."

Although young, Yuric knew right from wrong.

A savage beast like a raptor would hunt without a command from its keeper. Yuric understood how dangerous that was. Even if she was asleep, attacking other people's livestock as it pleased was... No matter how hungry Yuric was, even if the raptor had been thinking of her, she wouldn't be forgiven.

A fully trained beast didn't assail or eat something without its master's permission. The young, lonely Yuric's training may have been too trusting and lacked strictness.

Fortunately, as far as Yuric could see in the raptor's memories, it hadn't attacked any humans. Apparently, the farmer who came running at the racket had startled the beast, and it had fled here with this chicken in its mouth.

If it doesn't know the taste of human flesh, I don't think it'll be killed, but...

There was no way Yuric had the money to reimburse for the lost chickens.

If she was caught, she would have no choice but to relinquish the raptor.

"Found it! Over here!"

Just when Yuric was pondering running away, the sound of dogs barking and the shouts of men who seemed to be adventurers reached Yuric's ears.

"Raptor! Let's go!"

Yuric immediately jumped on the creature's back to leave the place behind.

"Nice try, chicken thief!" a man exclaimed.

A stone came flying at Yuric.

"Gah!"

She didn't know how powerful an adventurer the man was. Regardless, an adult had hurled a rock about the size of a fist at Yuric, who was still a child. The stone hit her left shoulder with a sickening crack, and she fell off the raptor.

"Strike! Once more!"

"Rar!"

The raptor, angry that its master had been injured, rushed at the adventurer with its teeth bared. This man probably wasn't especially strong. He couldn't deal with the raptor's speed and the way it opened its mouth to bite him, and all he did was recoil and cry, "Waugh!"

"N-no... *Stop*, raptor!"

If it attacked a human here, there was no turning back for the creature. If it struck a person without a command from its master, experienced the taste of human flesh, and learned it could overpower people, retraining it would be difficult. Sooner or later, it would probably be caught and culled.

Yuric had frantically stopped the raptor, but the adventurer, utterly ignorant of her efforts, began to beat the animal that had suddenly halted with his sword's sheath, and his comrades who came running threw a net over the animal so it couldn't escape.

"This thing nearly gave me a heart attack! Grah, how d'you like this?! Grah, just try to bite me again!"

The adventurer used his scabbard to beat the captive animal.

"Rar, rar, rar..."

"Stop! It can't fight back! Stop it, stop it!"

Holding her broken left shoulder, Yuric clung to the raptor, and the adventurer grabbed the front of her shirt and lifted her up.

"What was that, you little shit? You're its owner, thief!"

"I'll apologize! I'll pay them back! So please..."

"Hey, isn't this brat an animal tamer? We can make some good coin if we sell that kid."

"Oh yeah? I didn't know 'cause he's all dirty, but I bet we can get a lot more money from that than what we'd get from the chicken thief request."

"'Ey, I know a slave trader who'll buy."

Yuric had to escape.

These adventurers had no intention of listening to her, and at this rate, the raptor and Yuric would be sold apart. As Yuric fought desperately to loosen the hand that was gripping her, the adventurer's fist swung down at her.

"Quit strugglin'."

Bam, whack. The man's fist mercilessly struck her, ripped her worn-out clothing, and threw her to the ground. She'd managed to escape his grip, but after being hit so hard, Yuric couldn't even get up.

"Hey, ain't this a girl?"

"Hmm? Ooh, this'll be a profitable one. She's still a brat, but females fetch a high price!"

The men's hearty, vulgar laughter reverberated.

Filthy, foul people. I have to escape, no matter what it takes...

The fallen raptor caught in the net lay in Yuric's blurry line of sight.

"Rar..."

It, too, had been beaten and injured, yet it seemed to be worried about Yuric as it gazed at her.

She slowly stretched out her hand toward the raptor.

After being struck countless times and thrown to the ground, Yuric found that her right hand was wet from blood, perhaps from a cut somewhere. The raptor understood Yuric's intention after seeing her reach for it, and it twisted its body to push its forehead toward Yuric.

The adventurers were probably busy contriving to sell Yuric and the raptor. They didn't notice Yuric writing some sort of bloody letters on the raptor's forehead.

I did it...

All she had to do now was give the Order.

Yuric was still inexperienced as an animal tamer. Still, there was no doubt she had inherited this ability, which only the members of the borderland tribe possessed, along with that landscape she'd seen when she was very young.

The raptor, strengthened and turned savage by the animal tamer blood, would unquestionably devour the likes of these brutish adventurers. Yuric simply had to give the command.

The Order to *Go Wild, My Children* and devour these humans.

Although if she gave this instruction, there would be no turning back for either Yuric or the raptor.

"G... Go... Wild, My..."

Yuric's field of vision was blurry.

She didn't want to kill people. She didn't want to make the raptor devour people.

She just wanted to find her way back to that place...that horizon, the only thing remaining in her memory.

So why...

"I think you've gone far enough."

Before Yuric could send the raptor into a frenzy, a lone figure emerged from an alley in the slums.

"What was that, asshole?"

"What's with this guy?"

The adventurers drew their swords and threatened the man who'd suddenly entered the fray.

"You had best let this drop. I've called the guards. They'll probably be here at any moment. If you try to make a child like this a slave unjustly, you'll wind up forced into servitude yourselves when you're caught."

The man didn't seem to have a weapon, yet he didn't hesitate to approach the adventurers with their swords drawn. With a mask hiding his face and a hood low over his eyes, he had an intimidating air, suggesting he wasn't an ordinary citizen.

With seemingly no opening to take advantage of, the adventurers exchanged looks.

Clearly, they thought the man was bluffing. There was no way guards would come to the slums.

However, someone in the distance was definitely shouting, "Mr. Guaaard, this way, this way!"

"Hey, let's get outta here."

"Tch, count yerself lucky!"

Even if the guard was a lie, the man seemed to have other comrades. Causing even more of a commotion wasn't a good plan. The adventurers sheathed their swords and retreated in a hurry.

"Well now, they're the ones who should count themselves lucky. Can you stand? Ahh, they got your shoulder? **Heal.**"

After helping Yuric to her feet, the masked man used restorative magic on her broken left shoulder.

The voice calling for help appeared to have been a child putting on a performance, as he received a reward from the masked man and immediately disappeared into an alley.

"...Why did ya help us?" Yuric asked doubtfully. Somehow, she had a hunch this savior of hers wasn't a bad person. But the disguised hero had perceived what she'd been about to do.

"Because it would be troubling for a raptor to go into a frenzy here. You seem to be inexperienced. Causing a disturbance in the slums would be a nuisance to the other residents. Look, your raptor is very intimidating. Do me a favor and calm it down."

Now that the masked man mentioned it, the raptor had grown very agitated because Yuric's own anger had influenced it. The animal breathed wildly through its nose as it bared its fangs, and it seemed ready to indiscriminately accost even the man who had saved them.

"*Calm down*, calm down. It's all right now. Thank you for trying to save me. Thank you, it's all right now..."

"Rar..."

Yuric soothed the raptor as she removed the net and gave it plenty of pets on the head.

Both Yuric and her animal companion were beaten and

bruised, but the masked man's simple healing magic helped them recover quickly.

Thankfully, since those adventurers had intended to catch and sell the raptor, they hadn't injured it in any significant way.

"Now, this raptor is the one that attacked the chicken coop, correct? If I let you two off now, I'm sure it will cause more trouble. At this point, I believe the best plan is to quietly repay those you've wronged."

The masked man had a point. But the only things Yuric could pay with were herself or the raptor. She hung her head.

In response, Yuric's savior proposed, "Hmm, if this raptor can work, you can repay your debt in no time. Since its lack of complete training is evident, it can labor together with its animal tamer. That seems best. I'll handle the negotiations for you and get things set up."

The masked man arranged it so that Yuric and the raptor would work on that farm on the imperial capital's outskirts for about a month. The raptor got to eat the intestines of any livestock that was processed into raw meat. When weak monsters attacked the farm, the raptor would kill and devour them, too. It wasn't going hungry anymore.

Regular meals had thankfully calmed the creature, as the raptor not only protected the livestock from monsters, but it also began pulling wagons and allowing humans other than Yuric to ride it. No longer needing to supervise the raptor constantly, Yuric trained the homestead's watchdogs in her free time and performed medical examinations on the barnyard animals. She was even asked to come back for more work after she'd repaid her debt.

By the time Yuric's deficit was squared away, the raptor's training had been completed. Now, even without Yuric, it would obey the stock farmer and wouldn't go around snatching other people's chickens.

"Please be good to the raptor."

"Yes, we'll treat it with great care."

"Rar."

Yuric knew the raptor couldn't live in the imperial capital with her. She didn't even possess the means to provide daily food for it.

Understanding this, Yuric decided to leave the raptor in the farmer's care and return to the imperial capital alone, though the farmer made it plain that she was welcome back any time.

"Hello, Yuric. Good job at the farm. I know I said, 'If you have nowhere to go after you've finished your task, you should come to me,' but I'm surprised you actually came. I heard the stock farmer tried to convince you to stay."

"Visitin' the place every now and then'll be enough. I look forward to livin' with ya, Franz."

Yuric returned to the slums and lived with the masked man.

It was as though she'd been drawn to the bestial nature hidden under his facade.

Yuric was an animal tamer. She felt her instincts would develop more by living with a beast.

This guy isn't a bad person. I want to return to that place someday. But right now...

Yuric's intuition seemed to be correct. She'd lived with animals, as an animal, ever since she lost her mother. For the first time, Yuric now had a place she could go home to and a brief, humanlike peace.

07

...Another dream about Yuric? It felt so real.

Mariela awoke in the baggage-packed third floor of the southeast tower.

"...Another nostalgic dream. Why had I forgotten...?"

Yuric seemed to have risen at the same time, as she sat up while rubbing her eyes.

She mentioned something about a sentimental vision. Could it have been the same one Mariela just had?

While not certain, Mariela believed that was so. She sat up to listen. It seemed like the pouch at her waist had come open unnoticed, as some of its contents had fallen out—hand towel, potion vials that had been repacked with medicinal crystals, a small folding knife for cooking.

In addition to items such as those, the golden-brown stones had come free.

"Uh...?"

The scarlet-on-white rock was gone again. Thinking it had rolled somewhere, Mariela searched the area, but it was like it had simply vanished, as she couldn't find it.

"Mariela? What is it?"

"U-um. It's the white stone..." That's all Mariela said as she took a long, hard look at Yuric's face.

Pale skin and white hair. Yuric's scarlet eyes shining from

amid such light colors seemed bizarre. Mariela thought she was beautiful, but her appearance made her seem very nearly a wild animal.

These were the colors of an animal tamer. Weren't they just like those white stones with scarlet mixed in?

"...Say, Yuric. The dream you said you had, was it about meeting Franz in the imperial capital?" Mariela asked to confirm her belief.

"Yeah. Was I sleep talkin'?"

Mariela knew it.

Yuric had said, "I get the feelin' those black monsters are absorbin' somethin' when they stick to you."

And they'd obtained scarlet-on-white stones reminiscent of Yuric from defeated black monsters.

Now those stones were gone, and Mariela had a dream about Yuric's past.

A vision Yuric herself had said she'd forgotten.

"These rocks are memories the black monsters stole..."

When one of those creatures had clung to Yuric, it absorbed recollections of her past. The stolen memories became a stone in the monster, and after defeating it, they returned to Mariela and Yuric. The recollections that turned into rocks became dreams and were restored, but Yuric herself wasn't the only one who saw them; Mariela, who slept next to her, did, too.

"Hmm, guess anythin' goes in a world like this. Still, it's all a bit much to take in."

After hearing Mariela's explanation, Yuric gazed at the golden-brown stones with a troubled expression.

"Yeah. Sorry I peeped at your past like that... Next time we get a stone, I'll make sure to sleep in a different room."

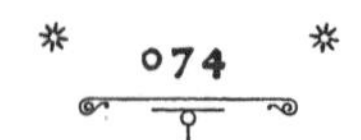

Yuric waved her hand and said, "I don't mind. I was just surprised," in response to Mariela's apology.

"But if that's how it is, why are these stones still here? And whose are they in the first place?"

"Hmm. Judgin' from the colors, I think they're Edgan's. As for why they're still here, it's 'cause he didn't sleep near us...maybe?"

They'd learned all sorts of things, but plenty of uncertainties still remained.

Before Mariela had found Yuric, the monsters the salamander defeated didn't drop any stones. Did they simply not have any, or could there be some requirement for them to drop the rocks?

"If that's true, it's good we defeated those things. I'm glad we made lots of fire bottles!"

Yuric gripped a fire bottle tightly. She seemed to like fire.

Behind them, Koo went "Rar!" and raised his tail, and even the salamander went "Rawr!" and blew flame from its mouth.

Everyone was raring to go. Mariela needed to be the calm one and responsibly manage the remaining fire bottles.

A person who appeared cool, vigorous, and had an extremely wicked tongue. Up to now, that's how Mariela saw Yuric, and she'd felt it was only natural for a member of the Black Iron Freight Corps to be like that, but now Yuric seemed a little sweeter.

"...I was pretty surprised. I didn't know you were a girl."

If she hadn't had those dreams, she probably wouldn't have noticed.

Certainly, Yuric was slender and graceful, but because of her sharp tongue and the way she could control raptors at will, Mariela had just assumed she was a boy.

"It's a secret, okay?" Now, even Yuric putting her index finger to her lips and saying that sort of thing seemed adorable to Mariela.

"Does everyone in the Black Iron Freight Corps know?"

"...Probably. Except for one."

They'd been traveling together for a long time. Anyone would've noticed by now. Those who didn't surely didn't have eyes or a brain.

"...Does Edgan know?"

"...Koo, heeey, food time!"

Koo opened his mouth wide on hearing the words *food time*, and in a fluster, Mariela had to stop Yuric from tossing Edgan's memory pearls into it. She managed to get them back and stowed them in her pouch again.

CHAPTER 2

The Calamity of Famine

01

On the third night, as soon as the water outside turned to mist, Mariela and Yuric rode on Koo, with the salamander on his head, and dashed westward.

They passed by the black monsters en route without stopping whenever possible as they ran.

The southwest tower they made for was where Yuric had first found herself.

The day they'd washed up in this world, Yuric ran down the tower in one go and arrived at this rampart passage before sundown.

The room on the fourth floor had few torches and was only dimly lit, and because the outside had been full of water, the north and east doors didn't open. The third floor had also been flooded, and Yuric had been unable to get down there. However, on her way down the tower, she could see a path leading to the temple from the center of the outer wall connecting east and west, and apparently, it was precisely sunset when she'd tried to dive down and investigate while there was still light.

On the third level, the outer circumference of the wall had collapsed and flooded. And in addition to the north and east doors, there seemed to be a staircase leading to the second floor.

The daylight had disappeared before Yuric dived down to the second level. The water had thinned and changed into a dense fog,

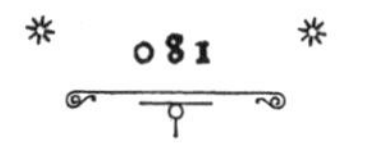

and before she knew it, she could breathe. Yuric had wondered what was going on and looked outside through a hole in the wall, where she saw several black monsters crawling up it.

Although she put up a fight with her whip, too many came in through the gap. After frantically shaking off several that attached themselves to her, Yuric had dashed up to the fourth floor, only to be met by a few more of those inky creatures.

Had the doors not initially opened because of water pressure, and had they now because the sea had vanished, or was there another reason? Regardless, they yielded, and Yuric moved to the east tower through the southeast one, where Mariela was at the time.

Mariela had gone down the tower and found her way to the fourth floor long after the sun set, so Yuric probably came to the southeast tower before Mariela reached the fourth floor. Mariela and Yuric speculated that Koo the raptor had sensed his master's magical power and was attacked by the black monsters that had been chasing her.

Mariela and the others had come here as a group of six people. And there were most likely six towers.

If they assumed each person had been brought to a different tower, where on earth could their other companions be?

When Mariela and Yuric used fire bottles to *Fire* the ebon creatures that were lurking just before the southwest tower, they obtained stones, just as they expected. There were two: One was the golden-brown kind that seemed to be Edgan's, and the other was gold on blue.

Perhaps the rock's shades informed Yuric of something, as she cried, "Mariela, hurry!" and ran for the fourth floor of the southwest tower while sending black monsters flying with her whip.

Yuric's impatience was apparent.

That blue stone was probably one of Franz's memories. Yuric taking no notice of the fact that they'd found a rock of Edgan's at the same time made Edgan, who was getting crazy over in the northeast tower even now, seem just the tiniest bit pitiable.

Black monsters were crawling up from a lower level toward the fourth floor of the southwest tower, which had few torches. The third floor was likely filled with the inky memory stealers. However, the group had fire bottles now, and the salamander would protect them from the flames, so it was possible for them to charge down.

But their destination was something to be discussed and decided on together. If even Edgan was having a tough fight, it was likely the other party members had come to harm, too. Mariela and Yuric would have to try to deliver fire bottles as soon as possible.

Yuric used her abilities to empower Koo's legs, and after the raptor quickly kicked open the door leading north, they hurried toward the west tower.

The fire bottles created fierce fire pillars at regular intervals and burned up the black monsters. The salamander not only protected the group from the flames, it also might have even been controlling the range of the blaze, as the ebon creatures that barred the way forward burned to nothing before the group ran through. Perhaps not all of the monsters carried stones, since Mariela and Yuric didn't spot any new ones before they reached the west tower.

When they forcefully opened the door to the west tower with a *bang!* and plunged inside, they found no lack of lit torches.

This room was probably safe. Maybe someone had taken refuge here.

"Is...is anyone here?!" Mariela's shout echoed for a time, but there was no reply.

"Yuric, let's go to the northwest tower. There's probably no one here, and even if there is, it's safe, so I think it's fine to leave this area for later."

"Got it!"

The raptor carrying Mariela and Yuric broke into a run again, sprinting toward the passage crowded with monsters darker than the night.

"Hii-yah!"

Although Mariela's fighting strength was nonexistent and her clumsiness second to none, the amount of magical power she possessed was outstanding. A fire bottle with as much energy as Mariela could put into it caught Yuric's wind magic and flew toward the creatures blocking their way. Upon explosion, the salamander stretched the pillar of fire even farther.

A second column of flame rose in the northeast as if in concord with Mariela and Yuric's own.

It was Edgan. He'd probably noticed the explosions along the third-floor passage of the northeast tower. Perhaps he'd been lured by the smell of food from the window. Might as well praise him for being so wild.

Undaunted, Mariela hurled another fire bottle.

Although she'd thought running through swirling flames would be terrifying, Mariela felt it was far more beautiful than she'd imagined. Thanks to the salamander's protection, it was bright and warm despite being nighttime, and that seemed to urge them forward toward their destination.

Mariela and the others exited the bright tunnel of flames, and just as they arrived at the northwest tower, that tunnel dispersed into thin air.

A gentle light shone in from the east.

"It's morning! This fast?! The water's gonna fill the place! And the door's closed!"

It would be unbearable to be locked out in a place like this. Mariela couldn't swim, and it didn't seem likely the salamander could exist in water.

Without even giving a thought to the black monsters sticking to them, they somehow managed to rush into the northwest tower, at which point the outside was filled with water. Just like in the northeast tower, the door connecting east and west on the fourth level of this tower was gone, and water was pouring in. Of course, the torches weren't lit, either. So the door may have been opened despite the fact that the place was nearly submerged.

The black monsters clinging to Mariela and Yuric practically melted away as they vanished when the water touched them. Although they looked like slimes, they apparently weren't aquatic creatures.

Knee-deep in rapidly materializing liquid that was rising from below, Mariela put the salamander, who hadn't yet gotten wet, on her head and shouted, "Yuric, we have to hurry upstairs!"

"Got it!"

Carrying Mariela and the others, Koo hurried up the tower at top speed to keep the salamander safe. It seemed like the mist steadily filled the place from below and turned into water when it reached a specific density.

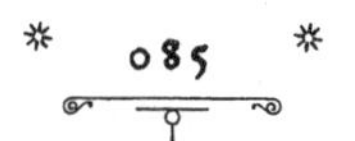

Koo's ascent would for sure earn him a gold medal if something like a raptor track-and-field competition existed. And that would be no surprise coming from the beast who had once rescued Mariela from a death lizard's blade. Koo usually fooled around, but he was the kind of raptor who did what needed to be done when push came to shove.

Koo ran all the way to a room in the middle of the northwest tower in one go, and after Mariela and Yuric confirmed the torches there were lit, Koo finally stopped running and dropped to the floor.

"Thanks, Koo. You've saved us so many times."

"Koo, you were great. Ya really are somethin'."

"Rawr, rawr raaawr."

The salamander jumped from the top of Mariela's head to Koo's and chattered as it tapped the raptor's head with its tail. Maybe it was saying "Thank you" or "Nice work!"

Koo seemed to be really pleased over being praised by both Mariela and the usually-strict Yuric. He was still panting as the raised tip of his tail quivered happily.

"I'll make us a feast today! Something that'll really perk us up."

"Raptors can't eat cooked stuff, y'know."

"...Rar."

"Rawr."

Koo made a disappointed noise as though he somehow comprehended Yuric's statement.

"Could Koo try it, at least?"

"Hmm, just a little. More important, ya should give him water with magical power in it."

Mariela stood up to give Koo some water when Yuric suddenly exclaimed "Shh!" and stopped her.

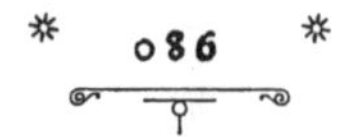

Mariela looked around to figure out why and found that Yuric, Koo, and the fire spirit salamander were all staring at the stairwell they'd climbed to get here. Koo appeared to be quieting his heavy breathing in preparation to start running at a moment's notice.

The area beneath those stairs ought to be half submerged.

The black monsters should have melted and disappeared when they touched the water, and the torches in the room were brightly lit. Mariela and Yuric had thought the chamber was safe.

But even Mariela could hear the sloshing of wet footsteps.

Some time had passed since today's flooding. Whatever was approaching had traveled through the water for quite a while.

Just as Mariela felt so tense that she might explode, Yuric shouted happily:

"Franz!"

"...So you're all right, Yuric."

It was indeed Franz.

The previously nervous Koo went "rarf" as he exhaled a long-held breath. It was such a relief that Mariela wanted to say "rarf" herself. However, Franz's behavior as he ascended the stairs while sopping wet struck Mariela as somewhat strange.

"Yuric, who is this girl...?"

"Uh, it's Mariela...?"

"Mariela... That's right. She's our current client."

Apparently, Franz had lost quite a bit of his memory. He couldn't remember anything about Mariela except that she was his client. Unlike Edgan, Franz was a healing mage, so he'd been unable to repel many of the black monsters.

"Franz... When night arrives, let's leave this place together!" Yuric took Franz's hand and tried to persuade him as she dried him off, but he shook his head and replied, "I can't do that."

"Why?! Don't tell me ya also think ya have to protect this place? That's impossible for a healing mage! Ya should leave that to Edgan!"

"This temple is connected to my roots. The blood flowing within me tells me to protect it."

Franz's eyes peeked out from his mask. Their color was the same gold as that in the stones Mariela's group had picked up along the way, but different from the gold eyes of Mariela's master. If Mariela had to say, she'd describe them as having a damp shine reminiscent of a reptile's, and the pupils were vertically long and narrow. If those stones had the same colors as Franz, surely the hair hidden under his hood was blue.

No matter how desperately Yuric urged him, Franz seemed to have no interest in leaving the tower. He stubbornly reiterated, "I'm staying here to protect the temple."

"Anyway, why don't we all have something to eat? Mr. Franz, are you hungry, too?"

"I'd appreciate that," Franz replied to Mariela's suggestion. While he seemed averse to leaving the tower, he was okay with passing the time with Mariela and Yuric until night arrived.

"Fish? I have some to add to that."

"I'll help ya carry it."

Yuric probably wanted to be with Franz, even if it was just for a short time.

Mariela left transporting the food from the top floor of the tower to Yuric, Franz, and Koo while she herself began cooking.

They'd left the monster fish she and Yuric had caught for Edgan, so there was little food remaining. The lean fish was rich, and Mariela could prepare it like meat depending on how she cooked it, so she decided to marinate it with garlic-like herbs and the seasonings she'd brought with her before roasting it. The aquatic plants Yuric had plucked along with those used for the fire bottles were just perfect for that.

As Mariela marinated the lean monster fish in a Transmutation Vessel, she gathered medicinal herbs from a window. It would be helpful to have more edible vegetation, and she'd be even more grateful if she had gepla seeds to make more fire bottles.

Unfortunately, the group's current floor was too deep to find gepla, but Mariela plucked those plants she could get cooking oil from. Their roots were edible as well. They were fibrous and would get stuck in one's teeth if eaten as is, but when Mariela cut them diagonally and fried them in oil, they took on a burdock-like flavor. The aquatic plant salad tasted a little bitter and monotonous, so the roots would make a good accent.

"Mariela, I'm starvin'."

As Mariela was using the salamander to dry the lean fish that had been marinated in the seasonings, Yuric and the others returned. From the look of it, they'd harvested what useful vegetation they could, too, which they'd piled onto Koo in back-breaking quantities.

"...Whoa, look at all that stuff. Koo, Franz, you guys're both musclemen."

They'd brought so much that Mariela reflexively uttered something silly.

It befit Koo, who was loaded with so many aquatic plants they practically reached the ceiling, but also Franz, who had lugged an enormous serpentine fish monster wrapped around his body.

"This tastes like chicken."

The monster looked more like a snake than a fish.

"Chicken... Deep-fried... To fry it in such a small amount of oil, I'd need to..."

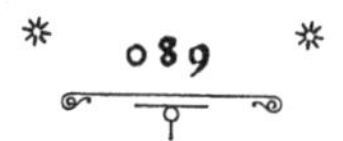

Mariela was in serious mode. As she pondered something, she gazed at the fish monster with the same intent expression as when she made potions.

"Mariela, I'll help."

"Thanks, Yuric. In that case, could you cut the snake monster into bite-size pieces?"

Two girls doing some outdoor cooking. If that was all there was to it, surely it would have been a charming scene, but a serpent that looked like it could have swallowed them whole lay before them. Franz did the work of slicing it lengthwise with a knife and tearing off the skin, but Yuric was the one who mercilessly butchered the pink flesh. Mariela tossed the cut meat and seasonings into a Transmutation Vessel with "Just a little **Pressurize**," then added flour she'd made from tubers and vigorously spun the entire Transmutation Vessel before shaping another one into a nozzle and using that to uniformly spray what little oil she had.

Mariela made full use of the transcendent high-grade potion creation techniques that only she could perform.

"Superheat."

The temperature was important for deep-frying food. Mariela had once made the Elixir, however, so cooking was rather simple by comparison. She listened carefully to the sound of the meat to make the outside crisp and the inside juicy, and she completed the dish by tweaking the heat to bring out the flavor without wasting a drop of the fish's oil. Meat was, in its own sense, a material. There was no way the ultimate alchemist, now quite hungry, couldn't draw out the best from such a substance.

It was only because Yuric and Franz were with Mariela that they could enjoy cuisine made of such advanced alchemy skills.

"It's good."

"Delicious! Franz, if ya come with us, ya could eat this kind of cooking every day."

"...That's a shame......... A real shame."

Mariela's transcendent alchemical meal and Yuric's cunning psychological attack caused Franz's strange sense of obligation to waver. The three spent their brief time together enjoying incredibly delicious food, but all the same, Franz persisted. "I'm staying," he insisted, refusing to travel with Mariela and Yuric.

That night, everyone decided to sleep in this room midway up the tower.

Mariela had Franz's stones in her pouch. If she slept here, she would probably glimpse some of his memories. With that in mind, she offered to spend the night on a floor above, but Franz and Yuric stopped her, saying it would be dangerous.

Mariela didn't explain the circumstances regarding the rocks to Franz. Yuric, who knew about these special dreams about the past, had said, "There's still a lot we don't know. Let's focus on determining exactly how we recover the stolen memories first." She seemed to think Mariela being present was one of the conditions for stolen recollections returning.

Mariela and the others fell asleep within the bright light shining in from outside the windows.

The dream of Franz that Mariela had was memories of carefree days he spent living with Yuric in his clinic in the slums of the imperial capital. The appearance of the simple infirmary and Yuric and Franz's modest living somehow reminded Mariela of when she had lived with her master in their Fell Forest cottage.

Although there were days with unreasonable demands from unpleasant customers and those when Franz and Yuric were looked down on for their race or appearance, they helped and supported each other. Together, they overcame all obstacles. It wasn't a one-sided relationship of Franz protecting Yuric, either. It was clear that Yuric's presence helped keep Franz going, too.

Ordinary days with nothing special to them.

Franz's memories brought a sense of nostalgia to Mariela.

I have to find my master...

Mariela reaffirmed her determination. The salamander, curled up beside her, watched her with its glistening golden eyes.

They had probably been impatient, Mariela thought.

Mariela wasn't strong enough to fight off monsters. If one that neither Yuric's whip nor fire bottles worked on appeared, they would have no choice but to flee.

Mariela had lived in the Fell Forest. She knew this better than anyone else, so she had been exercising caution up to this point. All she'd encountered thus far were those inky things that, despite being ominous and many, could be defeated with simple explosives, so she'd been convinced that only those black monsters appeared in this strange structure.

"Let's leave the exploration of the west tower for later and hurry to the second floor for now."

Mariela and Yuric had decided to remain in the northwest tower, partly due to Franz's memory having largely disappeared.

His recollections from the stone Mariela picked up had returned, but that was just a portion of what had been stolen away.

But more than that...

"Franz! Your face..."

When Mariela turned in the direction of Yuric's trembling voice, she saw that the other girl was about to remove Franz's mask.

The hair spilling from the lowered hood was the same blue as that of the memory stone. It was neatly trimmed and swept out behind him. Mariela didn't get a good look at the man's face, but he struck Mariela as much younger than she had thought, possibly closer in age to Sieg or Edgan.

Rather, he had a very calm air, so if you lined him up next to the overly excitable Edgan, he would probably seem far more mature.

But what surprised Mariela wasn't Franz's calm disposition. The same shade of blue as Franz's hair was also present on his forehead and the bridge of his nose. When Mariela squinted, she thought she could see scales.

Franz noticed Mariela's gaze and quickly returned the mask to his face, but the azure things peeked out from under the facade in spots around his eyes.

They say Franz has demi-human traits. But...his face. Weren't those scales...?

Franz had said that this mysterious place held some connection to his roots, and that he had to protect it and couldn't leave. Assuming what he spoke of was his demi-human blood, then perhaps this structure somehow gnawed at his heart and caused him to fight the black monsters here and lose his memories.

It's like he's being wholly remade...

The thought was enough to make Mariela shudder.

If Franz lost all his memories, what would become of him?

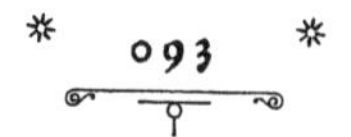

If Mariela had everything she could remember taken away, could she still say she was herself?

"Yuric, let's hurry."

"Got it."

After giving Franz fire bottles and food, the two girls rushed out of the northwest tower right at sunset.

Southward, southward, southward.

Yuric ran the raptor toward the southwest tower as they burned up black monsters with fire bottles.

En route, they passed through the west tower and continued to plunge toward the southwest one.

"Mariela. Fire bottle!"

"Okay!"

Mariela had gotten somewhat accustomed to handling the alchemical explosives. What's more, she had a fire spirit with her. The pillars of flame that rose up didn't burn even a single hair on her or Yuric's heads.

Mariela tossed a fire bottle into the third-floor room of the southwest tower, and the group flew into the enclosure not a moment later.

Just as Yuric had told her, part of the wall on this level had collapsed, and the black monsters were freely invading from the outside. If you looked at the tower from the exterior, you'd probably see flames jetting out from the collapsed parts of the building.

The blaze caused by Mariela's explosive immediately went out thanks to the salamander, but only the cinders of the wooden boxes and shelves, let alone of the monsters, remained on the third floor of the tower. That, and several spherical objects scattered on the floor.

"More stones... They're sooty and hard to see, but this one is..."

"Mariela, we can check those later. Let's hurry to the second floor."

How many rocks did that make? Mariela could check later. They needed to press ahead as much as they could.

After Mariela and Yuric collected the stones and put them away in a pouch, her group continued down to the floor below.

"There are...no stairs to the first floor, huh...?"

"This wasn't goin' to be that easy."

"Graaar..."

There were only doors leading to the north and east on the second level of the southwest tower—no steps to the first floor. To head for the temple, they would have to keep searching for a way down.

They hadn't expected smooth progress, so Mariela and Yuric weren't discouraged, but there was one creature who seemed fidgety with discomfiture.

"Koo, what's wrong? Ahh, the carpet? It's all right. No one'll get mad if we get it dirty."

A very expensive-looking rug had been laid out on the second floor of this tower, and Koo the raptor, who usually didn't go inside, was confused by the fluffy feeling under his feet.

"Rar!"

After Yuric told him it was acceptable to step on the carpet, Koo happily started kneading it on the spot and enjoyed its softness.

"There's something very different about this place."

It was not just the rug, but the materials and construction of

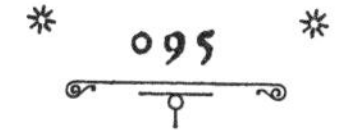

the chamber and doors were different from those on the third floor. Perhaps it was like a palace or temple from ancient times? The most splendid building Mariela knew of was the house of Margrave Schutzenwald, but the structure here seemed more magnificent and solemn.

"This room might be fancy, but there's nothin' here. Let's move on."

Koo was the only one enjoying the fluffiness of the carpet. Yuric promptly ran up to the door leading east and quietly opened it.

"Mariela, there's another room… As far as I can see, there doesn't seem to be any monsters, but the light's sparse, and I don't know if it's safe… Same for the north side."

Yuric opened the way to both halls and inspected them. Corridors with no additional rooms connected the towers from the third floor and above, but on the second, several extra chambers adjoined each hallway's respective inner side. What light came from them was sparse. Since the doors were illuminated, the only torches were probably near them. Extravagant carpets were also laid out in the corridors, and because they didn't look wet, neither hallway appeared to flood.

"If there are lights next to the door, I wonder if inside the room is safe?"

"Who knows? The door's normal-sized, so we won't be able to go in without getting off the raptor first."

Yuric took a step into the east-west hallway from the eastern passage she'd first opened. There was a row of doors on the north side—in other words, the left-hand side—and after several steps, she found that the first door appeared to be openable.

For now, Yuric decided to check what was on the other side of the door leading from the tower, and she took in the lay of the land as she moved forward. Thinking it was probably safe, Mariela and Koo also followed Yuric and stepped into the hallway from the southwest tower.

Windows were open on the right-hand side at fixed intervals; the outside was dark, so dawn hadn't yet arrived. From what they'd seen up to this point, black monsters should have been flooding the outside, yet none could be seen in either the southwest tower or this hallway.

Maybe this place was safe.

Just as Mariela and Yuric were beginning to think that, they heard a distant sound like something being struck.

Boooom, boooom, boooom.

"!!! That noise! It's gotta be Donnino."

The outside was dark, and the light in the corridor was unreliable. The weak illumination obscured the end of the hall stretching east, and Mariela and Yuric couldn't tell whether it continued to the southeast tower or if there was something in the way.

But they had heard the rhythmic sound of a hard impact from the other side of that hallway.

"Let's go, Yuric! There might be an exit. We can go outside since it's still nighttime!"

The two spurred Koo on without opening any of the doors and traveled at full speed east toward the noise.

Running through the straight, dark corridor with flickering torchlight here and there flying past them made it feel like a phantom world.

This strange place also seemed like someone's nightmare.

Booooom, booooom......

The concussive sounds, which had gotten louder as the group chased after them, suddenly stopped.

"The noise…! On the other side of that door!"

About halfway across the east-west corridor was a large double door. Unlike the other doors, this one was much more imposing, tall and wide enough for the girls to pass through while still on the raptor.

"That path to the temple started somewhere around here, right? Maybe we can find a way out!"

Perhaps a staircase leading down lay beyond these ornate doors. And surely there would be a door to that temple, too.

Maybe there was a chance they could reach the temple before dawn when the world would fill with water…

Mariela and Yuric had been in a hurry.

They'd seen Franz, who had lost his memories and whose very appearance was even changing.

And they had been careless because they'd easily dealt with the black monsters by using fire bottles.

They had grown comfortable in a structure they still understood very little about.

Why had the striking sounds stopped? Were the torches on both sides of this door lit? And was the color of the sky visible from the windows in the hallway the dark of night or the white of dawn…?

Paying none of that any heed, Mariela and Yuric chose to open the door.

Creak…

Leaving Mariela on Koo's back, Yuric nimbly dismounted and put a hand on the knob. The door opened with a smoothness that belied their sturdy appearance.

Just as they'd suspected, the area beyond the door was an

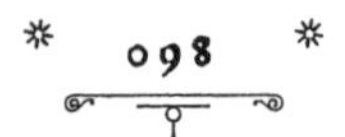

entrance hall that continued to the temple in the center. The second-floor hallway became a staircase on the other side of the door, joined with the steps from the southeast hallway at the landing, and went down to the first level.

That's how the structure had been built, anyway. Unfortunately, a large, imposing tree lay in front of the spot where the stairs joined, barring entry to Mariela and Yuric's destination.

"A tree...? It's like a wall..."

The branches of the tree, so enormous it touched the ceiling, spread out as if to obstruct all advances, and several other equally tall trees grew near it and blocked the stairs so the group couldn't go descend them from the west side. If they could pass through a gap in the many boughs, they'd probably be able to get outside, but winding ivy grew between the trees. If there was any way past the barricade, Mariela and Yuric didn't spot it.

The scent and sight of the greenery reminded them of the middle of a forest, but the unnatural density of the trees with a single giant one at their center also made it seem like a twisted hedge.

"We can't go outside from here. As for jumping to the lower floor..."

Yuric set foot into the room with the stairwell and looked down at the first floor from a railing.

"Heeey, anyone there?" Yuric called. When she did, someone near the foot of the steps answered.

"That you, Yuric?"

"Donnino?! You're down there?"

"Thank goodness you're okay, Mr. Donnino!" Mariela exclaimed on reflex. Those loud, concussive sounds from earlier really had been Donnino after all.

Donnino, who maintained the armored carriages in the Black Iron Freight Corps, wielded a hammer as a weapon and used his strong arms to smash his enemies. Although he wasn't the speedy type, in no way did that mean he was weak.

Despite this little reunion, what Donnino said next was a sharp and urgent command.

"Yuric, get away from there right now!"

At Donnino's shout, Yuric jumped back to the hallway side where Mariela was. In that instant…

The trees blocking Mariela and Yuric's path suddenly shook.

The ivy covering the giant tree and connecting it to the others around it rustled, and all at once, it cleared away like tied-up hair coming undone, exposing the tree's surface.

"Eek! A face?!"

Faster than Mariela's shriek, the loosened ivy wriggled like a living creature, lashed at the spot where Yuric had been mere moments before, and contorted from the recoil. If Yuric's retreat had been even a moment slower, the vines might have struck and torn her apart.

The exposed tree trunk had bloodred eyes, nostrils, and a mouth like a wound cut into flesh. The frightening being glared at Mariela and Yuric.

"This thing's a Necklace!" Yuric shouted after narrowly evading her demise.

A *Necklace*.

That was the common name given to a particular breed of face trees, monstrous plants with human faces.

Just as there are various types of ordinary trees, there is a great deal of diversity among monstrous ones. This one probably had a formal name given by scholars in the imperial capital, but to adventurers like Yuric, the official nomenclature was inconsequential. What kind of monster was it, and how should it be dealt with? Understanding those things was far more critical.

The common name Necklace also clearly expressed the special quality of this plant creature.

As both the facial expression that appeared on the trunk and the name suggested, this tree was said to be the vainest species. However, since no one had tried to communicate with this monster tree, there was no evidence to back up this claim.

Unlike typical face trees, which sometimes decorated themselves with hideous flowers or fruit, this one didn't bear either.

The expression of this austere tree seemed more jealous than any of its kind that Mariela had encountered before. Its inflamed eyes and its mouth, bright red like it had just drunk blood, made it look as though a vengeful spirit had possessed it.

And the creature used the ivy as limbs to indiscriminately attack people and beasts who passed by. To adorn itself, it hung a feeler from its neck like a pendant.

That's how this variant had earned the nickname "Necklace."

The monster couldn't use its roots to relocate, but its ivy was tough as steel, excelled at both offense and defense, and could move at will. The creature was belligerent and troublesome.

"Yuric, let's meet up at the west tower. Listen now, at midday. Come exactly at midday! Got it?!"

They couldn't see Donnino. But what they could hear were the clangs and crashes of something hard colliding. The sounds left Mariela and Yuric to infer that Donnino was battling the Necklace downstairs. He was probably distracting the monster to create an opening for Yuric and the rest to escape.

"Roger!" Yuric replied. The Necklace regarded not just

Donnino as prey, but Mariela and the rest as well, and its vines slithered after them.

"Rarar!"

Koo easily avoided the attack.

"Hurry and get outta here! That ivy isn't this thing's only weapon, so watch out! I'm gonna fall back, too!"

With that final warning, Donnino apparently began to retreat somewhere. Little by little, the sounds of battle grew more distant.

It didn't take long for Mariela and Yuric to discover what Donnino meant.

As though losing its temper over failing to ensnare Mariela and the others, the Necklace shook its entire body.

Thud, thud, thuuud.

Several objects fell from the Necklace's foliage that blotted out the chamber's ceiling.

If those bodies that writhed around had been smooth and white… Well, that still would've been more than deserving of a scream, but at least the things wouldn't have been so creepy looking.

Fur, spines, and poison.

Many legs, although they were very short, and strong teeth.

Were the black spots on their heads eyes, or just a pattern?

Mariela and Yuric couldn't tell, but they had a feeling like they had locked eyes with the repulsive things.

"Haah—"

Was it Mariela or Yuric who instinctively gasped?

With speed like a spinal reflex, Yuric leaped onto Koo and spurred him at full steam back the way they came. The giant things that had come from the Necklace gave chase with bizarre speed.

The large creatures, which looked like they could take off a

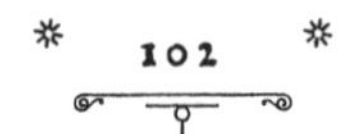

human head in a single bite, poured through the door and crawled out from the floor, walls, and ceiling.

"AAAAAUUUUUGHHHHH!!! HAIRY CATERPILLAAA-AAAARS!!!"

The girls' screams reverberated throughout the second-floor hallway they'd gone through so much to reach.

Caterpillar monsters—both the hairless and the hairy types—and treants had been closely involved with human life since time immemorial.

Of course, it depended on the type, but the lumber obtainable from treants was stiffer and more fireproof than ordinary wood and was traded as a high-class item. The thread that caterpillars spit was strong, thin, and warm, and its great elasticity and breathability made it prized as a material for high-performance cloth.

Incidentally, Mariela's tights she'd obtained in the Labyrinth City were also created from caterpillar silk, and they made her legs look curvier than they were. Magnificent functionality.

By the way, for some reason, Mariela had imagined caterpillar monsters to be roly-poly and somewhat charming, hairless caterpillars that munched grass and cutely spit out thread.

In reality, the caterpillars raised to produce silk for ordinary citizens' clothing were a type that was comparatively easy to

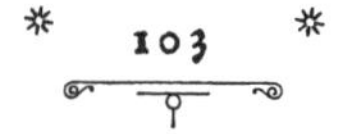

handle among their larger phyla. Not only were they giant—five times bigger than Mariela imagined and twenty times more grotesque—but they ate raw meat instead of grass. What's more, the thread was collected after they spit it out and scattered it all over when they went berserk and made "grrrgrrr" sounds, which was a frequent occurrence.

At the very least, that domestic breed didn't have strange patterns, somewhat fluffy hair, or spines that made you feel itchy just by looking at them, and they didn't send poisonous fibers flying in place of thread.

The domestic breed's appearance and attack methods were by no means as atrocious as the horde of approaching hairy caterpillars going "greeeeaaaaaaaaar" that were about to bite off the swaying tail of the raptor Mariela and Yuric rode.

"Mariela, fire bottle!"

Yuric looked like she was about to cry as she steered the raptor to the right and left while avoiding the toxic fibers.

"Okay!"

Mariela also looked like she could start sobbing at any moment as she threw a fire bottle while clinging to Yuric.

"Rawr!"

Thanks to the salamander, the flames from Mariela's explosive spread, filled the passage, and began engulfing the hairy caterpillars.

Although there were many rooms along the length of the hallway, Mariela's group had gone all the way to the room with the Necklace without checking any of them. They had opportunities to plunge into one of the rooms, but if the one they went into was dangerous, it would probably spell their doom.

That's why they now had to escape back to the southwest tower while fighting back with fire bottles.

Unfortunately, the alchemical explosives, their last ray of hope that had burned the black monsters to nothing, didn't seem to stop the hairy caterpillars. They broke through the blaze and extinguished it with their enormous bodies and sheer numbers as they continued to advance.

"Whoa! They're still coming! They're kinda smooth now!"

"Gaaah! They're still coming! They smell kinda tasty now!"

Aside from whether the hairy caterpillars with their lightly broiled exteriors were delicious, their spines had been burned away, eliminating the danger of toxic fibers, so the fire bottle hadn't been completely wasted. However, at the sight of the giant hairy caterpillars closing in, heedless of getting burned, the two girls went well beyond teary eyes.

"Whyyy, why aren't they burning?!!"

"Maybe…they're soggy?"

"Sog…?! Don't say that, Yuric!"

"You're the one who asked!"

Mariela and Yuric screamed in unison from atop Koo.

Was it that Yuric was girlish after all, or did she simply hate bugs? Few humans, regardless of fighting strength, would probably be able to stay calm at being chased by a large number of enormous hairy caterpillars, so maybe it was a reasonable reaction.

Perhaps because the blaze had scored them, the hairy insects at the front of the charge began to slow. Mariela's group put as much distance between themselves and the caterpillars as the chaos would let them, but that only lasted a moment.

Swoosh, tmp-tmp-tmp.

The uninjured monsters in the back trampled the ones who'd

stalled after being burned, closed in on Mariela's group, and sent poisonous fibers flying.

"Raaah!"

"! Koo!"

One of the toxic barbs pierced Koo's tail, and his speed dropped right away. Did this hairy caterpillar toxin paralyze its prey?

"Hang in there just a little longer!"

Mariela faced the monsters closing the distance before her eyes and threw fire bottles one after another at them.

The group was almost to the southwest tower. The fire bottles only had a slight effect on the frightening insects, but if their progress could be slowed even a little, maybe the group could make it to the tower.

"Rawr!"

The salamander on Koo's head cried out as though to encourage him.

"Grah, grah, grah."

Koo's breathing grew labored, but the raptor ran with the utmost effort despite his poor control over his legs.

The hairy caterpillars behind the group drew near, as if to devour the very space between them. So close were the insects now that Mariela and the others could feel the hot air coming off the monsters after they'd charged through the alchemical conflagration.

Even the hem of Mariela's cloak seemed to be getting scorched by the hot air. Mariela was clinging to Yuric so she wouldn't be thrown from the raptor, who was nearly tripping over himself, and she couldn't afford to look behind her. Even without risking a glance, she knew the terrible creatures were very nearly upon her.

"Har!"

Yuric's whip whirled and twined around the knob of the door several yards ahead of them.

The southwest tower was a hop, skip, and jump away. Yuric pulled on the whip to open the door, and Koo practically slid through as he plunged into it.

As soon as he was in the tower, he tripped over his own legs and collapsed. Both Mariela and Yuric were thrown from their mount and toppled onto the floor.

"Eek!"

Mariela let out a rare girlish shriek and rolled over and over like some sort of baby animal, while Yuric quickly righted herself after one tumble and yanked on the whip, still coiled around the doorknob, and shut the door. The coiled lash both pulled on the door and released the knob as though it were a living thing and returned to Yuric.

Ba-bam, bam, thud, thud, spatter, spatter, squelch.

Many collisions reverberated from the other side of the closed door, and then they heard what sounded like something being squished.

"...Whoa."

It was probably inevitable that the first thing out of Mariela's mouth after she unsteadily got to her feet with her cloak flipped over her head wasn't an astonished "We're saved!"

She didn't know whether the tower door was far sturdier than it looked or whether some mysterious power was at work, but Mariela and the others seemed to have escaped from the surging tide of hairy caterpillars. The awful crunching sounds on the other side of the door told one all they needed to know about what happened to those monsters at the front of the charge.

"Koo!"

"Mariela, hurry and use a potion!!!"

Yuric was far more worried about Koo than any splattered hairy caterpillars.

Koo's tail, which had been struck by a poisonous fiber, was turning a purplish red. Most urgent of all, it was swelling a great deal and very painful to look at. Koo himself lay in the same position he'd slid into and twitched repeatedly.

"Yuric, have him drink this for now!"

After Mariela handed a potion with recovery and detoxification effects to Yuric, she applied a cure potion to Koo's tail and neutralized the poisonous spine while washing it away.

"I think this is a type of toxin that numbs the body. All I can do with potions made from makeshift ingredients is alleviate it. If you have him rest for a few days, he'll probably recover, but..."

The concoctions Mariela had with her were imitations she'd made from the medicinal herbs she'd gathered around this structure, so their effects weren't powerful. The poison of the caterpillar monsters inhibited movement to make catching their prey that much easier, and since Mariela had neutralized it to some extent, Koo's heart wouldn't stop. However, it would be a considerable amount of time before he could walk.

"Wouldn't it be fine if we had the materials?"

"Yeah. But I don't think there are any above us..."

Up to this point, Mariela and Yuric had climbed a few towers and collected materials. Still, all the towers had offered similar vegetation, so even if they went up this tower, they probably wouldn't find the necessary medicinal herbs.

If so, there was only one way to go.

"Koo, we'll definitely be back, so wait here."

"Nrr...," Koo responded weakly.

He partially closed his eyes in apparent contentment at Yuric stroked his head.

Yuric and Mariela walked toward the one other door, which led north.

"This time we'll check the rooms."

"Yeah. Let's go through carefully."

The door on the east side had already quieted, but it was probably better not to approach it for a while. The hairy caterpillar monsters might be nearby, and even if they weren't, no doubt there was a terrible sight out there.

Mariela and Yuric opened the door to the north passage and slowly and quietly stepped into the hallway.

"No monsters. I'm gonna take the first door."

"Okay."

Ready to flee at a moment's notice, Yuric slowly and quietly turned the handle.

"...It's a...normal room?"

"It sure is. I wonder if this place is a workshop? Where could the craftsmen be?"

The first room in the northern hallway was an alchemy workshop resembling Carol's, with rows of glass and metal equipment.

Dried herbs lay in one corner of the room, and expensive materials in vials lined the shelves. Partially processed medicinal herbs had been left on the desk, and based on their condition, there seemed to have been someone here not too long ago. At present, the chamber's only occupants were Mariela and Yuric, however.

"...This all seems really convenient. You think this might help Koo, though?"

"Yeah. Probably. Let's see, is there treant fruit...? There is. Lund petioles, too. Hmm, they were processed poorly, but they might just barely work."

The curiously plentiful reagents had been handled sloppily. Since this place had materials for high-grade and specialized potions, it seemed to be the workshop of a capable alchemist. By Mariela's standards, this person was intermediate at best, however. Regardless, they seemed to be very well-off, as the room contained many complex and shiny magical tools.

But then, this was a typical workshop for an alchemist who could make high-grade potions. Regular alchemists didn't have restrictions on their Libraries. Even if the high-grade potions were crude, they would sell at a much higher price than mid-grade brews, so it was customary to make high-ranking concoctions with expensive tools to compensate for lack of ability. Since Mariela still hadn't completely shaken the sense that her own proficiency as an alchemist was average, she just felt uncomfortable.

"Mariela, there's lunamagia in the refrigeration magical tool over here!"

"Really?! It hasn't been processed yet. I might be able to manage with this."

With unprocessed lunamagia, it seemed like Mariela would be able to make a high-grade antidote of reasonably good quality.

Mariela expanded a Transmutation Vessel as she had done so many other times and, after completing a high-grade cure potion in the blink of an eye, she rushed back with Yuric to the southwest tower where Koo was waiting for them.

"Sorry to keep you waiting, Koo. Here, got you a potion!"

"Nrrr...nr? Raaar!"

"Whoa, Koo, ya perked up way too much."

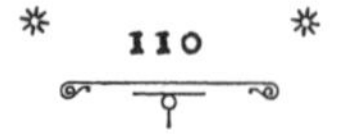

Just as you'd expect from one of Mariela's mixtures. Koo recovered on the spot, stood up, and began licking Yuric and Mariela.

"Thank goodness, Koo. But what were those venomous insects doing here?"

Yuric pondered briefly before answering Mariela's question.

"There were those big fish, even in the daytime. Are the black creatures the only ones that appear during the night?"

"So you're saying they weren't random in the places we've been to so far, and normal monsters are active even during the day?"

When Mariela looked out through the tower window, she saw that dawn had long since arrived, and large fish would occasionally pass by and stare at the group with goggly eyes as they swam around the tower.

All the aquatic monsters were so huge, they couldn't fit through the long and narrow windows, so they didn't attack. That was a poor comfort when one caught sight of their well-developed jaws and sharp, jagged teeth, though.

"Mariela, Donnino's waitin'. Let's keep goin'."

They were safe here, but they needed to meet up with Donnino.

He'd said "Let's meet up on the opposite side." Could he have had a reason for not designating the safe second floor of the southwest tower?

At the very least, he'd told Mariela and Yuric to meet up with him, so there was no doubt they could get to the first floor if they went through the north hallway.

"Okay. But, you know..."

After healing Koo and taking a short rest, Mariela began to ponder things a little.

The hairy caterpillars from earlier. Mariela hadn't thoroughly observed them, but she thought they were the larvae of

a poisonous moth species known as Mojolaus Meiyo. If so, they were the material for a particular potion. It wasn't one that could be used to attack, but there were those enemies that couldn't be defeated with fire bottles. It was better to have many means at their disposal.

Gathering what they could from the hairy caterpillars aside, what was in the numerous other rooms in this corridor?

The first chamber on the north side had been an alchemist's workshop. Would the other rooms prove as useful?

When did Mr. Donnino say to meet up with him, again...? Would it be okay to be a little late?

Although they'd made a promise with Donnino, finding their way there without being attacked by monsters was their first priority. A face tree and hairy caterpillars had already attacked them. There was no telling what awaited them ahead now.

Mariela suggested to Yuric that they discuss the plan from here on out.

"...We shouldn't go in there."

"But it might have some materials."

"Didn't we just decide *not* to go in there?"

The two began to argue in front of the western door where the insect monsters' corpses were scattered about.

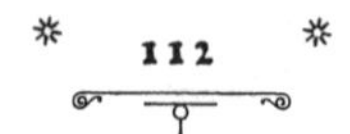

Yuric vehemently refused to go in, so Mariela slowly and quietly opened the door herself with reluctance.

She'd put her ear to it first but had caught no sound. Nonetheless, how many humans existed who could recognize the sound of crawling hairy caterpillars? Even if any of the things were scurrying about, there was no way Mariela could've heard them.

She quietly opened the door about four inches and tossed dried fish meat inside. If any of the insect monsters were left, they would likely rush to snatch it up. Mariela didn't detect movement. Thinking it was safe, she peered through the crack in the doorway and involuntarily muttered at the terrible spectacle.

"Whoa… It's like…magical power is being scraped and whittled away…"

If that was true of anything, it was likely sanity, not magical power.

Perhaps the surviving hairy caterpillars had returned to the Necklace, as Mariela didn't spot anything crawling around on the other side of the door. However, the phlegm as far as the eye could see and hairy caterpillar corpses everywhere made Mariela uncomfortable. Just that alone was unbearable, but even worse was the smell hanging over everything, and Mariela desperately suppressed the nausea welling up within her at the terrible, unfamiliar fishy smell.

"We at least gotta do something about this stink. Blech, they're too damp to use, too. For now, **Dehydrate, Ventilate**."

Mariela put in considerable magical power to dry the carcasses around her and blew them away with a puff of air. The west side of the hallway was now in a much better state, both visually and olfactorily.

"…Mariela, let's hurry and finish this up."

Perhaps she felt she couldn't afford to let Mariela do all the work, as Yuric reluctantly followed the alchemist's lead.

"Thanks, Yuric. Let's see, this…no good. Then, over there…"

The light coming in from the windows highlighted every detail of the caterpillar carcasses that one really didn't want to see.

Perhaps Mariela, who screamed when she thought of them as bugs, was fine when she thought of them as materials, since she inspected every corpse that hadn't been wholly crushed. Each time, she sighed. "I can't use this one, either."

"What're ya lookin' for?" Yuric asked. She was worried that if Mariela did everything herself, it would take too long, and the gruesome bugs would return.

"The intestines are located near the butt, but hairy caterpillars' organs are soft, so they were crushed in the impact and got all mixed together."

Yuric wished she hadn't asked.

"…In that case, wouldn't it be faster to search a bit farther along the hallway?"

Yuric put Mariela on Koo's back while avoiding looking at the hairy caterpillar carcasses as much as possible, then led her around the end of the heaps of phlegm and chunks of meat.

Thanks to Yuric's reluctant help, Mariela was able to obtain the reagents she sought, and she began to collect one other material in the room on the northwest side where she'd made the cure potion a short time ago.

"Mariela, are ya goin' to use the magical tools?"

"Yeah. I need these blowers."

"Then what're you cutting 'em up for?"

"I only need this one part."

Something got lost in translation between the two of them. Mariela collected only the blowers from the magical tools, and she used scissors to cut out the balloon parts that inflated and expelled air when you put magical power into them. Hence, it was only natural for Yuric to misunderstand.

The balloon pieces of the ventilation magical tools expanded when you poured magical power into them because they were made from the cheek pouches of creatures called *bravado frogs*. Despite technically being monsters, they were a weak variety, and they blew up their cheek pouches to astonishing sizes to make themselves appear stronger. The sturdiness of these sacs was evident from the fact that they didn't break even when given some pokes at maximum capacity. Still, the best characteristic of this material was that, even if it didn't suck in air, it would instantly inflate with wind magic if it was fed magical power.

The bravado frog's survival strategy was to deflect attacks with a sudden expansion of its cheeks. Then it would expel air to escape.

Magical tools for ventilation made use of this characteristic, but the balloons were still made from a living thing's skin, and a frog at that, so it wasn't like they could be used indefinitely. Most modern societies, including the Labyrinth City, had outgrown using these components, but for some reason, this workshop had ventilation tools that ran on this antiquated method. Naturally, there were several spare balloons for replacement.

Mariela used scissors to cut loose and collect the cheek pouches.

After drying them for a short time, she turned the cheek pouches into powder and boiled them in water loaded with Drops

of Life. What concentrated wind with magical power was the many cells within the cheek pouches, and if you heated them like this, they would turn clear and sticky and allow you to take out the individual cells. The work of diluting them with water filtered as much as possible, separating them, and then condensing them again was by all rights extremely time-consuming, but the process was basic.

"And nooow, those hairy caterpillar materials we..."

"Ya don't need to explain every li'l thing."

Mariela completed the new potion, albeit not without the occasional chiding from Yuric.

"Another alchemist's workshop?"

"What's goin' on with this place?"

After Mariela completed the potion, she and Yuric checked the rooms at regular intervals while making their way through the northern hallway. They were heading north to meet up with Donnino as soon as possible while inspecting the chambers to see if they could be used for shelter.

The pair didn't check all the rooms, but every single one they opened was an alchemist's workshop. What was the meaning of this? Just like the chamber they first went into, they all looked like people had been in them until just a little while ago, as they contained partially processed medicinal herbs and, on rare occasions, meals with steam rising from them.

There were no actual inhabitants to be found, though.

One other mysterious thing was that the materials Mariela processed into potions or crystallized could be taken out of the rooms, but if they took fully processed medicinal herbs from the rooms, they crumbled and vanished.

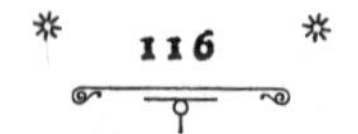

Although she couldn't take out the smoke bombs she'd made by simply kneading and mixing powdered medicinal herbs, those that Mariela repurposed by extracting the components and combining them again could be taken out even if she mixed in materials from a workshop.

Because they didn't get hungry again when they left a chamber after having a meal, the rooms seemed to have a rule that nothing could be taken from them unless it became Mariela's or Yuric's in some form.

Even the door of a chamber they left ajar so they could take refuge there at any time closed, pushing the baggage Mariela and Yuric had placed to keep it from shutting into the hallway, when they entered a different room.

The rooms had magical tools for illumination, lit lamps, and other lighting forms, so it wasn't as if they were dark. Without torches at regular intervals like the chambers in the towers, monsters could still invade. It was probably best to think of the spaces in this corridor as hiding places.

"Let's move as carefully as possible so we don't meet any unpleasant creatures."

"Sounds like a good idea."

Mariela and Yuric cautiously proceeded north as they scanned the interiors of the rooms.

It was a few hours after they'd left the southwest tower when they encountered an identical pair of double doors to the ones they'd found earlier. Distance-wise, it was right around the west tower.

Mariela and Yuric had rushed out of the northwest tower where Franz was as soon as night arrived, traveled through the southwest one, met Donnino in the south second-floor hallway, and were chased by hairy caterpillars. A lot of things had happened, and Mariela felt like a lot of time had passed, but since they hadn't taken any naps, she felt like this would be a good time for night to come.

Mariela gazed out the windows that were still bright after who knows how many hours.

What was it Donnino had said?

She was positive he'd stated, "Exactly at midday."

Didn't *exactly midday* mean noon in the normal world? Not here after the night had been shortened?

"Mariela, are ya goin' to open it?"

"Yeah."

Yuric's voice drowned out Mariela's ponderings, and she automatically agreed.

This time, she carefully opened the door just a little and peeked inside.

A bright light spilled through the crack.

"A greenhouse…or somethin' like that?"

"For a greenhouse, the trees sure are in rough shape, though."

Peeking through, the two saw a large atrium that began on the first floor of this tower. It was lusher than the entrance where the Necklace had attacked them, and it called to mind a botanical garden.

On the second floor, a passage went halfway around the wall before coming to an end, and it didn't connect to the northwest tower. Mariela couldn't see well because the trees were in the way, but there might have been a staircase in the middle going down.

The walls seemed to be made of marble or some other beautiful

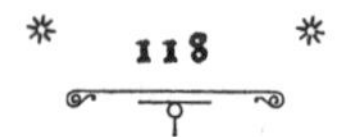

alabaster stone, and they looked far brighter than those in the rooms they'd seen up to this point. The width of the outer facade was the same as the previous tower chambers. Still, several splendid pillars in the inner court supported the tower that continued upward, and the room further expanded such that it protruded into the courtyard.

The walls on the courtyard side, built as a semicircle, were glass-sided, and the ceiling had a dome-like curve from around the middle of the second floor where Mariela's group was. The first floor had waterways and water fountains as well, and the fact that it was covered in trees and plants in a disorderly way gave it that ruined sort of beauty.

An abandoned garden. The room suited that feeling, and you could say the way the light, diffused through the water outside, poured in and filled the trees with a pale glow that seemed straight out of a fairytale.

Mariela and Yuric probably would have been captivated by that beauty if the plants growing in the chamber weren't all monsters, and if they hadn't all been broken off at the middle or cut up as though something sharp had gouged them.

"I wonder if Mr. Donnino fought here?"

Mariela opened the door a little more to get a better view of what remained of the timber, broken and piled up in disarray.

"The way they were defeated...doesn't look like Donnino's work..."

Yuric carefully peered in through the gap that now commanded a view of the room's left and right sides.

"Mr. Donnin—"

"Shh, Mariela, quiet!"

Yuric covered Mariela's mouth as she started calling Donnino.

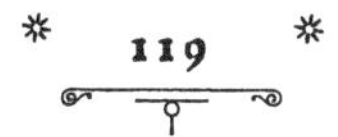

Yuric's gaze, which keenly surveyed the interior of the chamber as though seeing through the fallen timber, stopped at a point on the wall a little above the trees. From their perspective, the spot was left of center on their side of the room.

Since it wasn't right in front of them, they probably wouldn't have noticed unless they'd carefully looked around like this.

Something pitch-black clung to the pale surface of the wall on the outer facade side.

Many slender legs were folded up. It was impossible to say they were symmetrical. Several looked to have been severed, and others were bent in strange directions. If the body hadn't been swaying irregularly, it would have resembled the corpse of a spider.

The ebon thing was clinging to the smooth surface of the wall, swaying up and down with its stomach pressed to it.

If it were a normal spider, its head and chest would be joined, the legs would be attached to the cephalothorax, and it would have a large, puffy abdomen. However, this dark-colored creature had no midsection, and the cephalothorax was bulging like lumps had built up on it. The uneven surface gave the impression that something had chewed it.

Several streaks of liquid smoothly ran down the surface of the wall from below the black thing's stomach.

The thick substance was green or light yellow. The ebon creature slid its body downward as though to chase the liquid and audibly slurped it all up.

Yes, this unknown being *slurped.* It didn't lap the goop as beasts did with water. It drank as a person would have.

A *face* appeared from under the black something's cephalothorax, at the liquid's source. Perhaps it would be more accurate to call it a head, however.

Mariela and Yuric had seen both the spilled phlegm and that head before. So many had chased them. It was probably impossible for them to forget those enormous hairy caterpillars that had hunted them.

After the thing finished drinking the phlegm, it lifted its cephalothorax a bit and pressed its stomach against the hairy caterpillar again.

Squelch, squelch. Slurp, slurp, slurp. Drip, drip, driiip.

Unpleasant sounds reverberated despite the fact that it looked like the weird creature was merely pressing its body against the hairy caterpillar to crush it. There was an unmistakable sound of greedy chewing, as though it had been a long time since the thing had eaten.

"Mariela, get back!"

Yuric seized Mariela's arm and yanked her away.

Mariela wasn't sure exactly what happened in the next few dizzying moments.

What she could perceive in the rapidly moving scenery was the door of the west tower, which she swore had only been cracked, suddenly opening wide. She also made out the spiderlike being extending its long and narrow legs into the opening as though to block the light shining in.

The joints of the creature's limbs and the bottom of the cephalothorax turned in Mariela's direction. A slit in the cephalothorax widened like an expanding gash, and within that slit were sporadic teeth that resembled a human's.

And...

"H...ungry... Hungry, hungryyy..."

The maw that had greedily devoured the hairy caterpillar monster spoke.

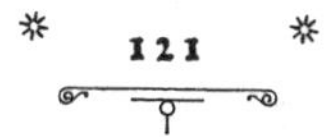

* * *

Was it flames emitted by the salamander on Mariela's head that dyed her field of vision red right before she was yanked back?

After falling on her backside, Mariela retreated by way of Koo, who grabbed her cloak's collar in his mouth and pulled her. After Yuric threw multiple potions and smoke bombs toward the door she'd been peeking through just a moment ago, the entire group plunged into a nearby room.

They put a broom through the ring-shaped handle of the door in place of a bolt, hoping that would keep it shut.

If a monster pulled on the door, such a thin stick would probably break easily, but it opened in the direction of the hallway. They couldn't pile up scattered items to bar entry.

Yuric stayed close to the door and strained her ears for sounds in the adjoining passage.

Mariela hadn't been able to sense the immediate danger, but Yuric had understood everything and leaped into this room.

The monster—let's call it the "black spider" for convenience—had finished eating the hairy caterpillar and decided Mariela's group was its new prey. The black spider had moved so swiftly that it'd been upon Mariela before she even knew what was happening. It had used its legs to throw the slightly ajar door wide open, and it had exposed the underside of its body to Mariela and Yuric.

That maw on its underside unmistakably had to be the creature's weak point.

If the mouth had possessed sharp fangs like a beast's, it might have seemed a more formidable point on its body. But what lay in the black spider's maw were rounded teeth like a human's, and the area around the mouth was shaped like lips.

The moment Yuric had thought it was over for them, the salamander on Mariela's head had spit out flames, and the black spider had recoiled in apparent fear.

Seizing upon that opportunity, Yuric had pulled Mariela back and hurled recently crafted potions made of hairy caterpillar phlegm and bravado frog cheek pouches at the black spider.

Fortunately, Mariela had recast their vials to be a lot thinner than usual. They broke easily upon impact against the spider, and their effectiveness could not be denied.

The liquid inside was scattered at an explosive speed and changed into thin white thread as though stretched out by the airflow. The way it ensnared its target as it spread was like a spider's web, but it covered the frightening monster like an insect cocoon.

These were *Potions of Binding.*

Those hairy caterpillars had been the variety that attacked with poisonous fibers rather than thread, but they still made cocoons. Mariela had made concoctions that combined the body fluids the monstrous insects used as the base of their cocoons with the rapid inflation property of bravado frogs.

Since the hairy caterpillars' organs were soft and fragile, obtaining the materials was difficult under normal circumstances, and they rarely appeared on the market, but the mixture was easy to use and effective against both people and monsters.

The Potions of Binding's effects seemed reliable, and they were able to buy the group time to escape by immobilizing the black spider, which had shown such nimbleness before. Simultaneously, Yuric had obstructed the creature's field of view with smoke bombs, so it couldn't have known which room they had taken refuge in.

It shouldn't know...

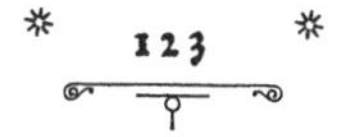

Yuric tried to convince herself as she listened carefully for sounds in the hallway.

That black spider was clumsy. Surely it would be incapable of finding her and Mariela.

Crunch, crunch, rip, rip, rip.

It sounded like the thing was biting a hole in something thin and tough—perhaps the Potions of Binding's restraints.

"...ungry... H...un... Hung..."

The voice gradually got closer. How did this black spider speak a human language? Swallowing that question, Mariela and even Koo lowered their voices and stayed motionless in one corner of the room.

"Hungry... Hungry... Hungry... Hungry..."

The sound of it scratching at the different entrances along the hallway echoed. Despite being capable of speech, the black spider may have only possessed low intelligence, as it didn't seize any door's handle. Instead, it seemed to be pushing its legs against and scratching at the barricades that would simply open if it only pulled on them.

Scratch, scratch, scratch.

"Hungry... Hungry..."

The voice of unsatisfied craving seemed to have finally reached the other side of their door.

"Hungry..."

Were Mariela and Yuric now only separated from that disgusting black spider by a thin layer of stone and wood? Was that gruesome maw that resembled a laceration waiting for them beyond the door?

Scratch, scratch, scratch......... Bang!

Whether it was by chance or by the powers of this world, the black spider's leg seemed to catch on the ring-shaped door handle.

Bang! Bang! Bang! Bang!

There came a cacophony as the creature tugged its limb back and forth. The broom handle that Yuric had used in place of a proper bolt began to strain and creak.

It's not gonna hold...

Yuric gripped her whip tightly, and Mariela held several potions at the ready.

The battle would have a low chance of success, but they didn't want to be devoured by such a vile monster.

Bang! Bang! Bang! Bang!

Bang-bang-bang-bang-bang-bang-bang-bang-bang-bang-bang-bang.

Bang.........

After the door made an especially loud noise, it unexpectedly fell silent.

What's goin' on?!

Yuric, who'd even held her breath, could hear a faint sound like something vibrating.

Bzbzbzbzbzbz......

Buzzing? That's...a killer bee or somethin'?

"Hungry... Hungr... H...un... Aa, aa..."

The humming of what seemed to be several bee monsters, the black spider's complaints of hunger, and the sounds of a scuffle between the two sides were intermittently audible.

And then—*splat, crunch*—there came the noises of repulsive mastication.

Apparently, the black spider had found a different meal.

Little by little, the sounds moved in the direction of the west tower, and when Yuric couldn't hear them anymore, she at last breathed a sigh of relief. They had made it.

Mariela shot a look asking if they'd escaped the danger, and Yuric silently nodded.

When Yuric looked at the door, she saw the broom had almost snapped. Just as she decided to look for a replacement, Yuric noticed her right hand was still wrapped tightly around the handle of her whip.

I gotta calm down...

She took a silent, deep breath to loosen the tension in her muscles. Mariela gingerly tiptoed up to her and held out a potion with recovery effects.

"Yuric, are you okay?" Mariela mouthed silently.

"I'm fine. But let's keep quiet for a little while," Yuric replied in much the same manner.

Any noise risked drawing the attention of that black spider. Both women kept quiet in fear of such an event. Mariela nodded in agreement with Yuric's proposal.

Eventually, the pair came across a long stirring rod discarded in one corner of the room. It looked to be a suitable bolt substitute, and they used it to secure the door. Then they huddled with Koo in a corner and waited for time to pass as they mentally kept their fingers crossed.

"Come exactly at midday," Donnino had said, most likely to warn them of this danger.

Donnino had far higher attack power than Yuric, but he wasn't the speedy type, so the black spider was probably tricky for him to deal with. Maybe that was why he'd avoided it and had wound up where the Necklace was.

Exactly at midday meant noon. So if we'd just been patient a little longer...

Donnino wouldn't have designated noon without reason.

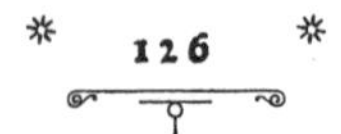

Mariela didn't know if the monster would be asleep or weakened, but if it being midday increased their chances of escaping from it, they had to buy a few more hours here.

Amid the quiet tranquility, where the only sounds were the breathing of her and her companions, Mariela took stock of the chamber.

This room also seemed to be an alchemist's workshop. The worktable installed in its center was a high-class item cut from a large slab of rock. It was the most durable kind when handling acidic slime liquid or various other corrosive materials.

However, it didn't have a uniform thickness, and the height was adjusted with something resembling plaster. Its glass, too, was low quality with air bubbles in it. All the objects in this chamber had been manufactured with low-level technology compared with those in the Labyrinth City.

This place probably...

Without speaking the answer that came to mind, Mariela shifted her gaze to outside the window. Through the long, narrow aperture, she could see the courtyard and the temple, both hazy due to the water.

Bit by bit, things resembling air bubbles flowed through the window into the water—like raindrops on an intensely windy day being blown away.

Several streaks traced diagonal lines on the window, and after meeting en route, they joined to become larger specks. When several combined and grew to be about as big as a grain of barley, it burbled and began to swim away from the window.

Huh, a baby monster...

Could the semitransparent little monster be eating the sediment that clouded the water? The sea outside the window was slightly cloudy, and Mariela couldn't find the nearly transparent small fry.

If so, it'll be dawn soon. I wonder if babies are born in the morning...

Maybe it wasn't the case for Yuric, who was used to traveling through the Fell Forest day and night with the Black Iron Freight Corps, but there was no way Mariela wouldn't be sleepy after moving around all night.

It was probably also because she'd relaxed a little after the extreme tension from up until a short while ago.

The salamander twined around her shoulders was nice and warm.

Before she knew it, Mariela fell asleep while absentmindedly gazing at the infant monsters being born and swimming away one after another.

It was the middle of a deep forest.

Had the trees been this big? Had the night been this dark?

A group of people wearing hoods low over their eyes were walking in the wood. Maybe it was more accurate to say they had strips of cloth around their heads instead of cowls. The attire of the people moving through the forest was too simple to rightly call clothing.

Were there only twenty of them? The group advanced while trembling at the sounds of a beast howling in the distance and an owl flapping its wings overhead.

The tree branches blocked even the moonlight, and the weeds growing thick further hampered the people, who were dull-witted compared to beasts.

If they happened to meet a monster, would they have any way to fight it?

A dreadful, frightening nighttime forest.

It seemed the only thing protecting the people from the night, from the forest, from the monsters, was the light of the lamp the person in the lead held aloft. The candle, painstakingly made from materials of the finest quality so the flame would stay lit for a long time, could be an offering to the fire spirits on its own.

Actually, what lit the tip of the candle in the lamp was a little fire spirit.

The spirit with fiery hair hovering around her who flickered and burned within the lamp seemed to be a very young individual, judging from her size. She was completely tired of the forever-unchanging woodland scenery, and every time she yawned from boredom, the flame wavered and almost disappeared.

Whether or not he could see the spirit, the person holding the lamp frantically chanted something to curry her favor every time the light wavered.

—Boooring. Now I get why the others told me not to do this.—

As she complained, the fire spirit waved her right hand to shoo something away. When she did, several beasts in the direction she waved her hand ran off into the forest.

Beasts and weak monsters feared flames. This was believed to be because spirits dwelled in flames and drove evil things away.

Despite complaining, it seemed this fire spirit was doing her job perfectly.

* * *

The group continued walking toward the depths of the forest with a number of short rests along the way. When the sun came out and revealed their figures, they proved to be extremely thin and dressed in clothes that couldn't be called proper garments. The weapons they carried were metal, but both their surfaces and their edges were dull.

They looked awful, but that didn't mean they were slaves.

They carried weapons, and they even wore ornaments made from bird feathers and the fangs and bones of beasts.

This was a very, very old memory.

A recollection from such an ancient time period that nothing—magic, technology, knowledge—had been developed, and people depended on the spirits' divine protection to survive.

On the way, monsters devoured two people, and another who suffered severe injury was left behind.

The fire spirit, who saw this from within the lamp, stopped her fickle wavering and protected the remaining humans with her small but powerful light.

Thus, the group reached their destination at last.

A clear, beautiful lake marked the sudden end of the deep forest.

No rivers could be seen flowing into or out of it. The water's calm surface, which resembled a large pool, reflected the surrounding forest like a mirror. The lake was so clear you could even count the rings of the fallen trees beneath its placid facade.

The tiny fire spirit gasped as she gazed at the center of the lake.

—Whoa… Beautiful.—

What she saw there was most likely the water spirit that ruled this lagoon. They possessed androgynous features and hair that cascaded down their back like water from melting snow. The creature's kind, pale blue eyes were reminiscent of the lake bottom.

Because of their appearance, they seemed to be a powerful spirit. One born a long, long time before the fire one in the lantern.

The lake spirit captivated the fire spirit, and as the latter stared unmovingly, the group of humans left both her and the lamp on a nearby rock. They then set to work purifying and making an offering to a simple altar that had been built by the pool. Once all preparations were complete, they initiated some sort of ritual.

The person who had walked at the head of the company and wore many adornments was probably a priest.

He chanted some words of prayer, and then a few people took over the recitation. Those in waiting behind them took out a tightly sealed box from the baggage they had brought.

The humans didn't seem to notice that, even with the lid closed, a black mist had begun to pour out of a crack in the container.

They might not have been able to see the fire spirit or the lake spirit, either.

When the priest unsealed the box, the interior turned white, or the dark spot rose up. The box contained many crops that had been eaten by insects and rotted, as well as something larger than two palms wrapped in enchanted cloth.

—Diseased crops. And...—

The fire spirit understood the reason the priest and the others had risked their lives to come here.

"...gry... Hu...y... ......"

The humans couldn't hear the whispers coming from the shadowy vapor. It was a form comprised of a disease that had rotted crops alive, and the remains of a baby who had perished of starvation as a result. The enchanted cloth seemed to have

gathered and confined in the remains the deep grudge of a person who died of hunger. The feelings of pestilence and human famine had mixed and formed this black mist.

The people had come here to exorcise the calamity that had struck their village.

With a reverent gesture, the priest placed the box overflowing with ominous vapor into a small boat they had prepared and sent it into the lake. The fire spirit looked in the direction of the lake spirit with worry.

Powerful and pure water prevented corruption from getting close. Suppose the contaminant was taken in, purified, and properly returned to the world. In that case, the lake spirit, the forest trees, or even living creatures could harbor it and gradually circulate it through the world. However, they would be corrupted themselves until the purification was complete.

It was the domain of fire spirits to excise vicious pollution like this. They burned and cleansed it with mighty hellfire and returned it to ashes. It was best to weaken its power and then slowly return it to the world. Of course, a tiny fire spirit didn't possess the strength to cleanse this much foul influence.

Despite the lack of wind, the boat carrying the diseased crops moved all the way to the center of the pool, where the lake spirit was located, and it sank into the water as though a hole had opened at the bottom.

"...gry... Ung...ry... Hu..."

The ebon corruption spread thinly into the lake, and fish that had gathered unnoticed picked at it until it disappeared. Undoubtedly the malefic influence had spread far and wide to all the creatures living in the water.

"The calamity in our village has been exorcised."

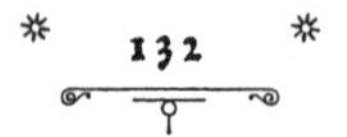

"The crops have been purified."

"Our suffering has passed."

The people chanted in unison. They picked up the lamp with the fire spirit once more and turned back the way they came.

—Hey, you okay?—

The fire spirit placed her hand on the glass of the lamp, worriedly watching the lake spirit.

The other creature didn't answer the fire spirit, who was so small she looked like she might be blown out in a single breath from the watery entity. However, before the water spirit disappeared into the lake, they smiled with the utmost gentleness.

06

That dream just now...what was that?

Mariela felt that this vision had also been someone's memory. This one, however, seemed to take place in an era from a very long time ago. Mariela herself had been born over two hundred years ago, but the attire she saw in the dream seemed from a far, far older time.

Mariela wondered if she should check the memory pearls, but since she'd collected them in a hurry yesterday, she didn't know how many there were, and she hadn't checked the colors of the sooty ones. Inspecting them now wouldn't reveal much.

"Mariela, you awake?"

Yuric, who'd been near the door keeping watch, returned.

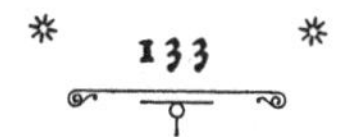

"Sorry for being the only one who fell asleep..."

"I'm used to it. It's more important for ya to recover your strength. It's almost time, so ya should at least have some water."

Had Yuric stayed up this whole time? If so, that meant only Mariela had that dream.

Did Yuric guess from the position of the sun, or did her biological clock tell her? Regardless, it was almost noon, as Yuric said; they should go meet up with Donnino soon.

That meant opening the door to the room with that black spider again.

Neither girl knew if the place they were in was safe, but they had no other path forward. Above all, they couldn't run away and leave Donnino behind on the first floor, where the escape route was blocked by the Necklace, while that black spider was wandering around.

"O-okay."

Mariela nodded resolutely.

"Ya should stay on standby on Koo," Yuric suggested with a little laugh at Mariela not taking a means of escape into consideration despite her lack of fighting power.

After the two girls ate premade sandwiches and washed them down with just a little water, they stood in front of that door once again while paying exhaustive attention to their surroundings. Mariela clung to Koo's back so she could flee whenever necessary, and Yuric stayed close enough to be able to jump on the raptor.

Fully alert, they opened the door as carefully as careful could be. On the other side, the place was more devastated than it had been a few hours ago. Perhaps the black spider had battled it out with some other monsters, as the tree-creatures growing in the room had been violently smashed, and most had collapsed. On a closer look, Mariela and Yuric found things resembling giant bee wings and insect legs in the aftermath.

They couldn't confirm the black spider's whereabouts.

Thanks to the tall, fallen tree monsters, they now had a good view of the inside of the room. Half of the passage that went about halfway around the wall was broken, including the handrail, and seemed dangerous, and the stairs that went downward were utterly destroyed and unusable.

Yuric slowly and quietly set foot in the west tower, where all was still.

From the other side of the broken heaps of timber, or the left or right. Maybe above the door she'd just passed through. Yuric gripped her whip and assumed a posture that would let her throw a potion no matter where the black spider jumped out.

Yuric was so tense she felt liable to snap, but suddenly, a voice from right below her broke through it.

"Yuric, you made it."

"Donnino! Your voice is so loud!"

Yuric was flustered, thinking the black spider had come.

"Ha-haaa, you came here during the night, didn't you? I thought I said to come exactly at midday. We should be fine at this hour. Come on in." Guessing the situation from Yuric's state, Donnino laughed heartily as he replied.

"What do ya mean?"

Slowly, quietly, Yuric entered the west tower. Mariela, who rode on Koo, followed at a slight distance. When they were all in the tower and got close to the partially destroyed handrail, they saw Donnino down in the first-floor section of the atrium.

"I'll tell you later. Bring me up to the second level. That black spider-looking thing ate my rope."

Mariela tied up rope ivy in a bundle to make a cord and fastened it to an intact part of the handrail. Donnino had a good physique and carried a heavy hammer, so if she didn't braid several rope ivies together, it wouldn't be strong enough.

"...ngry... Hu...y... *Sob, sob...*"

In the middle of preparing the tether, Mariela had the distinct feeling she heard a quiet call, practically a whisper.

"That voice!"

Mariela looked around in a panic. Yuric, too, seemed to have realized the identity of the speaker. She gripped her whip tight and warily examined their surroundings.

"Donnino! Behind ya!!!"

There it was. The black spider, looking up at them from behind Donnino. It had compressed its body to spring at his defenseless back.

"Don't worry."

But Donnino didn't seem panicked as he took a single swing of his hammer.

The black spider that had attacked Mariela's group with so much agility a few hours ago leaped at Donnino at a gentle speed, like a ball lobbed toward a child. The hammer repelled the monster, and it struck a wall.

"Hu...n...ngry... *Sob, sob...*"

On a closer look, its body was far smaller than it had been a few hours ago. Mariela couldn't make out any details of the creature, which was pitch-black all over, but most of its legs were gone or broken, and its torso had thinned considerably. Its uneven form gave off the impression of something that had been eaten.

"Monsters chewed it up, yet it still won't die..."

Donnino turned toward the black spider. The salamander on

Mariela's shoulder leaped off and landed on the top of the man's head.

"Whoa, what's this, now?"

The salamander lowered itself to peer into Donnino's face and spit out a small flame before his eyes.

"You wanna try burning it?" Donnino asked the salamander as he glanced up at it sitting on top of him.

The salamander went "rawr" as if in reply.

"Mr. Donnino, use this! It's a fire bottle."

After accepting the potion Mariela tossed over, Donnino approached the black spider and threw the vial at it. The salamander belched flame as though to act as the clincher.

"Hungry... ...ung... H... Hun... Aa, aa, aa..."

The black spider's body repeatedly quivered as it began to burn in the blaze.

This thing is the embodiment of famine and diseased crops I saw in my dream...

Mariela gazed fixedly at the smoldering black spider from the second floor.

A very long time ago, a plague must have spread through the crops of some village, and its people went hungry. Children, the elderly, and the weak began dying. Townsfolk exorcised the catastrophe in a lake deep in the forest where a spirit lived.

That was how the memory went.

If that was true, why was this frightening being of famine in this place?

There was no one to answer this question. The salamander on Donnino's head had crawled down next to the black spider. Once again, it blew flame at the terrifying monster, reducing it to ash.

CHAPTER 3

The Calamity of Disease

01

"The west tower is where I woke up. I went to the northwest one the same day, but Franz refused to budge from there, so I decided to head for the temple."

After Mariela and Yuric safely pulled up Donnino with the rope ivy, they returned to the seemingly safe southwest tower for the time being to eat and exchange information.

After parting with Franz, Donnino had gone down to the second floor of the southwest tower. He was probably trying to focus on the west tower, where he woke up, for exploration. Apparently, when he'd headed north before and reached the west tower, then descended to the first floor with rope, it happened to be noon when the black spider was less active.

"To think that kinda beastie that'll eat anything really exists. We'll all need to be careful."

According to Donnino, that starving black spider seemed to eat monsters indiscriminately. Curiously, monsters would ignore Donnino and attack the black spider when it appeared.

The horrible part was its appetite. No matter how many things it ate and how big its body grew, its hunger never seemed to be sated.

"I only survived thanks to those things eating each other."

Midday was when the black spider had gobbled up most of the other monsters and also when it was the most wounded and

unable to move. It was the safest time of day, when the black spider was weak and few other creatures were about.

Mariela and Yuric had seen during their second encounter with the black spider what it looked like after being eaten by other monsters. Even after sustaining such grievous injuries, the horrible thing refused to die. Instead, it had continued consuming the remains of whatever it could and waited for nighttime.

"In case you didn't know, night's real dangerous. That black spider comes back."

There was a fountain on the west tower's first floor, but those inky creatures gushed out through the sluice gate. And the black spider absorbed those, restored its devoured body and broken limbs, and rapidly resurrected. The reborn black spider was fast, and its attack power was enough to let it single-handedly consume all the creatures remaining on the first floor. Donnino was tough, but his speed was lacking, putting him at a disadvantage. Above all, no matter how much he struck and pulverized it, the black spider continued to attack him indefinitely as though it felt no pain. It was not the sort of opponent one wanted to face head-on.

The black spider seemed unable to open the large door to the second-floor hallway of the west tower, but the door on the first floor had broken and come off, so after devouring the remains of the tree and insect monsters in the west tower, the black spider wandered through the first level hallway in search of food.

"The Necklace sleeps at night, and since I couldn't open the door to the entrance hall, I stayed where the Necklace was. I was gonna make a hole in the Necklace's hedge during the night and slip out, but the sucker's tough."

The striking sounds Mariela and Yuric had heard were

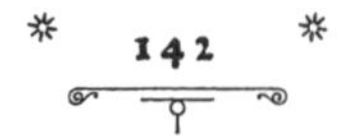

Donnino demolishing the Necklace's foliage. However, the ivy covering the Necklace's surface was as strong as steel, and Donnino hadn't been able to destroy it.

When the night was over, the Necklace would wake up, and the hairy caterpillars would attack. Although timing it was risky, if the hairy caterpillars and the black spider met, you could escape to another room while they were chewing on each other.

After each night passed, tree monsters suddenly sprouted and grew to be large trees, and insect monsters hatched from eggs and grew wings, filling the first floor. And the monsters and the black spider started eating each other again. This cycle of rebirth and predation seemed to loop every day.

"Maaan, the first decent meal in ages tastes so good," Donnino said as he sunk his teeth into the meat Mariela had cooked.

The two girls looked at each other for a moment, then forcibly diverted the conversation, which seemed about to shift to food.

What had Donnino been eating in a place with nothing but tree and insect monsters?

Donnino seemed to be in his late thirties, but even if you said he was in his fifties, his personality smacked so much of a middle-aged man it wouldn't seem incongruous, and he also had a wild feeling about him. He'd probably eat anything if push came to shove, but Mariela and Yuric didn't want to entertain that notion.

"Anyhow, I'm glad you're safe, Mr. Donnino. And if we can find Mr. Grandel..."

Grandel was the only one still missing. If they each woke up in a different tower, Grandel should have been in the east one, but where on earth could he be now?

"Grandel's probably over there."

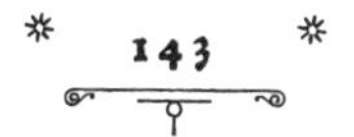

Donnino took out a folding telescope from his tool bag and indicated a place near the east tower through the window.

"Whoa, you're right..."

"There's water outside. Can he breathe?"

Mariela and Yuric alternately identified the heavy armor for use on a raptor that Grandel had been riding inside. It had sunk into the courtyard near the east tower, and a giant snakelike creature had coiled itself around it.

A lone, giant fish was swimming up to it.

The upper half of the coiled snake's body cut through the water and sunk its teeth into the fish's abdomen.

"Whoaaa, Yuric, look."

Yuric received the telescope from Mariela, checked the upper half of the coiled snake's body, and sighed.

"Mm. That's a subspecies of lamia. It's got six arms, and I think it's a fairly advanced kind..."

It was so long, it could easily reach the second floor of one of the structures even if the lower half of its body stayed wrapped around the heavy armor Grandel was in. It seemed unthinkable that there could be a lamia so enormous.

"Monsters get eaten by the black things during the night, but it seems like that lamia got that huge because it's got Grandel's shield protecting it. The fact that it's still wrapped around the armor probably means Grandel's fine, but..."

"Donnino, think ya can kill that thing?"

"Not by myself, that's for sure. I need someone who can stop it from moving. Too bad Edgan ain't here."

Yuric and Donnino pondered strategy for a moment. That lamia seemed to be quite the formidable opponent.

Apparently, they could manage somehow if Edgan was with

them, but if he left the northeast tower, a horde of black monsters would probably surge out from the north side where the defense had weakened. Could Franz hold out on his own?

"If it's a snake, there are a few potions that seem like they could be helpful, but..."

The concoctions Mariela proposed were ones that either emitted an odor snakes hated, threw their vibration-sensing organs out of order, or robbed them of their body heat and stalled their movements.

All of them were for terrestrial snake creatures, but this lamia was likely amphibious, and it might also hunt prey using sight in addition to sensing vibration. Given that it was such an advanced type, one had to wonder how effective Mariela's potions would even be.

Above all, she lacked a bit of each of the materials, and it seemed unlikely they could obtain them on the west side.

"At any rate, we can't do anything until we move to the east side. We'll rest here until the sun goes down and move once it's nighttime."

"Got it."

They ate when they could eat and slept whenever possible.

With warrior-like judgment, Donnino was about to throw himself down and fall asleep on the spot, and Mariela hurriedly produced rocks from her pouch.

"Mr. Donnino, here. I think these are your memory stones."

The ones Mariela took out had more subdued colors than Edgan's: a chic light brown and dark brown. There were two of them.

"Memory stones? What're those?"

Mariela told him about what they'd learned up to this point. Mariela and Yuric didn't understand the conditions for recovering the stones, but the memories would definitely return if everyone gathered and slept in the same room, and in that case, Mariela and Yuric would get a glimpse of Donnino's past.

"I see. But, young lady, isn't it best not to see people's memories? You'll end up biting off more than you can chew."

Donnino accepted the memory stones from Mariela and tucked them away in a pocket.

"I'll rest by myself in some random room. Hey, memories ain't all good. It doesn't make a difference to me if I don't get one or two of 'em back."

After saying this, he opened the north door and disappeared into a nearby room.

—Yo, long time no see.—

—You come so often, yet you never tire of it.—

How many times had she met the lake spirit now?

The other fire spirits felt this work of staying in the lamp and going through the forest was boring, and they hated it, but this one didn't feel that way.

When she thought about how she'd get to meet that lake spirit, the sluggish trek through the dark woods felt as brief as a wink, and on the way home, she thought of that beautiful creature until she arrived back in the city.

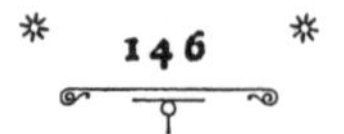

These days, the place where the humans lived had too many people to call it a village.

The question of how much time had passed was utterly meaningless to the fire spirit. If she couldn't obtain nourishment or got tired of existing, she would vanish from this world and return to the ley line. That was how it was for a spirit. Birth, existing, vanishing. Everything had equal worth, and at the same time, was uniformly worthless.

Spirits had no physical bodies to begin with. They came into existence easily, they changed quickly, and they vanished swiftly. Their consciousness was never exactly the same each time, but if you compared it to humans, it was something akin to whether or not they remembered what they ate yesterday.

However, the rare one existed who had found something that became their foundation.

For example, a sacred tree spirit or the like would take lodging in a newly sprouted sacred tree sapling and exist with it in the physical world. If a spirit didn't dwell within a sacred tree, it would never grow, and if the tree died, its inhabitant would similarly vanish. The rare mature sacred tree spirits separated from their plant and existed independently, but that was a scarce example and unlikely to happen under ordinary circumstances.

In particular, fire spirits were fickle and prone to change, and as exemplified by the phenomenon known as flame, not many maintained themselves indefinitely. Those few were ones who inhabited ceaselessly burning volcano craters or magma rivers deep underground, so a fire spirit who continued to exist while moving from light to light in a city was exceedingly rare.

Since she usually hid herself in small streetlamps, the fire spirit herself hadn't realized it, but after continuing to exist for a long time, she was no longer so transient that she could be extinguished with a single breath from the lake spirit.

That was how she managed to exchange words with the lake spirit while the humans were performing their ritual.

—The city of people is fascinating.—

To a spirit, the only difference between humans and other animals was whether they walked on two legs or four, so while adults and children could be differentiated, it was difficult to tell individuals apart. But as this fire spirit continued to exist, she gained an interest in the way people lived.

She could've sworn that up until quite recently, they'd lived in wooden houses, riddled with cracks, that could quickly be burned to nothing. Yet now they resided in domiciles made not just of wood, but plaster coatings and stone, and the only places fire spirits could dwell were in lamps, furnaces, and near fireplaces. Large iron-melting kilns had been built on the mountain a short distance away at some point, and that had recently become a popular spot among fire spirits.

The fire spirit happily talked about the process of baking bread, where springy batter expanded to become fluffy and delicious-looking in kilns; festivals where people surrounded a large bonfire and got really lively; and the way warriors fought with a torch in one hand when they drove back monsters attacking the city.

The spirit that lived in this lake listened to these tales with a gentle expression.

—If you are able to find them that endearing, then I, too, can treasure them.—

With a smile, the lake spirit drew the pitch-black corruption the humans had brought toward the water.

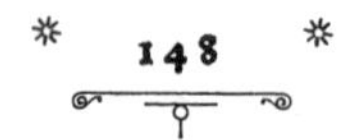

"It… …hu… …don't…"

Human life was very busy, and its changes were dizzying. Right now, the fire spirit only knew joy, sadness, anger, and suffering as variations of emotion. Just as she watched the changing of the seasons, she observed people's transitions with great interest.

Of course, many human feelings weren't positive. Such things gathered together and affected both people and the world negatively—as corruption. It killed crops, distorted the weather, and summoned epidemics.

Perhaps the corruption in humans was extremely strong, as only those with extraordinary abilities could see it, and when those kinds of people purified that malign presence, the fire spirit always helped.

Of course, there were things her power couldn't touch.

Today's corruption was an example of that. A terrible disease had spread extensively and caused people to vomit blood and die.

A sick person who shivered, not wanting to die.

A mother who feared for the young children she'd leave behind even as she heaved blood.

Sick people were stripped of all they had by traders who sold fake medicine or by greedy healing mages.

Folks who didn't know that poorly employed restorative magic would only ward off the symptoms of a disease for a short time used it to drag out the little remaining strength the ill had, merely appearing to heal them, and prolonged their suffering.

The powerful plague that wouldn't subside began to turn the healthy against the ill.

Diseased people were burned alive, and young children were treated as sick and beaten to death.

Even the healing mages and alchemists who examined the ill were thought to carry the plague and stoned.

"It hurts. It hurts. I don't want to die."

There was no way mere practitioners and spirits could do anything about such agonized cries.

The ark carrying the corruption sank into the water at the lake spirit's feet.

To slowly return it to the world at the deep, unseen bottom.

03

"This place is a real mess."

In front of the enormous box blocking the staircase to the second floor on the third level of the southeast tower, Donnino gripped his hammer tight.

"Think ya can handle it?"

"Sure can. Splinters might go flyin'. You two should head up to the fourth floor."

After Mariela's group had caught a nap until nightfall in the southwest tower, they'd returned to the southeast tower through the passage on the fourth level. Perhaps due to the effects of the fire bottles, the night was short, and since they had to slow down to make sure Donnino could keep up, they'd just gotten back to the southeast tower when it brightened outside.

In any case, the group needed to go down to the second floor

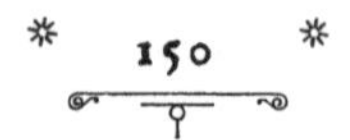

in this southeast tower to get to the temple in the center, and they could get to the northeast tower where Edgan was through the third-level hallway. Mariela's silence wasn't because they could get trapped in this tower or because they were losing time.

The answer seemed so close to her now, yet it still remained elusive. While frustrated, the alchemist kept her thoughts to herself.

Mr. Donnino and Yuric both said they didn't have any dreams during that nap...

Donnino had insisted he hadn't dreamed about the past and showed her the memory stones. This proved that memories wouldn't come back simply by bringing the rocks and their owner together. Of course, there was a possibility those stones didn't belong to Donnino, though.

Yuric also said she didn't have any dreams this time...

If Yuric didn't have any, whose dream could that have been, and why did Mariela alone see it?

Bang, smash. Crunch, crunch, crunch.

"Whoa, this's bad."

Mariela's thoughts were interrupted by sounds of destruction and Donnino's voice from the floor below.

"Donnino, what's goin' on?"

"Whatever this is, cleaning it up's gonna be tough, Yuric."

Mariela followed Yuric down to the third floor, saw the large number of scattered potions there, and thought, *Ahh, I knew it.*

The things had filled the towering box that blocked the stairs to the second floor. It need scarcely be said how many there were. Over half of the potion vials had broken and mixed together from the impact of the container's destruction, but all of them were concoctions that had sold well two hundred years ago.

"For now, I'll dry the place. **Dehydrate.**"

In one go, Mariela's *Dehydrate* dried up all the potions that had soaked the room.

"Ooh, not bad, young lady."

Donnino's exclamation of wonder wasn't mere flattery. Evaporating that large a quantity of liquid all at once wasn't a feat just anyone could pull off. If it had been normal water, even Mariela, who boasted immense magical power, probably couldn't have dried it this easily.

Just like I thought. These are...

Potions often had their medicinal efficacy extracted after Drops of Life was dissolved into magically created water. In other words, the liquid the brews were composed of was originally magical power.

The water was created with magic because it was easier to exert influence on something made with your own magical power in the processes that followed. For example, when drying spilled water, there was a world of difference in the time and magical energy it took to dry well water versus magically created liquid.

These are potions I made.

The fact that they were concoctions Mariela had made herself was why she'd been able to *Dehydrate* them so effortlessly.

Mariela looked around the room and realized she had some recollection of the numerous cheap sundries packed into the boxes there.

Surely these are from the orphanage that looked after me...

Mariela was convinced. This southeast tower was a tower of her memories.

"Ow!"

"That's what ya get for daydreamin'. There's lots of potions here, so get that healed up."

A glass shard had cut Mariela's hand as she cleaned up the broken vials.

The expanding drop of blood and the throbbing pain in Mariela's fingertip told her this world wasn't a dream.

The answer was close at hand.

Feeling that was the case, Mariela went down to the second floor with the others after gathering the broken potion vials to one side and clearing a path to the stairs down.

The second floor had the same carpeting and identical construction to the southwest side. Rooms lined the hallway, and most likely the entrance was at the end of the west side. A place like an atrium with a greenhouse was at the end of the north side.

"I don't think it's dangerous if we don't open the door at the end, so I'm thinking I'll go around to the rooms and make potions."

At Mariela's suggestion, the three split up. Donnino went north to investigate the situation of the first floor from the east tower, and Yuric rode Koo up the stairs to replenish their fire bottles and food.

Now on her own, Mariela opened the door of the room closest to the north side.

"I knew it..."

It was Mariela's workshop, which should have been in the Labyrinth City.

"Slaken's...not here..."

She didn't know whether it was because Slaken was a living thing or because this was a reproduction of the room after Sieg had taken out Slaken. However, the rearing vessel for the artificial slime made of kraken somatic sells was empty, and Slaken's viscous liquid was collecting at the bottom.

The shelves were lined with a variety of crystallized medicinal herbs, and the selection was most likely better than in any of the other rooms. Since the Labyrinth had been defeated and materials were growing scarcer, Mariela had bought as much as she could while they were still available.

Even so, there were things it lacked.

"If this room exists, surely Lady Carol's workshop should be around here, too, don't you think?"

"Rawr."

The salamander on Mariela's shoulder made a noise in response to her question. It was incredibly reassuring to have this fiery lizard around. Its presence really reminded Mariela of someone.

After gazing at the small spirit moving its big, round, golden eyes about for a little while, Mariela left her workshop for the moment and went to search the other chambers.

Donnino was in the second-floor hallway leading to the east tower.

Strong light shone in through the windows, and the monster fish swimming nearby sometimes cast shadows.

"The monsters should be resurrecting now. If this side is like the west side, the black thing'll probably be out and about. But as long as I don't bump into it, it'll be busy with the other creatures and won't notice me here. Perfect for scoutin'."

After confirming Mariela and Yuric weren't nearby and thus no harm would befall them, Donnino approached the east tower's entrance.

No sounds could be heard from the other side of the door. There probably weren't any battles happening nearby. Even so, after carefully and silently opening the door, Donnino reflexively groaned at the scene and smell on the other side.

"...What an awful stench. What's goin' on with this place?"

A narrow, complex cave system lay beyond.

The west side had been an atrium with a wide, dome-shaped ceiling, yet dark red, fish-smelling things completely covered the expansive surface area in this place, and Donnino could see white objects here and there.

"Is this...carrion?"

When he touched it, the crimson surface of the wall conveyed elasticity and coldness through his glove. Since it had no warmth, this was probably the flesh of something dead. Donnino pulled his hand away and found dark red fluid still clinging to this fingertips.

"At any rate, it sure does reek."

It was an unspeakably foul odor, one that was a mélange of orcs, goblins, blood and internal organs, and rotten meat.

After covering his mouth with a cloth, Donnino traipsed farther into the cave.

Both the floor and the walls of the chamber were formed of squishy lumps of meat. While there wasn't sound footing, there were solid objects here and there that helped support Donnino, and his feet didn't sink.

"There're even bones here...?"

The white objects that protruded in places were probably skeletal remains. Thanks to his goggles that granted night vision, Donnino had no problem seeing.

Perhaps for the benefit of whatever made this chamber its stronghold, a liquid different from the blood oozed here and there and emitted phosphorescent light. It wasn't enough for the naked eye to see, but it could ensure sufficient visibility with the help of night-vision magic. As Donnino advanced through the cave, the flesh's color changed here and there, making it appear as though several types of creatures were mixed into it.

Donnino could stand up straight and walk in the wider parts of the passage, but it was so tight that he had to bend his knees and drop his rump to move forward when it narrowed.

If he happened to meet monsters in a confined spot like this, the hammer wielder wouldn't be able to fight sufficiently. Fortunately, the compact passage didn't last long, and Donnino soon arrived in a small room that afforded more space. Many paths branched from this new chamber, and there were hole-like passages above and below. Donnino surmised that this network of caverns stretched in all directions.

Several small rooms lay ahead in this one, and another kind of smell wafted from them.

"What's that? Melting flesh?"

There was a pool with what looked like a muddy blend of melted skin and blood. The flesh-liquid swelled like foaming gas, and some of the bubbles bloomed like they were being torn and emitted screams like "aaa" or "gyaaa."

A baby's first cry.

The pieces of meat crawling from the flesh pool suddenly grew

limbs, opened eyes, and made unpleasant cries as they crawled toward the deeper parts of the cave system, apparently not catching sight of Donnino.

"Is this a monster nursery? I've never heard of things bein' born like that before. Were those goblins?"

As Donnino followed the newborn goblins and progressed through the cave system, their numbers increased. All of them seemed to regard Donnino as nothing more than a part of the caves, and the small ones slipped between his legs and proceeded deeper. As they went on, the chambers widened little by little, and newborn creatures with large bodies such as orcs and wolves mingled with the goblins. All the monsters were the kinds that ate weird food and had potent reproductive power like those that could be found in the Fell Forest or the shallow strata of the Labyrinth.

The monsters surged from the cave system laid out like a spiderweb toward what was probably the center of the east tower's first floor. Even if Donnino covered his mouth, breathing was difficult due to the stink of the cave itself and the monsters, as well as the unbearable stench wafting from ahead of them. Donnino crawled into a hole in a place a little higher up to escape from the monsters' odor, because he felt a slight, cool breeze from there. This sort of cave had air holes.

"Pwah, this's unbearable..." Donnino, having managed to catch his breath at last in this small pocket of fresh air, cursed this place.

The room had air holes stretching vertically that were so thin, not even a newborn goblin could pass through them, and the fresh breeze was flowing down from above. When he looked down the one shaft that connected directly to the lower floor, Donnino saw that the monsters seemed to be marching toward the central part of the first level.

"Wuzzat?"

The air hole was narrow, denying Donnino a full picture.

What he could glean from the fragmentary field of view was monsters attacking a giant round object that looked like it had been painted pitch-black.

The spherical, ebon object appeared filled to bursting, like a ripe pomegranate.

Donnino could only see a portion of the black pomegranate through the air hole, and he couldn't tell if it was turning into a tree or what the parts of it he couldn't see were.

Donnino did identify monsters jumping and snapping one after another at the creature's stretched-full skin, however. They resembled ants swarming over a sweet fruit that had fallen to the ground.

Rrrip.

Without any warning, the black pomegranate's flesh split.

What spilled out from it wasn't fruit, but countless black rats.

The momentum of the overflowing vermin was like that of water breaching a dam, and although the monsters had been swarming the black pomegranate up until just now, the mass of rats swallowed them up after it burst.

"This's real bad."

Donnino rushed back the way he'd come with incredible agility considering his solid build.

This cave system was complex, and it was difficult to tell one passage from another, but Donnino had left scratches on the walls so he would know the way back. Dark red liquid oozed from the scars that looked like lacerations. Though grotesque, they were landmarks for the way back, so Donnino relied on them as he hurriedly returned the way he came with the momentum of a startled hare.

Monster howls and the noise of swarming rats echoed from the chambers at Donnino's back.

Munch-munch, munch-munch.

An unpleasant sound reverberated in the carrion caves.

05

"Here, Mr. Donnino, drink this."

Donnino had somehow escaped from the east tower's cavern system and reunited with Mariela and Yuric in the southeast tower. Seeing how sickly he looked, Mariela offered him a potion.

"Phew, thanks, young lady. Finally feels like I can take a breather."

After downing the concoction he'd accepted from Mariela without confirming what kind it was, Donnino caught his breath and then began to explain what he'd seen in the east tower.

"There's likely some type of strange disease in there."

Donnino had confirmed as much with his eyes and ears. He'd witnessed the rats spilling out of the black pomegranate touch the monsters, which then collapsed as blood gushed from not just their mouths, noses, eyes, and ears, but from anything you could call a pore. And he'd heard the chewing of the rats devouring those bleeding creatures' corpses.

"Donnino's not infected, is he?" asked Yuric.

"He just drank a cure potion, so he'll be fine," Mariela answered. She'd anticipated what lay ahead.

Because she now had a rough guess of what this place was and whose memory she'd seen in her most recent dream.

"I know a potion that works on diseases," she said. Yuric, who saw her sparkling golden eyes, felt she'd caught a glimpse of the face of Mariela's master, Freyja, because it seemed like Mariela could see what was going to happen.

"What Mr. Donnino just drank was a special-grade cure potion. It'll cure any disease then and there, and the person who imbibes it won't get infected for a few days. I'll throw this into the monster nursery."

Mariela conveyed her strategy as she whittled a white horn.

The group was in one of the alchemist workshops up on the second floor. It was the first time Yuric and Donnino had ever been in this particular one, but Mariela had been here many times. Among the expensive materials on display, the one categorized as the highest quality was what Mariela was whittling currently: a unicorn horn.

Out of the many ways Caroline's uncle, Ruiz, tried to communicate the secret art of the Sacrificials to the Aguinas family, only one had been successful—concealing it in this unicorn horn.

After hearing this story, Mariela was shown the real thing, and she knew where it was stored. Yes, this place was Caroline's workshop.

She added the unicorn horn she'd whittled down with a gold file into lynus wheat vinegar and began to dissolve it. This vinegar was pure, made only of lynus wheat, which could naturally store Drops of Life, and the grain itself was also used as a raw material by removing the germs and polishing its surface. It could be refined into vinegar after a short time by putting it in a Transmutation Vessel with air and Drops of Life.

The special-grade cure potions that used unicorn horns really couldn't abide any impurities mixed in during the creation process. As such, it was necessary to perform the transmutation in a two-layered Transmutation Vessel without removing it once.

"And this time, I'll add crystallized shinogira root to it and combine it with a dissolved ley-line shard."

Mariela had made ten potions while the group had been split up, plus an additional twenty now. This many ought to be enough.

After countless monsters—mainly goblins—had been birthed in the carrion caves, they would prey on the black rats, which were far greater in number. The goblins that ate the little animals would immediately spurt blood from not only their eyes, noses, and mouths, but even their pores due to the plague spread by the rats, and after they crumbled and died like their flesh was melting, they became food for the vermin. The whole situation was hellish.

The black rats devoured the dead monsters and the caves themselves, so it seemed like even the terrain was changing as new passages took form and uneaten carrion coagulated to become part of the floor.

The group decided that Mariela, who was no match for the rats, would stay with Koo in the safe southeast tower. Yuric and Donnino would throw the completed special-grade cure potions into the countless monster nurseries in the carrion caverns.

The potions would grant the newly birthed monsters in the

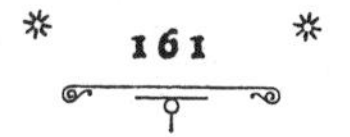

nurseries a resistance to the plague, albeit only as long as the effects of Mariela's concoctions lasted. Thus, even if they ate the black rats, they wouldn't immediately die. Over time, the balance in the caves would probably invert, and the rats would be exterminated.

However, since there wouldn't be much potion per monster, one had to wonder if the effects of the alchemical mixture would even last half a day.

It was certain that the number of both goblins and rats would significantly decrease in the next few hours.

"All we can do now is wait."

"Rar."

The raptor Koo brought his face close to Mariela, who felt just a little helpless, as though to say everything would be okay.

"Thanks, Koo."

Now it was just Mariela and Koo. The salamander had gone to the carrion caves, riding on Yuric's shoulder. Whether it was worried about Yuric's fighting power or it just wanted to go to the tunnels was unclear. It had voluntarily moved to her shoulder.

"Oh, hello. Are ya comin' with us?"

Since her animal training skills didn't work on the salamander, a spirit, Yuric couldn't converse with it, but she looked thrilled. Yuric must have been an animal lover through and through.

"Surely I'm not wrong about using those potions..."

Mariela had turned all the materials Yuric had gathered for her into fire bottles, and she'd also cooked some monster meat.

Not knowing what to do with herself, Mariela reclined on Koo, who was seated, and waited for Donnino and Yuric to return.

06

"Mariela, Mariela, wake up. It's time."

"Wha—? Yuric, did I fall asleep?"

Yuric shook Mariela awake, and Mariela rubbed her eyes as she sat up. Apparently, she'd been resting. And it seemed to have been a deep sleep, as she'd completely recovered her magical power.

I didn't have any dreams...

Mariela straightened up her outfit as the salamander, who had returned to its usual place on her shoulder unnoticed, licked her cheeks to tell her to wash her face.

"Around what time is it?"

"Probably about noon."

Donnino answered Mariela's question as he chewed a lump of monster meat. Although Mariela's biological clock was entirely out of whack due to the extremely short nights, Donnino and Yuric had been living on the road for a long time, and their senses of time seemed to be very accurate.

At Yuric's recommendation, Mariela had just a light meal in case she vomited from the smell, while Donnino and Yuric partook of their food with gusto. Afterward, the trio headed for the carrion caves in the east tower to check the potions' effect.

"Well, I'll be damned. Who woulda thought it'd go this well?"

Mariela gave a vague, disingenuous laugh in response to Donnino's surprised muttering as she gazed at the lump before them, which resembled a nearly rotten pomegranate that had ripened and fallen from a tree. She hadn't spoken of her dream about the plague. Since the others hadn't said anything about it, either, Mariela was probably the only one who had seen that vision.

Mariela's master had told her about that disease once.

It had run rampant a very, very long time ago.

In those days, potion technology hadn't yet discovered mixtures that could cure disease, and no one knew that if healing magic was used poorly, even the sickness would be restored.

That's why people intending to cure the illness misused restorative spells, whittled away the stamina of the sick in vain, and unwittingly spread the infection. Those who feared the incurable disease quarantined people who showed symptoms from the city along with their families and incinerated the sick's houses, possessions, and even their livestock. Despite the afflicted being quarantined, no one cared for them. It was functionally just leaving those poor folks to die.

Of course, it wasn't as though no research was done on illnesses. Money was freely poured into study on potions that could cure plagues, and at last, a single brew was completed. The disease abated thanks to that mixture, which became the prototype for high-grade cure potions, but by then, the city's population had decreased to less than half of what it had been.

High-grade cure potions were potent. So there could be no doubt about their effects if they were special-grade. Moreover, this time Mariela had added crystallized shinogira root. Shinogira was a purple flower that bloomed rarely in tropical forests, and both its petals and particularly its roots possessed powerful antibacterial properties. Even in the subtropical strata of the Labyrinth crawling with monsters that spread disease, it was said you'd be fine if you simply drank from a body of water where shinogira was growing on its banks.

The components extracted from shinogira root had many impurities, so it wasn't generally mixed with the unicorn horns used as materials for special-grade cure potions. However, since Mariela blended it in as medicinal crystals containing no impurities, she successfully created the potions.

You could say these were special-grade potions specialized for this disease.

Their effect was tremendous: The goblins generated from the nurseries the potions had been thrown into were eating the plague-spreading black rats without contracting it themselves. Several surviving goblins had attacked Mariela's group along the way, but they were still just weak monsters at the end of the day. With one swing from Donnino, they were reduced to being part of the cave system. The party had expected the surviving monsters to attack and threw the potions only into nurseries that birthed goblins, so you could say this also went as planned.

When Mariela and her companions at last reached the lowest level of this system of caverns, they found corpses of goblins whose potions had worn off collapsed in heaps. The giant pomegranate-like lump Donnino had spoken of lay at the center, and it blew out a rotten smell as though it was breathing.

The fissure the black rats had spilled from ran in four directions from the bottom like a split, ripened fruit, exposing its dark red interior. Could the dark red fibrous tissue growing densely within be cilia? Gooey liquid resembling bloody pus that coiled and squirmed indicated that the thing wasn't entirely dead yet.

The group could hear a noise from the riven pomegranate-like lump, which expanded as though breathing and spit out a rotten odor. It resembled the sound of wind blowing and reverberating through the caves made of dead flesh, and Mariela heard it as the following:

"It hurts. It hurts. I don't want to die."

"Your lives and your bodies aren't in this world. You've already been released..."

Mariela opened a special-grade cure potion and threw it into the black pomegranate.

In that instant, the thing stiffened like a fruit contracting, as though its insides were being squeezed out, and then it drooped like the skin of produce that had lost its interior and stopped moving.

The black pomegranate rapidly shriveled and dried up, and it felt as though the group had seen a fruit ripening, rotting, and decomposing at an accelerated speed.

"It... ...rts. I... ant... die."

Did that sound have the tone of wind blowing through the carrion caves?

When Donnino and Yuric threw fire bottles at the black pomegranate, flames swallowed up the surroundings.

"Even if the salamander's protectin' us, we'll be baked at this rate. Let's pull out for now."

At Donnino's orders, the party beat a retreat from the carrion caves. Only the salamander on Mariela's shoulder as she rushed for the exit was staring at the burning black pomegranate.

07

"Now, we gotta decide on our next plan soon."

The group briefly returned to the second floor of the southeast tower and discussed the strategy from here on out.

Whether they were going to help Grandel or simply move forward, they needed to get to the courtyard.

If they simply went to the courtyard, the best course was to wait on the south side where the entrance was and go outside at dusk when the Necklace went dormant.

"There might still be monsters or the black spider on the first floor."

"Right, I'll go check for that when the fire's died down. But the problem's that snake woman. The one with Grandel. It's probably no big deal if we leave that alone, but… Young lady, do you have all the materials for a potion that might work on a snake?"

Mariela shook her head at Donnino's question.

"I'm missing one reagent, but if we search the first floor, I think we'll almost certainly find it."

"Almost certainly, huh…?"

Donnino glanced in the direction of the east tower. After he'd returned from scouting, he'd most likely contracted something. Mariela had offered him a potion as though she could tell. It almost seemed like she'd even known how to defeat the disease nesting in the carrion caves.

That's why Mariela saying that she would obtain the final material on the first floor, which they hadn't yet been to, had a mysteriously persuasive power.

"You decide, young lady," Donnino said to Mariela. "That lamia's too much for me on my own. Do we call Edgan, or do we open the way with potions? Either way, it'll take too much time. Edgan's not around, and we don't have any potions made yet."

The surest way to rescue Grandel was to rely on Edgan. As much as they hated to admit it, there was no doubt that Edgan's fighting power as an A-Ranker would bring down even the likes of that titanic lamia. However, if they asked him for help, there would no longer be sufficient defense in the north. How long could Franz hold out by himself?

Mariela shifted her attention to Yuric, who was facing north and looking a little restless.

Was she fretting over Franz or Edgan?

Mariela was certain Yuric was worried about Grandel, too, but it seemed like she had greater concerns than that.

"Mr. Donnino, Yuric..." Mariela began to outline their plan going forward.

CHAPTER 4

The Gentleman and the Serpent

Siegmund was beside himself.

"M… Mariela!"

Not much time had passed since Mariela had run away from home.

With his Spirit Eye open, Sieg scoured every nook and cranny of Sunlight's Canopy for Mariela. Unable to just sit by and watch, one of the regulars, Old Man Ghark, called to him.

"What's the matter, sonny?"

"Mari… Mari… Mariela!"

"So that's it. Your wife's gone and run out on ya."

"No, Mr. Gordon. Mr. Sieg hasn't proposed to Miss Mari yet."

Sieg, who had promptly begun saying nothing but "Mariela" despite the fact that not much time had passed since she'd left, was incapable of explaining, so Gordon had drawn his own conclusions. Sherry, who'd returned from school, made a cruel amendment to the explanation. Merle, the housewife intelligence agent, also latched onto this conversation.

"Oh? Weren't you plannin' to propose soon? I was wonderin' if you'd made a complete mess of it and got dumped."

"!!!"

It was nothing short of what one would expect from a person in the know. She'd delivered the topic Sieg least wanted anyone to touch on with exquisite timing.

At this, Sieg's face paled.

It had been a year since the Labyrinth was killed. Things had been extremely busy back then.

Although the number of alchemists in the Labyrinth City had increased, Mariela was the only one who could create special-grade potions. She was still a rare breed, and the groups trying to have her work for them via kidnapping, blackmail, false friendship, or seduction were too numerous to count. Of course, Sieg stopped these things before they happened, either single-handedly or with the help of Margrave Schutzenwald or the Aguinas family. Sieg had tried his best to keep Mariela safe, but maybe he'd been a bit too overprotective.

Although Mariela had been in many dangerous situations, she never experienced the suspension bridge effect because Sieg always safeguarded her from behind the scenes. She'd grown quite comfortable with Sieg, who was something like a parent watching over their child.

Far from the relationship being carefree, it had become care*less*.

At a glance, the relationship between the two seemed rather harmonious. Although they weren't hitched, they had a calmness like an old couple who'd been married for a long time.

There's no point in saying Sieg was too lazy—after all, the regulars of Sunlight's Canopy, including Sherry, Emily, and Merle, had been saying that plenty.

Maybe he was nervous about the way things were going, or perhaps his facade was cracking just a little, leading him to ask himself if he could even take any more of this. Siegmund, who had appeared to think he had all the time in the world, finally got off his laurels.

In the year since the subjugation of the Labyrinth, Mariela's alchemist training goals and stock of special-grade potions were more or less in order, and Sieg had intended to make a move to improve their worn-out relationship when Mariela's life had settled down.

Had Sieg failed, or did he make a mistake in the preliminary step?

Even the intelligence agent Merle couldn't understand Sieg's explanation when all he spoke was Mariela-ese, but news like "Siegmund got dumped" running amok through the Labyrinth City would be awful for the poor hunter. This was no time for Sieg to be forgetting what he'd fought, bled, and killed for.

"M... M... M... N... Not yet. We just had a little fight..."

"Ah, he spoke."

"In that case, go after her right now and make up! She'll surely forgive you if you offer a heartfelt apology."

Amber lit a fire under Sieg, who had finally regained his words and his wits.

"I understand." Sieg nodded vigorously. Amber often told off her husband, Dick, who repeatedly did stupid things, but she always accepted his earnest apologies. Her words carried weight with Sieg.

"Siggy, do you know where Mari is?" Emily asked, puzzled.

Sieg nodded, said, "Don't worry. I have my ways," then headed for the rear garden.

"Illuminaria! Illuminaria, I need your help!"

—What is it? Geez...—

After wasting his Spirit Eye and summoning the sacred tree spirit Illuminaria, Sieg rushed to make preparations to pursue Mariela.

"Siggy sure is slow, isn't he?"

"Right? And I can't believe he got so carried away he made Miss Mari angry enough to run away from home in the first place."

"Right? I heard women hate men who act like their boyfriend right away."

"Right?"

As Sieg grumbled quietly after Emily and Sherry deliberately badmouthed him loud enough for him to hear, he finally departed Sunlight's Canopy.

"I knew it'd be here..."

Mariela and the others had made their way to the first floor after the fire in the carrion caves went out.

It must have been around noon by the time they'd reached the first floor of the southeast tower after cooling and ventilating the nearly airtight cave system. Koo had come through the tunnels after Donnino had made them wide and tall enough for a raptor. After trekking through the hot caverns, Mariela urged the others to rest, saying, "It's probably safe from here on." She searched the rooms in the vicinity of this tower by herself and soon found what she'd been looking for.

This tower had Mariela's workshop from Sunlight's Canopy. She'd thought there was no doubt it would also have this room, where she'd spent a very long time and learned alchemy.

"I lost it without warning in the Stampede... Brings back memories."

The cottage in the Fell Forest where Mariela had lived with her master two hundred years ago. It was there, the same as it had been.

The dim, confined abode was made more cramped by the medicinal herbs off-handedly left here and there. Yet it lacked even the bare minimum of household items necessary for daily life, and it was a dreary place that resembled a storage shed.

To Mariela, it had only been a few years since she'd lived in that little cottage all alone, but when she stood in this place once more, all she recalled were the hectic and joyous days she'd spent with her master when she was very young. Compared with now, her life back then was rather uneventful, but she also felt that was when she was most content.

Was it really this dark...?

Mariela felt like it had been far brighter and warmer when her master was there.

In which case, this place was likely a reproduction of the room from when Mariela lived alone.

Although Sunlight's Canopy, where she lived with Sieg, was chilly and made of stone, for some reason it was very cozy and comforting. She'd almost forgotten what it felt like being here.

Most of Mariela's life had been spent at this cottage, so it was full of memories and utterly sentimental.

But she neither wanted to go back to it nor felt like she had come home.

This little cottage in the Fell Forest was an important place that remained in Mariela's memories, but she accepted with a strange feeling that it was no longer her home.

"No matter what kind of world this is, the potions made here have an effect for sure, so I gotta use what I can… Oh, there it is!"

Mariela took out a bundle wrapped several times around in cloth from the top of the food storage cabinet near the sink. This object that leaked cool air was *Ice Spirit's Kiss*. It was a frost-like plant that clung to things like tree trunks and windows on frosty mornings. Since it melted when sunlight touched it, Mariela got up early on chilly winter mornings before the sun rose and went around checking for it. Collecting it was frigid, tough work, but processing and selling Ice Spirit's Kiss had provided her a good source of income in the summer.

The name was based on the legend "If an ice spirit kisses you, it will steal your body heat, and you'll die," and the object did indeed steal heat.

The aboveground parts resembling semitransparent vines were cold as ice, but they melted and disappeared if a certain amount of heat was applied to them after collection. Since the material was sensitive to both light and heat, you had to store it securely, but Icy Wind Potions, which improved the effects of Ice Spirit's Kiss, had been sold at a reasonable price in the summer as potions that could cool the air in a room for about half a day.

"There were no magical cooling tools two hundred years ago, after all."

Since there were devices for keeping rooms comfortable now, the potions were hardly necessary anymore, but two hundred years ago, they were an essential revenue source for Mariela during the hotter months of the year.

"Still, this pantry's pretty bare."

The cooling box the Ice Spirit's Kiss had been stored in was made to preserve food with ice. With the Ice Spirit's Kiss taking up space in the container, however, there was only a small area in it where food could be kept. Ironically, Mariela's diet had been so poor that she hadn't even needed the entire available spot in the cooling box. It wasn't so bad when her master was there and they had charred monster meat and souvenirs she'd brought from somewhere, but Mariela had lived very modestly when she was by herself.

"I feel like the things in it were slightly more varied when my master was there, but still, it was nothing but weird monster meat… Even so, every day was fun with her around, you know?"

"Rawr."

The salamander on Mariela's neck responded to her mutterings.

Hectic, precious days gone. A warm time in her life.

I have to repay her…

Mariela made a note of this and set about making an Icy Wind Potion.

Night came yet again—one of many by this point.

Mariela and the others confirmed it was now dark outside the windows and passed through the door leading to the entrance hall, where the tree monster, the Necklace, was encamped.

Since it had roots, it couldn't travel itself, but it was a fashionable tree monster that manipulated vines as hard as steel and tried to catch people by the neck and decorate itself with them.

Much like humans who enjoyed excessive decorations, this Necklace, too, had a slightly peculiar hobby: keeping hairy caterpillar monsters as pets. No one knew if they were famous among tree monsters as rare pets, but Mariela and the others hardly enjoyed the nasty bugs. In particular, the experience of being chased by hairy caterpillars seemed to have left Yuric deeply scarred, and their current strategy was tailored to avoid as much fighting as possible.

As though it took the term *beauty sleep* seriously, the tree monster slept soundly and returned to being just a plant while the sun was down. Mariela's group slowly and quietly approached the door at the center of the entrance so as not to rouse the fearsome monster.

The solid door, much taller than Mariela and the others, opened outward without a sound when they pushed it.

The party had traveled along the top of the outer wall many times over, and it wasn't the first time they'd been outside. Still, they felt suffocated by the heavy air. It was more than the fact that it was heavy and damp.

They were underwater. Everything in this world of water had drifted down from the surface and accumulated here.

Dark madness mingled with the moist air. Mariela, Yuric, and Donnino could no longer feel the kindness of the water that reflected light and nurtured monsters. A white building with many jade, dome-shaped ceilings piled on top of each other towered at the center of the courtyard. Now that there was no illumination, it was utterly dark and oppressive, as though it were leaning on them.

"That's gotta be the temple." Mariela had felt that way since she'd first seen the building. But what on earth was it a temple to?

Surely the answers to everything awaited them inside the structure. Unfortunately, that wasn't where they were headed.

"It's over there. Let's move," Donnino called to Mariela, who was looking up at the temple.

They left the path leading to the temple and made for the

east side of the courtyard. That was where they hoped to find the trapped Grandel.

As the group proceeded through the damp, oppressive air, black monsters appeared around them like sludge swirling up from the bottom of the water. The creatures lifted their bodies like rolling, muddy goo, and Mariela, Yuric, and Donnino hurled fire bottles at them.

"We can't waste time on the small fries. Hurry up."

Their goal was the base of the east tower. The raptor carrying Mariela and Yuric matched Donnino's pace as he ran with his heavy hammer, and the girls tossed alchemical explosives at the black monsters to keep them in check.

"I see it! Grandel's armor!"

"The lamia's there, too! The night is short, so let's hurry!"

The lamia slowly lifted her head as she scowled at the uninvited guests.

Seeing how big she was from up close took their breath away.

"Shaa, sha."

The lamia made menacing sounds, and Donnino kept her in check with his hammer as Mariela and Yuric threw potions at her. The concoctions sapped her body heat and hindered her movement, but they weren't enough to stop such a powerful monster.

Donnino raised his hammer overhead and struck at the lamia. Mariela and Yuric seized that opening to throw more Icy Wind Potions at the creature's tail and body. The numerous Icy Wind Potions freely hurled at the lamia worked well enough that even Donnino could dodge her attacks. He avoided or deflected strikes from the lamia's six arms with his hammer as he slowly drew her away from Grandel.

"Now! The tail's separated from the armor!"

The instant the lamia's tail, which had been twined around Grandel's heavy armor, released it, Yuric and Mariela rushed forward. The pair jumped from the raptor and past the half-frozen lamia, though the giant creature still tried to stop them with its tail. Yuric used her whip to parry the attack, and Mariela took that opportunity to open Grandel's heavy armor from the outside.

"Mr. Grandel! Hurry!"

The armor, custom-made by Donnino, had been built to affix to a raptor with Grandel inside. Grandel couldn't move around while wearing it, but it came with two hatches that could be opened both from the inside and outside. Mariela opened the outside lock on one of them and told Grandel they'd come to help him. That was when…

"Shhhaaaaa!"

"Guh!"

Mariela turned her head at the lamia's menacing sound that shook the courtyard and saw the monster blow Donnino away with a single attack. Now free of distraction, it turned its attention to Yuric, who'd been handling the tail, attacking her with water magic.

"Yuric!!!" Mariela cried. No one had expected the lamia to be capable of casting spells.

The many half-moon-shaped water attacks launched at Yuric were likely sharp blades of liquid. Yuric instinctively ducked and avoided the lamia's spells.

Not a moment later, Yuric came to realize that she hadn't necessarily avoided them.

Behind Yuric, who had desperately jumped away, black shadows resembling people on horses rose and didn't show a hint of flinching upon taking a blow from the sharp water blades.

When Mariela and the others had opened the door to that shrine in that marshland in the Fell Forest, the end of the rope they'd pulled on the door with was fastened to the heavy armor Grandel was holed up in.

They'd used it as a weight.

If he'd gotten out of his iron suit back then, Grandel probably wouldn't have been sitting at the bottom of the water in the courtyard for days. Unfortunately, he'd been pulled into this world of water in his heavy armor, along with everyone else.

"Ohhh. What is happening?"

All Grandel could do was watch as everyone sank toward the bottom of the water.

Even when he'd tried to escape, he couldn't open the armor on his own, perhaps due to water pressure.

The other mysterious thing was that although this metal suit was sophisticated, it had an opening for visibility, and the joints weren't airtight. Yet no water entered it.

When Grandel had calmly examined the situation to discern what was happening, it seemed to him that his comrades were sinking. It was as though they were all being carried in the same direction toward a temple of a style that Grandel had never seen before, surrounded by ramparts and six towers.

As they got closer to the structure, one party member, then another, was carried to the top floor of a tower.

"It appears everyone is being taken to the top level of a different tower. Hrm, so I am going to that one?"

Perhaps his comrades had been overwhelmed by the water and rendered unconscious, because they didn't fight against the current as they disappeared into the towers through open windows at the top of each.

"They don't appear to be terribly complicated buildings. If so, we will be able to come together again before long."

Just as Grandel murmured this…

Bam.

Grandel's heavy armor got stuck in a window.

"Oh? I'm not going in?"

The armor was massive. It had been carried diagonally and should have smoothly entered the tower through the window, but it got stuck with a *thud* and then scraped the tower's outer wall as it sank toward the courtyard on the first floor.

His comrades in the Black Iron Freight Corps had mocked the metallic suit Grandel used for being "box armor" and the like. At a glance, it was awkward, rough, full-body metal protection, the likes of which might be worn by heavy infantry.

Moreover, it was enormous. It was so big that the slender Grandel could have fit two of himself inside it, and it was even too tall for him. The surface, the underside, and the joints were all made of metal plates.

Any knowledgeable eye looking over the armor would realize that the joints, which should have been crafted with ease of movement as a priority, had a particular gimmick to them.

To tell the truth, the armor Grandel wore was not expected to move at all.

Its sophisticated design allowed it to be affixed on the back of a raptor and had the joints move on their own to match the raptor's movements and keep balance. Although its structure allowed one to escape from it if they so chose, it wasn't so different from being packed in a box.

Grandel was so physically frail that he couldn't even hold a shield. If he couldn't move with even moderate equipment, then prioritizing survival regardless of the avenue of attack was clearly the way to go. With this in mind, Donnino had put his hobby to full use and had completed this heavy, boxlike armor.

Although the product forced inconvenience on Grandel, livability was taken into consideration accordingly: The interior was lined with a soft and fluffy material, and a stockpile of food, albeit a small one, was built in. The box-shaped container even included a small window for exchanging goods.

As luck would have it, edible aquatic plants also grew in this courtyard, and Grandel, who had a small appetite to begin with and ate mainly vegetables, didn't starve.

"I'm bored..."

During the day, the place filled with water, and Grandel couldn't leave the armor due to the pressure. At night, black monsters surrounded him, meaning he couldn't risk leaving then, either. Fortunately, Grandel's shield skills seemed to be effective against the inky creatures, as they didn't enter through gaps in the armor or attack, but even though he was safe, Grandel was also stuck.

It was a small, lone snake that brought him comfort.

"A monster, I believe. Still, it's quite charming."

The white serpent had a pair of pectoral fin-shaped protrusions, and the tip of its tail, its fins, and the area around its head were all pale pink. It was a very, very small snake, only long enough to circle one of Grandel's slender arms once.

It had probably gotten lost not long after it was born.

Although tiny, the creature threatened Grandel with *shaa, shaa* sounds. When he tore up some meat from his rations and fed it to the creature, its abdomen swelled, and it curled up in Grandel's hand, where it fell asleep.

It was only one day that Grandel had direct contact with the serpent. The following day, it had grown so large it couldn't fit into the aperture in the armor anymore.

Did it think of Grandel as its parent for giving it food, or did it understand it wouldn't be attacked if it coiled around his armor? The snake eventually wrapped around Grandel and stayed there, eating those memory stealers.

Every time morning came, monsters were born and the world became an ocean. Grandel watched the black creatures disappear like sludge dissolving and the newborn monsters eating them and growing rapidly. At night, the inky creatures surged from the north and both ate and were eaten by the new monsters, and most of the latter died out during the night.

However, only the snake, protected by Grandel's shield skills, survived repeated encounters with the black blobs, and it continued to grow at such a rate that it would be more accurate to say it was evolving.

How many days had passed by the time the tail that had once barely fit around Grandel's slender arm grew large enough to twine around his armor over and over?

How long had it been since the last time Grandel saw another human peek through a hatch in his armor?

How much time had gone by before the ebon creatures resembling a group of cavalry materialized to rout the black monsters the lamia was effortlessly defeating?

Day by day, the lamia was growing into an immense and powerful monster.

However, the ebon cavalry swallowed both the surrounding monsters and the inky memory thieves like a surging tide, and the battle repeated every night.

It was as though they didn't know what it was to perish, and they knew no retreat. The ebon cavalry was like the ravages of war born from foolish humans.

The shadow of war closed in.

When dawn broke and the water returned, the dark raiders curled up their bodies and stopped moving as though balking at being melted by the water, but when night arrived, they awoke without fail and overran the area.

Perhaps because they were getting practice, their movements sharpened every night. No matter how much stronger the lamia became, she couldn't bring down the ebon cavalry.

Exactly how long this had been happening was unclear by the eve when Mariela's group appeared before Grandel and the lamia.

04

Mariela thought the black shadows that appeared behind Yuric looked like a troop of horseback riders standing out against backlight.

Even when they were at a standstill, the way their shapes changed moment to moment made them seem more like a mass of multiple people than a uniform group. The humanoid upper bodies, straddling shadows with multiple legs reminiscent of horses, carried long weapons akin to spears.

Invaders...? It's like a war...

Mariela had already realized these shadowy monsters were the incarnation of a past calamity.

She'd seen famine and plague. This new entity was the ravages of an ancient war.

Before the dark raiders' weapons could strike Yuric, the lamia's water blades pummeled them repeatedly.

The liquid razors tore the cavalry's front row to pieces. However, the line behind it immediately replaced them, and the company's numbers didn't change. Their ranks had seemingly replenished when no one was looking. The shadowy figures readied their spears.

They probably decided the lamia was their enemy, as the cavalry unleashed spear attacks at her in perfect coordination.

"Shhaaa, sha!"

The lamia tried to mow down the attacks with her tail, but it had grown stiff due to the Icy Wind Potions and couldn't move properly, so the only thing she accomplished was being a shield against the spears.

"Mariela, get Grandel now!"

Yuric's shout brought Mariela back to her senses. She opened the door on the back of Grandel's heavy armor and called to him.

"Mr. Grandel, Mr. Grandel, hurry!"

"Oh, it's Miss Mariela. My apologies, but would you have a potion handy? I've been in this position for a long time and am unable to move."

Grandel's face appeared from within the metal container. His voice was extremely low, and his slender frame seemed even thinner now. He'd lived on preserved food and aquatic plants for a long while. That he was so weakened was only logical. Even so, Grandel understood well enough what was going on. He drained the potion he was given with a bleak expression, then smoothly slipped out of his armor with umbrella in hand.

"Let's go now."

Grandel began running toward the lamia.

Although he'd recovered with the potion, that didn't mean he regained his lost body weight. Grandel's legs were weak, and his breath was ragged after only a bit of movement.

He was so frail that he should have taken the opportunity to retreat while the lamia and the black monsters were fighting.

But Grandel had broken into a run.

The normal monsters born during the day attacked the black creatures that came at night, but that didn't mean they were allies. Mariela and Yuric knew that well from their miserable time being chased by the Necklace and the hairy caterpillars.

Grandel was a former member of the Labyrinth Suppression Forces and had faced many fearsome beings as part of the Black Iron Freight Corps. At the end of the day, monsters were monsters, and Grandel understood they couldn't coexist with humans.

However, even knowing all that, he'd started running.

Because in the days Grandel had spent with the lamia, he had a feeling the creature possessed some power of communication. The glances he'd exchanged with the massive thing made him sure of it.

Maybe it was only that their interests had coincidentally aligned. But the lamia hadn't tried to hurt Grandel. If she'd constricted him with that powerful tail, there was no doubt his heavy armor would have been crushed the moment his skill ran out.

That was enough to spur on Grandel. He was a gentleman and a "legendary hero."

"**Shield.**"

The ebon cavalry changed and rained countless spears down on Grandel as he rushed toward the lamia.

Using his opened umbrella in place of a shield, he warded off the polearms, but the cloth of the umbrella was torn to pieces from just that one attack, and the impact sent Grandel flying.

Toward the lamia.

Grandel's shield skills were powerful, but the man himself was light and frail. So even if he could defend against a strike, he couldn't reciprocate that energy.

Grandel controlled the angle at which he took the attack and even made use of the impact that sent him flying so he would come to rest in front of the lamia.

"That did the trick. **Earth Wall, Shield.**"

He could no longer use the umbrella. Grandel, clad in lightweight equipment like an ordinary citizen might wear to go harvesting, formed a wall with earth magic, then used his Shield skill to construct a simple barrier from the top.

Grandel's Shield skill completely blocked the attack from the dark raiders, which should have finished the lamia off. Unfortunately, Grandel wasn't a mage, so his conjured barricade was fragile. It collapsed after absorbing the impact of the many spears.

The lamia used the dust cloud from the collapsing wall of earth as a smoke screen to rain down blades of water on the charging soldiers.

Although the ebon cavalry was torn to pieces, they didn't seem agitated in the least, and they were already preparing their next assault.

Grandel's assistance had improved the situation for the moment, but how much longer could he endure the attacks from the shadowy army?

"Guess we got no choice. We'll help you, Grandel. Hey now, don't hiss at me, snake lady."

With a sidelong glance at the lamia giving a short, menacing sound, Donnino got in position next to Grandel. Mariela and Yuric also moved next to the snakelike monster as they threw fire bottles to keep the gathering inky blob creatures in check.

Grandel's Earth Wall and Shield skill blocked the dark raiders' attacks aimed at the lamia, and the lamia's water blades and Donnino's hammer counterattacked. Mariela and Yuric hurled fire bottles at the slime-like black monsters, which were steadily increasing in number, to keep them in check so they wouldn't surround the group.

The viscous memory stealers burned well.

The entire courtyard was already a sea of fire, and the shadowy riders emerging from it were like an advancing army.

“——————————!!”

A sound loud enough to rupture one’s eardrums reverberated through the courtyard.

It was the bellow of the ebon cavalry—a war cry and the howl of beasts.

The thunderous roar shook the air and caused Mariela to freeze. When she looked around, she saw that the amorphous, shadowy cavalry quivered as its members roused themselves and stood from within the flames.

“G-goblins…?”

Smirking black shadows carried weapons that were somewhere between swords and poles.

Mariela thought the figures, mad with the pleasure of pillaging, the excitement of murder, and the joy of devastation, were like an attacking swarm of goblins.

“No. Those things, those kinda things, could surely only be humans,” Yuric disagreed.

The flames from the likes of fire bottles burned up their fuel and could only last a short time. The army trampled over and extinguished the weakened blaze as they surrounded Mariela and Yuric, and there was no way Yuric could deal with the likes of them alone.

Grandel, who was defending against the black raiders’ attacks, was probably close to his magical power and stamina’s limits. The wounds Donnino and the lamia suffered were steadily getting worse, and the circle of monsters surrounding Mariela and Yuric was gradually tightening.

I can at least heal them…

Mariela turned around to use restorative potions on Donnino and the lamia. There she saw the dark raiders, which still should have been farther away, closing in like a tsunami.

Grin.

Mariela thought the ebon things, which seemed to lack eyes and noses, were contorting their faces with glee.

Black spears rained down. The many polearms easily crushed Grandel's Earth Wall. Just as their blades were about to pierce Donnino, Grandel, and the lamia, however…

"Eek ook!"

Something descended from the sky.

"Eek ook, eek, eek ook, *ook*!"

"Whaaaaaa—?!"

"…He's finally gone back to the wild?"

The one who came from the sky, or to be precise, from the northeast tower via the outer wall, was a monkey. Wait, no, it was Edgan, who should have been human.

"Why is he saying 'eek, eek'?"

"He probably lost too much of his memory and went back to bein' a monkey!"

What in the world? Did people revert to monkeys when they lost too much of themselves?

Or was that only the case for Edgan?

Edgan still had to count as a member of the human race, technically. He was a bit dirty, but it was unmistakably him. The fact

that he was drooling slightly was not because he'd become a beast, but because his eyes were locked on the lamia's chest.

Even if he had turned into a monkey, he held his dual swords properly in his hands and slashed at the dark raiders with flames surrounding his left arm and wind on his right—his Dual Sword Elements skill.

"Edgan, to think you would have learned how to shorten your skill chants! That's our captain!" Grandel exclaimed, offering a compliment that would have pleased Edgan had he been lucid.

"No, that ain't what's surprisin'," Donnino replied calmly.

"Hrm. It is important to be aware that chanting is not language, but a recitation...," Grandel murmured thoughtfully.

"That may be true, but that's not what I'm talkin' about, either! **Meg-ham!**"

As he quipped, Donnino spoke an abbreviated Mega Hammer that was either intoned in a strange accent or a simple mispronunciation. Regardless, the skill was executed beautifully. As one might've expected from the guy in charge of maintaining the armored carriages in the Black Iron Freight Corps, Donnino seemed quite dexterous, but it was embarrassing for the people nearby to hear this chanting. Perhaps the man himself also thought it was unacceptable, as he corrected himself back to saying the usual "Mega Hammer" from the second attack onward.

"Hum. I can't let myself be outdone! **Wall Shield.**"

Grandel, being who he was, chanted the earth magic *Earth Wall* and the shield skill Shield in combination to form a magnificent barrier of dirt and stone. After having come this far, you might say it was a new composite skill. That was a "legendary hero" for you. His potential was staggering.

Although he didn't speak in a human tongue, the A-Ranker's

appearance seemed to be heartening to everyone. The sight of Edgan springing around with inhuman jumping power and routing the dark raiders seemed to give everyone their strength back.

Mariela said, "I'm sorry for attacking you before," and sprinkled a potion on the lamia to heal her wounds. She didn't know whether the creature forgave her and Yuric for their earlier friendly fire, but the lamia kept attacking the ebon cavalry while Grandel deftly protected her from any incoming attacks. Donnino and Yuric mowed down the approaching infantry, and Mariela threw fire bottles.

The tables had turned.

"Ook!"

There was even leeway for Edgan to blow a kiss at the lamia in his spare moments and for the lamia to hiss a genuine threat to him in return as she wriggled her six arms.

"Eek ook!"

He certainly was *ook*-cited. He was having a ball.

"Not that! The enemy, the black monsters are closin' in!!!"

Could Yuric, as an animal tamer, somehow understand Edgan's monkey speech?

When everyone looked at the area around the collapsed outer wall to the north where Yuric pointed, they saw creatures darker than night surging into the courtyard where Mariela and the others were.

Had Edgan come running to help the two girls, Mariela and Yuric, as well as his comrades in the Black Iron Freight Corps, or had he simply wanted to get acquainted with the feminine lamia? Either way, it doesn't do well to dwell on the likes of Erotigan's easy to understand behavioral principles, but there was no doubt that everyone owed the man their lives. However, he'd been protecting the north side, and due to his absence, the inky memory

stealers were heading for this courtyard. They looked to be moving for the temple in the center. The things surged like water that had just broken through a dam.

"This's bad."

"Let us withdraw for now!"

"Ook."

Edgan's animal cry was the only *ook*-citing thing, and even he wore a serious expression like everyone else.

They all turned on their heels and began running toward the entrance on the south side of the outer wall.

But could any of them escape from the horde that gave chase?

Although the door was only a short jog away, the distance between it and Mariela's group felt infinite, and even the damp air of the courtyard seemed to be hindering them. Would Mariela and her friends be consumed like debris against a crashing wave? Perhaps their memories and existences were doomed to be scattered and lost.

Mariela was about to be overwhelmed by the looming despair when…

"Groooooooar!"

A wyvern? A dragon? A roar reverberated from the northwest.

A tornado whirled from the direction of the cry, swallowing the sea of darkness behind Mariela and carrying it far away into the sky.

A thunderous breeze blew.

The gale caused by the whirlwind whistled past Mariela and the others. It was powerful and rapidly grew stronger. It even made breathing difficult, as though one had been submerged. Invited by the presence of water, the humidity gathered like a dense fog, and a light shone in through the darkness above.

"It's morning, the water's comin'!" Donnino shouted and immediately threw the fire bottle at his waist with all he had before hoisting Grandel onto his shoulder and breaking into a sprint toward the entrance. "Let's hurry back!"

"Rar!"

The one who responded to Donnino's shout wasn't Yuric, who was completely mesmerized as she stared at the tornado, but the raptor Koo, who carried her and Mariela. He took care not to let them fall as he scattered trampled black monsters and dashed toward the entrance.

"Eek ook, eek, eek ook, ook, *ook*!"

Ape-gan...no, Edgan, who had been holding back the dark raiders, drove his Dual Sword Elements into them as though to finish them off. Then, for some reason, he ran up the wall and returned to the northeast tower, the opposite direction from Mariela and the others.

Night shifting into morning and the world filling with water took a very short amount of time.

The whole group rushed toward the outer wall entrance to escape from the rising sea.

Grandel, who had exhausted his stamina, lifted his head and looked in the lamia's direction, despite being carried by Donnino. As though she noticed his gaze, the lamia stopped attacking the black raiders for just an instant and turned to watch Grandel depart.

Grandel saw the lamia gazing at him from beyond the white fog that was growing ever denser.

And, in the instant the lamia's caution lessened, the ebon cavalry, which had decided the defenseless Grandel and the rest were their prey, began to charge.

"This won't do! They're coming!"

"Gh, we don't have time to fight! We gotta run at full speed!!!"

Despite losing many of their ranks to fire bottles and Edgan's attacks, the dark raiders charged the group with bizarre speed. How could anyone possibly stop things that felt neither pain nor fear?

"**Wall, Wall!** It's no good!"

Grandel's Earth Wall had been able to keep the shadowy warriors in check precisely because he'd combined it with Shield. And his Shield skill was worthless when its target was far away from him.

The likes of a fragile heap of stone and dirt could only serve as a blinder, and the dark raiders were rapidly closing the distance as they approached.

"I'm no good at swimmin'."

"I am the same."

"Mr. Donnino?! Mr. Grandel?!"

In order to keep the ebon cavalry in check and let Mariela and Yuric escape, Donnino stopped and assumed a stance with his hammer. Grandel, whom he'd been carrying, landed on the ground and used his remaining magical power to erect an Earth Wall and reinforce it with his Shield skill to stop the raiders' charge.

The black raiders' attack should have instantly reached them.

"What...?"

"Hey, Grandel, that's..."

At the unexpected halt of the pursuit, Grandel peeked past the Earth Wall.

"Oh...ohhh, the lamia..."

The lamia, which he had spent the last few days with and had been fighting with until just a short time ago, twined around and constricted the shadowy soldiers to stop their charge.

However, the dark raiders refused to relent, even with a lamia crushing them.

They penetrated the lamia's body, and black spears pierced through from the inner side.

"Sha, shhaaa!"

Although blood spilled from her and she became more and more like a pincushion, the lamia's grip didn't weaken.

"What are you doing, lamia? Stop this at once."

Even if the massive monster didn't understand Grandel's words, perhaps she understood his feelings.

The lamia lifted her head to look at Grandel, then bent her upper body back and forth and tightly hugged herself with her six arms, as though to restrain her own body.

"Ssshhhhaaaaaaaaa!!!" she screamed to the heavens. Grandel thought that voice sounded more like the agonizing death of a maiden than an intimidating snake.

"Lamia!"

Advanced snake monsters sometimes had the power of petrification.

Some species cursed humans to turn them to stone and then decorated or ate them.

But had there ever been a serpent that turned itself to stone to help humans?

"Let's move, Grandel. The water's comin'. There's no time."

Donnino hoisted the dumbfounded Grandel once again and rushed for the exterior wall entrance.

The courtyard filled with water, and the black creatures began to vanish like they were melting.

Soon, monsters would be born anew in the gentle light.

It was morning, a sight Grandel had seen many times with the lamia.

The dawning sun hadn't yet reached the courtyard surrounded by the outer wall, but the light brightening the sky reflected off the dense fog, and for a moment, this confined world sparkled white, as though the night's corruption had been purified.

The fog changed into water, which quietly began to fill the world and engulf everything.

Within that silent ocean, the lamia, now stone and still wrapped around the ebon cavalry, stood in silence.

06

"No time to wallow in sentimentality. We gotta retreat before the Necklace wakes up!"

At Donnino's command, Mariela and the rest left the entrance and rushed into the hallway. Grandel and Yuric remained quiet. Their thoughts were elsewhere for a little while.

The group somehow made it back to the first level of the southeast tower and took a deep breath in the brief moment of safety.

"Thank goodness. We saved Mr. Grandel..."

Mariela was happy at the man's safe return, but Grandel looked unwell. While the potion he'd imbibed earlier had helped,

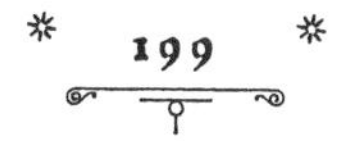

his weakened body wasn't back to normal, and he seemed unable to completely absorb the fact that the lamia, a monster, had sacrificed herself to save him.

They'd confirmed Edgan was uninjured, but he seemed to have lost almost all his memories. Even so, Edgan was still Edgan, and he somehow looked like he was having fun, so his situation didn't seem serious. But the fact that he'd forgotten human language and turned into a monkey wasn't a predicament that could be overlooked. What's more…

"That tornado… That was Franz," Yuric muttered as she stared northwest.

The roar that seemed to summon the tornado wasn't that of a person.

What in the world had happened to Franz?

Even Edgan, an A-Ranker with high attack power, had lost himself and become apelike. Franz may have forgotten even more than Edgan, so what remained of him?

"We can't leave those two the way they are."

They had to get the pair's memories back, even if it was just a few.

"Right. Shall we split into two groups here? The young lady and Yuric, and Grandel and I. We'll go help those guys," Donnino proposed.

But Mariela knew. She'd realized by now the conditions for regaining memories lost here.

The pair couldn't regain recollections at the same time.

Edgan, or Franz? While they were helping one, what would befall the other?

"I'm headin' out to help Franz by myself… Sorry, Mariela." Yuric's words were neither a proposal nor a request, but a decision.

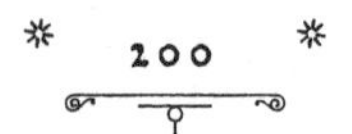

She'd probably long since prepared herself. Even though they were in the middle of a job, Yuric decided to help Franz.

"We'll go together, Yuric. Maybe I'll get in the way, but surely I can also help." Mariela grasped the other girl's hand.

"Thanks, Mariela. But this is our problem. I can't put ya in danger for my own convenience in the middle of a job."

As a Black Iron Freight Corps member, Yuric turned Mariela down, saying she couldn't drag a client into peril.

"What're you talking about?! I can't just ignore this. We're friends, aren't we?!"

If it was a question of danger, Mariela had already been exposed to plenty of that. More often than not, it was Mariela who led others into risky situations. In response, Yuric looked at her blankly.

"......Friends?"

"......Huh? Am I wrong?"

Could it have been just Mariela who thought they were that close?

As the tense atmosphere softened into a more complex feeling, Mariela's thoughts revolved at high speed.

Mariela knew hardly anything about Yuric and Franz. She'd spent a short time with them since she'd first met the Black Iron Freight Corps in the Labyrinth City, and she'd gotten a peek at their memories in this world. That was all.

In particular, Franz's memories had been of his daily life with Yuric in the imperial capital, and Mariela couldn't even guess how that whirlwind from before was connected to him. All Mariela could imagine was what Yuric thought of Franz in that state.

But Mariela felt that knowing someone well might not be necessary.

The time she'd spent with Yuric wandering around in this

world of water hadn't been so bad. If it weren't for the danger, she probably would have even thought it was fun. Even if she didn't know her companion well, and they didn't have anything in common, being together was kind of enjoyable. While living in the Labyrinth City, Mariela had come to know the concept of getting along with such companions.

"If you have one meal with someone, you're already friends."

Mariela's master had once said something like that, but was that actually a rule she'd come up with herself?

Mariela somehow grew a bit embarrassed in the ensuing silence and stole a glance at Yuric. Yuric, too, seemed bashful as she answered in a low voice, "You're not wrong."

"I'm so glad..."

Since there had been a strange pause, Mariela thought she'd made a slightly embarrassing mistake.

"...I'm not."

Yuric pouted very slightly, and when Mariela looked where she was glancing, she saw Donnino and Grandel, the two middle-aged men, watching the friendship drama between the two girls with uncomfortably warm smiles.

It was just a bit before sundown when Mariela and Yuric, who had relied on those two middle-aged men and Ape-gan—no, Edgan—reached the third-floor entry to the southwest tower through the third-level hallway.

Mariela had wanted to sleep a little on the way and learn something about the ebon cavalry through a memory, but healing Grandel with potions and replenishing fire bottles took longer than she'd expected.

"Mariela, we're goin' to run at full speed. Hold on tight."

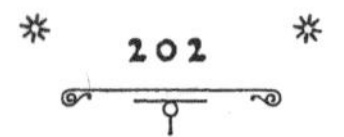

"Okay, got it!"

When night came, Mariela and Yuric traveled on Koo up to the southwest tower's fourth floor and headed for the northwest tower via the outer wall.

Up to this point, the northwest tower's vicinity had been brimming with those inky memory stealers. However, there were surprisingly few now, and Mariela and Yuric were able to approach the tower without effort.

Mariela had an uncomfortable hunch. Although they progressed smoothly, uneasiness gnawed at her heart.

How many times had they seen this landscape?

The light of the torches filtering from the tower dimly defined the outline of the outer wall in the night.

What crawled along that dim, outer barricade as though they were about to swallow even the light itself were monsters blacker than night. The things seemed to be closing in like a tide that filled the other side of the outer wall.

Every now and then, a plume of flame erupted on the largely collapsed east side of the outer wall. Maybe Edgan, or Donnino and Grandel, who had hastened there, were using fire bottles.

As though in concord with that, what lay just a little before the northwest tower Mariela and Yuric were heading for was...

"Franz!!!" Yuric exclaimed.

Did the silhouette that emerged from the darkness truly look like Franz to her?

The fists flying out from the figure in a doubled-over posture moved so fast, Mariela couldn't perceive them. The barehanded attacks tore the black monsters to pieces. The leaps that propelled the person were far quicker than those of any adventurer Mariela knew.

Since he was so far away, it was all Mariela could do not to lose sight of him. The man's agile, rugged, powerful movements seemed more appropriate for a beast. To Mariela, they appeared beyond what any human should have been capable of.

Perhaps Franz had heard Yuric's voice, as his head turned in their direction. She couldn't confirm the face from far away, but she had a feeling she was gazing at something unfamiliar.

From behind him, inky creatures rushed at Franz like a tsunami to crush him.

"Franz, watch out!!!" Yuric screamed as loud as she could. There came a whirlwind that swept away the monsters and an inhuman roar that drowned out Yuric's voice.

"*Roooooar*, graaaaaah!"

"Franz! Franz!"

"Yuric! It's too dangerous!"

Mariela desperately stopped Yuric, who looked like she was about to leap down from the raptor and break into a run.

"Let go, Mariela! Franz is...!!!"

Mariela clung to Yuric to try and stop her. The raptor's rider was no longer leading him, and as soon as he slowed down in apparent bewilderment, a great number of tornadoes centered on Franz swept both the raptor and the girls into the air.

"Aaah!"

Below, Mariela could spy what lay beyond the outer wall. A dark path split the forest, stretching out like an endless plain, and it led to the temple.

There was an obsidian torrent of catastrophe surging toward the temple through gaps in the broken outer wall.

It lumbered toward the helpless Mariela and Yuric like a living creature, and at the moment when it seemed the sinister turbid waters would engulf them, Mariela realized she was frightened.

It wasn't the terror of preparing to die when facing monsters, but rather a fear of clammy entwinement, of her life being gnawed at from the inside, of being forced into an existence worse than death.

Mariela felt the jet-blackness streaming in her direction like a wild river was a human heart distorted with anger, pain, sorrow, anguish, tyranny, hate, lunacy, and desire.

The twisted ebon current undulated.

The mass of black monsters gradually rose to swallow Mariela and Yuric all at once.

Hungry to savor another's misfortune, black arms stretched toward the two to taste and deplete their joy and sorrow and all the memories they held in their hearts, the memories that made them who they were.

"I'm scared, I'm scared, I'm scared. Help me, help me… Sieg!!!"

In that instant, the sky and the earth shook as though the world were transforming.

Dazzling light abruptly spelled the end of the night that seemed to have just begun.

Pure water flooded the world, and the rapids washed away the black monsters. Mariela and Yuric felt like something was holding onto them as everything else shook violently.

Amid the dizzying metamorphosis was Yuric mumbling "Franz…" and a seventh tower appearing in the broken northern outer wall as if to plug it up.

…You're late.

Although Mariela felt a touch of bitterness, she was relieved. She yielded her consciousness to someone's memory streaming into her.

The village elder had said this place was once a verdant land.

A man, the last one born in this dry land, didn't know how far back in the distant past that was.

An endless horizon interweaving blue sky and scorched earth.

That seemed to be the state of the world the man knew.

When was the last time it had rained?

The man sowed seeds in the parched earth again today.

He made scratches in the dirt and dripped his own blood there.

"Surfeit Heal."

Through healing magic that caused cells to excessively propagate, the blood spilled on the ground multiplied, decomposed, and changed into soil that brought a little blessing to the plants.

The sown seeds grew literally from the man's blood and bore the tiniest bit of fruit.

"This place, too, will soon be swallowed by the desert..."

All land in the surrounding area was slowly becoming a red desert.

Before long, the ground here would turn to sand.

The fruits on the crops were thin, and no matter how much one planted, the plants wouldn't so much as sprout unless you put magical power into them.

It was now only a matter of time before the tribe of men returned to the parched earth.

"How long will we cling to this land? This place has been abandoned, and we have been forsaken."

The elders only shook their heads feebly at the man's words.

"If that's the case, we have committed some kind of wrongdoing, and this is our punishment. Our flesh sprouted in this land, and our lives sprang forth from the earth. Our lot is to die in obscurity here. Everything is as the water spirit who governs this ley line wills it."

The tribe of men descended from water dragons had their blood to thank for their long lives and their tenacity.

They enriched the barren land that ordinary creatures couldn't live on and survived off meager nourishment using blood and magical power.

The red desert was their gravestone.

They slowly starved, died, dried up, and returned to the sands.

This was the final land of the tribe bound by the chains of their faith.

It was said that the man's clan used to worship the water spirit governing this ley line and received its divine protection in return.

The youngest man in the tribe hadn't been told about when the water spirit disappeared.

No one in the clan knew why or where the spirit who had governed the land and the people disappeared.

The tribe clung to this barren earth, believing the spirit would return someday, and now they merely awaited their end.

The frail women had already died out, and the man who was last to be born had no one to live with besides the decaying old men.

"The red desert is proof of our tribe's blood. Our desire is to return to the earth here. But, young man, you should depart from this place. The water spirit will surely forgive you, the one born last."

After bidding farewell to the final elder who returned to the earth, the man left the red desert behind.

He walked and walked, yet the unchanging view continued.

The cloudless bright blue sky was probably far more azure and clear than the sea he'd heard about in tales.

The man recalled the fairy tale about how the unobstructed blue sky was a cruel sun god's garments.

The deity had grown angry and burned the land to nothing because it stained the hem of his beautiful blue attire.

In this world, the moon goddess, who ruled over death, was far gentler than the sun.

With enough of a chill to freeze you, she granted you eternal sleep, release from the hardship known as life.

Just when the man began to believe that the divine protection of the water spirit was truly gone forever, and that this parched land and cruel sky were all there was, he saw a change in the distant horizon.

Mountains.

In the far-off mountain range, sand, not water, flowed like a river from between the peaks and into the desert. However, the man's energy returned at the sight of the clouds drifting in the sky above them.

There were clouds. In other words, rain fell in those mountains.

The man no longer recalled how long he'd been traveling. Regardless, he moved forward, crossing arid, rocky mountains and pushing through a dry lake of salt as it rustled at his feet. The pool of salt was white and bone-dry. No vegetation grew around it, but water soon gushed forth when he dug into it. The water was briny at that point and couldn't be drunk, but it evaporated in the heat of the day and changed into cool, fresh water at night.

It was indeed a miracle that the man who followed the shadows the clouds cast and ate sparsely growing herbs and beasts running among the rocks as he roamed found his way to a river. He followed the winding thing, clouded with fine sand, upstream, and he grasped the truth of his birthplace when he finally reached its source.

The one who dwelled in the headwaters was the water spirit his tribe had longed after.

The moment they met, the man knew the spirit was the focus of the faith engraved in his own blood.

"O water spirit, pure, loving master and origin of life, why did you abandon us? Please, heal our land with your mighty power once more."

After finally finding the life giver, it was all he could do to ask it to restore the land.

—Descendant of water, our youngest child. You have done well to reach this place after all your suffering. However, I am not the water spirit you and your people know.—

This creature told the man that it had no connection to him and that the one who had protected his birthplace disappeared a very long time ago.

—We are born, and we disappear. Our transitions are not fixed. I was born in this source and am merely one spirit who exists for a brief time. A change occurred in the ley line in your land once, did it not? When one considers the timeline of the world, it is not an unusual occurrence. When the flow of a ley line changes, spirits lose their power. Even water will fade away.—

"Then where did our water spirit go? How will it restore our land?"

—The spirit of that land no longer exists in the world. Even people are born and eventually die, do they not? This is no different. Human child descended from water, the water in this place, too, will soon fade. Go, seek water. Even if there is no spirit, the kindness of water will never run dry.—

There was a drought in the land that had led to the slow death of the man's tribe.

And not due to any wrongdoing they had committed. It wasn't a punishment or anything of the sort.

The ley-line change was simply a natural disaster, no different from an earthquake or a storm, that caused the land to wither.

"If so, why were my people such prisoners in that land? We were abandoned and forgotten, yet what is this feeling that consumes my heart…?"

The man's journey wasn't over.

This was a distant memory engraved in blood…

08

"It seems the blood of dragons flows within me," Franz told Mariela and Yuric after he awoke.

The memory of a man who sought the water spirit. Franz explained it was his ancestor's memory, engraved into his blood.

Franz's face was hidden by the hood worn low over his eyes and couldn't be clearly seen, but the little bit that was visible was covered in blue scales down to the bottom of his neck. The tips of his boots had torn, and sharp talons extended from them. Sharp claws on fingers covered in scales had cut through his armored gloves.

Most likely, Franz had lost too many of his own recollections, and his dragon blood had run rampant.

"Strangely, my memories of my time with Yuric in the imperial capital remained. So I think I never completely lost my self."

Franz's recollections that remained were the ones he recovered when Yuric and Mariela saw him a few days ago. Apparently, once you regained a memory, you wouldn't lose it again. If they hadn't visited the northwest tower back then, Franz might have wholly transformed into a dragon.

Perhaps due to the effects of his metamorphosis, Franz was able to spend a long time underwater, and apparently, he had brought Mariela and the others, who were caught up in the tornado, to the northwest tower. The salamander, who had been clinging to Mariela's shoulder, may have crawled into her cloak, since it looked unharmed as it clambered up the raptor Koo.

"Franz, are ya all right?"

The worried Yuric nestled up to Franz without showing the slightest fear of his scaly face or sharp claws. Mariela felt this wasn't her usual boyish appearance, but that of a mature girl.

"Sorry I made you worry, Yuric. I'm a little confused, maybe due to remembering past events all at once, but I'm all right now."

Mariela and Yuric had brought Franz's memory stones, and Franz himself seemed to have collected some, too. He probably hadn't regained all he had lost, but he seemed to be far more like himself than he had been before.

"Will your appearance...never go back to the way it was...?" Mariela asked timidly.

Yuric didn't seem to mind at all, but the limbs that had exceeded human size and the face that most likely had a different silhouette now would probably make it difficult for him to live in the imperial capital or the Labyrinth City.

"I think it's a temporary thing. My demi-dragon ancestor didn't look like this. However, this isn't without benefit. It's granted me some offensive abilities. It would probably be better to stay like this for the time being."

Franz seemed to think he could return to normal, and Mariela recalled the dream she'd had not long ago.

The recollections of Franz that Mariela had gotten a glimpse of weren't just those of his ancestor.

It was probably a case of genetic throwback. None of Franz's forebears had scales. At least, there'd been no mention of it in his family's oral history.

Franz's father loved his son's aptitude for healing magic, but his mother shunned him as a "lizard boy." The memories Mariela witnessed had included a heartbreaking one of a young boy who begged for his mother's love by whittling down his own face with an edged tool and regenerating it with magic.

Surfeit Heal wasn't merely healing magic. This unique spell was innate to the blood of demi-dragons, and it reflected the will of the practitioner when it restored the subject. Of course, since that wasn't his natural form, the skin the young Franz generated by carving up his own face grew back all its scales within a few weeks due to his body's tenacious recovery abilities.

I wonder if Yuric saw Franz's memories...

It was probably natural for a man who grew up being despised as a “lizard” to be comfortable living with a girl who loved beasts more than people.

Mariela couldn’t guess from the way Yuric nestled close to Franz whether she had seen Franz’s past.

Maybe Franz’s history doesn’t matter to Yuric.

If it was necessary, the pair would discuss it, because they lived together. Even Mariela had had that sort of experience.

“Even so…”

Franz had saved them after regaining a bit of his sanity, but what had sparked that? And why had dawn arrived so suddenly?

Mariela turned her gaze away from the endlessly flirting Yuric and Franz and walked toward a window.

Maybe…

She had a guess. That said, just how many days had it been?

It was quite likely the flow of time differed between here and the real world, but that sort of thing was irrelevant. If feelings could be resolved with logic, surely the world would be forever peaceful and boring.

“There it is, a seventh.”

The passage connecting east and west on the north side had largely collapsed along with the wall and cut off the route. When night came, the black monsters would close in like an avalanche from there, but a new tower stood in the middle of the collapsed outer wall.

After glancing at Franz and Yuric in their own little world, Mariela faced the seventh tower and thought to herself, *Maybe I’ll listen to his explanation now…*

What had happened to Mariela’s extreme stupidity back when she had rushed out of Sunlight’s Canopy? Was the unsociable Yuric’s lovey-dovey behavior affecting her?

CHAPTER 5

The Tale of the Fire Spirit

Siegmund was an unlucky person.

His looks and intellect weren't bad, and his combat abilities were A Rank. Whether or not his personality was agreeable depended on the person. Still, he endeavored not to be haughty, lazy, or negligent. To be a man honest enough not to make Mariela feel uncomfortable, faithful enough not to make her feel insecure, and attractive enough that she wouldn't look away from him.

At least the man himself believed that, and superficially, he conducted himself as planned.

So people in the Labyrinth City who were somewhat acquainted with him considered Sieg to be the ideal young man.

As far as Mariela went, she saw through his diligent attempts to keep up appearances and appeal to her, but she viewed both his facade and his true side favorably. In other words, the people around Siegmund, Mariela included, recognized him as quite the high-spec man.

If one had to name the most unfortunate thing about Sieg, it would be his bad luck rather than his tendency to deviate somewhat from the sphere of common sense when it came to Mariela.

Even if he had angered Mariela, there was plenty of room for an explanation. He'd simply had no chance to defend himself due to a series of regrettable incidents coming one after another.

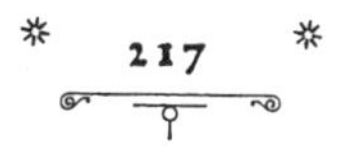

If he properly clarified and apologized from the bottom of his heart, surely Mariela would forgive him.

Thinking as much, Sieg had gone after her, venturing deep into the Fell Forest, but…

"This place is…a tower?!"

He could've sworn he'd been in a marshland in the Fell Forest. The instant he'd laid his hands on a door within a shrine there, he had a sensation like an earthquake. Sieg had felt as though he would lose consciousness from extreme vertigo, so he'd reflexively shut his eyes, and upon opening them, he was in a tower.

Damp air blew in through the tower's many windows, and outside was pitch-dark, without a single visible star, but he could faintly feel Mariela's magical power from far below him.

"!!! Mariela! I'm coming!"

Sieg practically flew down the stairs that led to a spiral staircase running along the round tower's inner wall.

"Two doors… Which one?!"

Sieg reached the fourth floor—though he didn't know what level it was—at an astonishing speed, and he'd lost track of the direction Mariela was in due to going around and around on the coiled steps.

"Her magical power is… It's no use. It's too scattered…"

A storm blew violently outside, perhaps created by magical power. It drowned out Mariela's energy, as she wasn't using it. Hoping to locate her visually instead, Sieg invoked his Spirit Eye while scanning the outside through a suitable window. Before long, he spotted a place resembling a spacious courtyard and a building resembling a temple towering in the center.

"?! Gh!"

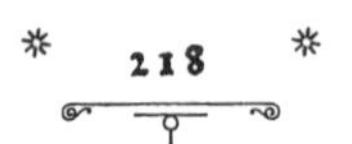

As soon as Sieg's Spirit Eye perceived the temple in the center, his magical power was absorbed in the direction of the temple via his Spirit Eye, like it was being dragged out of him.

At the same time, the dark water was rapidly filling the world, centered on the temple.

"Water?! Damn it, I'm trapped!"

The image of rising water reflected in his Spirit Eye made Sieg feel he needed to get out of there right away. At present, he stood in the chamber of a tower with two doors opposite each other. There was also a staircase leading down, but since Mariela wasn't in this tower, descending didn't seem very valuable to Sieg.

Right or left? Mariela had to be on the other side of one of the doors.

The wind blowing in through the windows seemed to signal that the water was rising more and more. Sieg didn't have a moment to lose.

"Mariela! Guide me!!!"

His mind made up, Sieg rushed for one of the doors and flew out into a passage on the outer wall.

The outside was filled with damp air too dense to be called mist, enough so that even breathing was difficult. Moreover, the barricade connecting the tower Sieg had been in with the neighboring one had collapsed, and there was a considerable distance between them. Even if Sieg tried to leap the gap, jumping from the fourth floor he was on now to the exposed third floor hallway would be the best he could manage. In other words, after he jumped once, he didn't know if he would be able to return to this tower.

Sieg's path was clear.

He'd already decided on this door with the conviction that it would lead him to Mariela.

And there was no longer any time to waver on that point.

"Ahh, the hell with it!"

Sieg leaped over to the hallway connecting to the neighboring tower and ran through it. He understood from the weight of the air coiling around his body that the water was approaching the area around him.

As far as Sieg was concerned, the fact that the door to the tower he finally reached was broken might have been his only bit of luck. When he got there, the vicinity was filled with water, and if the door hadn't been broken, he probably wouldn't have been able to open it due to the water pressure.

Sieg somehow managed to slip into the tower, and he swam to the floor above, seeking air.

"Pfaw, the room is flooded, but the top of the tower isn't...?"

If the chamber above wasn't underwater, surely Mariela was at the top of this tower.

Siegmund thought this way, trusted his luck in this way, and he ran up the spiral staircase without catching his breath.

Mariela had to be there.

What should he say in apology? How should he explain?

No, since this was Mariela, maybe she would warmly embrace him simply because he'd followed her this far.

No doubt about it.

Surely, Sieg would be able to see her smiling face.

Mariela, Mariela, Mariela...

Siegmund was an unlucky person.

At least to the point where it got a laugh from those around him.

"Eek ook!"

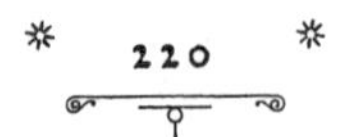

After running up the tower, what Sieg found wasn't Mariela, but Edgan making monkey noises. Sieg's expression was so comical it made Grandel and Donnino, who happened to be there, too, think, *I'm glad we accepted this job.*

"Ook?"

"...Mariela."

"Eek ook, eek, eek ook!"

"...Mariela."

Did Sieg belong to the society of peculiar animals like Edgan?

Although Sieg hadn't lost a single memory, was the shock so nasty that he'd been robbed of his sanity?

Mariela had no such miraculous power that could answer Siegmund's plea of "Mariela, guide me," and above all, she'd run away from home in anger and had no reason to help him. If the regulars from Sunlight's Canopy were here, there was no doubt they'd be eating this up with their eyes as they treated themselves to tea and cakes.

"Don't be so discouraged. Comin' this direction, well, I can only say it was bad luck, but you can go outside when the night arrives. You'll be able to meet up with the young lady before long."

"Indeed. There is no woman in the world who wouldn't be delighted you came all this way to get her."

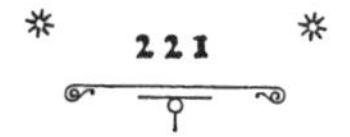

"Ook!"

Grandel and Donnino consoled Sieg, who couldn't hide his dismay.

The male-only room gave a shabby impression, but its occupants were quite gentlemanly. Well, the last one was really just a nuisance.

"So Mariela is safe, huh…?"

At last, Sieg raised his head and asked a question in a weak voice. While Grandel and Donnino were surprised he wasn't using Mariela-ese, they replied, "She's safe. She's doing great," and began to explain the situation.

"In other words, we can only go outside during the night, and that window of opportunity is short?"

"Exactly. The plan is to meet Yuric and the others in the southeast tower."

"Ook."

"What about information on the enemy? Anything other than having black, sticky bodies?"

"There are also normal monsters, which generate and grow in the daytime. They seem to be hostile toward the ebon ones, and they prioritize them when attacking."

"Eek ook."

"Then the problem is simply the sheer number of those inky things…?"

"Well, there're several black monsters that look like bigwigs. We dealt with the main enemies, but there's this one really nasty group in the courtyard. Right now, a petrified lamia is keepin' 'em in check, but we don't know how many nights that'll last. Well, now that you're here, Sieg, we can probably handle anything that comes our way."

"Eek *ook!*"

Sieg, Donnino, and Grandel exchanged information while Edgan interjected in monkey language on every little thing. Perhaps he was trying to converse, but he kept getting up into Sieg's face and peering into his eyes, which got very annoying.

"...So Edgan lost his memories, huh?"

"..."

"..."

"Eek, eek!"

The fact that a person lost their past when a black monster latched onto them had already been made clear to Sieg, but no one had an answer regarding Edgan's present condition except Edgan himself.

Edgan had been following Sieg around for a little while now. Sieg didn't know whether Edgan remembered they had been friends, or whether he'd come to ridicule Sieg with all his might for Sieg's expression of despair when he saw Edgan and realized he'd magnificently made the wrong choice.

Ape-gan...no, Edgan...had once taken all comers in matters of the heart and chased women relentlessly, but ever since the Labyrinth's subjugation, his sole speck of sense was not to get involved with married women or women who already had lovers. Yet, even if it was by her request, Edgan had led Mariela away from Sieg. He deserved death.

Well, Sieg was the only one who believed that, but if Edgan was really Sieg's friend, he should have dissuaded Mariela from running off, or called Sieg, or something similar.

No matter how much Sieg was to blame, it was just a few hours between when they had the fight and when Mariela ran away from home. Sieg hadn't been given a chance to defend himself, nor had he even been contacted, and he seriously thought about reexamining his friendship with Edgan.

Although, no matter what Edgan said now, no one would understand.

Even now, Edgan was trying to open the large pack Sieg had brought with him, and Sieg was firing arrows at him. Of course, he wasn't firing them in earnest, so Edgan agilely dodged them with *eeks* and *ooks*. He appeared to be teasing poor Siegmund.

Sieg glanced at the *eek-eeking* Edgan, who was clearly enjoying himself, and let out a sigh.

"Well, if we can make it to the spirit temple in the center, Edgan will probably turn out fine, too."

Donnino and Grandel reacted to Sieg's nonchalant comment.

"Spirit temple?"

"Are you saying this is a spirit realm?"

"Eek, eek ook?"

"Uh, yeah. It's most likely a water spirit. The instant I looked at the temple with my Spirit Eye, a considerable amount of my magical power was taken, so I think it's quite a high-ranking spirit."

"Eek ook!"

Sieg had revealed some critical information, and Edgan ruined the seriousness with his *ook-ooking.*

Was he *ook-ooking*, or was he *ook*-cited? Or could it be both? Either way, the monkey's friend was steadily getting sick of it.

Grandel and Donnino discussed things like "When the place is full of water, do the black monsters not appear because of the spirit's divine protection or something similar?" as though they understood and accepted what Sieg told them.

The fact that the night ended yesterday as soon as Sieg arrived in this world may have been because Sieg's magical power was summoned from his Spirit Eye and forcibly purified the corruption. Although, they didn't know whether the water spirit intended to help Mariela and the other humans or whether it had its own agenda.

Sieg waited impatiently for night to arrive as he gazed at Edgan, who had wandered into Sieg's field of vision as he talked to the two middle-aged men, with a faraway look.

At that same moment, Mariela was...

"Mr. Franz, could you swim like a fish the way you are right now?"

"No. I can stay underwater for a long time and move quite freely through it, but I don't have gills."

"Mariela, what do ya intend to make Franz do?"

Mariela and the others of her group entertained such topics as they absentmindedly gazed at the ocean outside and waited for nighttime.

Perhaps because the group had burned and purified the calamities of famine and disease, normal monsters seemed to be gaining strength in the world of water. The fish monsters were clearly much larger than those swimming around when the group had first arrived in this structure. Mariela thought she saw a whale creature calmly floating by above them, though she only knew of whales from stories.

"That's a whale monster, right?"

"Hmm? Ah, that's right. It seems young still, though... Never thought that was even impossible."

"It's huuuge for just a baby. About thirty feet long."

Despite having many dreams of Franz's lost memories, Mariela and the others hadn't been asleep any longer than usual. They had a lot of downtime on their hands as they waited for night.

Until just a short while ago, Franz had been checking for a way to the north tower—the newly generated one—by leveraging his special characteristics that enabled underwater activity. The north side's outer wall was fragmented en route, and the north tower towered in the center, but it seemed the divided wall hadn't been restored, and the gap between the tower and the outer wall was a little too wide to jump. In other words, Mariela and the others couldn't get to the new tower from the northwest one where they were, and they would have to go around the south side to reach the northeast tower.

"Hmm, I wonder if what we need is a whatchamacallit and a thingamajig. Mr. Donnino could make that one thing, and I should be able to make that other thing if we go to the first floor..."

"What are ya plannin' this time?"

Mariela talking about "whatchamacallits" and "thingamajigs" made her seem like a senile old lady. Although Yuric was puzzled, she offered, "If there's somethin' ya need, I'll go look for it."

"Thank you! The main part will be after we meet up with everyone, but right now, I'd like to get as much rope ivy and gepla as possible—the materials for fire bottles."

"Got it."

"I'll help, Yuric."

Yuric and Franz boarded the raptor to go collect the materials, and Mariela waved to them, saying, "I'll make something delicious for when you get back."

"I want to eat somethin' fried again!"

"I'm looking forward to it."

Yuric and Franz's reactions were extremely positive.

Mariela's alchemical cooking had a superb level of heat and was more delicious than when she prepared things with her fully equipped kitchen in Sunlight's Canopy. Dishes eaten on the road were seasoned with exercise and impressive vistas. It made the flavor of even commonplace foods better. And if the taste of the dish itself was good to begin with, then so much the better.

At the same time Edgan was saying "ook, ook" in the northeast tower, two people in the northwest tower were similarly *ook*-cited.

After seeing off Yuric and Franz, Mariela quickly finished her preparations, hugged the salamander, who was watching for a chance to snatch a bit of food, threw herself down on the spot, and curled up.

"Would you tell me just a little bit?"

"Ar..."

Could that have been a reply to Mariela's muttering? The salamander made a small noise, then the two of them closed their eyes.

Ahh, one of those dreams again... I knew it.

It was a vision about traveling through the dark forest protected by the fire spirit's lamp.

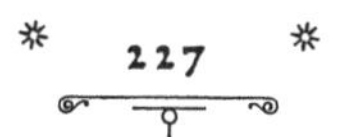

How much time had passed since the last dream? The woods appeared even denser, and it weighed on travelers' hearts like the trees hanging over them.

The darkness of the night made the trees' shapes, which twisted as though to block the people moving through the forest, feel even more terrifying. How many times had there been pilgrimages to the lake since that first, fateful ritual? Travelers carved a narrow path through the thickets and scrubs.

Was this place always so hostile? They looked like regular trees before...

No sooner had Mariela thought the woods seemed familiar than a pack of forest wolves attacked.

—Damn mutts!—

The fire spirit lighting the ceremonial lamp swayed in irritation as she waved her hands to drive away the beasts, but she hadn't quite materialized. The best she could do with her meager power was to dazzle the crazed monsters and weaken their attacks.

"Forest wolves! Get in formation! Don't forget the monster-warding potions!"

This group of travelers had weapons and armor that was far superior to the people Mariela had seen in the first dream of this place. Of course, compared with the equipment from the era of the Kingdom of Endalsia, let alone what the Labyrinth City's adventurers wore, the gear was inferior. The armor was clumsy and lacked maneuverability, and the weapons were extremely blunt.

Even so, a squadron of humans wasn't going to be overtaken by a few forest wolves. The travelers set to exterminating the monsters with swords and spells.

—You won't get in the way of us seeing each other after so long!—

It had been a very long time since the fire spirit had been to that lake.

Both human technology and the city had flourished more and more. There were stockpiles of food in case of famine and methods for creating potions that cured illnesses. People's dependence on the spirits had gradually lessened.

Many more humans now lived in the city, and from the fire spirit's point of view, they were as cramped as a flock of sheep. What made her the most uncomfortable was that black mist-like corruption had become visible in the city here and there as the number of humans increased.

Filthy, shadowy vapor gushed into the city with every foul word someone spat, and with the tears of sorrow and anger that spilled from their eyes. The air in the large settlement felt stagnant to the fire spirit.

The fire spirit, who had continued to exist for a long time, understood that they were words of resentment and tears of bitterness. She understood that if the corruption accumulated and wasn't purified, something terrible would happen.

That's why she endeavored to purify the desecration as she moved from lamp to lamp in the city. However, this sprawling settlement, with its brilliant lights that stayed on all night, was full of gold and silver treasures more dazzling than any lamp. No matter how much corruption she expunged, the desecration gushing out from gaps in the gold, and the people themselves, never ran out.

Although more corruption surged forth than the fire spirit could purify, it never thickened beyond a certain point. The same could not be said of where the desecration flowed to: the lake. That had long troubled the fire spirit.

She couldn't suppress her worry over the black corruption

floating both ahead and behind them on the road, as though both pursuing the people hurrying toward the lake and guiding them.

The air of the forest, which had once been deeply peaceful, was now gloomy and damp like the breath of an enormous monster inviting unwary folks into the abyss. The woodland creatures that had once been gentle now had bloodshot eyes and attacked the humans without heeding the fire spirit's attempts to restrain them.

The fire spirit had become aware this place was no longer the place she once knew, but she felt compelled to ascertain with her own eyes what awaited beyond this point.

The dark forest suddenly came to an end—to convey the truth to the fire spirit.

—Why...?—

The water's surface, darker than the night itself, lay amid a silvery shaft of moonlight. The jet-black lake seemed to swallow up both the lunar glow and the illumination from the fire spirit's lamp. The lake spirit slowly emerged in the very center, sluggishly moving their body, which looked like it was drenched in ink.

Was this the same place?

The fire spirit could have sworn the lake was so clear the first time she'd come here that she could easily count the rings of the trees submerged in its depths. The bottom of the pool had been visible when the lake took in the corruption of disease, too.

—It's been a long time. I thought you had already disappeared.—

Though their body was dyed obsidian with desecration, though their eyes were blackened and dull, the fire spirit still thought the lake spirit was beautiful.

—I won't go out. I won't ever go out. Not now or in the future. Never ever. Because I… I will purify the corruption…—

As soon as she said this, the fire spirit looked back at the group she'd come with and scowled at today's "offering."

In that instant, the flames of a torch spread to the box of the offering the group carried, and it violently burst into flames.

"Wah, the fire!"

"What is this? Hurry and put it out!"

"B-but it was dried, and the fire is spreading fast…"

"Help!" "It hurts!" "The monsterrrs!" "Open the gaaate!"

The shrieks from the offering went unheard by those who'd carried it here. The voices of people crying, shouting, and unanimously begging for help.

—Did monsters attack you this time?—

—Yeah. There's a ton of them in the forest. They surged into the city. I managed to drive 'em away, but a great many humans died.—

The only ones who'd fallen to the monsters were the poor who resided outside the outer wall. The people who possessed the brilliant gold and silver treasure were able to escape harm within the sturdy castle barricades, protected by brawny soldiers.

The rich ignored the voices of those who banged on the outer wall and pleaded for sanctuary, and they watched the monsters eat them alive.

The offering housed the resentment and anger exploited destitute, and the horror and grief of being attacked and eaten by monsters.

—Your bodies and souls are no longer in this world. I'll burn all those painful feelings to nothing. You can turn to cinders and return to a brand-new, colorless, shapeless state, and melt into the atmosphere.—

—You once looked like you could be blown out with a breath, and now you've become so strong...—

The fire spirit smiled happily at the lake spirit's earnest voice. She turned to look at them, and her expression froze.

—Why? Why is corruption still streaming in?—

She realized the black desecration endlessly drifting on the road that led from the city to the lake was flowing straight into the water.

—A path was made. People were coming to me to purify corruption long before you and I met. Yet, though I am the spirit who rules over the ley line of this forest, I have not the power to expunge desecration. This misconception people have was likely born out of their repeated visits to me.—

Over the centuries, humans had formed the notion that this lake was the place corruption returned to.

—Thus, they created a path for the defilement to move through, and it began to flow here like this.—

No anger or sadness could be seen in the lake spirit regarding the pool's corruption, and their own, as they calmly spoke.

They simply received the desecration that streamed in just as they received the rainwater that fell from the heavens, the moonlight that poured down, and the fallen leaves of the trees.

—But, but... If that much corruption collects...—

The fire spirit understood why the trees and the monsters in the forest had transformed. This lake led to the forest's ley line. The corruption that streamed in circulated through the woods and spread to all the trees and animals. The creatures that lived in and loved the forest likely wished to carry the desecration in themselves rather than have it pollute the lake.

—Even if I become twisted and dark, things in the forest will not change. They will just become a little bit mischievous.—

It was said corrupted magical power coagulated and formed monsters. That wasn't a lie. Creatures that took so much corruption into their bodies, it overtook them changed into monsters.

Corruption was, in short, the negative emotions people emitted.

It wasn't possible for monsters that had taken in such a thing and transformed to love humans.

Monsters didn't hate people. People hated people.

The lake spirit calmly told the fire spirit that if it hadn't been for humans, things in the forest would never have changed.

—Even so! That doesn't mean they're not tormented by the emotions in their hearts!—

The lake spirit smiled gently, looking at the fire one as she shouted.

—The structure has already been remade. Do not be anxious. Even if we go mad from the corruption, our existences are but a gentle breeze rippling the water in the eternal flow of time. Unless something unexpected occurs, our peace will not be threatened. It would be best for you to go, dear flame. You are too dazzling for me as I am now.—

After those final words, the lake spirit disappeared into the water, and no matter how much the fire spirit screamed and called to them, the jet-black surface, which didn't even reflect the moon, simply wavered gently.

The fire spirit couldn't forget the lake spirit's gaze, radiant like a gentle night, nor the color of the eyes, black as the abyss. In their final moments, the spirit had turned that look upon the humans before sinking, never to be seen again.

"Ah, I knew it was you, Sieg."

"Mariela! You're safe!"

"Ook!"

"Yeah, Yuric and the others protected me."

"I see… Mariela, I'm so sorry…"

"Eek ook."

The following night, Mariela and Sieg safely reunited at last.

With the loss of the two gatekeepers, Franz and Edgan, the night seemed to have gotten longer. With Franz running alongside the raptor, Mariela's group was able to make it all the way to the southeast tower before dawn came.

Thanks to the newly created north tower, the surging black monsters had abated, but how long would that last? Despite such concerns, Sieg, Mariela, and all the Black Iron Freight Corps members were delighted to at last be back together.

"Mariela, um, I…"

"Eek, eek ook, eek, eek."

They'd finally reunited, yet because a certain monkey kept butting in, the conversation didn't progress at all.

The two couldn't even make up, let alone exchange information. Sieg wanted to apologize and receive Mariela's forgiveness properly, but Edgan, who had been thrusting himself between them with *eeks* and *ooks* for a while now, managed to hinder Sieg at every attempt.

"Oy, Edgan! Get lost!"

Sieg snapped at last and tried to catch Edgan, but all this did was delight the latter. Sieg chased after the monkey, who *ook*-citedly and happily ran amok.

"They sure get along, don't they?"

Mariela smiled as she gazed at the two, but she was distracted.

The spirit's dreams shouldn't have ended with last night's vision. What in the world were the dark raiders in the courtyard…?

They could help the petrified lamia. It was a simple petrification, but in the unlikely event it was a curse, Mariela also prepared a curse-removal potion, the same kind she'd once made for Leonhardt.

The real trouble was the ebon cavalry. Even with the lamia, Mariela wasn't confident in her side's victory. And the black monsters seemed to pour into the temple every night. Her conjecture from the spirit dream was that the swarm of black monsters flowing toward the temple was a mass of corruption. It had to be beyond any one person's capabilities, let alone Mariela's, to change an established current that may as well have been a raging river.

Just because they rush to the temple in the center doesn't mean it's their goal, though…

Mariela was thinking hard. Sieg, misunderstanding this as her still being upset, looked for a chance to apologize in a fluster, and the monkey pulled all the pranks he could.

"Ahhh, you are so annoyin'!"

The one who ran out of patience wasn't Sieg, whom Edgan was pestering, but Yuric, who was watching.

Crack!

Everyone reflexively straightened at the high-pitched sound of Yuric's whip striking the floor.

"Edgan! Down!"

"Ook!"

Mariela and Sieg were simply surprised at the sudden reverberating whip sound, but the effect on the monkey and the raptor was immediate. Edgan straightened up at the cracking of the lash, and when he was told "down," he sat next to Koo.

"Animal tamer skills really do work..."

"Edgan, you..."

Mariela was astonished. And Sieg rubbed his eyes in disbelief. Where had his irritation from a moment ago gone? He seemed to have thought the monkey thing was just a facade.

"Edgan, drink."

"Ook..."

Yuric placed a potion in front of Edgan, who had grown obedient due to her animal tamer skill. Edgan timidly lifted the concoction, then sniffed it and held it up to the light as though he wondered what it was.

"I said *drink*!"

"Ook!"

"Sir, yes, sir!" No back talk was tolerated in Yuric's boot camp. If you showed even the slightest hesitation, her cutting whip would come flying. Well, since Yuric was a girl, maybe it should be "Yes, ma'am." Edgan wasn't speaking a human language, so who can say what the particulars of his reply were?

After giving a relatively good response for a monkey, Edgan drained the potion in one gulp, immediately fell backward with a thud while still in the drinking pose, and stopped moving.

"I knew a potion of Mariela's would work well."

"Yuric, what kind of potion was that?"

"A fast-actin' sleep one. I had Mariela make it in case ya wouldn't move from the tower, Franz."

"Wha...?"

Yuric answered Franz's question without showing the least bit of shame. Depending on the circumstances, Franz could have wound up being dragged along unconscious after being fed a potion. Yuric's calm answer made Franz a bit at a loss for words.

"Mariela, return Edgan's memories right now. I can't take this anymore."

"Yeah. We have to do our best for him."

"It's still a rough idea, but...," Mariela began. She seemed to have some sort of plan in mind.

After hearing the outline of the strategy, Donnino, Grandel, and Franz hurriedly headed out to gather the needed materials so as not to anger Yuric further.

"I'll keep watch here to make sure Edgan doesn't go wild."

Yuric's words gave Mariela peace of mind, and she lay down next to Edgan. When she did, Sieg wedged his way between them with a sullen expression and lay down, too.

"Sieg?"

".........You shouldn't be alone with him."

Sieg wore an expression as though he'd just bitten down on a bug as he gave his short objection, looking neither at Mariela nor at Edgan, but at the ceiling. Although it was to restore Edgan's memories, the idea of letting Edgan and Mariela sleep next to each other was detestable. Obvious jealousy.

"Hee-hee. Then you, too, Sieg. Here, a sleeping potion. One sip is enough."

Mariela, who felt a little awkward seeing Sieg like this, took a sip of the potion, placed the warm salamander on her stomach, and closed her eyes as a laugh slipped out of her.

At the sight of the three lying parallel with Sieg in the middle, Yuric scratched her head and wondered how it had come to this. Edgan, who was sound asleep, scratched his rump now and then as he drooled.

Unconsciousness came immediately.

The smiling face of a woman with soft-looking reddish-brown hair told Mariela this was a memory from Edgan's past.

How gently and warmly this person smiled.

Mariela's master, too, had given her tender smiles when she was little, but this seemed to her far more pleasant, and full of never-ending love.

Eliade.

To Edgan, the woman with reddish-brown hair and eyes was the kindest and most beautiful creature in the world.

His mother, and the first person he ever killed...

Edgan wasn't even ten years old at the time. He went to search for his mother, who had gone into the shallow strata of the Labyrinth and hadn't come home by dinnertime. He'd heard by chance

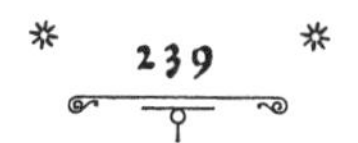

that a man-eating plant monster had appeared in a higher stratum where it was ordinarily safe for his mother, who couldn't fight, to go gathering.

The woman often went to harvest nuts and edible mushrooms in those strata so the growing Edgan could eat his fill, regardless of the flavor.

Edgan rushed to her usual gathering spot, where potato-like plants could be collected, and there he found his mother *in full bloom*.

At the time, Edgan didn't know what kind of monster it was, but it was a man-eating plant that ate its prey alive and sucked its blood to make its flowers blossom.

The body was standing upright, held in place by vampiric roots extending from its feet into the ground and by branches growing inside it. The skin, having been drained of blood, was so pale it was as though it had never known the touch of the sun, and the large, bright red flowers that broke through the woman's flesh here and there beautifully highlighted Edgan's mother, as if she was wearing a gorgeous dress.

Edgan remembered how beautiful it looked to his very young self.

And he could never forget the screams that felt like they were tearing him to pieces.

"IT HURTS IT HURTS IT HURTS IT HURTS IT HURTS IT HUUUUUURTS!!!"

His mother was still alive, tormented by the pain of being eaten from the inside and the agony of blooming flowers breaking through her skin.

Crack.

With a sound like joints disconnecting, his mother's back *lengthened.*

The piercing screams no longer formed human words.

Edgan learned many years later that this plant grew from components it secreted when it sensed pain. At the time, Edgan didn't know why his mother was still alive in this horrid state, but he could understand that she was beyond saving and that this pain wouldn't stop until the little remaining life she had came to an end.

That's why. Because he loved his mother.

Edgan picked up the hatchet his mother had brought for gathering and swung it at her.

The young Edgan was short. Even if he'd leaped, he had neither the leg strength nor the arm strength to cut off her head in one stroke.

Horrid screams carved themselves into Edgan's mind, as did the sensation of swinging the hatchet over and over again as he cried and shrieked.

"Aaaaaaaaaaaaaaaaaaaaaah!!!"

"Eeeeeeeeeeeeeeeeeeee...!!!"

The pair's screams blended together into a gruesome chorus that Edgan could still hear to this day.

But Edgan could also never forget the smiling face of his mother as she uttered her last words: "Thank you."

Eliade.

To Edgan, the woman with reddish-brown hair and eyes was the most beautiful and kind creature in the world.

Hollis.

Edgan's enchanting, cheerful, adorable first love had blond hair and light brown skin.

He'd met her in the Labyrinth Suppression Forces, and due to her caring and frank personality, she and the newly enlisted Edgan soon grew close.

Hollis was senior to Edgan and stronger than him. She teased, "You're hopeless," when Edgan couldn't handle his dual swords well, and she laughed happily when he got worked up over the needling.

Hollis had developed warrior-like arm and shoulder muscles, and her favorite civilian outfit was a rather lovely dress. She was a very sweet person who'd hung her head and said, "It doesn't suit me, though."

When Edgan had grinned and replied, "It looks good on you," Hollis's ears turned bright red, and she grew bashful.

Every time they fought in the Labyrinth, she'd earn a new scar, and gradually, her many wounds began to peek through the sleeves and hem of her dress, yet to Edgan, Hollis's loveliness remained unchanged.

Hollis's delighted look every time Edgan whispered how cute she was and her attempts to conceal her bashfulness weren't flattery, and they showed her sweetness more and more.

As long as she was herself, Hollis's loveliness would never change to Edgan.

Yes, even when her legs decayed, and her skin gradually began to turn bluish-black from her feet to her head due to poison from the Labyrinth.

Potions had run dry in the Labyrinth City. They were something supplied to the army's elite, not to the reserve forces.

The toxin was so volatile that standard medicine was

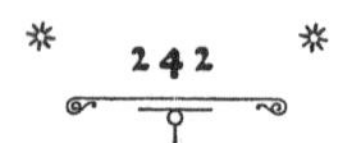

ineffective, and there wasn't enough time to take Hollis to the imperial capital to receive treatment.

"Send me off before...my face changes color. While that dress still looks good on me...as you've told me so many times it does."

Edgan wanted to grant Hollis's wish, to save her from the poison that ate into her mind and body, yet his hand shook, and he couldn't steady his aim.

"You're...still hopeless with dual swords..."

Hollis endured pain so intense that even breathing was difficult as she flashed Edgan her usual smile. Unfortunately, Edgan was unable to return the expression.

"I'm glad I can die...the way I was when you told me I was cute..."

After leaving these words with him, Hollis, smiling, passed on.

Her last wish granted, Edgan dressed her in her favorite outfit and told her, "You're so cute. It looks good on you."

The setting sun dyed Hollis's light brown face red, making her look like she was smiling bashfully.

Hollis.

Blond hair and light brown skin. She was cheerful and adorable right to the end.

Milmette, Margarita, Doris, Alma.

They all had their circumstances, yet they all believed in a better future.

Elda, Irene, Johanna, Camila.

They all had their merits, and were very adorable.

Clarissa, Lise, Sophie, Rosa.

They all smiled at him, yet no one stayed by his side.

Therese, Wilma, Clarina, Natasha.

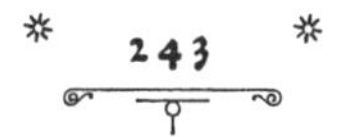

Edgan asked them for love. He wanted them to beam when they saw him.

His mother, burned into his eyelids, smiled only when they did. Her excruciating screams paused.

Laugh, heal me, love me—

My equally kind, equally beloved femme fatales—

It should have been so peaceful.

"Eeeeeeeeeeeeeeeeeeee...!!"

Yet they didn't stop the ear-piercing screams of the blooming flowers...

06

What horrible memories...

As she slowly sat back up, Mariela wondered if Edgan would be better off forgetting such things. Suddenly, Sieg embraced Edgan and began crying his eyes out.

"Edgaaan! Edgan, you were in so much paaaaaaain!!!"

"Whoa, Sieg. I...don't swing that way..."

"Your words came back, too! I'm so glad! I'm so glaaad!!!"

"Y-yeah..."

Sieg's time as a slave hadn't dulled the emotional sensitivity his upbringing had instilled in him. He was a hectic man with various preoccupations who devoted himself to Mariela, the girl who had saved his life and who he felt was a goddess and his destiny.

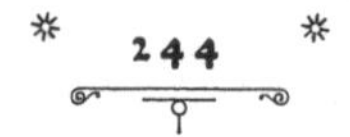

Regardless of whether it was because he was occupied with Mariela or not, Sieg was typically silent. This led many to believe he was a levelheaded sort of man, but that wasn't the case.

Even if Mariela was quiet and engrossed in something, her actions were comical and gave her a funny image. So Sieg simply appeared to be a relatively calm, cool, and collected man by comparison because he was always with her. To tell the truth, Sieg was more introspective and more sensitive than Mariela, perhaps only because of his Spirit Eye.

Conversely, Mariela was less sympathetic. She recognized the memories she'd seen up to this point—Yuric's and Franz's, the ones about past calamities that seemed to be the fire spirit's, and all the others—as the playbacks of people's pasts. Although she grieved at how heartbreaking the tragic ones were, she didn't get too attached. But then, as a high-ranking alchemist, Mariela perceived existence not just through senses like vision and hearing, but also through the state of Drops of Life, so it might have been difficult for her to feel moved by images alone.

Unlike Mariela, who could classify the memories of the past as "things that happened in someone else's history," Sieg seemed to have empathized completely. He'd been crying for a while now, enough to cause a great flood.

Even the salamander, who should have been with Mariela, might have been drawn in by Sieg. It had climbed up on Edgan's shoulder and licked his cheek as though to comfort him.

"Siiieg, would you calm down a bit?"

"But, but, Edgan. If something like that happened to Mariela, I surely wouldn't be able to bear it..."

Apparently, Sieg had substituted Mariela for all the women in Edgan's memories who'd suffered unnatural deaths. Despite not being real, to Sieg it seemed that Mariela had suffered endless terrible fates. One would think that Sieg would have envisioned himself gallantly coming to Mariela's rescue before things got that bad.

"Well...it's good ya get along. Edgan, this means you're a human again?" asked Yuric as she turned to look at the three. She'd remained awake to keep watch. Then she nodded slightly and cracked her whip to confirm whether he was back to his old self.

"Edgan, and Sieg, that's enough!"

At Yuric's shout, Sieg came to his senses, hurriedly straightened himself, and moved to Mariela's side, but Edgan stood stiffly at attention, so maybe just a tiny bit of his monkey side remained.

In any case, the group finally had enough fighting power to execute Mariela's plan.

Sieg and Edgan. The two A-Rankers had assembled.

There was no need to delay the gathering of the more dangerous materials any longer with these two around.

"Thank goodness. With this, I'm sure we'll manage somehow!"

Mariela had the notable characteristic of being able to obtain anything if she asked these two for it.

"Umm, Mariela? What're you planning to make us do?" Edgan, who had been rounded up for miserable material gathering in the past, asked in fear.

"It's not a snowy mountain this time, so it's fine! First, I need wood."

Mariela smiled innocently, while Yuric grinned wickedly.

So it not being cold automatically made things okay? Sieg and Edgan didn't really understand Mariela's criteria, but there was no way the two would do something as terrifying as destroying the two girls' smiles.

"Leave it to us, Mariela! We can get anything."

"Hey, Sieg, you're promising too much..."

"Edgan, wouldn't it have been nice if you'd said even a single word to me before you accepted Mariela's request? I think so."

Sieg had been in tears over Edgan's circumstances, but apparently he still held a grudge about Edgan accepting Mariela's running-away-from-home appeal without even briefly consulting him.

"Come to think of it, I was mad at Sieg," Mariela muttered, as though Sieg's careless remark had made her remember. "After we've gotten out of here, let's have a proper *talk*, okay, Sieg?"

"Okay..."

Mariela, too, apparently wouldn't just forgive Sieg as things stood, even though he came all the way here to rescue her.

"Pfff, tee-hee. Sieg, you're dead meeeat."

"Shut up! Edgan, we're going!"

Although Sieg was frightened of Mariela's smile, he seized Edgan and departed for the southeast tower.

Thus, the pair's harsh hunting began.

"Whoa, they're huge! Whoa, gross!"

As the steellike vines whooshed around, Edgan found footholds

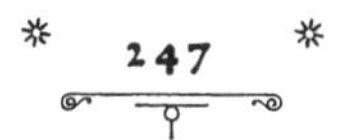

left and right, even on the walls, and dodged attacks as he waited for an opening, while Sieg ruthlessly sniped giant hairy caterpillars in silence.

The pair were in the entrance hall at the center of the first and second floors on the south side.

That's right, the room with the tree monster, the Necklace.

Just as there were many types of plants, there were many types of monsters. Some were even capable of speech. The Necklace wasn't, but it was a nasty monster that freely manipulated parasitic vines like feelers, caught its prey with them like a whip, and decorated itself with them in truly poor taste. These tendrils were tough as steel and wrapped around the trunk in place of armor to thwart attacks.

As further proof of its poor fashion sense, the mass of hairy caterpillars the Necklace kept in its branches grew to between three and six feet long as soon as it shook them out and then attacked their prey. The insects themselves weren't especially strong, but because they sent poisonous fibers flying with a viscerally unacceptable visual effect, a lightweight short-range attacker like Edgan wanted to keep away from them as much as possible.

"Mr. Donnino said the Necklace's wood is very solid and extremely flexible, so it would be perfect."

Mariela had seen off Sieg and Edgan after conveying this snippet of Donnino's extensive knowledge of timber.

The Necklace was too large to walk, but it could move its appendages. It was undoubtedly sturdy, and flexible as well. Its wood was indeed a high-class item, but the tradeoff was that it was a difficult creature to subjugate. It had melee attacks with its whiplike vines and long-range attacks with its mass of hairy caterpillars. How in the world could one take on such an opponent?

Lightning or fire would end the battle pretty quickly but would render the wood useless.

"Gah, Sieg, be a little more careful! The juice! The juice is flying at meee!!!"

"I can't do anything about that! It's a trait of these insecticide potions!"

The insecticide potions called *bug bombs* that Mariela had given the two men as a countermeasure against the hairy caterpillars were made by mixing originally low-grade items with special-grade materials to boost their effects. In other words, they were Mariela's specially adapted concoctions, whose increased potency alone made them special-grade equivalent.

"The Fell Forest had a lot of bugs, so I came up with many different insecticide potions to protect my medicinal herb garden. This is the first time I've increased the power to special-grade, but it should totally be effective!"

Just as Mariela had said, the bug bombs were indeed impressive.

Boom, boom, boom-boom! Using arrows dipped in the mixture, Sieg made every last one of the hairy caterpillars explode.

It was a tragedy. Every time one of the insects burst open, yellow body fluids splattered all about.

Since defeating a giant hairy caterpillar in a single blow required some amount of power from the Spirit Eye, this potion that made arrows poisonous was very helpful in curbing Sieg's magical power consumption. Even so, the bug bombs were better banned or kept a secret. If they fell into the hands of a brat, the kid would probably immensely enjoy making insects explode.

When Mariela lived in the Fell Forest cottage, she didn't have the leisure to play around with making bugs burst open, but the stench of dead insects scattered around the area had the convenient side effect of keeping others out of their away.

Where on earth was the Necklace keeping that many hairy caterpillars? Did they grow at ultra-high speeds after hatching? The tree monster sicced the hairy caterpillars on Sieg and Edgan one after another, and Sieg's envenomed arrows caused them to pop.

Even Edgan, dodging attacks from the Necklace and the hairy caterpillars, couldn't read the trajectory of Sieg's arrows, despite them both being A-Rankers. He got heavily drenched in insect body fluids. Wherever he jumped, *goosh!* And again, wherever he landed, *splat!*

"This gunk stinks! It smells like buuugs! Siiieg, are you listening?! You couldn't possibly be doing this on purpose, right?!"

After confirming that Edgan, who was angrily *oo*king from a distance, was filthy, Sieg nodded as if to say "hmm" and signaled to him.

"...Would now be a good time? All right, Edgan, I'll cover you. Bring down the Necklace!"

"Wha?!"

Sparing no time, Sieg turned his arrows on the Necklace, loosing many in quick succession.

The projectiles struck the monster's numerous vines with fearsome accuracy and pinned them back.

"Now, Edgan! The Necklace is wide open!"

For an instant, the Necklace, with all its vines pulled up and away by arrows, was completely defenseless.

"Nice one, Sieg! But the bugs... Huh?!"

Shockingly, the hairy caterpillar monsters seemed to be avoiding Edgan and advancing on Sieg, who stood at a distance with his bow at the ready.

"So that's it! They hate the smell of the bug juice..."

"Hurry, Edgan! While I lure the hairy caterpillars!"

"!!! Got it, Sieg!!!"

"I'll draw them away, so you deliver the final blow" sounded a little like a plot point in a story of friendship. It also seemed like a line that monkey-Edgan would be pleased to hear.

This noble-path-like development completely revved up Edgan, and he began to attack the Necklace with full force.

"My left arm is a pedestal for gales, my right arm a pedestal for adamantine. Abide in me! **Dual Sword Elements!!!**"

Edgan tempered his dual swords with the earth element and increased their momentum with the wind element. Then he began to strike at the Necklace's trunk. The sharpness of Edgan's weapons cleaved through the steellike vines, and their momentum whittled down the large tree as surely as any ax. If the monster had been an animal, the blow would have torn its flesh to pieces and even severed its bones; however, it couldn't possibly sever a thick thing like the Necklace that easily.

"Not good enough?!"

Any other creature would have weakened after being struck so powerfully, but the Necklace had no sense of pain, and to make matters worse, the only emotion it did have was anger.

The tree monster lifted its hideously warped eyes, which resembled cracks in the bark, and screwed up its ugly mouth, then unwrapped all the vines that had been coiled around its trunk and bent backward to strike Edgan at range with its full power.

"Damn!"

The vines Sieg had pinned back were free and moving to strike Edgan. Even if he avoided those initial hits, the second group of tendrils that had been wrapped around the trunk wouldn't miss him.

Despite the vines that spread like a net to block his retreat, Edgan searched for a way to recover from the hopeless development. He stood ready for the Necklace's next attack, knowing that if he couldn't escape, all he could do was take the monster down first.

All the Necklace's tendrils were being used offensively, and its trunk was unguarded.

What would happen sooner: Edgan slicing through the Necklace's trunk, or the Necklace's vines knocking down Edgan and smashing all of his bones into tiny pieces?

Thunk.

In that life-and-death moment, a dull, powerful sound that originated neither from Edgan's swords nor from the Necklace's verdant lashes echoed through the chamber. Instantly, the great monster became nothing but a mere tree.

A single spirit arrow had ended the perilous struggle between Edgan and the Necklace.

"...Wha? Huh?"

Dumbfounded by the abrupt end to the battle, Edgan gazed at the now-motionless Necklace, which had an arrow shaft blooming from the base of a branch above its eyes on the top part of the trunk. Gravity pulled down the vines that had been poised to kill, and they became entangled in foliage.

Siegmund had been waiting for the instant the Necklace unraveled all the tendrils protecting its trunk.

For a split second, the Necklace had bent back its trunk and exposed its weak point, the base of a branch where its magical gem was located. Normally, that vital area was concealed behind vines and foliage.

Every type of monster had a magical gem.

These stones, which were compact, portable, and could be sold at a high price, were not only essential spoils of battle—they were also the source of a monster's power and its weak point. The Necklace's magical gem had been shot through, and its life as a monster had ended in a single blow. It was now just a tree.

The location of a monster's magical gem varied from one individual to the next, and although the approximate area for a given species was known, you wouldn't know the exact spot without dismantling the creature's corpse. Typically, smashing a magical gem halved the hunting profits, so using it as a one-shot kill was a rarely considered option save for exceptional situations where other materials were prioritized, as was currently the case. Sieg's Spirit Eye enabled him to locate the magical gem and shoot the weak point, which had only been left defenseless for an instant.

"Hey, Siiieg? Was this how you planned it all along?"

"Gh, Edgan, there are still hairy caterpillars left! Help me out!"

Although Sieg had the leeway to relentlessly pierce the approaching hairy caterpillars at a distance and even magnificently sidestep the bug juice that came flying at him, he didn't answer Edgan's question.

He pretended to be in a tough spot against the large army of monsters, but his acting was a bit too shoddy.

"Hey, enough about finishing them off. Maybe, just maybe, you were squishing those bugs just to throw their nasty gunk on me? Hmmm? Siiieg?"

"Uh-oh, this is bad! Poisonous fibers!" Sieg exclaimed, wholly monotone.

By the way, the venomous barbs flying at Sieg never reached him because the wind created with one swing of his bow was enough to turn them away. To conserve magical power, Sieg only used his Spirit Eye a little bit, but it was enough to make the fight a relatively leisurely one for him.

"Why, you! I'm gonna cover you in bug juice so you'll get dumped!!! **Wind Edge!!!**"

"Don't say something like that and jinx it!!! It's your fault for taking Mariela out in the first place!!! **Wind Wall!!!**"

Complain, complain, complain; wah, wah, wah.

The men's stupid quarrel, harsher than their battle with the Necklace, continued until the entire mass of hairy caterpillars had been squashed, and they were both covered in insect guts.

Although Sieg and Edgan had defeated the Necklace, Mariela and Yuric told them they stank when they returned covered in bug juice. Until Mariela made a deodorizing potion, the pair weren't allowed in the room and were made to stand in the hallway.

08

"This's better lumber than I thought it would be! And the vines seem usable enough. Sorry, but could you lend me a hand, Grandel and Franz? Yuric, there should be a workshop ahead where we can process these. Use the raptor to transport them there. Edgan and Sieg, you can rest for a bit."

Delighted at the quality of the Necklace's wood, Donnino set about assigning tasks to everyone.

Edgan and Sieg, released from their job at last, groaned in reply and happily sank to the floor. Apparently, cutting down and processing the Necklace had been exhausting.

"Since we don't have an ax, there's no way around it," Donnino had said, and so Sieg and Edgan had used their mythril longsword and dual swords, respectively, to break the wood down per Donnino's instructions. Since the weapons weren't meant for such work, it was terribly tiring.

Swords made to cut up monsters, and especially animals, weren't suited for chopping trees. Thin, sharp blades could easily be chipped and blunted by solid, thick wood.

That's why Sieg and Edgan applied magical power to their blades to strengthen them before splitting the timber, but apparently, both the unfamiliar motions of cutting and processing wood and the use of magical power over a long period of time were quite tiring, and the pair didn't seem to have any energy left to bicker.

"Sieg, Edgan, I'm going to leave your meals here, so eat and then rest a little."

Mariela recommended the pair have some food, then quietly left the room.

There was still something she needed to confirm.

"It's been a long time since I slept here."

The place Mariela had chosen in the hopes of having a dream was the room that was a re-creation of the cottage in the Fell Forest where she'd lived with her master two hundred years ago. Mariela had come previously to make potions, so she knew where it was, and she'd also confirmed the route's safety.

The Fell Forest cottage was tiny; all it had was a bedroom and a chamber that served as a workshop, kitchen, and living room.

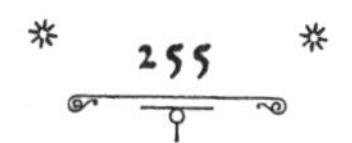

"I think I slept in the same bed as my master when she first took me in."

How long was it before they slept separately?

Mariela's master had given reasons like "It's too hot" and "You want your own room, right?" but had she really needed to go as far as partitioning such a cramped space with a small dresser for them to sleep apart?

"Raaawr."

The salamander wriggled around as if to say it wasn't sleepy yet, and Mariela hugged it tight and whispered, "You can't escape," before crawling into her master's familiar bed.

The city burned.

The people burned.

The world was filled with lamentations.

Fire spirits who had newly come into being didn't possess the humans' knowledge of good and evil; they merely gathered where there was fuel, crowded together, became hellfire, and engulfed the entire city.

The fire spirit became aware for the first time that the blood of the people put to the sword was as red as fire.

Voices of people crying and shouting, shrieks of those frantically trying to escape, cries of many begging for help.

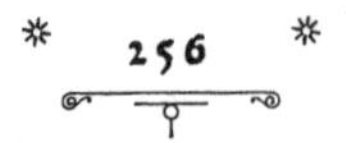

Despite being of the same species as those suffering, some humans ignored or otherwise took delight in these terrible sounds, transforming them into wails of death. There was fighting with blades, sounds of heavy boots, and elated shouts.

People were killing people.

Humans were burning a human city.

The tragic sight was one that human history might remember for many generations, but to the many spirits who gazed at this terrible spectacle, it was like watching a storm as they thought, *So this is the kind of creature humans are.*

While many lives were being lost, the death toll didn't reach that of an earthquake or a volcanic eruption. To the spirits, it seemed hardly any different from an ant's nest being attacked by a different kind of ant.

Except for a lone fire spirit...

—No, no. You mustn't die this way. Anger, sorrow, so many dark emotions are flowing in one after another...!!!—

The road had already become a black river. The dark emotions humans called corruption or curses passed through the woods they called the Fell Forest and streamed toward that lake.

A small amount would have been fine.

The corruption was melting into the water and spreading throughout the entire Fell Forest. And it came to rest inside the trees and the animals of the woods. More than half of the creatures living in the Fell Forest had turned into monsters. The beings known as monsters had wild temperaments and strong bodies, but excepting those features, they weren't any different from any other animal that was born, ate, was eaten, reproduced, aged, and died.

Despite the desecration dwelling within them that consumed

their minds and bodies, they purified it throughout their lifetimes until, at last, they returned to the ley line.

The balance between the human city and the Fell Forest had been passably maintained until the attack on the former. The corruption generated by the humans had been purified by fire as much as possible, but beyond that, the Fell Forest itself functioned well as a purging mechanism.

Unfortunately, no matter what, there was no way to completely staunch the flow of corruption from a calamity as terrible as an enormous settlement being attacked and razed to the ground.

—This is bad. This amount is unacceptable. If this much desecration streams into it, that lake, that spirit will…—

In the eyes of many spirits, the foolish act of war, in which people fought and killed, resembled animals preying on one another, albeit on a large scale. However, no other creatures besides humans raised their voices in resentment like this. No other animals cursed the enemies trying to take everything from them with feelings of anger, resentment, grief, and sorrow and spread corruption.

—No!—

An ebon, sootlike substance rose up everywhere, from burnt corpses to collapsed houses.

—No, I don't want to let it through!—

Ghosts, unaware of their deaths, roamed through the city and groaned in miserable agony, cursing all around them.

—I don't want to let it pollute that lake spirit any more than this…!!!—

Spirits were simply there.

They merely dwelled in the blowing wind and burning fire, flowed with the water, and nurtured life along with the soil. By all

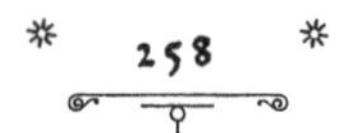

rights, neither happiness nor unhappiness, nor even knowledge of good and evil, existed within such things.

Spirits existed regardless of whether the current of abundant rivers watered the earth and lights illuminated cities brimming with life, or drought caused the land to dry up, ponds to vanish, forests to catch fire, and many lives to be lost.

They accepted everything as it was, and it was that nature that should have rendered them incapable of a strong desire for anything.

If a spirit truly wished something, if it sacrificed something for that aspiration, it was likely no longer just a spirit, the embodiment of a phenomenon. If it gained a "self," it could never again simply dwell in the city lights or return to being a mere flame that swayed and was snuffed.

That fire had a wish and wanted desperately to see it realized.

After existing for so long, that fire spirit now held the power necessary to grant her own request, albeit through only a single method.

—I won't let it through. I'll burn it all to nothing.—

Because she, a fire, possessed no other way to do so.

The spirit would furiously burn the city to the ground. The people, the houses, the food, the treasures.

The flame decided she would turn the humans to cinders. Enemies and allies, the living and the dead.

The force of the rampaging blaze, the tempest-like fury, engulfed everything belonging to the humans, from prayers to curses, like a muddy stream and scorched it until it was merely ashes.

—Burn it, burn it, burn everything. I won't let even a fragment of a curse or a sliver of corruption reach that lake...!!!—

The flame even enveloped many fire spirits, burning brighter and spreading farther.

Black smoke and soot blew upward.

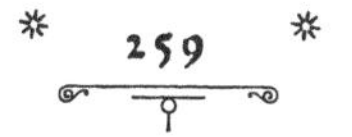

Fiery pillars sprouted so that not even ash and cinder could escape, dyeing the clouds crimson.

Whether the terrible sounds were those of humans screaming or the city collapsing, no one could be certain.

However, even a conflagration of this scale couldn't stop the air currents or change a river's course.

The shadowy corruption that slipped through gaps in the purifying hands of the blaze, the people's feelings of grief, sadness, resentment, and anger at this tragedy, with no place to go, streamed toward that lake as water flowed from a high place to a low one.

—I won't let it get away. I won't let it through. No, no, this can't be happening!—

The inferno that engulfed the city and razed it to nothing stretched itself all the way to the forest, chasing after the cascade of desecration.

The flame had a wish. She wanted nothing more than for the lake spirit to know no further pollution or suffering.

She was aware that she'd assigned value to something. The fire spirit had judged the negative emotions humans produced to be filthy and evil.

Thoughts about what was superior and inferior had entered her mind. She'd had ideas about determining good and evil. The lake spirit was precious, and the fire spirit didn't concern herself with the lives of the people who had polluted it. Hers was a self-righteous desire to help the lake spirit, even if that meant sacrificing others to the flames.

—I'm coming for you.—

The fire spirit understood that she wished to see the lake spirit. She understood the nature of her own feelings in sparing no effort to muster her power for the lake spirit's sake.

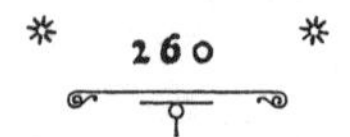

That was why she torched houses, shops, roads, and the city.

The forest smoldered, insects crumbled, animals burned, and people died.

She consumed infants, the elderly, men, women, the living, the dead, everyone, and sent them back to the ley line.

And at last, the fire spirit reached the lake in the Fell Forest. Incinerating everything indiscriminately was simply part of the phenomenon known as fire.

—To burn and cleanse the corruption. So no more of it will come here. So it won't corrupt you any further…!!!—

On the bank of the pitch-black pool, the fire spirit screamed as she seared the corruption that coiled around in bits and pieces.

—Is that truly what you plan to do…?—

Like a black lagoon inverting and rising, the lake spirit floated up from the surface of the water and asked the fire spirit this question with the calmness of the night. Their dark hue made it clear to the fire spirit that she'd been too late. Helping that beautiful creature was beyond her power.

—If the corruption flows into me, then so be it. Is it not the way of we spirits to accept things as they are and simply exist?—

The lake spirit's form was dyed so ebon from the desecration they had taken in that it took the fire spirit's breath away, yet the lake spirit neither resented nor hated the humans who had twisted them so.

Monsters attacked people simply because the corruption within them that detested humans compelled them to do so.

Sparks crackled and spilled from the fire spirit's eyes in place of tears at how much the lake spirit had changed. Their black eyes motionlessly gazed at her and smiled just a little.

—Your feelings toward me are warm. Your unsettled heart

rampaging in anger, sorrow, and suffering is the very embodiment of flame. But have you not realized? Thinking of another and mustering strength for their sake is the way of a human heart.—

At this, the fire spirit gasped and then put words together as though she were squeezing them out of herself.

—If I have a human heart, then you're the one who gave it to me...—

Crackling embers streamed from the fire spirit's eyes, and something powerful clawed at her heart. Though buried beneath so much dark corruption that the lake spirit's life seemed a flickering thing beneath it, the sight seemed both like a light forever illuminating the shadow of night and a short-lived flower that bloomed and fell. The lake spirit thought it beautiful.

They moved toward the fire spirit as though they were gliding across the water's surface and stretched their arms toward the fierce, fickle, flickering flame.

—Come.—

The lake spirit beckoned to the ebon desecration that coiled around the fire spirit even as her body incinerated the ominous substance.

—No! You mustn't take any more...—

—I do not mind. It seems that I, too, desire to take in your corruption.—

The two spirits stretched their arms toward each other so naturally that it wasn't clear who did so first, and their palms pressed against one another. Even before their fingertips touched, the lake spirit's digits fizzled to steam and rose into the air, while the fire spirit's own began to wane.

No matter how long they existed, no matter how much power a spirit possessed, water and fire never made contact.

As long as water was water and fire was fire, the spirits were bound to their nature.

—Even so, I want to purify your corruption. How do I do it...?—

—That is a wish that surpasses what a spirit is capable of.—

The lake spirit laughed that it was impossible, and instead of responding, the fire spirit asked for something else.

—Hey, would you tell me your name? Even if you're corrupted, you remain noble. If I know what to call you, no matter where we are or what we become, our hearts will be connected. And I want you to remember my name and my feelings.—

Then the fire spirit introduced herself to the lake spirit.

—I... My name is Freyja, spirit of flames.—

—That is an excellent moniker worthy of your fierceness. Then I, too, will give my name. It is...—

The name the lake spirit gave evoked their crystal-clear waters of days past. Freyja yearned to return the lake spirit to the way they used to be back when she'd first met them.

10

"I figured as much...," Mariela muttered after waking in the bed in the cottage of the gloomy Fell Forest.

This place, where memories of Mariela's master dwelled, tore at the girl's heart all the more.

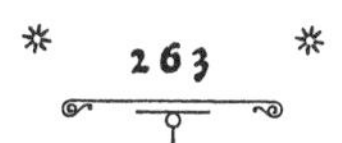

Drop, drip-drip.

Tears spilled from Mariela's eyes and began to leave spots on the sheets.

"I was fine with the other visions, but..."

Considering its distance from the Fell Forest, that ancient city had probably been in the place that was now called the imperial capital.

Mariela had never been to the imperial capital, but she had a vague understanding that the war she'd witnessed had occurred more than a few hundred years ago.

If so, just how long had her master been alive?

When she thought about that, Mariela grew so sad that her chest tightened, and large tears spilled from her eyes as she continued to hold the salamander tight.

Mariela recalled the day her master left the Labyrinth City.

"I can't stand all the melancholy."

Freyja had said those words with a laugh, but how many people had she left behind—who now only existed in her recollections of them?

Undoubtedly, Freyja had taken on countless pupils, raised them, and said farewell when they'd died.

It had all been for the sake of just one, solitary spirit whom she'd offered her heart to...

"Awr."

As Mariela quietly sobbed, the salamander licked away her tears to comfort her.

CHAPTER 6

The Calamity of War

"This weapon isn't in my area of expertise, but I think it's usable enough."

Using the Necklace's lumber, Donnino had made a ballista, a large-scale bow that was supposed to be useful in castle sieges. He'd spent all night making it, but because Sieg, Edgan, Franz, and Grandel had been fighting in the courtyard with many fire bottles in hand, dawn had arrived earlier than usual.

If they continued to battle here like this, they might be able to eventually purify all the corruption, but keeping this up seemed unreasonable.

"Still, I think this is the best way," Mariela said. Her strategy lacked a clincher, but everyone else had accepted it readily enough. Although none of the others had an alternate plan, the fact that Mariela seemed to have discovered something before proposing her tactic was probably a significant factor in why they went along with it.

They mounted the ballista Donnino made at the top of the southeast tower, where Mariela had first awoken, to obtain the materials they needed when they used it. When Mariela peeked out through the large windows, she saw a massive fish leisurely swimming through the clear water, shimmering in the sunshine. The creature seemed to be enjoying itself.

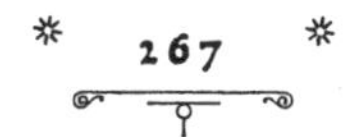

"What a strange sight. This looks like fresh water, but isn't that a saltwater fish?"

Sieg's comment was sensible, but not very imaginative.

Next to them, Grandel and Donnino commented on passing sea creatures as though they were already ingredients, saying this one was delicious when roasted or that one was exquisite in a sauce of melted innards. They had no sentimentality, either.

"Siiieg, you gotta think fuzzier. This is an awesome world where a tiny snake can become a lamia with big hooters. The salty taste is probably unavoidable, but overlooking that is easy, since it's a fish and a monster. Better yet, I wonder if there are any cute mermaids?"

Apparently, Edgan thought this world was "awesome." The only half-human creature he'd seen so far was the one lamia, and as for mermaids, it was questionable whether they were monsters or demi-humans.

"People don't say 'hooters' anymore, you know?"

"Edgan's an old man. Gross."

The two girls, both possessed of flat-chested beauty, gave sly remarks.

"Well, this *is* a world where a human can revert to a monkey..." Sieg, who somewhat agreed with fuzzy Edgan's fuzzy opinion, said something uncalled-for as he set an arrow, or rather, a harpoon, into the ballista and began to make adjustments.

"Isn't that fish a little close?" Mariela wondered aloud.

"I'm lurin' it this way, so it's fine. Oh! Edgan, there's a mermaid over there!" Had Yuric planned her answer, or had it been spontaneous?

"Seriously?! Where, wheeere—? Gah! Isn't that a bit too cliché? *Glug, glug.*"

"Rar!"

Whether Edgan understood it was a gag and merely humored it, or he couldn't resist looking for a mermaid at the mention of one even if it was a lie, he rushed over to the window and peeked out in the direction Yuric had indicated. In that instant, Koo shoved him into the water with a splash.

Perhaps it seemed fun to the raptor, as Koo even stuck his tail out the window and began provoking monster fish by fluttering the appendage and splashing around as he trilled. Edgan struggled to escape as he spun around and around in the churning water.

He certainly made for lively bait.

The struggling Edgan must have looked tasty, because several monster fish made a big splash as they charged at him with incredible momentum.

"All right, Sieg. It's your turn."

"Got it."

Sieg faced the charging creatures and took aim with the ballista.

Donnino was responsible for maintaining the armored carriages in the Black Iron Freight Corps. Since the wagons were equipped with bow guns, he had a rough understanding of a ballista's structure, as well. The ballista, which had been made from whittled wood from the Necklace for its body and vines for its bowstring, seemed complete at a glance.

The ballista, a stationary, large-scale weapon, typically made use of minute mechanisms that enabled adjustments to the height and angle of the fixed pedestal and allowed one to pull the bowstring. Donnino, not being a weapon craftsman, couldn't make something so complex in only a day, so he'd planned for Sieg's physical strength as an A-Ranker and his Spirit Eye to make up for the lack of that kind of fine control.

"It's quite a strange thing. But with this kind of power…," Sieg muttered. The harpoon he fired passed within inches of Edgan, who had finally been released from the water currents and had his hands on the window frame in an attempt to get back into the tower. Far from simply piercing the approaching fish from mouth to tail, the harpoon speared them through and kept on going.

"That Spirit Eye thing really is slapdash," uttered Donnino, shocked at seeing the aquatic monsters turn into minced meat with a single shot.

Even the slipshod ballista would always hit the bull's-eye with the Spirit Eye's divine protection behind it—even underwater. It was as though the ocean changed its current so as not to dampen the harpoon's momentum and even corrected the projectile's course.

"Now, now. We'll still be able to claim our catch, so it all turned out well enough." Grandel soothed poor Donnino, who was thinking he'd made that ballista in vain.

"*Pant, pant*, I thought I was gonna drown… Sieg, do you usually shoot so close to your friends?!"

"You're quite the handsome fellow now that you're dripping wet, Edgan!"

As expected, Edgan was huffy, and Sieg praised him and flashed a thumbs-up with a smile on his face. "Hooters" was stale, but so was this. Their matching old-fashionedness was one more reason they got along.

"…That's enough, you two. It's coming. Hide your magical power."

Edgan and Sieg had been about to start goofing around as

they often did, but at a word from Franz, who was looking up through the window, they snapped to attention.

Many of the giant fish were gathering, lured by the others that had been torn to shreds by the test fire a moment ago and now resembled ground meat. Bait-gan had just been the opening performance. These newly attracted fish were the real lures.

They were quite a distance from the tower, but the sight of countless carnivorous creatures, far larger than normal ones at several yards each, swarming around the chum and keeping each other in check as they devoured it, was quite an impressive spectacle. However, a shadow that eclipsed them all was swiftly approaching from somewhere deep in the distance of the endless ocean.

"It's huuuge. Can we seriously bring it down?" Edgan's remark wasn't without merit.

A whale the size of a sailing vessel was drawing near. Upon close inspection, one realized that it was very different from whales detailed in reference books. What made it stand out was undoubtedly its giant mouth. It resembled a deep-sea fish's maw that was a third the size of its entire body. Compared to normal whales, which filtered seawater and ingested tiny creatures, this monster, a *Gladere*, survived by absorbing magical power in the sea. The amount required to maintain its large build was tremendous, so it could only inhabit areas of the ocean with dense magical power, and it didn't attack ordinary fish that had no magic.

If it weren't for that, the whale monster would have hunted every fish in the world to extinction.

No sooner did the Gladere indent its stomach and contract its entire body than it suddenly dived down all at once at a bizarre speed.

It was surprisingly nimble for a creature so large. And its

enormous mouth swallowed all the fish monsters feeding on the bait faster than they could scatter and escape.

The Gladere's biggest boons were its mouth, which could eat and tear up anything, and its mobility.

A special subcutaneous layer of fat and the Gladere's magical power enabled radical density changes that allowed the creature to swim swiftly. When it rose toward the surface, the whale monster expanded to attain buoyancy, and when it dived down, it became as dense and heavy as lead, moving at formidable speed.

By the time you noticed its rapid approach from overhead or the ocean floor, it was already too late. No sea life existed that could escape a Gladere.

Moreover, although a Gladere was a monster that subsisted solely on magical power, it could swallow plants, and even wood.

A significant number of large, goggly fish shifted around.

The Gladere had found its next prey.

It opened its big mouth wide and charged toward the tower. Sieg and the others may have been the first ones to see its massive snapping maw, which could shred anything.

"Gaaah, gross!" Edgan screamed reflexively.

Within that deep-sea-fishlike mouth were several more mouths. More precisely, the Gladere had multiple sets of teeth. If you compared it to a human's, what the Gladere had parted were its lips. And there were many more sets along the throat, as well. Moreover, the rough rows seemed to have multiple joints, and each tooth was clenched separately.

The Gladere charged forward to crunch up both the tower and the group alike, and a single arrow shining in rainbow colors grazed its mouth.

It was a spirit arrow charged with plenty of magical power via the Spirit Eye. Sieg had preserved his magical power during the fight with the Necklace for this express purpose.

The power of spirits was a little different from average magical power, but that evidently made it irresistible food to the Gladere. The moment when the creature shifted its mouth in the direction of the arrow to catch it…

With a *fsh*, the ballista's giant harpoon pierced the titanic whale's largest jaw joint.

Roooooar.

The Gladere's scream traveled through the water and shook the tower.

"Eek!"

"Mariela! Are you all right?!"

"She's fine. Let's get outta here. Sieg, keep your eyes on the monster and take it down, would ya?"

Despite the fact that they were in combat, Sieg had spun around in response to Mariela's unusually adorable shriek. It was shameful how transparent he was in wanting to show her his good side and score points with her.

Yuric, who had grown close to Mariela while Sieg took his sweet time getting here, put Mariela on Koo and began evacuating to a safe lower floor. Yuric, noticing Sieg's gaze, gave a broad, meaningful grin.

"Hey, Mariela, hold on tight."

"Okay!"

Mariela remained unaware of both Sieg's gaze and Yuric's ulterior motive. She wrapped her arms around the waist of the girl she'd become great friends with and hugged her close so she wouldn't be thrown off.

"Grr…"

Yuric laughed at Sieg's grumble.

Sieg only barely managed to keep himself from uttering something like "You little brat...," but his expression was that of a villain no matter how you looked at it.

He had reverted entirely to the scumbag he'd been before he became a slave. A Siegbag.

Two girls clinging to each other on a raptor was a charming sight, but Sieg hadn't realized Yuric was female. From his point of view, it looked like Mariela had been stolen after he'd dared to take his eyes off of her for a moment. Yuric's less curvy body played a huge part in fooling Sieg.

Incidentally, there was no way Edgan would ignore the fact that jealousy was showing on Sieg's face, and he sauntered around the other man with an *extremely* happy expression—retribution for earlier.

"Hey, hey, Sieg, buddy. Attractive men are the ones who work hard *behind* the scenes, you know."

"Shut up, Edgan. You're one to talk."

"Stop messing around, both of you. Here it comes!"

The instant Franz reined in the pair, a loud *boom* that shook the tower pierced the air. The Gladere, which had been hit by the harpoon, hurled itself into the tower. Surprisingly, all that came of it was that thundering sound. Even with the whale ramming the structure, it remained firm.

"Hoh-hoh, leave it to my Shield."

From armored carriages to umbrellas, earth walls to tower edifices, if it was a solid body he could touch, Grandel could make it into a shield. He chuckled with a placid expression.

"Donnino, pull the rope now!"

"Right!"

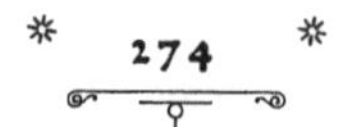

Donnino and Franz showed off their strong arms by pulling the tether attached to the harpoon and dragging the Gladere toward them so it couldn't escape.

"Welp, guess that's our cue, Sieg."

"...I'll end this right now!!!"

Edgan reluctantly grabbed a harpoon, and Sieg, who glared with eyes full of murderous intent, loaded the ballista.

The Gladere was called a "demon of the sea," a title that evoked a tough fight. However, Sieg shot the thing through, nailing joints and weak points. In the blink of an eye, the whale monster was a lifeless pincushion.

"Sieg's merciless..."

"Mariela! It's overrrrrrr!"

As soon as he defeated the monster, Sieg disregarded both Edgan and his prey and ran down to the lower floor, where Mariela and Yuric were waiting.

Whenever Sieg finally learned that Yuric was a girl, he would undoubtedly have a comical expression.

"Let's go."

Everyone gathered at the entrance hall nodded at Mariela's declaration.

It wouldn't be long until the sun set, and the water that

obstructed the group's path would disappear. Was the water that imprisoned them in this world hindering them, or was it protecting them from the black monsters?

That, too, would become clear after they crossed the courtyard beyond this point and finally reached the temple in the center.

To do this, the group needed to defeat the creatures that had taken the form of the ravages of war—the ones the petrified lamia was keeping in check.

When they opened this door, it would begin.

The final battle...

When the Labyrinth Suppression Forces' elite soldiers had captured the Labyrinth's lowest strata, they had come prepared with enough equipment to challenge a stratum boss several times over. In contrast, the party here sported only a few people who could fight. Admittedly, perhaps it was a bit too early to judge on numbers alone. Leonhardt's troops may have been many, but potions had greatly bolstered their strength.

Siegmund, wielder of the Spirit Eye and critical figure in the Labyrinth subjugation, was here. So was Edgan, who, despite being unable to join the Labyrinth Suppression Forces because of personal reasons, had grown as an A-Ranker and was a User of All who could utilize two elements simultaneously.

What's more, not only did this little band have Franz, who had transformed into a demi-dragon and was now more powerful as a result, but Yuric, Donnino, and Grandel. If the group assessed their opponents and exhaustively prepared, the likes of the black monsters were nothing for them to fear.

Mariela looked around at her reassuring allies, all of whom wore determined expressions: Sieg, Edgan, Franz, Donnino, Grandel, Yuric—and a barrel.

A barrel, another barrel, and another, bottles, a barrel, another barrel, bottles, more bottles, and more bottles.

"...We gathered a lot more than I thought."

"The more we have, the better."

That's right. This was the beginning of the end, and preparation was essential. Nonetheless, the quantities of casks and alcohol bottles were so massive they couldn't all fit on the raptor, and everyone had been made to carry one or two. It gave the whole thing the air of a large delivery more than a climactic engagement.

Donnino had used the remaining wood from the Necklace to make a narrow, two-wheeled carrier akin to a wagon, which Koo now pulled, and a large number of barrels had been loaded on it. The sides had walls to keep the cargo from falling, and it could defend against attacks with Grandel on board, making it an exceptional product. However, Yuric, who operated the cart piled with cargo, was the spitting image of a delivery boy no matter how you looked at it.

"It's got better maneuverability than I thought. If we just gave it the imperial capital's latest wheel bearings and plate springs and processed the tires, it seems like it could be quite fast." Although they were on the brink of a fierce battle, Donnino seemed extremely pleased with his craft. He talked at length about the friction and speed of wooden slide bearings. After they returned home safely, maybe he'd start a "Black Iron Express Delivery" service.

In any case, Mariela and the others had a large number of barrels and an equally sizable amount of bottles.

The liquid filling them had been collected from the Gladere.

The processing hadn't required much time because Mariela had made full use of her excess magical power to mince, boil, and separate the thick hide and skull interior all in one go in a

Transmutation Vessel. Sieg and Edgan had exerted considerable effort keeping the fish monsters away from the Gladere's corpse while Franz had butchered it, however. Moving the many casks of the refined product had been hard work, too.

With the Necklace's defeat, it had become possible to travel through the buildings from the west tower to the east one. Still, Mariela couldn't help but gape at how many barrels and bottles had been strewn about, mostly in the southeast tower. Had her master really drunk all of their contents?

Or could it be that Freyja had planned this…?

No, I gotta focus.

Mariela lightly shook her head to drive away her idle thoughts as she walked toward the door that led to the courtyard.

There was a dampness that seemed to fill even their lungs with water, and then there came a darkness that covered the world. The dreams felt like an abstract of this world to Mariela.

"Let's get started."

"Ya should be careful, too, Mariela. Let's go, Koo!"

"Rar!"

The raptor began to run, towing the wagon holding Franz and Yuric. The rest of the group took that as the signal to charge through the entrance.

"Right, take these, Sieg!"

"Okay, Donnino, bring them! Now, Edgan, get these to the other end!"

"Right! Leave it to me."

Donnino picked up the barrels and bottles that had been placed in the entrance hall and handed them off to Sieg. After accepting them, Sieg took in the situation, indicated to Edgan where to carry them, and handed them to him. After that, Edgan shouldered the containers with a "Hup, ho!" and took them where they needed to go.

Grandel, who couldn't carry anything heavier than an umbrella, was in charge of holding the door, and Mariela, possessed of even less fighting power, was responsible for cheering on Sieg at his side, one of the safest places to be.

Sieg used his bow to repel the inky memory stealers that seemed to ooze in from time to time. The haphazard way he pierced multiple monsters with single shots to look cool to Mariela, who was next to him, may have been overdoing it just a little.

"Phew, *pant*. Heeey, Sieg, wanna switch for a bit?"

The difference in the amount of exercise the two were getting—Sieg shooting a bow and Edgan running around the vast courtyard carrying barrels while avoiding black monsters—was excessive.

"You don't have any ranged attacks, right? Here, take this to the other side."

"You can do it, Edgan!"

"Leave it to me, Mariela!"

"I'd expect no less from you!" Sieg praised as he handed a barrel to his friend. Just what aspect of Edgan did he expect no less of? Was Sieg merely praising Edgan because he was useful in this moment? Edgan only realized as much after Yuric and the others had finished loading casks on the north side and returned after emptying the remaining contents to connect the spots where the barrels had been placed.

"Mr. Grandel, here, this is a cure potion that removes petrification. One for curse removal, too, just in case. After that, please use a high-grade cure potion on her."

"You have my gratitude. Saving the serpent who did as much for us seems only fair."

Mariela gave Grandel a potion to remove the lamia's petrification.

The snake monster had grown next to Grandel in this courtyard and had even fought alongside him. Her reason for coiling around and holding back the ebon raiders may have only been destiny or some manner of instinct, but Mariela and Grandel believed the lamia had also sought to help Grandel. She'd spent several days with him, after all.

The shadowy warriors had begun to struggle after noticing the presence of Mariela and the other humans. Many cracks were appearing in the petrified lamia's body, and they occasionally spread with creaking sounds and minute vibrations.

"You did very well."

As everyone stood ready to battle the ebon raiders after completing their preparations, Grandel expressed his gratitude to the lamia while sprinkling the high-grade cure potion over her. Immediately, blood began to circulate through the lamia's skin and change its color from cold stone to that of living flesh. The chips and fissures that had developed during the creature's time as a statue changed to lacerations, which then started bleeding as the petrification dissolved.

When Grandel applied a high-grade cure potion to heal those wounds, her skin became smooth on the spot, and the lamia took a breath—"Shaa…"—as light returned to her eyes and she gazed at Grandel.

So we didn't need a curse-removal potion after all…

The lamia's petrification was gone. The bound ebon raiders were probably rushing out even now. Amid such a tense situation, Mariela realized that a curse-removal potion hadn't been necessary.

There were two types of petrification: one where someone's condition was merely altered, and another where a curse turned them to stone. In the case of the former, it only took a high-grade cure potion to heal. However, lifting petrification inflicted by a curse required either a curse-removal potion or a similar ceremony.

Back when a basilisk had cursed Leonhardt, he'd nearly died because neither was available to him. Fortunately, Mariela's potion had saved him. In the Labyrinth City, which was the monsters' territory at the time, performing a ritual to excise the affliction wasn't possible, because such ceremonies required the spirits' power.

Except for one instance where Freyja burned and purified Robert's curse, rendering him unable to move, in a back alley of the Labyrinth City. Mariela already had the answer as to why her master had been able to do that.

I feel like the spirit of this place wouldn't just leave someone petrified.

That lake spirit didn't seem like they would ignore the maladies of others. Above all, it felt very unlikely that the monsters here would use curses at all.

When Mariela and the others had found their way to the marshland in the Fell Forest that connected to this world, the powerful-looking monster on the opposite shore had disappeared into the forest without attacking Mariela or the others. The creatures here would probably never contaminate that marsh, this world of water, or the lake spirit.

You could say the proof of such was the lamia silencing herself as soon as she noticed the spirit power dwelling within Sieg's

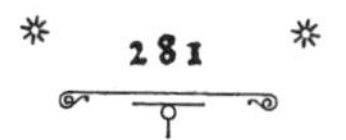

nocked arrow. She uncoiled herself from around the ebon raiders and glided as she retreated to a spot somewhat close to Grandel but more than far enough away from the shadowy warriors.

In a flash, Sieg fired a spirit arrow, and roars echoed throughout the courtyard.

Were the ebon raiders pleased with having found an enemy to fight, or were they screaming in pain and anger from the spirit arrow boring large holes into their torsos?

Either way, the shadowy things spread out like they were crumbling, and then they sprouted thornlike legs and spears and changed into the shapes of infantry or cavalry as they swayed and shook.

It's just like that nightmare...

The animals and spirits who'd witnessed that war may have considered that ancient conflict no different than this. There was no doubt the people who survived that battle had nightmares like this for the rest of their lives.

Perhaps the ebon raiders had been storing power while the lamia had held them, because they somehow swelled to the size of an army corps in an instant as they absorbed the inky memory stealers that cropped up here and there.

Even the spirit arrow Sieg fired hardly did any damage to them, perhaps because they were water entities, the predominant element in this place. All the wounds the projectile inflicted were engulfed, and no trace of them remained.

The human shapes that arose from the shadowy things were like a stampede overrunning a city, the speed of their proliferation was like some unknown monster, and the way they spread so much they couldn't be escaped from was like a surging curse.

To make matters worse, viscous memory thieves closed in on

Mariela and the others from the collapsed north side of the ramparts like an avalanche.

How could they stop something like this? Was there any way to turn such an overwhelming tide and purify the raiders?

"Now! Launch the fire!"

"Yup!"

At Sieg's signal, Edgan charged his dual swords with flame, and Sieg nocked a burning arrow. Yuric, Franz, Donnino, Grandel, and even Mariela hurled fire magic of various sizes at the trails of liquid they had drawn to connect the barrels and bottles they'd placed.

Mariela was the only one to use lifestyle magic to make a flame. Even throwing a lit stick would have been more efficient, but let's not dwell on that. She was giving it her best effort and didn't notice her own uselessness, and the other members weren't depending on the likes of Mariela's fire magic in the first place. Her participation mattered more than her tangible contribution.

The scattered paths of liquid ignited at the touch of flame, and the blaze spread toward the barrels.

Whale oil.

It had been extracted from the Gladere. Oil collected from whales was the most suitable kind for lamps. Before magical tool technology, lanterns lit without a supply of magical power were the norm, and whale oil, which could be acquired in large quantities compared with other fuel, was distributed far and wide in urban areas with large populations.

The ebon raiders flinched for an instant at the bright light that flared up like a torch, but they wavered in a crooked way, as though they were grinning, and immediately trampled the blaze as they began advancing on Mariela's group.

It was as if they were saying torches and lights that illuminated cities were nothing compared to the fierceness of the conflagration that would reduce such structures to nothing. The shadowy warriors stepped into the fire that dyed the surroundings red with no hesitation. And despite changing their course to get around the flames, the inky monsters didn't stop, either.

If it were mere whale oil, the blaze undoubtedly would have been snuffed.

However, this wasn't mere whale oil. Mariela and the others didn't spend the whole night whaling and refining for such a humdrum substance. The Gladere's oil was a special, rare type that burned for a long time at smaller quantities than the oil of normal whales. What's more, it stayed ignited for an even longer time at a low temperature if lit with a small amount of magical power, and for a short time at an extremely high temperature if set aflame with a large amount.

And when it came to fire…

Mariela forcefully seized the salamander, who had been, up until that moment, wrapped around her shoulders just like a scarf, and threw it at the barrels that had burst into flames.

"Raaawr?!"

The spirit must not have expected this turn of events, as both its eyes and its mouth opened wide as if to say, "Huh? Wait, here?!"

Facing the now airborne lizard, Mariela shouted with all her might, imbuing the cry with all her magical power. Any less wouldn't have reached Mariela's master, who was up ahead, through the Nexus that connected Mariela to the ley line.

"Come forth! Spirit of flames, Freyja!!!"

In that instant, a flame pillar enormous enough to blow away both the ebon raiders and the inky memory stealers erupted from the courtyard.

Addled from the loss of all her magical power, Mariela, who had escaped the flames as though a barrier protected her, saw the figure of her master, Freyja, standing within the blaze and heard her voice.

“*Fire!*”

“Master, stop saying that as your first line.”

In an instant, Freyja had burned both the shadowy soldiers and the viscous monsters to nothing with incredible firepower. Unfortunately, her entry line was so stupid that it could have reduced the minds of Mariela and the others to cinders.

“Maaan, that was amaaazing! I should have known the firepower from that Gladere’s high-class oil would be something else! And your reserves of magical power, Mariela. Aw man, suuuch strength! I never would’ve thought of that.”

“Aah geez, Master. Morning’ll be here soon, and the water, too, so we’re going to the temple right now!”

Freyja’s barrier protected Mariela and the others, so they didn’t feel the heat, but everything beyond was like a scene from hell.

What the heck is with this shield? A long time ago, my master said flames felt warm even without touching them directly because heat is transmitted by "conduction" and "radiation." This barrier is transparent, but I wonder if it cuts off things like radiation, too. Come to think of it, Transmutation Vessels don't make my hands get hot or cold even if I increase or decrease their temperatures. Could this be a type of Transmutation Vessel, too? No, that can't be...

Outside, Mariela and the others could hear cries that sounded something like "guuuh..." or "gaaah...," and the ebon raiders twisted their bodies as they burned in the blaze, but Mariela's thoughts had completely wandered off.

I wonder why my master is wearing clothes...

Mariela had been convinced the salamander was her master, but the possibility of Freyja appearing stark naked hadn't even occurred to her until the small lizard had instantaneously turned into a manifestation of her master clad in fluttering clothes.

The fact that Mariela had violently thrown Freyja proved that pupils truly were a product of their teachers.

Of course, even if she had appeared stark naked, this is Freyja we're talking about, so she probably would have given the same grandiose speech, and Mariela would have hastily made her put on clothes.

As Mariela was imagining Sieg pretending to hide his face as he peeked between his fingers with his Spirit Eye and Erotigan staring without even trying to disguise it, her master interrupted her lengthy train of thought.

"Mariela, when did you notice? I thought for sure I'd fool you if I took the form of your spirit friend."

"I thought something was off ever since the salamander

showed up without me calling it. When we first got here, it showed up seemingly all on its own. It also remained incarnated for way too long, no matter how I tried to justify it. But the point when I knew for sure was…that dream."

"Oopsiiie. You tried to summon it, huh? This place is the domain of the lake spirit, so ordinary fire spirits won't come here. You have to call them with an offering, or conjure a special one like me, the great Freyja. By the way, the real salamander went home, so there's no need to worry. Aah, I should've disappeared once or twice to really sell it. I mean, you were hardly surprised at all, huh?"

"It's because you're you. This isn't nearly as shocking as when I found out you couldn't make potions any better than mid-grade despite being my master."

Freyja talked Mariela's head off as if she was happy to use her mouth again after finally returning to human form, and Mariela pulled her along as she rushed for the water temple in the center of the courtyard.

"Ah, wait, wait. Those things'll come back if you don't properly burn them. We gotta torch them good before *that one regains sanity* and the place fills with water. Come, many many flames, come, many many flames… Oh right, they're already here. Hup. **Summon Fire Blast! Fire!**"

"What's with that half-baked chant…?"

With Mariela still perplexed, Freyja once again struck the shadowy soldiers with maximum hellfire, and the ebon figures that had been squirming in the large blaze were wholly burned away and turned into dust.

During the famine and the plague, Master burned every last one of the black monsters. Maybe the tower rooms with lit torches were safe because...

Mariela thought back on all the salamander's unnatural behavior ever since arriving in this strange place. Meanwhile, the ebon raiders, which had previously seemed an unstoppable force, were swallowed up in flame and reduced to ash.

"Hey, we gotta go right now; the water's coming."

Despite Mariela urging her to hurry up before, it was now Freyja, finished with her work, who turned to Sieg and the others and beckoned them to shake a leg.

The other members, including Sieg, hadn't anticipated this turn of events at all. They'd witnessed Freyja's appearance with mouths agape. At the fiery woman's instructions, however, they all regained their senses.

"Huh? Whaaa—?! Freyja?! Uh, but she was that salamander until just now..."

"Calm down, Edgan. This is normal."

"Huh? A lizard...in clothes... The thing that...licked...my cheek..."

"Don't think too hard about it. Let's go."

They needed to get going, but Edgan had been overwhelmed by confusion. Actually, you could say he was possessed of a very clear head at that moment. Despite the approaching danger, he managed to think about a lizard wearing clothes.

"So my master was originally a fire spirit. Even now, she somewhat resembles one, I guess," Mariela explained to the flummoxed Edgan. The man had been totally thrown for a loop. Freyja had been a lizard, totally not Edgan's type at all. But then she'd transformed into a beautiful woman, the perfect fit for him.

"Ummm, errr, uhhh. Ah, Edgan. That's right." As was quickly becoming tradition, Freyja seemed to have forgotten poor Edgan. Her golden eyes glittered as she searched the Akashic records for it, then she replied as if she'd recalled the man's name herself.

Sieg looked at Freyja first with his Spirit Eye, then covered it and used his normal one, over and over. Although he possessed the Spirit Eye, even he hadn't suspected Freyja's true nature. However, his time living with her had helped him develop a considerable tolerance to Freyja's antics. This left him with enough composure to lead Edgan as he followed after Mariela and the others.

As for Yuric and the rest, they didn't seem to understand the situation at all. Donnino removed his spectacles, wiped them off, and looked at Freyja again. Grandel was content with not understanding, and he simply turned toward the lamia and said good-bye to her. She responded with a menacing "Shaaa."

"Hoh-hoh, that's quite frigid of you. So are you the hot and cold type, then?" Grandel asked with a chuckle, although the lamia had never once shown a "hot" side. Well, perhaps she was doing so now, since she remained close to Grandel and neither attacked nor fled.

"Ra-rar! Rar!"

"H-hey, Koo, no jumping!"

Perhaps Koo the raptor thought he could also turn into a human, because he started jumping around on the spot, jostling the cart hitched to him. Yuric and Franz, who almost tumbled off, had to restrain him.

"Look ou—"

Sieg's excessively large rucksack, which had been placed in the raptor's wagon, also went flying, and Sieg caught it in a fluster right before it hit the ground.

Despite the red-hot hellfire still blazing outside the barrier, everyone was involved in their own personal chaos.

"Now then, it's time to give the solution to this riddle."

The one who put an end to the discord with a brief comment was the woman who'd started it in the first place, Freyja.

"Now, where should I start...? Heh-heh, you don't need to make that face. I won't dodge questions."

Freyja laughed at the rather exasperated Mariela, who stared wide-eyed at her master like she wouldn't look away even for a moment.

"Mariela, your eyes will dry out if you keep them open like that...," Sieg remarked. Mariela was staring at her master so much it caused him to worry.

In protest, Mariela muttered, "But...," as she looked down just a little.

Her master said, "Hey," and offered Mariela her hand with an expression like she was soothing an upset child. Mariela took Freyja's hand and at last blinked several times.

Freyja always came running when Mariela needed help, but she never spoke about herself. Not only that—she'd abruptly left for parts unknown. If Mariela took her eyes off Freyja again, she felt like the woman might really disappear for good this time. That was why Mariela stared as hard as she did. After Freyja's favorite pupil had followed her all the way here, however, she seemed inclined to explain things at last. Freyja tugged on Mariela's hand as she led the whole group straight toward the temple in the center of the courtyard.

04

"A long time ago, before humans created what you call countries, this place wasn't the Fell Forest, but a regular, plentiful wood."

The temple door, so gigantic you had to look up to see its peak, opened without a sound just from Freyja holding her hand out.

A sixteen-foot-wide hallway extended left and right past the entrance, and just beyond the doorway was a garden decorated with streams and flowering plants. Mariela surveyed the area and saw blue sky peeking out from overhead. When she wondered if they were outside and gave it another look, she noticed the faint outline of a domed ceiling at a height that was several stories tall. The azure above seemed to be a painting on the top of the atrium.

This temple had a symmetrical structure, and there were exits at both ends of the hallway the group now stood in. A splendid door was also visible on the opposite side of the garden, likely the heart of the temple.

The corridor's ceiling was about as high as that of a chamber or assembly hall, but as far as Mariela could tell from looking at the atrium's garden, there seemed to be an upper floor. All the many pillars supporting the high roof had been cut from huge rocks that sported natural bands of lateral color. This gradation resembled geological strata, and to Mariela, it seemed like the memory of the earth that stretched far below the Fell Forest.

A roughly waist-high wall separated the hallway everyone

was in from the indoor garden, and it looked like they could reach the door to the heart of the temple in the shortest amount of time by climbing over the barricade and crossing the garden. However, Mariela hesitated even to stretch her arm toward the picturesque landscape, let alone set foot inside it.

What a truly peaceful place.

This world of water in itself wasn't noisy, but even so, one undoubtedly felt the presence of monsters. Although this garden was a beautiful place where copious flowers bloomed, not a single leaf nor petal stirred, and Mariela could sense neither the chirping of birds nor the beating wings of butterflies.

This place lacked the smell of earth, the scent of greenery, and the sound of running water, so it seemed like an elaborate model or a pop-up picture book.

"This way," Freyja called to Mariela and the others, who beheld the incredible vista, and she began walking briskly down the corridor.

"Way back when, the marshland you guys found was a clear, beautiful lake. Its sublime elegance far surpassed this garden. When you saw it from far away, the water's surface reflected the surrounding woods like a mirror, and up close, it was so glassy you could see to the bottom. The sight of light shining on that lake was so divine that any flame would cower at its radiance."

Sieg, Yuric, and the others looked incredulous, unable to imagine the fantastical sight that Freyja described from the gloomy marshland they'd visited earlier, but Mariela had seen it within her master's dreams.

"A lake spirit who ruled over this ley line, the one of the Fell Forest, resided there. This was a very long time before the ley line of the Labyrinth City and its surroundings was ruled by Endalsia.

You probably know that the Fell Forest and the land around the Labyrinth City share the same ley line. Yet doesn't it strike you as odd that you can understand the language of the spirits in the Labyrinth City but not in the Fell Forest?"

Freyja's scarf fluttered as she strolled along, and the decorations on it rustled quietly. The accessory's golden color added a new hue to the bright garden they saw from the dim hallway and breathed life into the still world for just an instant.

Without stopping or waiting for an answer, Freyja continued.

"That's because even with the same ley line, the warden can differ from place to place. It's a common thing. Managing a vast range is tough for spirits—they're noncommittal beings to begin with. Back then, the lake spirit here had already gone completely to the monsters' side, and the humans' patron, Endalsia, took over managing things."

The information in Freyja's speech was so significant it would have put a complete end to the long-standing dispute between scholars in the imperial capital if they heard it. However, it was less impactful for those present, and they followed after Freyja one by one while surveying their surroundings with curiosity, as though they were on a sightseeing tour.

"Now that you mention it, when I was little, I thought it was strange that I could make potions in both the Fell Forest and the Kingdom of Endalsia even though the forest was the monsters' domain and the kingdom was the humans'..." Mariela, an alchemist, managed to follow Freyja's exposition.

"Ahh, Mariela, I think you did say something like that once. But you trusted me when I said it was because we were near the Kingdom of Endalsia. Thank goodness you were such an accepting child!"

Mariela had slightly mixed feelings in response to her laughing master, and she wasn't sure if she was being praised or mocked for having been so simpleminded. Wanting to get back to the original topic, she urged Freyja to continue. "And then?"

"This is a closed lake, so it isn't connected to any rivers. Well, it's more accurate to say the pool rests above a spot where underground water wells up. The river near the sandpit goes underground, right? This place is far downstream of that. That water vein bumps into a rock, causing part of it to gather in one spot. That sand filters the water, leaving it very clear. The underground stream is abundant. Spirits live in it, too. That's why this lake, which receives blessings from the forest, has never dried up. But since humans long ago didn't know how water veins flowed, people in those days saw this as a very mystical place that would purify anything."

Mariela recalled her first dream. In that vision, the people, still inexperienced, had relied on the small fire spirit to reach the lake so they could purify the famine.

"That's why they came here to exorcise the corruption, right?"

Freyja nodded at Mariela's question.

"Every time there was starvation, disease, or any other calamity, the humans passed through the forest to get to this lake and purify the corruption. It was thus that they survived."

After Freyja placed her hands on the door at the end of the hallway, she glanced back at the garden. Mariela also looked behind her and realized the beautiful landscape had transformed.

It wasn't a case of the seasons changing. Because the place that had been a beautiful garden had transformed into a deep, gloomy, yet magnificent forest reminiscent of Freyja's story just now.

"Now, in here."

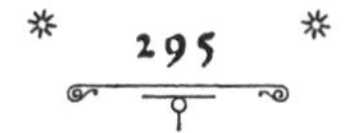

Beyond the door Freyja ushered everyone through was a huge library packed with books that reached the ceiling on the left and right walls. Overflowing shelves of incongruous sizes were lined up even in the center of the spacious hallway, and heaps of tomes and discarded volumes were also stacked on the floor.

"This is magnificent!"

Grandel, who had some appreciation for literature, opened his eyes wide at the incredible collection as he tugged at his mustache. Meanwhile, Edgan, who would fall asleep in three seconds if he opened a book that wasn't erotic, gave a big yawn at the smell of paper and ink blanketing the place, despite the fact that he wasn't reading anything.

Sieg surveyed at the interior of the room and then turned toward Mariela with a slightly dubious expression. Perhaps the girl had realized something, because she returned his glance with a slight nod.

"None of the humans in the imperial capital remember this lake anymore, but frequent visits to this place to purify corruption eventually formed a kind of path—the road the desecration streamed through. That's why the corruption generated in the vicinity of the imperial capital now flows here of its own accord even without anyone doing anything."

Freyja continued to talk as they passed through many rooms. They went through doors; they climbed up and down stairs. Every chamber was a library crammed with a massive quantity of books, and although Mariela was aware there were a lot, the letters were blurry or appeared to be volumes she was unfamiliar with no matter which one she examined. Try though she did, Mariela couldn't tell what kind of books they were.

"This lake was for sure more beautiful than any other, but it wasn't a miraculous place that could heal and purify. Yet corruption streamed in and accumulated more and more, and the pool became a mass of desecration. This forest, the creatures within it, and this land that harbored the lake all bore the corruption and became the Fell Forest."

"Then what of the lake spirit?!"

It was Franz who broke the astonished silence with his impatient question. He'd been feeling restless ever since he'd entered the temple.

"The spirit is fine. It wasn't a problem at all—neither to the spirit nor to the monsters. Whether there was corruption or not. You understand that, don't you?"

If it rains, the earth will be wet, and if it dries up, life will come to an end. Spirits simply accepted things as they were.

If there was corruption, they would simply take it in and slowly send it back to the ley line.

If the desecration became too much, monsters would be generated in large numbers and attack human settlements, but this wasn't so different from a plague or a famine.

"Even if they were engulfed by corrupted thoughts and lost their sanity, both the monsters and the spirits of the forest simply accepted it, just like an elderly person accepts their own death. From the perspective of the lake spirit, there was no problem."

Freyja halted and slowly turned to look back at Franz.

"Franz, your worries and resentment come from the human sense of values. Do you get what I'm saying? Spirits are like that by nature."

At the question, Franz bit his lip. Even if he understood in his head, he couldn't accept it. Freyja continued as though she sympathized with those feelings.

"But, you know, there was someone who hated that. 'I want to return you to when you were pure, clean, and corruption-free. I want you to be your true self and to exist with you.' There was someone who wished for such things."

Freyja spread both her hands.

She shone red as though illuminated by flames, and the others realized their surroundings had grown so dim, they couldn't see. Some of the nearby books remained faintly visible, but it was impossible to tell how large a place they were in now. Everyone had a feeling like they were in an endlessly vast chamber, even though they should have known otherwise.

"Now, Mariela, my pupil who reached this deep place in the Fell Forest. This is as far as I can guide you. This is the heart, the real situation. The truth is here, but to those who don't even understand what they don't know, it's like looking at a book in the darkness. They won't glean anything."

Freyja's hair began to billow, despite the lack of wind. It was reminiscent of burning fire.

"Now, tell me the answer. Where is this place? What is this world? Take everything you've learned and present the key to the exit."

Their surroundings were already pitch-dark, and Mariela couldn't see anyone, not even Sieg. All that remained was Freyja. The woman's eyes seemed to blaze in the darkness. Coupled with her slender pupils, they gave Freyja the countenance of an unfamiliar entity.

"It's pointless to try and scare me." Mariela, however, responded to her master as she usually did. "This place isn't our territory or anything. It's Akashic records, right?"

As though to show that Mariela's answer was correct, the

lamps in the black room lit up one after another, and the rest of the group, as well as the surrounding chamber, became visible again.

"Mariela?! This place?"

The first one to react to Mariela's response was Sieg, who had been dubiously surveying their surroundings since the moment he'd entered. To his Spirit Eye, the strange library had looked like far more than a mere collection of books.

"Probably, Sieg. I don't know how, and I can't be sure what sort of condition the lake spirit is in now, but if we're in the Akashic records, then the memories of the true heart of the spirit should be here. The recollections of the lake spirit, Lyro Paja, who rules over the Fell Forest's ley line."

The instant Mariela spoke that name, a gust of wind blew through the room.

She'd presented the key, and the door opened.

Book pages were ruffled and flipped, and many were torn out altogether.

It was like a sudden breeze had blown through trees and carried their leaves away.

Mariela and the others reflexively closed their eyes at the unexpected strong gale, and when they opened them again, they found themselves not in a library as they had been before, but a dense forest.

They were all familiar with the twisted trunks that writhed in pain and the gloomy leaves of the timber in the Fell Forest, but the trees here stretched straight up, seeking light, and those who beheld this place's verdant colors felt as though their hearts were being cleansed. Surely the Fell Forest had looked as marvelous as this before the corruption had altered it.

Stretching out before Mariela and the rest of the group was a placid, mystical lake.

Not a single ripple could be seen on the water's surface, as though the sudden breeze just now had been a lie. It reflected the surrounding greenery and made it seem like the forest continued below their feet.

The scene was far more normal and natural than the world of water or the Fell Forest, but it curiously felt more wondrous to Mariela and the others.

"There's no doubting it. This is the place I sought..."

"Franz!"

Yuric clung to Franz's arm as he began walking feebly toward the lake. Yuric's touch returned Franz to his senses, and he muttered, "Sorry, Yuric. I'm okay." However, he couldn't take his eyes from the lake. In particular, he was transfixed by the figure standing at its center.

"Lyro Paja. Long time no see," Freyja said to the figure standing still on the water's surface. It was the lake spirit, Lyro Paja. Freyja sounded both joyful and sad.

Freyja had her back to Mariela and the others, and only Lyro Paja could see her expression. Still, the sight of Freyja stretching out her arms on the bank of the lake tied Mariela's heart in knots.

—O flame, is it true you used the time that seemed so long to you for my sake?—

The spirit's voice was calm.

Like a waterfall threading its way down through rocks, their hair flowed and spread down toward the lake's surface and became one with the water, further enhancing their neutral features, which looked neither male nor female.

Perhaps because of the corruption, the being's hair was dyed a deep color like black or navy blue. It resembled a stream at night rather than the transparent hue Mariela had seen in her first dream. Mariela felt the hair made Lyro Paja seem somewhat like a living creature with body heat rather than like an uninteresting object resembling clear water.

Lyro Paja's eyes, which evoked a deep abyss Mariela felt like she was about to fall into, shifted from Freyja to Mariela, then Sieg, Franz, Edgan, and the others in turn.

—Did you purify my corruption along with these children of humanity? You've always been fond of people.—

"Yeah. My pupil and her buddies. You feel it, right? They're all very good boys and girls."

It was Freyja and Lyro Paja's first meeting in many years. The pair were in their own little world on the lakeshore.

It was a scene resembling fine glasswork that seemed like it could be broken simply by approaching it.

Unsurprisingly, the tone-deaf Edgan butted in even though the tension was so thick, you could cut it with a knife.

"Umm, is that gorgeous person there Freyja's girlfriend or something?"

For Erotigan, the most important pieces of information seemed to be Lyro Paja's gender and relationship with Freyja.

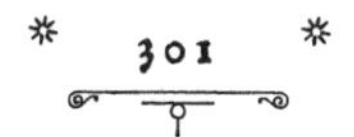

"Learn to read the room, Edgan."

"Ya really are the worst."

"Sometimes, in life, you must learn not to get involved."

As Sieg intervened in a fluster, Yuric shot Edgan an icy gaze, and Grandel delivered the coup de grâce. Freyja turned in Edgan's direction.

"By nature, spirits have no gender."

Her broad grin exemplified the master Mariela knew so well, and for some reason, this came as a relief to the young alchemist. Evidently, even Edgan's monkey attributes had their uses.

"It's not my intention to interrupt your reunion, but I would like an explanation, if possible. Even if you say this place is the Akashic records, that's not something those unfamiliar with the subject matter can follow."

Taking it as a blessing that the mood had changed, Franz continued the conversation. Every word was filled with respect for the lake spirit, Lyro Paja. Yuric looked up at Franz anxiously as she held his hand.

"That's easier said than done. Mm, Mariela, you explain it."

It was possible that Freyja wasn't aware of what Franz and the others didn't know. To her, both this place and the world where people lived were equally normal, and apparently, she couldn't guess the misgivings Franz and the others who had gotten mixed up with this place had.

Mariela, whom Freyja had delegated the response to, placed her forefinger on her chin and went "mmm" as she considered briefly before beginning her explanation on the Akashic records.

"Umm, the Akashic records is like a place where every piece of the world's information is recorded? It's said appraisal skills access this place."

"Information? Then are our bodies here not real?"

Franz let fly a pointed question at Mariela's incoherent detailing, and just as Mariela floundered to reply, Freyja cut in.

"This place isn't the Akashic records themselves, but rather a space with all kinds of information related to Lyro Paja over there that I anchored to the present world with my superior magic. You can think of it as one of the spaces between the material world and the spirit one. Your bodies are the real deal, and although its speed is different, time does flow here. I'm sleeping under the Magic Circle of Suspended Animation, so my body doesn't age. It's just my soul that's here."

Freyja's supplementary explanation was one that would help you understand further, until you thought about it carefully and then didn't comprehend at all. However, when she said, "Look, worlds are continuous even if they seem to be separate," those who had cocked their heads in befuddlement now nodded in understanding.

"Then what about the towers we woke up in? Things I was familiar with were scattered all about that place. It's not a big deal, but I can't say givin' forms to people's memories is the best hobby," Donnino remarked, offering his honest opinion.

When he joined up with Mariela and the others, Donnino had declined to have his memories peeped at, but he may have realized something when he investigated the tower he woke up in.

"Donnino, you're rather shy despite your appearance. Heh-heh, no need to glare at me like that. I wasn't expecting visitors, so the most reliable way to enable you all to be here was to send you to the memory towers. The Akashic records contain all information, but y'know, that doesn't mean beings like humans can comprehend it all. If dozens of people were speaking in foreign languages all at once, you wouldn't be able to understand them, right? It would sound no different than simple noise. If you get used to noise, it doesn't bother you. If your name is called, you can hear it even in the middle of such a cacophony. I connected you guys with things you're familiar with so you could remain here."

The towers, which equaled the number of humans present, functioned as anchors to this realm for Mariela and the others.

"Guuulp, gulp."

Koo, incapable of understanding speech, was doing as he pleased, drinking water from the lake. Seeing this, Freyja laughed and admitted, "Your memories weren't enough to make a tower from, so you gave me the most trouble."

"Do the black monsters steal memories because they're influenced by the nature of the Akashic records storing information...?" Sieg asked knowingly.

"The memories from the ones I defeated were released on the spot, and you'll get the memories you recovered back through dreams. I've got the ones that haven't returned to you yet, too, so don't worry," Freyja replied.

Was the reason they couldn't recover any memory stones when the salamander defeated black monsters because the recollections were immediately set free? And did Mariela see everyone's memories in her dreams only because her master in salamander form was with her? When they had no memory stones, she'd had visions of her master's past. Mariela had thought this to be because she was connected to the ley line, and thus her master, through her Nexus. After realizing how it worked, Mariela had seized the salamander and slept with it in her arms.

"Ya can just leave Edgan's memories the way they are."

"Hey, Yuric, losing my dazzling memories of love would be a loss for mankind!"

"Are you fine with Lady Frey seeing those memories, too?"

"Ha! Sieg, you're smart! ...Whoa, I just can't decide."

To Mariela, who'd glimpsed Edgan's tragic past, Yuric's icy words weren't as funny as they usually were. Edgan had remained unflapped and had whispered to Sieg, however, so perhaps Edgan's history held more than sad memories. Maybe it contained many inconsequential Edgan-esque ones, too.

At the conversation between Edgan and the others, Freyja and Lyro Paja looked at each other and smiled. They seemed to be enjoying Edgan Theater.

"Then, maybe, were the alchemist workshops on the first and second floors Libraries?"

Freyja nodded in response to Mariela's question.

"The Libraries are also part of the Akashic records. The world is overflowing with all kinds of knowledge, and you can get your hands on whatever you want to know to a certain extent, but there's no way to learn everything. If you're not aware there's a continent on the other side of the ocean, you'd never expect there's another kind of people who live there, or that they possess a different language and culture, right? What is way, way high up in the sky, and what kind of creatures live in the deep chasms of the sea? Human knowledge comprises only a tiny bit of the world, and they aren't even aware of how little it is. Libraries contain information restricted to matters of alchemy from that greater sea of knowledge, and they can be accessed through alchemy skills."

Mariela nodded in understanding at her master's explanation.

"In other words, the first and second floors of the outer wall were strongly influenced by the Libraries and old memories of the Fell Forest, while our memories strongly influenced the towers.

And that's why there were memories of famine and plague on the first and second floors...? Master, after you defeated the calamity monsters, you diligently burned them. And morning coming and the world filling with water after we defeated lots of those inky monsters was because the corruption decreased and Lyro Paja was returning to their true self, right?"

Freyja's mouth gaped at Mariela's deduction.

"...Look at how smart you've gotten, Mariela!!!"

Freyja's rude remark came out of her like she was squeezing it out. Even worse, everyone, even Sieg, nodded in agreement.

"You're so rude," Mariela replied, but the edges of her mouth turned up in the shape of a smile, revealing that she was quite pleased. "Hee-hee. I knew you didn't live all that time just to defeat the Labyrinth and help the Labyrinth City, Master. I don't know if you just happened to help the City because you had the chance or if it was a part of your plan, though. You know, for a long while, I was bothered by what you said when you left. You told me we'd meet again during my lifetime. Oh yeah, the alchemists in the Library. So that's why...?"

Mariela's words made her master awkwardly avert her gaze.

"It's fine. What you really planned was to come right before I died, right? If so, I don't have a problem with that. But, you know, you're so distant. I wanted to talk to you, and I wanted you to tell me about many more things. I don't want to hear you say we'll only see each other one more time. Don't you want to spend a bunch of time with me?"

"Yeah. I'm sorry, Mariela."

Mariela saw that Sieg and the others were confused, and she laughed.

"See, in the deepest part of the Labyrinth, you gave me all

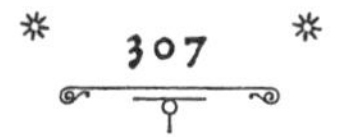

your alchemy experience, right, Master? Likewise, all your former pupils gave you theirs before they died. And I will, too."

"How did you...?"

There was only one answer.

"It was all to save the lake spirit, right, Master?" Mariela inquired. She wore a smile that suggested she didn't harbor the slightest bit of blame toward Freyja, who would someday take away her alchemy experience. Rather, Mariela seemed to accept the world as it was, like spirits did.

Once, the fire spirit who possessed a human heart had desperately sought a way to free the lake spirit.

However, beings who simply existed in the world and had no physical body didn't have the power to intervene in the world themselves and couldn't cause change. Even if that fire spirit stirred up an inferno and incinerated everything, she couldn't purify the lake spirit steeped in corruption, nor staunch the flow of desecration that still streamed into the being.

That's why she incarnated by feeding on the many humans who had been destroyed in her own blaze, and thus she gained a finite life in this world as a being who wasn't a spirit.

After acquiring a corporeal form, Freyja could no longer exist with flames, but she was able to borrow the power of the spirits

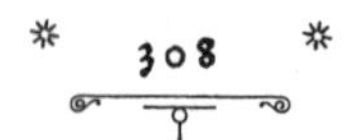

in exchange for offerings. Above all, she harbored her own will in her heart, acted of her own accord, and had the power to change the world. She wasn't a vague, never-ending being that came into existence and disappeared like a spirit. Freyja had form, a beginning and an end, a life and a death. She had watched things for a long time as a spirit, and she took in stride even the deluge of information known as the Akashic records, something a human wouldn't have been able to achieve at all. Piece by piece, Freyja was able to learn the process needed to make her wish come true.

It was incidental and splintered, like pieces of a poem engraved on leaves that sometimes lightly fluttered down before one's eyes, but Freyja had followed the bread crumbs up to this point.

Perhaps because she had started her existence as a spirit, her body aged far slower than those of humans, but even Freyja's life had a limit. That's why she separated from her body with a Magic Circle of Suspended Animation when she didn't need to be in the world of humans and worked hard to purify the corruption in this realm of the lake spirit.

Only when she understood her next step did she awaken and intervene with the physical world.

For example, taking in and raising Mariela as her pupil during the Kingdom of Endalsia's final years and waking up once again in the present world to guide Mariela and the others to the deepest part of the Labyrinth were likely necessary steps in the process of saving Lyro Paja.

"The Elixir is the ultimate secret medicine that can be made by removing the corruption from the core of a labyrinth. And I thought if I achieved that, I would discover how to purify this ley line, too, but..."

Freyja smiled sadly. The information she was able to acquire from the Akashic records wasn't complete, and it wasn't as though she could predict everything. It was like reading a story about saving Lyro Paja. She could only turn the pages one by one and put into practice what was written on them. Freyja didn't know the details of the tale, and she couldn't even turn to the next chapter on her own.

"I'd rather my alchemy experience was put to use before I die, and even now, I want to help as much as I can, but...I'm sorry. I made the Elixir by sending home the corruption in the ley line's core, but its destination was the ley line, so..." Mariela's words were hesitant.

It had merely been a case of transferring the corruption, not purifying it.

"No, that was enough. Thanks to you and the others coming and completely burning away those black monsters, most of the accumulated corruption has been cleansed. Right now, I'm able to manifest because you summoned me, but y'know, normally I'm in my soul form, and my body is in suspended animation, so I can only use power gained from the ley line through my Nexus. The power of a physical body really is something. The best I could do while incorporeal was to keep the corruption from increasing. No way could I have eased Lyro's burden this much like that. I was able to speak with Lyro again after a long time, too. Since the corruption gets in the way at night and the water gets in the way during the day, I was never able to get far on my own," Freyja said.

—I would also like to extend my gratitude for this brief rendezvous, pupil of Freyja.—

Did Lyro Paja really bear no grudge against humans despite it being their fault that the spirit had been tainted with corruption and had even lost their sanity?

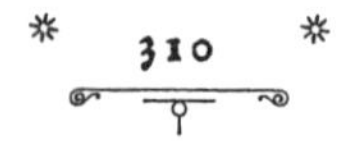

People hate people. Just as Lyro welcomed this concept that Mariela had seen in her dream, Lyro Paja accepted the human, Mariela, as Freyja's pupil.

"But won't new corruption keep flowing in?"

The spirit Freyja had fought so long to save resided in a mass of desecration. Thanks to Mariela's group defeating the memory stealers, a considerable amount of corruption had been purified, but as long as the spirit existed with that lake, they would be polluted again, and this place would probably sink into the darkness of night many times again.

In this realm, connected to information about Lyro Paja recorded in the Akashic records, no matter how many times the lake spirit lost their true character, they could regain it as long as the desecration was exorcised.

Thus, Freyja had lived for a long, long time to someday acquire a way to purify all the corruption and its source and save Lyro Paja.

"It seems this era wasn't the one where I'd find a way to free Lyro. Surely I'll find it someday, though. I'm sure of it. Don't make that face, Mariela. I've lived a long time, and that will continue. I might get to meet your children, grandchildren, or even their descendants. It's a lot of fun to have connections with people and watch the world change."

As long as Lyro Paja was a lake spirit bound to this ley line, they couldn't be saved.

At the very least, a way to do so didn't exist right now.

Burdened by this knowledge though she was, Freyja flashed her usual smile.

Although it was a grin Mariela was intimately familiar with, her heart ached, and she couldn't bear to gaze at Freyja's expression for long. She couldn't count how many ways her master had helped her, yet Mariela now found herself incapable of giving Freyja something in return. Even though Mariela had made the Elixir and was the most extraordinary alchemist, it still wasn't of any help. When Mariela thought about that, it quickly became too much to bear, and she hung her head and clenched her hands.

"...Now, it's about time for you to go home. Could I ask that Peeping Tom spirit over there to guide you all on your way? Come out, Illuminaria. I'll burn you, y'know? ...What? You have no power to manifest? Sieg, share a bit of your magical power."

Freyja's gaze shifted to the baggage Sieg carried on his back.

Immediately, everyone else turned to look at the large jar Sieg took out of his rucksack.

"Wha, Slaken?! How did he get so huge? And what's with that branch?!"

"Umm, Mariela. I missed my chance to explain before, but this is what happened..."

What occupied more than half of Sieg's rucksack was a jar containing the slime, which had swelled to about a hundred times its original size. Although it used to be an adorable Slime-in-a-Vial that could fit within two palms, it was so big now it required a barrel or a bathtub.

It was the second coming of the giant slime. A soft-bodied creature of this size honestly didn't seem cute at all.

And although the nucleus didn't seem to be injured, a sacred tree branch with two leaves was stuck into the top of it and shook back and forth.

As Sieg sent magical power from his Spirit Eye into the branch, he began his explanation, which smacked very slightly of an excuse, to the astonished Mariela.

"Mariela, both Slaken and Illuminaria are familiar with your magical power, right? So if you put in a branch of Illuminaria's like this..."

—It can move under my control!—

"Slaken spoke?! No, wait, that voice is...Illuminaria?!"

After receiving Mariela's magical power, a thumb-sized Illuminaria stood at the tip of the branch lodged in Slaken.

"Illuminaria guided me here."

—Because there are so many sacred trees in the Fell Forest! I figured out Mariela's location through the network they form. Amazing, right?—

"Um, so. I thought you might get mad at me, but there was something I wanted to get from the bottom of a lake in the Labyrinth... I consulted with Illuminaria, and she got it for me like this, but when she returned, Slaken's body was..."

—It was the first time it had been outside in forever, so it got excited. It went a liiittle wild and overate. Since it's got kraken in it, this creature can do quite a lot underwater.—

Shake, shake, shake.

The sacred tree branch stuck in Slaken shook proudly.

—Hey, don't shake. Stop it!—

Since Illuminaria was angry, it seemed to be Slaken who was shaking the twig. With Illuminaria's branch stuck in Slaken, could it be possible for them to strive for a mutual understanding?

"What?!"

The devastatingly serious atmosphere had relaxed for just a moment.

Mariela's voice, lower and unhappier than anyone had heard it before, echoed in the area.

The strength of the anger dwelling in that tone caused not

only Sieg, but Illuminaria to seize up, and even Slaken stopped moving its branch.

"Sieg, Illuminaria, aren't you being selfish? You took Slaken without telling anyone? And to the Labyrinth? It ate too much, and there were monsters there, right? You took it to such a dangerous place! Besides, Slaken has a Magic Circle of Subordination carved into its nucleus, so it'll die if I don't give it magical power! You know that, right?!"

Mariela was *furious.*

Sieg briefly glanced toward Mariela to offer an excuse, but when he saw her eyebrows curved upward in rage, he quickly shrank back.

For some reason, even Freyja, who was behind Mariela and shouldn't have been able to see her expression, straightened up and temporarily paused the conversation she'd been having.

Was the mild-mannered Mariela always this frightening?

Sieg had been born with the Spirit Eye and thus had been treated like a pampered prince during his upbringing, so not even his father had ever been this cross with him.

He'd suffered greatly under his master during his time as a debt laborer, but that was a different perspective. In this moment, Mariela might've been more terrifying than the wyvern that had taken Sieg's Spirit Eye.

"Are you gonna say something?!"

"Ah, I'm sorry!"

—I'm sorry!—

Shake, shake.

The two people(?) and one creature, no, one branch, all apologized in response to Mariela's rebuke.

"You're gonna get a major talking-to later… Slaken, have some

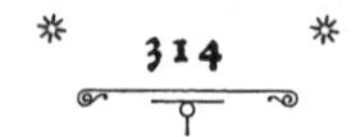

magical power. You're hungry, aren't you? I'll make sure these two go without dinner and Drops of Life-infused water for a little while. Ahhh, what should I do? You've gotten so big. I can't keep you in Sunlight's Canopy like this..."

Ignoring Sieg and Illuminaria, bowed at a right angle and frozen in apologetic postures at the words *go without dinner*, Mariela gave magical power to Slaken through the giant jar. Illuminaria and Sieg could siphon from the ley line or go out to eat, respectively, so they were capable of feeding themselves, but the meals they got from Mariela were that much more delicious.

Since Slaken madly shook the sacred tree branch lodged in him in joy, he probably was hungry after all. On a closer look, some Mariela memorabilia that Sieg had been carefully saving had accumulated undissolved at the bottom of the jar. Slaken had probably been receiving magical power from Mariela's discarded items and potions. Still, it couldn't have been all too much. Even though Slaken had eaten Sieg's Mariela memorabilia, this was karma for his mistakes, so Mariela ignored both them and him.

—Mariela. The nucleus stayed small because it didn't have enough magical power, so it should return to normal if you chop up the body.—

"'Chop up'? Will it be okay if we do something like that, Illuminaria?"

—Yeah. If you give it enough magical power, it won't die!—

Illuminaria, wanting to help Mariela and avoid the *going without dinner* punishment, hastily offered a solution.

"Really? Thank goodness."

Mariela had been furious for a moment, but Slaken was safe, and apparently, it could be returned to what it once was.

After hearing that, Mariela felt a little relieved, and she finally noticed the gazes of those around her and remembered her surroundings.

"I'm sorry, Master. I completely got lost in my own thing..."

"Naaah, you really impressed me, Maricla! I should expect no less from my pupil!"

—The flame had told me the children of humanity were fascinating, but this was undoubtedly an enjoyable time.—

The comments from the pair of spirits who turned toward Mariela when she apologized were like words of parting, and Mariela suddenly became aware of her own powerlessness.

As long as Lyro Paja is a spirit bound to this ley line, they can't be saved...

Illuminaria, who was relieved that Mariela's anger had been diverted, remained on the edge of the alchemist's peripheral vision. Although she was a sacred tree spirit who couldn't move from the place she was planted, she could remotely control a human pet at will and travel away from the tree.

If I don't give her a good scolding, she's liable to go out of her own accord again. Even my master used to be a fire spirit and always strolled around as she pleased. Selfish, irresponsible, incarnation and possession; her existence itself is careless. I wonder if that's what it is to be a spirit... Wait, huh?

Mariela looked at Slaken and Illuminaria, then Freyja and Lyro Paja.

"Lyro Paja, you live in this lake, but since you're a lake spirit, that means you're a water spirit, right?"

—Yes.—

At Lyro Paja's response, Mariela asked the question she had hit upon.

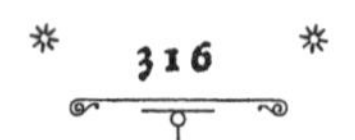

"Lyro Paja, is it possible for you to stop being a spirit?"

Asking something similar to a human would be absurd, but Mariela's master was person-like, and she was capable of something similar. Even Illuminaria, who was young by spirit standards, had come to a place like this despite being a sacred tree spirit. She'd used a branch as an intermediary to possess a slime.

What's more, Sieg's ancestor Endalsia, the queen of the forest spirits, had eventually become the warden of the ley line as a spirit, but she'd also produced a child with a human hunter. Surely, she had to have been something similar to a human during her time with her beloved.

"You know, spirits are pretty careless. I mean, their existence, the way they are."

—A careless...existence...—

As one might've expected, Lyro Paja was speechless at Mariela's frank words.

It was just by happenstance that the spirits around Mariela were oddballs. Not all of them were so eccentric after all.

"Well, you're close with Master. I wonder why you couldn't incarnate and move from this lake...?"

The corruption in the imperial capital streamed into this pool because a path for it had unknowingly been carved.

As long as Lyro Paja was a lake spirit bound to this ley line, they couldn't be saved.

But if Lyro Paja could leave this lake...

"!!! So that's how we do it!" Wondering why she hadn't thought of Mariela's solution herself, Freyja clapped her hands.

—I oversee this ley line, however...— Lyro Paja's response was more respectable. Apparently, not *all* spirits were that careless.

"The Labyrinth City doesn't currently have a warden, you

know? And my master seems like she was an incredible spirit, but did she oversee the imperial capital's ley line?"

"Nope. I was incredible, but managing a ley line is a bother, so I've never done it. The imperial capital seemed like it'd be just as annoying because it's packed with humans, and I wouldn't be able to stabilize it."

Freyja's answer was just about what Mariela predicted. She had a feeling there was some information mixed in that she shouldn't hear, but she let that pass and thought, *I knew it. My master would never do something that seemed so difficult.*

"Hey, there seem to be a lot of places without a warden nowadays."

—Mm, however…—

Lyro Paja had never considered giving up overseeing the ley line, and they didn't seem to be following Mariela's proposal.

"What would happen if you stopped being the ley line's warden? Everyone in the forest has taken on their share of the corruption, right?"

—The corruption flowing into the lake would coil up and most likely no longer diffuse evenly. Many monsters would arise from the pool of desecration, and a stampede may occur.—

"A stampede happened two hundred years ago even though you were here, didn't it?"

—Monsters will overflow if the corruption ever becomes too much, as well. Endalsia's actions led to a series of events that caused the negativity to grow too great to hold back.—

"So you're saying if there's no warden, the corruption will accumulate and cause frequent stampedes of a much smaller scale?"

—Indeed.—

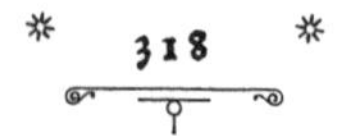

After listening to the conversation between Lyro Paja and Mariela, Sieg whispered to Edgan:

"If that's the case, I think the imperial capital and the Labyrinth City could both cope fine… What do you think, Edgan?"

"Mm? Well, it might be fine, no? Ever since the Labyrinth City became the humans' territory, Haage's lamented that we can't have the Orc Festival anymore. It might actually be a good thing…"

Lyro Paja showed concern toward the humans, but the subject of the spirit's fear was nothing more than an omen of a new festival for the present Labyrinth City. The people of the city had become a bit too robust.

Lyro Paja had an expression implying they couldn't comprehend the humans who, recalling the Orc Festival, exclaimed, "I hope tasty monsters come!" with delighted looks on their faces.

Confused, Lyro Paja murmured, —Festival?—

Freyja happily declared, "Booze!"

"Then, if we can manage the corruption, the spirits of this forest can take on the oversight of the ley line, right? That's how it is in the Labyrinth City. Illuminaria, there are a lot of sacred trees in the Fell Forest, right? You said you used them to find me. In that case, there must be tons of spirits like you, right?"

—Yeah. None of them are as powerful as Queen Endalsia, but in terms of sheer numbers, the place is full of them, and they grow along the ley line. All the forest children are easygoing, though. Their roots are connected to a spot deep in the ley line, so they can communicate even if they leave, and if there's no warden, they'd likely work hard to manage the ley line to keep themselves from withering.—

After hearing Illuminaria's response, Mariela turned to gaze at Lyro Paja. Her eyes made her look like she wanted to say something very badly.

A look could speak as well as mouths, and Mariela seemed to be conveying harsh remarks that she couldn't put into words. Something like "Taking on a responsibility so large all by yourself was never possible," or "It seems like things'll be fine even without you," or "How about learning from my master's example and living carelessly?"

"Lyro, come with me!"

Freyja's method of coercion was far less complicated. She splashed into the lake and opened her arms in Lyro Paja's direction.

—Frey… I…—

Freyja faced Lyro Paja straight on.

Lyro Paja looked down at the lake, then at the forest beyond, as though avoiding Freyja's gaze.

Although Mariela and the others couldn't see them, there were probably beasts and monsters in the forest, so many that the Fell Forest practically overflowed with them.

—I share the corruption with this forest and the monsters, and I cannot abandon them like Endalsia did.—

"So then just live in the forest. It's all right. I'll be fine in the woods. But how about you quit carrying this burden alone?"

Lyro Paja's choice differed from that of Endalsia, that spirit who once fell in love with a human hunter, decided to live with people, and isolated herself from the monsters. Lyro Paja had existed with corruption alongside the monsters of the Fell Forest for many years. As such, they couldn't give up everything for a single person, Freyja, who had spent so much time among humans.

Freyja, understanding as much, accepted Lyro Paja's choice as a matter of course.

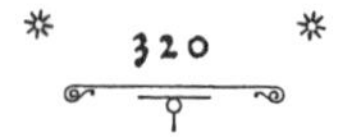

"I wonder why I never noticed. And here I've become so close to humans, got a ton of knowledge from the Akashic records, and was even called the Calamity Sage. Maybe I'm still a spirit at my core."

The flame neither faltered nor hesitated anymore.

"Lyro, I wanted to do something about you shouldering the corruption all by yourself, but I didn't think of your ruling over the ley line on your own as the problem. If a fire happened in the forest, the trees there would burn. It's a lot like that. I was convinced that things were static. Surely, the spirits living in this forest think the same way. You oversee the ley line, take the majority of the corruption that streams in, and purify the entire wood. Since it's been that way for such a long, long time, I thought it ever would be. You've always thought that way, too, even at the cost of your true character..."

Faster than Freyja could say "I'm sorry," Lyro Paja touched their right hand to Freyja's cheek.

—It seems the one who has lost their real self isn't me, but you.—

When Freyja laid her own hand over Lyro Paja's, ripples spread from where her fingers made contact. Even though Freyja had taken human shape, Lyro Paja's body was entirely water, and perhaps it felt like liquid as well.

Freyja's fingertips moved as though she were caressing the surface of a pond, and she formed words that sounded like sighs.

"Aah, I wish I could touch you, Lyro... More properly, that is. You don't have to become a human. You can live with the trees and the monsters in the Fell Forest forever. Everyone can do their part for the corruption and the ley line. It'll be all right. Monsters are really strong creatures, and the trees aren't weak saplings. It's already a magnificent forest. It will surely persist, even without you shouldering everything by yourself."

Freyja's golden eyes reflected Lyro Paja.

Her smiling face shone like her glittering golden eyes. It was reminiscent of the lit lamp the humans who feared the darkness held up a very, very long time ago, and it made Lyro Paja recall the day they first met—when Freyja was a tiny fire spirit.

Although she used to be such a small glow, now she sent light all the way to the deep, dark bottom of the water.

Mariela and the others gazed at Lyro Paja from behind Freyja. They resembled the humans who had crossed the forest many times to reach this lake, but they were far stronger, and they possessed the power to survive.

—......I suppose you're right. Perhaps they no longer need help.—

And thus, the lake spirit Lyro Paja decided to close the book on the current state of themself and the world.

"Are you *really* sure this kind of material is okay?"

—So much so that I consider it excessive for a temporary body.—

Mariela was a bit perplexed after Lyro Paja told her the substance to be used for their incarnation.

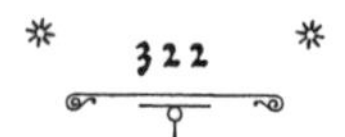

"Hey, when I decided I couldn't stay as a spirit if I wanted to help Lyro, I was born from ashes, you know? My body came together with a *rumble-rumble-rumble* feeling, so unsurprisingly, I was in a rush. I remember thinking I wanted to wear fluttery clothes and be pampered. As you can see, I wound up with a pretty nice form!"

—Apparently, when Queen Endalsia thought "I love you, I love you, I love you" toward the hunter, she'd become a human before she even knew what had happened. Well, we dwell in sacred trees, so in a way, sacred tree spirits start out incarnated.—

Freyja and Illuminaria gave rough accounts of their incarnation experiences as the former struck a swaying pose that was more octopus-like than sexy. They should have been very precious stories, but both were so disappointing, it was hard to choose which one was worse.

In particular, what was with this "nice form" of Freyja's? The pencil-shaped Mariela felt excessively irritated because her master was a beautiful woman with such a curvy body.

Mariela had thought Freyja to be a careless human, but she'd actually been irresponsible since the day she was born. The details of what led to her incarnation should have been quite serious, but Freyja kept to vagueness about her own desires, only saying things like "fluttery clothes" and "being pampered."

"Spirits really are reckless after all..."

Mariela threw a cold gaze at the strange creature she called her master as she turned toward Lyro Paja to prepare for their incarnation.

"Let's see, we should confirm the plan. First, I'll make a core and transfer some of Lyro Paja's existence and magical power into it. As long as Lyro Paja can adapt to the core, the body will be very accommodating, and then I'll chop off Slaken's oversized, sticky body and use that."

—Yes, that's right.—

"Lyro's a diligent being and finicky about incarnation specifications, too."

Freyja teased them as being choosy, but the material they'd settled upon was horrible. In the midst of what had shifted all at once into the usual, carefree atmosphere, Mariela was the only one who was diligently going over everything.

Lyro Paja had come from the center of the lake to the waterside, where Mariela and the others were. In front of the spirit, Franz fidgeted over and over again while Donnino and Grandel held him back. Yuric, who was restless with worrying over Franz, had seemingly gone soft in her animal taming skills, as she was desperately trying to bring back Koo, who'd begun happily chasing after small fish in the lake.

As for Sieg, the one who should have been the most reliable…

"Congratulations, Lady Frey. Lyro, I am Siegmund, a companion of Mariela's."

With a full business smile, he presented himself as an agreeable youth in the hope of scoring points with the being who might become Mariela's adoptive parent's spouse.

"Ummm, Lyro, are you Freyja's honey? Her hubby? Or, would the two of you hubba-hubba with me?!" Next to Sieg, Edgan was making his usual sort of fuss. He was using a lot of *H* words. Since spirits had no gender, Erotigan would have no issue if Lyro became a woman when they incarnated. In fact, Edgan endorsed it. The strange cry of "Become a woman, become a woman" in Mariela's ear was getting obnoxious.

So tiring and tedious.

It was just like the atmosphere at a school in the Labyrinth City right before one of Mariela's lessons began.

Smack! Mariela clapped her hands, then turned to her out-of-control companions and declared, "Attention, everyone! We're going to begin making the core now," just like when she began one of her classes.

"Let's see, Lyro Paja has been immersed in corruption for a long time, so wouldn't the spirit adapt better to their new form if I added just a tiny bit of the source of human sin when I make the core? I'm going to take just a little bit of everyone's memories."

"Source of sin…? By memories, do you mean the memory stones?" asked Franz, who had listened to Mariela's explanation the most earnestly. It might have been because of the instinct that compelled him to be useful to the water spirit.

—Indeed. The memories of your blood are particularly troublesome. If that quality is passed on to your descendants, it may cause trouble for me. There is Greed in those feelings.—

"I see… All right. I am grateful for your benevolence."

If Franz offered the memories of his blood, he would lose his longing impulses regarding the water spirit—the emotion that had sprung up from within Franz and roused him so. Although the feeling was extremely troublesome, it was also an important part of Franz. But after looking first at the water spirit, whom his blood sought, then at Yuric, who stood next to him with a worried look, Franz resolved himself to offer his memories.

"It's all right, Yuric. My future is mine to make. You'll be there to help me with it from time to time, too, won't you?"

"Of course, Franz!"

After happily nodding at Franz's decision, Yuric turned a gaze of gratitude and just a little anger toward Lyro Paja, who was taking away Franz's memories.

"What should I offer?"

Don't be so angry, handler of beasts. I shall take a little of the Wrath overflowing from your small body. No matter how much you hate them, the children of humanity must live among one another. It would be better if you loved humans a little more.—

As though to interrupt Lyro Paja to keep the spirit from saying "And not just the man next to you," Yuric replied in a fluster, "Okay!"

"Then, what shall we surrender to you?" Grandel inquired.

"Could you do it without needless lecturing?" Donnino added.

—Envy and Sloth.—

Lyro Paja requested Envy from the mild-mannered gentleman Grandel and Sloth from the diligent Donnino, who maintained the Black Iron Freight Corps's armored carriages.

They hadn't identified Donnino's tower, but expensive-looking bottles of alcohol and perfume containing colored water and cheap aromas, respectively, as well as worn-out silverware and clothing, had been in Grandel's tower. Yuric had commented, "Show-off" upon beholding it all.

Mariela wore some incomprehensible expression as she looked at Grandel, which caused just a bit of discomfort to show on his face.

"My family has been a distinguished one of shield knights for generations. Throughout the years, we had all inherited superior shield skills. However, ever since my great-grandfather's time, the children born to my family have always been frail. No matter how excellent one's skills are, you cannot do as much as you'd like with a body like this. It took me a very long time to realize that things such as bloodlines, honor, and prestige were foolish."

In his usual fashion, Grandel chuckled as he tugged at his handlebar mustache.

"That's like me. Have you ever heard of a 'Jack of all trades, master of none'? I can't go beyond what ordinary people can do and become top-notch at something. Aah, it's a crushing feeling, Sloth. But I understood. I couldn't perfect anything for the life of me." Donnino scratched at his head before continuing, "If somethin' like that is fine with you, by all means, take it."

Catching a glimpse of the trauma of an older, more experienced person was somehow unsettling.

The one who destroyed the suddenly heavy atmosphere was, as expected, Edgan.

"I'll give you my overflowing love!"

—Yes, I shall receive Lust from you.—

"Huh?! Lust?!"

"That makes sense," Mariela replied in agreement.

"He's the worst," Yuric judged, harsh as ever.

"That's great, Edgan! Someone finally accepted your affections!" As if to say it didn't matter what happened afterward as long as the situation at hand was settled, Sieg gave the sort of equivocal coaxing he often did when Edgan was around. It hardly seemed like the remarks of a true friend. Perhaps some of Sieg's bad habits from his younger days had inconveniently surfaced for a fleeting moment.

And to Sieg, Lyro Paja said...

—Sieg, was it? I shall receive Pride from you.—

"Ha-ha-ha—pr—ha-ha-ha—ide! Ha-ha-ha! Sieg, he said you're arrogant. You're so important! The great Sieg! How's that treat you?"

"Shut up, Erotigan."

Sieg cast his eyes downward and bit his lip at Edgan's roars of laughter. Even Mariela said to Sieg, "It wasn't nice to take Slaken out on your own," leaving the poor man at a loss for words.

"I'm the last one. What should I give you?" Mariela inquired.

—Gluttony.—

"Bwah?!"

As the last one of the group, Mariela gave her memory of her irresistible "snack meals"—Gluttony—and all seven human sin sources were assembled. Lyro Paja easily removed the memory stones from Mariela and the others by touching their foreheads. The spirit's cool fingertips felt like drops of water trickling down their brows. Like a bead of liquid, each memory rolled down its respective person's forehead and fell into its owner's hands as a stone.

"Because this place is the Akashic records, taking memories in and out is simple. Even though Lyro said they were receiving your memories, that doesn't mean they'll be entirely gone, like what happened with the black monsters. They'll still remain as information. The change should be negligible in your daily life."

Just like Freyja explained it, Mariela didn't forget the fact that she'd greedily indulged in snacks while Sieg and the others were absent, even after her memories of Gluttony were drawn out of her. However, the particulars of the sweets she'd scarfed down became vague, and Mariela had trouble recalling their taste. It was as though the recollection of that time had become somewhat ambiguous and changed into someone else's, leaving Mariela to guess at how she felt back then.

Even after Mariela safely returned home, she would probably

want to eat sweets, but maybe in the future, she wouldn't devour pastries like she was filling the holes in her heart.

Mariela had a somewhat ominous feeling.

Everyone probably had similar sentiments. They all gazed keenly at their memory stones.

"Say, Master. These are bad human memories, right? If I use things like that to make the core, will Lyro Paja be okay? You said Lyro Paja will stay in the Fell Forest, but won't they despise us humans? And Lyro Paja also said it would be a 'temporary body.' In other words, they won't last long with this core, right?" Mariela asked Freyja, with the Gluttony memory in her hand.

Lyro Paja had suffered for a long time because of human corruption. Wanting the spirit to be fond of humans was presumptuous, but if possible, Mariela didn't want Lyro Paja to hate them. And the spirit's expression, *temporary body*, made Mariela feel uneasy.

"The memories from all of you will be fine. These are recollections of wrongdoing, but y'know, they're not entirely corrupt. They also contain joy, sorrow, and feelings of consideration for others. Those memories hold the good and bad points of humanity, so the temporary body will still last a long time. I'm positive it'll do the trick."

Freyja answered Mariela's concerns with a grin. She was full of confidence.

I can't help feeling unsure...

Previously, Mariela would have taken her master's words at face value and believed that pure smile. However, the Mariela who had created the Elixir in the deepest part of the Labyrinth and had become the ultimate alchemist would not be deceived.

"Master, you said 'Mariela will be able to make the Elixir' similarly, but if you remember, I was just short on experience. What would've happened if I hadn't had the ley-line shard Lynx gave me...?"

"Well, that, uh, was part of the final miracle..."

"You don't know, do you? What I mean is, it's better to do things properly so you'll be fine even without a miracle. Lyro Paja is finally going to incarnate, but what would you do if they became an enemy of the humans? Lyro Paja is close to monsters, while you're similar to humans, right? Do you want a huge battle to happen between you?! If so, that would cause a new crisis in the Labyrinth City, wouldn't it?! We can't take that chance!"

"Guh... I'm lost for words."

"And yet you said that aloud. Really, Master!"

Somehow, Mariela was talking down to Freyja. Her attack power exceeded what had been her greatest offensive skill up to that point, the "No Dinner for You!" maneuver.

With this, the pampered child Sieg would probably have to prepare himself to be dominated by Mariela for the rest of his life. He didn't realize it himself, but he'd already become a perfect doormat.

—There is truth to your pupil's words. It would probably be best to add some sort of goodness to the core.—

Mariela nodded at the prudent Lyro Paja's words and thought briefly about what would be suitable.

"Something good... Something good..." Mariela looked around the area.

Freyja and Illuminaria, filled with confidence in their own merits, were looking over at Mariela as they chuckled among themselves. For better or worse, humans had been too much of a bad influence on those two, and they were quite likely to have taken on bad habits. Even by this point, they'd both amassed the quirks of various overly eccentric characters. The final piece probably needed to be something purer.

At first, the plan had been to create a core by adding memories of wrongdoing from Mariela and the others to a ley-line shard the size of a fist that had formed at the bottom of this lake. Mariela could feel a strong force from the ley-line shard, though not as much as from the Core of the Labyrinth, as well as the presence of water.

A ley-line shard was a lump of energy, an object that disappeared once it was used up.

Even the memories of Mariela and the others that would be added to it took the shape of stones in this world, but they were formless by nature. After Lyro Paja incarnated, the spirit would probably take in energy through meals, but was it really okay to have a core made of things that were unreliable as physical substances?

As if that wasn't enough, Mariela had a hunch the properties of a ley line with the presence of water and those of the group's memories differed. Could there be something with a more reliable existence that could adapt to both liquid and Mariela's group and also possessed powerful innate goodness…?

I feel like…there's gotta be something…

Mariela's waist pouch rustled as she rummaged through it.

What rolled out from the bottom of the satchel she always wore was a pale, transparent, wondrous stone that emitted light like the moon's.

"I wonder if we could use this?"

"Is that a mermaid's tear, Mariela?! That's such a high-grade item!"

—Moreover, it is filled with feelings of gratitude. A rare object, indeed.—

Freyja and Lyro Paja were astonished at the marvelous stone Mariela had produced.

The tears mermaids shed changed into stones. That legend was true, and very few of these scarce, valuable jewels were circulated in the world. The only way to obtain one was to either find it washed up on a beach by chance or to harvest it from a captured mermaid. In the latter case, it was easy to imagine what the apprehended mermaid went through. For that reason, mermaids' existence had become half legend, and when a certain quantity of mermaid's tears appeared on the market, it was whispered that the creatures were real.

Mariela had met one such mermaid before.

That was around the time when the Labyrinth Suppression Forces had just subjugated the Sea-Floating Pillar. Mariela and the Black Iron Freight Corps were invited to the beach cavern on the Labyrinth's fifty-fourth stratum.

Mariela had gone into the sea while Sieg and Lynx, tired from their fun, were asleep. What awaited her at the place she floated to as though invited was an injured mermaid who couldn't return home.

After Mariela had healed the mermaid's wounds with a potion, the creature returned to the sea, but afterward, Mariela had discovered a single mermaid's tear in her pouch.

It was a token of thanks.

Mermaids weren't monsters, but people in a different form. Because they were hunted for their tears, Mariela felt sorry for them, and thus never told Sieg about her encounter with one mermaid. However, this seemed as good a time as any to make use of the tear.

"Then it's an item that's inherently good, compatible with the water spirit Lyro, and filled with gratitude."

—I have no objection to using it as a core, but it has high worth to humans, too, does it not?—

If it was suitable for Lyro Paja...

"There's no reason for me to keep it." Mariela blew on the mermaid's tear and wiped it with a hand towel. Since she'd left it in her pouch, there was dust and dirt on it. The jewel was undoubtedly worth a small fortune. Was it really all right for this girl to be treating it so mundanely?

Mariela's efforts somehow made the little object shine like a pearl again in no time. Everyone was in agreement, and the tear was chosen as the core's final piece.

"Well then, first, the mermaid's tear and the ley-line shard..."

Just by bringing the extra-large ley-line shard Lyro Paja gave Mariela near the small mermaid's tear, the latter sucked up the former. Items belonging to the same water element seemed to be extremely compatible. The mermaid's tear, no bigger than the tip of one's finger, swelled to the size of a plum after absorbing the ley-line core, and it changed from the color of the moon to a blue reminiscent of a deep body of water. Most likely, no one would have been able to guess from its soft appearance—like liquid wrapped in a transparent membrane—that it had once been a mermaid's tear.

Next was adding the memories from Mariela and the other humans. Although not as compatible as the ley-line shard and the mermaid's tear had been, Mariela could sense that the memory of Greed from Franz's blood was strongly drawn to the powerful presence of water.

While everyone was quietly gazing at the blue core in Mariela's hand, Mariela brought the Greed recollection close to it.

"The first one'll be the hardest, but y'know, if the memory is drawn to it this much, the rest'll probably go smoothly." Just as Freyja said, when the powerful desire for the water spirit Franz had inherited from his forebears touched the blue core possessing the heart of water, it instantly dissolved and mixed into it.

"Next, Wrath."

The memory of Yuric, who preferred beasts over humans, wasn't bad in terms of compatibility. She relaxed around Franz more than anyone else, and because his memory had blended in first, hers was able to mix in smoothly as well.

"This's going better than I thought. Now that we've made it this far, the rest should be simple," Freyja declared. She was right. The memory stones of Envy, Sloth, Lust, and Pride melted as if they were following the connections between the people. With the final addition of Mariela's Gluttony memory, Lyro Paja's new core was complete.

—Ahh, it has turned out well. Now I will surely be able to get along with humans. I am grateful.—

After accepting the completed core, Lyro Paja swallowed it. Immediately, the spirit's current form began to break down. The transformation started from Lyro Paja's head, as though matching the core's path from mouth to stomach, and the spirit returned to the water.

"Lyro..."

The core fell onto the lakeshore where Lyro Paja had just stood. Freyja picked it up and gently placed it on top of the portion of Slaken's sticky body that had been cut off earlier.

The shaking of the viscous material, centered on the core, was like the surface of a pond quivering, and the core began to sink into it. After it reached the very center, both the body and the core rose up like a geyser, changing shape before everyone's eyes. The mass took the form of Lyro Paja, who had just been standing on the lake not a few moments earlier.

"Lyro! Ahh, you finally incarnated!"

Lyro Paja accepted Freyja's embrace.

The spirit was no longer in an indefinite frame that looked like it would melt away.

"Ahh, Frey. I feel so impaired by how limited this physical body is, yet I can move freely in it."

Freyja was the first person Lyro Paja touched and held close, and Mariela was overjoyed.

It was a touching sight. So much so that it seemed like Mariela might get teary-eyed.

How could the mystical sight of an incarnation and the fact that a fire spirit and water spirit could at last hold each other after so long not be moving?

Mariela's eyes reflected the beautiful pool deep in the forest and the two human figures holding each other tight amid that scenery.

If this wasn't beautiful, nothing was.

If it hadn't been for the background noise of the perverted monkey thoughtlessly chanting, "Become a woman, become a woman," there's no doubt it would have been truly perfect.

"Edgan handed over his Lust memory, but he seems exactly the same..."

"I'm not gonna lose my identity after something like that!" Edgan paid no heed to the icy looks he was getting from Mariela and the others. Perhaps one should have expected as much from a man who'd overcome many cold places like the stratum of ice and snow and the Ahriman Springs in winter.

"It seems your memory was rejected. 'That much isn't needed.' Edgan, what do you think about going to search for an identity somewhere else?" Sieg's comment was rather direct. He refused to say something equivocal like "That's our Edgan! People who don't doubt themselves are popular!" as he usually did.

Although Sieg still relied on others to attain his goals, his arrogance had evidently quieted down, and he'd become somewhat of a gentleman.

"Well? Well? Lyro Paja properly turned into a woman, right?! Lyro Paja!!!"

"H-hey, Edgan, read the room a little!"

Completely ignoring Sieg's attempt to hold him back, Edgan went to confirm Lyro Paja's gender, and what awaited him was...

Lyro Paja gazed at Edgan, who was fixated on sex, with extreme curiosity and gave a rather bland reply. "Slimes are agender. I am neither one."

How exactly was one to behave in this situation? Edgan's pondering was easy to see through. Sieg clapped him on the shoulder and shook his head.

"Lay off this unsightly behavior, Edgan."

"Guh!"

Siegmund had scored a critical hit. That much was due course for a bow user. His shot had been ruthlessly trained on Edgan's weak spot.

However, Edgan also had considerable defensive power, and he moved to counterattack.

"What about you, Sieg? Well? You're a grown man who removed the obstacles in your way, yet making that final leap still seems too much for you, huh? You're a master of ranged combat, right? Why not take the castle in one shot? I mean, why did you take Slaken out? Are you still ignoring what's important?"

"Agh. You say that, but there are too many people around in Sunlight's Canopy! How can I close the emotional gap when there's never a chance?!"

"Create your own opportunity!"

Dual wielders were quite troublesome. At the sudden ferocious rush, Sieg showered Edgan with shots.

It was a violent exchange of verbal blows, but the pair also seemed like close friends to onlookers.

Sieg and Edgan look like they're having fun.

As Mariela gently squeezed the soft Slaken, who had reverted to the size of her palm, she turned her gaze back to Lyro Paja and Freyja. She saw the incarnated former-spirit duo flirting as they sought physical contact. Nearby, even the usually reserved Yuric was conversing with Franz with more intimacy than usual.

"Franz, are you okay?"

"Sorry for worrying you."

The old man duo with no partners, Grandel and Donnino, were completely prepared to return home and had begun to search the area for something to take back with them from this mysterious world.

"...Wanna go home soon, Slaken?"

Mariela suggested heading back not to Sieg, but to Slaken.

Curiously, Mariela felt exhausted. She had initially run away from home because Sieg had thrown Slaken away. Of course, taking Slaken out on his own was probably enough of a reason to get angry, but since the creature was unharmed, Mariela wasn't mad enough not to go back to Sunlight's Canopy. In addition, finding her master was a better than expected level of achievement, worthy of a gold star if Mariela were a student.

"Next time we have a fight, Sieg, you can be the one who leaves!"

Mariela, whose self-confidence had increased after a real sense of personal growth, clenched her small fist.

She didn't look mighty at all, but her will undeniably was.

Freyja was in her own little world with the newly incarnated Lyro Paja, and Mariela felt very uncomfortable with how many people were present. It seemed that in the future, at least for a while, it would be better to drive out Sieg than for Mariela to run back to her master when she and Sieg fought.

After returning Slaken to its jar, Mariela said, "Illuminaria, please show us the way home," and fastened the bag with the giant jar inside to Koo's back.

"Wait, Mariela. At least let me explain. I don't want things to end like this," Sieg pleaded as he ran over. There was a little earnestness in his expression.

Mariela was already quickly preparing to make the return trip on her own. She could easily see through Sieg's outward facade, but this time she sensed he had made up his mind about something. Apparently, he'd talked with Edgan and come to a decision.

"What, Sieg? Even if you apologize, you're still going without dinner, you know?"

Despite Sieg's appeal, Mariela kept him in check by implying she didn't want to forgive him for taking Slaken out. She'd only recently realized that Sieg behaved like a spoiled child if he was pampered. When push came to shove, she needed to be strict with him.

Although Sieg groaned at Mariela's cold treatment, he didn't falter. Instead, he got down on one knee in front of Mariela and dug through his pocket for something. "I had Slaken search for this blue stone at the bottom of the lake in the Labyrinth. I… I hope you'll accept it," he admitted. Sieg was offering Mariela a ring with a blue jewel the same color as his left eye.

"Sieg's finally doing it…!!!" While no one said this aloud, it was obvious that everyone was thinking as much.

With this, the former-spirit duo and Yuric and Franz, who were all busy flirting, couldn't help but stop and watch with intense interest. Admittedly, Sieg's proposal came without any lead-up, but since the other party was Mariela, something like this might've been perfect.

Mariela was an alchemist who really did rank practicality above aesthetics and food above romance. Faced with this ring, however, the girl looked taken aback. She'd expressly lost her memory of her excessive appetite. It sure would have been nice if her interest in love had been awakened in exchange.

"What…? Um, Sieg, thank you? It's a super pretty ring… But it's not my birthday, so what's it for?"

"?!!"

Mariela stared at the trinket in her hand with confusion, and Sieg was struck silent at the reaction.

And Freyja stole up from behind unnoticed.

"Didn't you know, Sieg? The custom of giving a ring only started about a hundred years ago."

"!!!"

At Freyja's words, which she delivered with a huge smile, the crestfallen Sieg fell onto his hands and knees.

A hundred years ago... Mariela went into suspended animation two hundred years ago, so does she not know the significance of this gesture...?

"This is what happens when you think you can just wing it and expect it'll turn out fine, Master Siiieg!" The way Edgan made fun of Sieg while looking extremely delighted was detestable.

"Well then, shall we head for home?"

"Yeah."

"This whole adventure's been a real hoot, know what I mean?"

Before Sieg could explain the importance of the ring, Mariela gave the order to withdraw, and everyone began to prepare for the trip back to the Labyrinth City.

Sieg's do-or-die event had turned into a mere present-giving ceremony.

"When we get back... When we get back, I'll do it properly this time, so..."

Ignoring Sieg, who was grumbling quietly to himself, everyone else started walking.

"Sieg, you're gonna get left behind! Hurry up, this way!"

Mariela waved to him with an impatient expression.

Although Mariela surely didn't know its significance, the ring the color of Sieg's eye had wound up on the fourth finger of her left hand before he realized it.

EPILOGUE

People, Monsters, and Spirits

"After the spirit lake became a mere pool, the Fell Forest grew just a bit more unstable than it had been before, and sometimes monsters appeared en masse. However, every time this happened, the nearby humans, who'd grown quite strong in recent years, took this as a time for profit and rose up to drive away the rampaging creatures. In a way, both people and monsters were able to live happily.

"How much time has passed since that last adventure?

"A lone youth sped out of the Labyrinth City's gate again today.

"Bow in hand, this child, an alchemist with a Spirit Eye, worked hard to gather materials, as he did every day.

"Thanks to his hunting skills—teachings that had been passed down for generations—and his knowledge of alchemy, he was able to travel deep into the Fell Forest to gather valuable components. His companions were a small salamander and a spirit who dwelled in the twig of a sacred tree. They were a bit mischievous, but the youth was sure to enjoy many adventures with his trustworthy companions in the days to come."

"Is...is that...the predetermined future written in the Akashic records?! That kid is mine and Mariela's...?"

"Sooo, how about it? If I have some booze, I might remember."

"Sieg, no daytime drinking! And...Master, why are you here

in Sunlight's Canopy? Oh, Lyro Paja, please make yourself at home."

Not much time had passed since the spirit lake incident, and Mariela, who had finished the preparations for lunch, looked back at the dining table where the two former spirits were nonchalantly mingling with Sieg, who was setting the table, and the guards.

During lunchtime at Sunlight's Canopy, regulars of the shop and soldiers who protected the city came to the kitchen in turns and enjoyed proper meals, so a little fluctuation in the number of people was nothing unusual. However, the pair of former spirits blended in so well that Mariela reflexively did a double take.

Sieg didn't know whether the story Freyja told him was a fib or not. She was scheming to get Sieg to bust out some booze during midday. Meanwhile, Lyro Paja looked around the inside of the shop with curiosity.

Lyro Paja was now a being similar to a monster with a slime as their base, but that didn't mean their skin was transparent. Other than the creature's pale skin and their hair being too long, Lyro Paja's outward appearance wasn't terribly different from that of a human, and the spirit seemed like they could pass for an unusual demi-human.

After returning from the spirit lake's realm, Freyja and Lyro Paja didn't go back to the Labyrinth City with Mariela and the others.

"I do not plan to carry the burden alone, but I cannot bring myself to be the only one to escape the corruption. Moreover, this body was created from a slime. If I had to pick a side, I'd say I'm closer to a monster. Thanks to this core created from all of your memories, I was able to experience the feelings of madness and love behind your desires, as well as good intentions and gratitude. However, I believe if I remain in your company overlong, I'll be engulfed in corruption. A human city is not appropriate for me. Frey's pupil and comrades, I will be watching over you from the abyss in the Fell Forest. If fate wills it, we shall meet again."

"In other words, good job, Mariela. Come pay us a visit soon!"

Monsters couldn't coexist with humans. That was the way of things, and Mariela had expected the diligent Lyro Paja to go deep into the Fell Forest and her careless master to follow after them as she waved, but…

"Master, this visit is way too soon… Is Lyro Paja okay in a place full of humans like this? Won't they want to attack us?"

What about the corruption? Would Lyro Paja turn into a monster and be unable to resist attacking Mariela and the others?

Mariela was worried, and to her, Lyro Paja looked vaguely restless and fidgety.

"The truth is, I've adapted very well to this body. Not only because of the memories and ley-line shard, but also because of the water-aligned physical object known as a mermaid's tear that you added to the core."

"I'm…glad?" Although Mariela thought the appearance of Lyro Paja fidgeting and talking was strange, she made interjections to show she was paying attention.

"And, you know, this body once belonged to your subservient monster called Slaken, yes? It has a habit from that time, or perhaps you could say a desire…"

"Okay…"

Fidget-fidget-fidget, fidget-fidget-fidget.

"Could you give me water with magical power in it?!" After acting suspiciously for a while, Lyro Paja at last blurted out what they wanted from Mariela.

"Sure?!"

Had the mystical, magnificent lake spirit Lyro Paja always been like this? Or could they have inherited Mariela's Gluttony memory and become a complete gourmand?

Lyro Paja drained a full bucket of water that Mariela infused with plenty of magical power. Next to them, Freyja, who had successfully cajoled Sieg, was gulping down alcohol.

"Ahhh! That's the stuff."

"Ahhh! I feel rejuvenated."

The two former spirits' shamefulness stuck out all the more due to how beautiful they were. Although fire and water were conflicting elements, the pair looked remarkably similar now.

"Man, there's no booze in the Fell Forest. And neither Lyro nor I can cook, so I don't get to eat anything good. Lyro's a slime and seems to be fine with anything, though."

"I am not 'fine with anything.' I'm picky about magical power."

The pair, who sucked down their respective drinks in similar poses, talked congenially with each other.

According to the conversation they had while enjoying Mariela's homemade lunch, Lyro Paja wouldn't go hungry even without Mariela's magical power, unlike Slaken. However, every once in a while, they seemed to crave it excessively. Apparently, it was like someone who ate only pasta developing a craving for bread.

"I get it. I've got a desire for booze, too."

Mariela didn't think her master should lump her own constant thirst for alcohol in with Lyro's wants.

Mariela had worried Lyro's craving for human magical power

meant they would eventually eat people for a snack, but apparently, the taste of magical power taken by force and of that given freely were somehow different. As far as Lyro Paja could tell from the magical power of animals and monsters they'd tried, the energy offered with calls of "Soup's onnn!" was full of love and had a unique flavor. Lyro seemed to have inherited the desire for the taste of tenderness that Mariela showered on Slaken.

"The presence of fire is too strong in my magical power, so Lyro won't eat it even if I go 'Say aaah.'"

"You did that, Master...?"

Freyja was shameful, but Mariela was the one who was embarrassed after hearing her master's admission.

Apart from their eating habits, life in the Fell Forest seemed to be very pleasant for the two former spirits.

For their dwelling, Freyja had called for a *Talk* with a suitable sacred tree while flashing her fiery power, and it changed an old tree with a large hollow into a construct resembling a house. Lyro Paja slept in a swaying hammock they'd asked an orb-weaving spider to make for them.

Their mushroom chairs were soft and comfortable to sit on, but the shrub they'd made into a table had grown four legs and sometimes wandered off, which was a pain. Freyja and Lyro said they had few objects in their place, and it was dreary, so they were gathering the light of the stars to decorate it with. What exactly did that look like, though? Mariela grew excited just from listening to them. She wanted to visit them once.

As Lyro Paja was similar to a monster, there were times when corruption streamed into the former spirit. However, the quantity was minimal compared with the past, and, perhaps thanks to their core, Freyja, who was very human-like, didn't seem to irritate them.

"My master doesn't annoy you? Are you some kind of saint?"

Mariela was astonished. If someone was fine being with her troublesome master around the clock, didn't that mean Mariela was far more corrupted than them?

"Well, I'm the one who gets bothered, actually."

Lyro Paja had always been rather serious and straightforward. They weren't picky about what they ate aside from Mariela's magical power, and they seemed to be enjoying life in a physical body as they wandered through the Fell Forest all day long. At night, they listened to the murmuring of streams or gazed at the stars.

For better or worse, Lyro's spirit characteristics remained strong, and though the creature's core had been created from human sin, they led a clean, former-spirit lifestyle. It was no wonder the pleasure-seeking Freyja found that dissatisfying.

"I thought I'd teach Lyro about amusements, so that's why we came here today!"

Since when had Sunlight's Canopy been a recreational facility? Even Illuminaria was looking pleased as she stealthily peeked in through the skylight.

"So? Anything happen after that whole debacle?" Entertainment-starved Freyja made a beeline for the real question at hand.

With her master listening intently, Mariela recounted what the Black Iron Freight Corps members had been up to since the journey to the lake world. Partway through, however, Mariela wondered if Freyja had been asking about her and Sieg.

"It hasn't been *that* long, but Yuric and Mr. Franz seem to want to go on a journey to search for the place Yuric was born. Not right away, though. They said they would leave after they gathered information and saved up enough for travel expenses. They're getting along well together. Mr. Grandel said the next time he goes to the imperial capital, he would visit his parents for the first time in a long while. Mr. Donnino seems to be spending a lot of time in the dwarven city recently to improve his armored carriage skills."

The Black Iron Freight Corps members who had each offered a little of their memories were confronting their problems head-on and taking new steps forward.

Edgan, the simple, carefree man who would make love with anyone, anytime, anywhere, was no exception. He seemed to be in the middle of negotiating in turn with each of the women who had come to extort him by using the blood relation potions he'd received as compensation for escorting Mariela.

"I don't think they'd try to trick me if they were already well-off," Edgan had said. In the end, he wound up giving a bit of money to the women who'd duped him. It was very like Edgan.

"Come to think of it, Edgan mentioned something odd recently," Sieg recalled in a mutter.

"Ohhh, is that right?" Freyja pressed.

"He said that the screams he'd always heard before while he was alone had stopped. Maybe because of that, he's become better-behaved with women."

"So *what he got* paid off," Freyja stated while licking the corners of her mouth. The act somehow reminded Mariela of the salamander licking Edgan's cheek. Maybe Freyja had done something to soften Edgan's painful memories back then.

"So? What about you guys?"

"...My punishment of going without dinner just ended, finally."

Freyja roared with laughter at Sieg's miserable reply.

The guards who had been eating with them left in a hurry, giving some excuse that their training later would be relentless if they participated in the conversation. This gesture helped preserve Sieg's honor. Yet he still looked depressed that his relationship with the most important person to him, Mariela, wasn't progressing at all.

Mariela always wore the ring she got from Sieg on the fourth finger of her left hand, but only Sieg seemed not to have realized what that meant.

"Because… Well…what could I have said with all those people around? It was too much pressure." This was the explanation Mariela had given Amber and Merle after their sharp eyes had spotted the ring.

Unfortunately, Sieg remained unaware.

Even if it was a custom that didn't exist two hundred years ago, Mariela had spent plenty of time in this era and had modern female friends. She'd played dumb in the heat of the moment, but Mariela was still a young woman. It seemed ridiculous to assume she didn't know the meaning of Sieg's gift.

"Well, keep at it! We'll visit again, and I'll be expecting some fun stories when we do!"

After saying this, Freyja and Lyro traded rare materials that could only be found in the deep parts of the Fell Forest for a large quantity of food, alcohol, and magical power-infused water from Mariela, then returned to the woods.

"It's hardly a trip at all if we go this way. With Lyro, it's over in the blink of an eye."

Freyja and Lyro Paja's road home was the cellar of Sunlight's Canopy, which connected to the underground Aqueduct.

Undoubtedly, the two former spirits would enliven Sunlight's Canopy as regular customers through this private passage from here on out.

That night…

"Mariela, I have something important I want to talk with you about. Would you come to the roof with me?"

Sieg's mind was made up.

The idea of the roof as a place with a decent atmosphere and neither customers nor guards had a bit of a no-effort feel to it, but since the two had spent the night Lynx died sitting here together, it probably wasn't a poor choice of locale for a heavy conversation.

"Sieg? Wow, it's so pretty!" Mariela exclaimed in admiration. She'd come up to find that the rooftop, usually brimming with a lived-in feel due to the sheets and Mariela's and Sieg's underwear hanging up to dry, had been thoroughly cleaned up and was now covered in lit candles.

The tapers weren't the monster-warding ones sold at Sunlight's Canopy. Rather, Sieg had gone and bought them from another shop, and they had a fashionable feeling to them.

The roof was spacious, and the sight of the many lit candles filling its entirety resembled both a sky full of stars and the depths of the ley line. It was utterly magical.

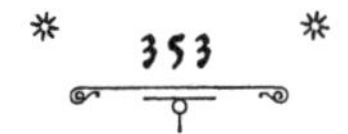

In the center of the swaying lights, Siegmund held out his hand to Mariela.

Mariela stepped up to Sieg as she was beckoned, and she softly placed her left hand on the one Sieg offered to her.

"Mariela… I…"

Sieg got down on one knee and attempted to speak the words he'd surely practiced many times over.

However, much to a certain hunter's chagrin, fire spirits, having been enlivened by Freyja's visit, took lodging in the lights on the roof to watch the pair. Similarly, Illuminaria once again peeked with an excited expression from a sacred tree branch that came up to the roof. This made it difficult to say if Sieg's proposal went entirely as planned.

The ring on Mariela's left hand with the jewel the color of Sieg's eye shimmered as it reflected the infinite light of the night sky and the candles.

BONUS CHAPTER

The Unlimited Meat Festival

01

"Guuuuuuuuys, sgfuhrgiuhuhgFujiko!!!"

"Huuuoooooooh, sgfuhrgiuhuhgFujiko!!!"

It was annoying how the guys kept yelling "Fujiko, Fujiko" excessively.

That didn't mean a beautiful woman named Fujiko from a foreign country was coming.

Outside the Labyrinth City's outer wall, young adventurers had formed ranks and were waiting impatiently for a stampede of monsters.

Everyone's morale was bizarrely high.

They were too excited to be articulate, but they still seemed completely prepared. The younger ones, in particular, wore polished armor that sparkled, and for some reason, even their hairdos were perfect. Some warriors were checking their appearances in their swords, polished like mirrors.

Although they scowled at the Fell Forest, sometimes they glanced back toward the outer wall, where a group of carefree, dressed-up women were.

Boom-boom-boooooom!

The earth shook. The ominous phenomenon caused everyone to straighten up.

The Fell Forest shook, and its trees toppled. It was a pack of rampaging monsters. There was only a single word to describe

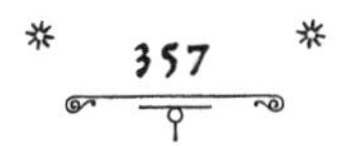

when monsters that typically kept to themselves began to charge in large numbers.

"Now, it's begun! The first Labyrinth City battle. Who will fell the most monsters and win the best prizes?! We'll stop the clock when the stampede quiets down! I, Lightning Empress Elsee, and..."

"...I, Haage the Limit Breaker, will serve as commentators! All right, everyone, let's goooooo!!!"

"Fujikoooooooooooooo!!!"

The roar of monsters that shook the earth and the men's call of "Fujiko" made for very clashing battle cries. Unmarried young ladies cast passionate glances from the safety of the side-lines. Those wives in attendance gave overbearing looks to their spouses, commanding them to get some good food.

That's right, this was the Unlimited Meat Festival, a celebration newly created in the Labyrinth City. It had replaced the Orc Festival, and it made for an efficient marriage of romantic rendezvous and survival.

It had been fine up until the Labyrinth City united to kill the Labyrinth and the entire region returned to human hands, but the orc subjugation, also known as the Meat Festival, ended in utter failure that year. Hungry orcs had come now and then before the start of winter, but they were few enough in number that the patrolling

City Defense Squad could exterminate them, and despite the long wait, no hordes of orcs came to the Labyrinth City.

This meant that the Meat Festival, the dating event young men and women looked forward to, wasn't held last year.

The Labyrinth Suppression Forces, who had killed the Labyrinth and now had so much time and physical strength to spare that they didn't know what to do with it all, forced their way into the Fell Forest and hunted edible monsters with reckless abandon. Thanks to this, no one was in want of food during the colder months, but the more satisfied they were in life's necessities, the more the Labyrinth City's up-and-coming generation acted out.

Blood pumped, bodies danced, meat was plentiful, and lovers burst into song. A festival that provided such things was indispensable.

Leonhardt had been at his wit's end dealing with the unexpected side effects of peace. With exquisite timing, a message from Mariela arrived in his office, stating that a stampede may happen soon.

If this had been any other settlement, people probably would have panicked at the unthinkable disaster. However, if you ran in the right circles, you'd know that the sacred tree spirit Illuminaria knew both the scale and the time. Moreover, instead of happening at fixed intervals, the stampede's scale was entirely manageable for the Labyrinth City with its many seasoned warriors.

"In which case, wouldn't it be an efficient hunt...?"

Although Leonhardt, who'd heard the origins of the Fell Forest and "The Legend of the Fire and Water Spirits," felt a little guilty about treating a stampede like a commonplace event, he readily agreed to the proposal of a new Meat Festival for the stampede suppression.

* * *

At Leonhardt's request, the influential people of the event-starved Labyrinth City banded together to make a plan. Even during the early starting stages, there was great excitement about this new Meat Festival.

"First, the important thing is to lure out the monsters."

Leonhardt nodded in agreement with Teluther's extremely respectable opinion.

Teluther was instantly overjoyed at having received approval from the general and broke into a huge grin. From there, he broke into a stream of the usual sort of stuff he babbled about, so we'll skip over that. Halfway-developed agricultural land was selected as the battlefield so the monsters flooding in from the Fell Forest could be defeated without causing harm to the Labyrinth City.

Monsters' aggression during a stampede outweighed the effects of monster-warding potions. It was necessary to scatter concoctions monsters hated over an extensive area of the forest to guide them to the desired location. Unfortunately, now that the Labyrinth City was the domain of people, bromominthra, an ingredient in monster-warding potions, didn't grow quite so abundantly anymore, so there weren't enough of the concoctions to go around.

Although its effects weren't as potent, Leonhardt's committee chose holy water as a substitute. It had been instrumental in the battle with the King of Cursed Serpents, and it did have enough efficacy to steer monsters one way or another. Holy water had an effect on corruption, and it was used primarily to protect against curses. Monsters had corruption within them and instinctively hated holy water.

The ingredients for it were sacred tree morning dew, salt purified by a spirit, and the hair of a maiden.

They gathered the sacred tree morning dew after splashing the sacred tree with so much water that Illuminaria begged, "Stooop, it's going to swell up."

As for the salt, Mariela summoned the salamander, Sieg asked it to purify the stuff, and the spirit, full of energy, went *—Fire!—*

Lastly, the hair of a maiden…

"In that case, let us summon a famous beautician from the imperial capital!"

A free hair salon exclusive to teen girls from had been opened per Caroline's proposal, and a suitable amount of the necessary component had been gathered over the last few years.

Through the skill of the famous beautician, girls transformed from unsophisticated children to precocious ladies. The city was all at once awash with refined maidens. There was no way adult women would overlook such a change.

Weishardt suggested opening a children's hair salon, which was up and running sooner than expected. Scores of young ladies and wives stormed the place, hoping to have the famous beautician get them looking spectacular for the festival. They didn't even seem to mind being charged. The place became extremely popular.

Not only did it cover the beautician's wages, but there was also enough revenue to allow the opening of a free medical clinic for the duration of the festival.

Caroline had always been talented, but ever since her engagement to Weishardt, she'd been refining both her business acumen and her beauty.

She sparkled so much in happiness that Mariela added her to her Big Three Dazzling People list.

By the way, the other two people on this list were Haage and the electrifying Elmera.

The fact that she was making such a list showed Mariela to be a disappointing person, as always. Still, thanks to the practical alchemy class she held on making holy water, her students came to acknowledge her preeminence.

The container storing a large quantity of sacred tree morning dew was a large bathtub in the public bathhouse that had been built in the vicinity of the Labyrinth. Mariela had mixed this large quantity in one go with a "Mix it round and rouuund" in a flat voice while hoisting it up like a waterspout. Upon seeing this display of her magical power, the portion of her students who had made fun of her as a "plebeian" and "mediocre" completely changed their tunes.

Sieg, who had proposed this class, grinned broadly and whispered, "Just as planned." Weishardt, who had been concerned about the formation of alchemist cliques in the Labyrinth City, was equally pleased. Mariela and Caroline happily enjoyed their tea together as they watched the pair, and they both remarked, "What an evil expression."

The trees of the Fell Forest shook, and out came a horde of killer bees. Each of the insects was roughly the size of a dog or a cat, and their weapons were stingers whose size needn't be mentioned.

They attacked left and right with their envenomed barbs, flying in a way that was surely impossible for a bird.

After the movement of their pitiable prey was stopped by the poison, the bees either devoured the food on the spot or carried it to their nests for their larvae. Moreover, the brutal monsters acted in groups, so in the unlikely event you met them in the Fell Forest, you would have to prepare to die.

"Uh-ohhh, it's killer bees from the very start. This is inconvenient—you can't eat 'em!"

"You can eat them if they're skillfully butchered, but the exoskeleton is tough and hard to cut, and the poison sacs sell at a high price, so it's better to just harvest their materials."

"...They're edible?"

"I recommend deep-frying the adult ones. Incidentally, the pupae are the most delicious, but during a stampede, the larva experience abnormal growth and rapidly mature, leaving the nests empty. I can sense how keen the Fell Forest is not to let us eat so easily. Such a shame!"

Commentators Haage and Elmera seemed to be treating the insect swarms as a disappointment because they weren't a reliable food source. Were they okay with eating bugs so long as they tasted good?

Let's not forget it was the Labyrinth City that was under attack. What was with that comment about the Fell Forest not letting them eat so easily? Weren't the commentators a little too complacent?

"Good gracious, I'd like to remind all of you to collect the stingers, too. They contain rare metals. Rock Wheel will buy all of them without exception." Whether he was giving play-by-play or spectating, Marrock had jammed himself into a seat in the commentators' booth and shrewdly announced he would buy up materials. Meanwhile, mages and archers, whose forte was ranged attacks, were steadily reducing the killer bees' numbers. Things were going well so far.

However, the adventurers, distracted by their flying foes, weren't paying attention to their feet. Plant vine monsters known as creepers had snuck up to them unnoticed. By all rights, they shouldn't have had such long vines. It seemed these monsters, too, had grown rapidly due to the stampede. They twined around the legs of those adventurers fighting in the front row.

"Whoa, where'd they come from?!"

The warriors who finally noticed their legs were entangled worked to free themselves. That momentary gap of time was enough for a mixed group of forest wolves and black wolves to charge out of the Fell Forest. While most of the killer bees had been dealt with, the wolves took advantage of the opening created by the creepers grabbing people in the front row to attack, and chaos spread through the Labyrinth City's forces.

"Ow, ow, ow, it's biting me!"

"Hey, don't forget about the killer bees!"

Even with diminished ranks, the venomous insects swooped down from above.

What cut a swath through the Fell Forest trees and caused earth tremors when it appeared—as though to twist the knife in the battle lines that had instantly fallen into chaos—was an enormous bull monster with eight legs and four horns.

Out of the four spikes, two short ones on its forehead pointed straight forward, and the remaining two stretched from each side of its cranium to about shoulder width before curving forward.

Its body, several times larger than a normal bull, was not only enormous, but it also looked extraordinarily thick and weighty. If not for its eight thick legs, it undoubtedly wouldn't have been able to stand.

"My, how unusual. A mincer. A delicious monster has appeared at last, but..."

"It might be a bit problematic in this free-for-all."

As you can imagine from their large build, mincers weren't quick-witted or agile monsters. If they crashed into you from the front, you'd be reduced to minced meat, but they took time to accelerate, and once they started running, it was difficult for them to change course. Usually, it wouldn't be hard to avoid their charge, but right now, the bees overhead and the wolves underfoot were making sport of the adventurers. Everything was a distracting disarray.

"Mroooooooooo!"

Its eyes turned bloodshot red from the excitement of finding prey: humans. The mincer was so agitated that monster-warding potions had no effect on it, and it charged with the intimidating air of a siege weapon. As if that alone wasn't enough, there were two others with it.

The momentum sent adventurers flying, and the unlucky ones were torn to pieces by its four horns.

"Waaaaaugh!!!"

What had happened to the festive atmosphere? The mincers' momentum wouldn't abate just by sending adventurers, wolves, and creeper vines alike flying. They were headed straight for the Labyrinth City's outer wall.

Those thick, brutal horns would surely leave far more than a few scuffs.

"It really is a stampede. Does that mean it'll be tough to deal with…?"

Leonhardt, who was giving directions at his headquarters, lifted his arm straight up and ordered the Labyrinth Suppression Forces to move out. They'd been on standby in the rear to prioritize the festival's goal, but perhaps the time for fun and games was over.

The ones who appeared before the charging mincers on Leonhardt's orders were the three captains of the Labyrinth Suppression Forces who had won rock-paper-scissors. With the shield knight Wolfgang at the center, Dick and a long sword user reinforced each side.

The first ones to move were the spearman, Dick, and the long sword user. Although the pair had different weapon specialties, they got on well. After exchanging quick looks, they drew their respective armaments at roughly the same time and sliced off the four front legs of the mincers on either side.

Just because the massive monsters had lost their front legs didn't mean they would immediately stop.

With thunderous sounds, the creatures pitched forward. One faceplanted into the dirt and slid several yards before finally coming to a stop, while the other unluckily got a horn stuck in the ground and turned a somersault, which caused its neck to twist and its life to end.

Tremendously high-ranking fighting power was undoubtedly something, but ending things in the blink of an eye lacked entertainment value.

"That's the Labyrinth Suppression Forces for you! They handily settled the problem!"

It was unknown whether Wolfgang had heard Elmera's remark

or if he was simply a natural performer. Regardless, Wolfgang assumed an exaggerated stance with his shield, grunted, "Hurr-rgh!" and magnificently stopped the remaining mincer's charge.

"I-incredible!"

"I knew the Labyrinth Suppression Forces could handle it!"

"...Ow, ow, ow, wolves are biting me!"

Several adventurers who'd grown wide-eyed in wonder and become distracted screamed as wolves gnawed on them. Meanwhile, Wolfgang, who had caught the mincer's charge, cried, "Hooooh!" and thrust it away.

On a closer look at the mincer that had fallen to the ground with a heavy *thud*, the two horns on its forehead were broken, the forehead itself was unnaturally dented, and blood foamed from its mouth. Centering the impact on its horns had caused its skull to collapse.

"Woooooo!"

"Eeeeee!"

The three warriors raised their hands in response to cheers from both the adventurers and the spectating women as they returned to the Labyrinth Suppression Forces.

"Unfortunately, all those guys are married!"

One should've expected no less from Haage. Although even married people wanted some attention, if only a little, he just had to say something superfluous.

Thanks to the Labyrinth Suppression Forces' intervention, the adventurers in disarray rallied, the restless mood was swept away, and everyone felt more enthused about the battle. But there was no way the flood of monsters from the Fell Forest would end there.

As if to say the preliminary test was over, numerous earth dragons created tremors as they emerged from the forest. Weak monsters like goblins and orcs rushed out from both sides of the earth dragons, perhaps to claim their share in the hunting grounds that the large-scale beasts had so graciously trampled down.

And weren't those things in the sky wyverns, which usually fed on goblins and orcs, heading this way like they were chasing their prey?

"Labyrinth Suppression Forces, forward! Clean up those earth dragons!"

Under Leonhardt's command, the Labyrinth Suppression Forces formed ranks and advanced toward the earth dragons.

"The Labyrinth Suppression Forces have taken the field due to the appearance of powerful enemies! All adventurers, please promptly move to the outer wall to protect it."

Per Elmera's announcement, the adventurers made way for the Labyrinth Suppression Forces. They weaved through the earth dragons to subjugate the small fries about to invade the Labyrinth City.

If you couldn't at least grasp that an earth dragon was a powerful monster just from facing it, you couldn't call yourself an adventurer no matter how much of a beginner you were. The relieving of those on the front lines had also been decided and agreed upon in advance.

"Ice Field."

Weishardt and the other members of the mage unit froze the earth. Aside from the physical attacks from the earth dragons' huge bodies, their stone lances were a nuisance. The lances that protruded from underfoot generated rapidly, and even if you dodged the first wave, the place you ended up would probably be changing into a pincushion.

By freezing the ground with *Ice Field*, you could slow the rate at which the stone lances were generated. The cracks in the frozen water would make it easy to guess the trajectory of the lances.

"Hrrrah!"

With a *thud*, hammer-wielding soldiers struck the bulging cracks in the earth and thwarted the initial wave of stone lances, which would make the defeat of the earth dragons much easier.

Nevertheless, earth dragons' scales were tough, too. Clumsy attacks probably wouldn't even leave a scratch on them, especially on their backs. If there had only been one earth dragon, it would have been possible to surround and defeat it. But perhaps due to the effects of the stampede, earth dragons that generally didn't group together had gathered in a pack of about a dozen, so the warriors were quite likely to be attacked by another individual while they were taking time to surround the first.

The only soft areas they had were their eyes, which were small when compared with their big bodies. Of course, hitting an earth dragon's eye with pinpoint accuracy was a feat akin to threading a moving needle.

Such a feat had to be impossible, and yet…

Whoosh, whoosh, whoosh.

The Labyrinth City had a single bow master with extraordinary finesse.

If Sieg didn't participate here, the "going without dinner punishment" would probably be waiting for him back home. He'd temporarily joined the Labyrinth Suppression Forces in exchange for the best cuts of earth dragon meat. One should've expected no less from his cunning in choosing this method to reliably bring home the most delicious meat rather than trying to do so through participating as a solo adventurer.

"Nice shot! Nice shot! He—you know—he lives in...sbhgblg..."

Excited by influential adventurer Sieg's participation, Teluther barged into the commentator's seat and seized the megaphone. Just as he was about to leak Sieg's personal information, members of the City Defense Squad covered his mouth and took him away.

Both the battlefield and the spectator seating area were alive with excitement and chaos.

Sieg's arrows magnificently crushed the eyes of the earth dragons. They threw their heads back in pain, and the instant they blindly raged and exposed their relatively soft flanks and bellies, soldiers from the Labyrinth Suppression Forces stabbed their weak points.

Although this was the first time such a large pack of earth dragons had been engaged, the Forces were experienced with fighting the creatures after their expeditions into the Fell Forest. In a group battle in an open space where Malraux's telepathic communication was also effective, the odds were in the Labyrinth Suppression Forces' favor. Despite taking attacks and sustaining some damage from the earth dragons that came after, the Forces steadily consigned the monsters to oblivion.

"Ballista unit, aim for the wyverns! Don't fall behind, City Defense Squad!"

The ones who shot down the wyverns coming at them from above were snipers of the City Defense Squad.

Under the command of Captain Kyte, mighty arrows were fired from ballistae installed on top of the outer wall and brought down wyverns one after another. Although the City Defense Squad's contributions were significant, the top of any high wall was inconspicuous and lacked showmanship. That much was typical for the City Defense Squad, though.

* * *

As the Labyrinth Suppression Forces steadily defeated the earth dragons, the novice adventurers retreated from the battlefront and played an active part in confronting the orcs and goblins targeting the Labyrinth City. Maybe being close to the spectator seating area made them more motivated after all.

Intermediate adventurers split into groups to defeat the slightly higher-level monsters and the wyverns that had fallen to the ground and were still breathing. The intermediate adventurers, whom you could call veterans, had both stable fighting styles and stable private lives, so they were steadily earning the fruits of battle and making money.

A raptor-drawn two-wheel barrow weaved its way between those adventurers and the Labyrinth Suppression Forces to retrieve the injured people it sometimes found.

You could probably call the steel frame and its large metal tires with sharp spearheads attached a chariot. The body, tailor-made for the operator, had the Black Iron Freight Corps's mark engraved on it.

The one operating the chariot and showing off tricky moves by sliding the tires with a screech and tilting it nearly lateral was Yuric. It was an attack vehicle with no load-carrying tray, only a coach box.

Depending on an animal tamer's skill, they could harmonize quite well with a chariot, let alone with the animal pulling it. The high-performance frame specializing in drivability made sport of forest and black wolves alike, and the spears attached to the wheels turned orcs into ground meat.

The raptor pulling the frame and relentlessly inciting monsters by sloshing them with mud just before a turn and hitting them with his tail was unmistakably Koo. You could tell even from a distance that he was having fun. Ever energetic, that one.

After Yuric and Koo had lured in prey, Grandel's armored chariot slayed them.

Unlike Yuric's cart, which emphasized mobility, Grandel's was built for defensive power, so with its thick armoring and the armor Grandel himself wore, it was heavy. You couldn't expect much speed from it. However, its sophisticated engineering, created by Donnino and the dwarves, allowed the operator to steer it without the techniques Yuric possessed. It was quite a simple matter to make the tires slide and slam the vehicle's body into monsters.

"Shield Bash."

Had the "legendary hero" transformed into some sort of gallant rider? Could you even call a ramming attack using the frame of a chariot a Shield Bash in the first place?

Grandel already treated anything that could protect against attacks a shield, and if he could operate it, could he append the "Bash"? If he kept this up, it seemed like he might be able to magically send wind into his umbrella and take flight one day soon.

Monsters were dancing through the air after being sent flying by Grandel's chariot. Donnino and Franz took that opportunity to coordinate and recover the injured in their chariots with load-carrying trays. Incidentally, Newie and Nick were the ones operating these chariots, and Donnino and Franz tossed fallen adventurers into the tray while using a hammer and bare hands respectively to knock out the sporadic monsters that remained.

"I'm glad our masters are participating in this subjugation, too," Newie remarked.

"And here I thought they'd be dissatisfied with the weaker types," Nick replied.

Their vocal cords had been healed after the Labyrinth City became the people's domain again and Mariela being an alchemist was no longer a secret.

"We put way too much money into these chariots, y'know!" Donnino groaned.

"This vehicle was worth it, Donnino. It hardly shakes at all, and it's fast. Even better, Yuric seems to be having fun. The retaining fee we got from the Labyrinth Suppression Forces wasn't bad at all, and this is a good setting for the chariots' debut, don't you think?" Franz answered with a smile.

This time, the Black Iron Freight Corps's job was to recover the injured and take them to the clinic. It was the perfect chance to show off their new vehicles, too, and it seemed like they'd be flooded with more and more work from here on out.

That left one guy unaccounted for—Edgan, the captain of the Black Iron Freight Corps. He should have been in the fray with everyone else, but...

"Waaaugh, ow, ow, ouch, I said *ouch*. I give up, I give up—really. I'm sorryyy!!!"

"There's no need to be shy, Edgan. No seriously injured people have arrived yet. I'll take the opportunity to give your body a tune-up. You can loaf around here. You have the time, don't you?"

The profits from the temporary hair salon that had been opened to supply materials for the holy water had been allocated to a clinic established for the duration of the Meat Festival.

The medical center was the perfect place to get in touch with wounded adventurers, making it a popular spot for women seeking dates. You could say the site was an "extra chance" in a sense.

Beautiful young ladies would personally give you potions and heal both your mind and body. There would be time to exchange names, and romantic encounters seemed likely.

That is, if Nierenberg, the most brilliant medical technician in the Labyrinth City and the good luck charm of Sunlight's Canopy, wasn't lying in wait like a final boss in case seriously injured people arrived.

The plan for this festival had been worked out to the finest detail. This sort of thing was within expectations. Any fool who decided to come to the clinic despite not having significant injuries would feel more pain than had they fought instead.

Leonhardt, who wanted to minimize the number of victims and allow many the chance to go all out against monsters, had the housewife intelligence agent Merle spread information throughout the city about the clinic, which was like a booby-trapped treasure chest. That's why the only one to brazenly come to the clinic despite having no injuries and be moved to tears by Nierenberg's "medical examination" due to a lack of access to information was, as expected, our Edgan.

The battle of monsters and humans ended at last around dusk.

Monsters intermittently came from the Fell Forest to attack for a little while, so more soldiers than usual took turns standing guard, but swarms of monsters no longer came.

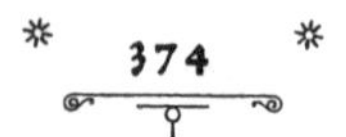

All the adventurers who participated in the battle were gathering on the main road to receive rewards corresponding to their battle achievements.

"Please present the lanterns you received before the start of the event."

The ones saying this and accepting lanterns from the adventurers were the regulars of Sunlight's Canopy.

A small candle lantern had been fastened to the waist of each adventurer. They were distributed before the start of the Meat Festival.

They included wind guards, but if you looked closely at the flames, which didn't go out even from the violent movements of the adventurers, you would see a tiny fire spirit dwelling in each of them, who bent forward from the candlewick to gaze outside with great interest.

These were special items called spirit candles, which were also votive offerings to the spirits that dwelled within them.

"You knooow, calling a ton of spirits requires a gift. Specifically, *al-co-hol.*"

"The offering is the spirit candle, right?"

It was Freyja, also known as the former great fire spirit, who ignited the spirit candles while ignoring Mariela's retort and drinking booze straight from the bottle right before the celebration.

"Come, many many flames, come, many many flames… This is a pain, so *Fire!*"

It was no longer a chant at all, but Freyja's enthusiastic *Fire!* caused tiny, weak flame spirits to light the mass of spirit candles all at once.

"Listen up, don't disappear until you come back here. Cling

to it with all your willpower. If you disappear...you know what'll happen, right?!"

After Freyja's threat, the tiny spirits doggedly clung to the candlewicks. They all did really well.

Each fire spirit was responsible for counting how many monsters the adventurer who wore its lantern defeated. They also helped keep their assigned humans safe from the monsters, if only a little. All the adventurers took care not to let their lanterns' flames go out.

Sunlight's Canopy regulars had a curious affinity with the fire spirits, perhaps because of their contact with Freyja. In particular, Emily, Sherry, Pallois, and Elio, whom Freyja had given lessons to, could hear the spirits' voices much more than other people, so they served as assistants in the unlikely event something shady happened. Thankfully, there were no incidents of someone stealing and presenting another's lantern.

Most of the fire spirits resembled ordinary flames and simply remained lit in silence, but an adventurer who had made friends with his spirit during the battle turned to it as he awaited his turn and asked, "Hey, you can count, right?"

The tiny spirit answered, —One, twooo...,— then —One, two, threeee...,— but since the adventurer didn't hear a number higher than three, he was a bit worried.

"How many monsters were defeated?"

—A looot!— —A lot.— —A *lot.*—

Emily's question got a rather ambiguous answer. The tiny fire spirits who couldn't count higher than three all said the same thing.

They happily answered that the adventurers who fought alongside them defeated many monsters, and they seemed to feel accomplished, but this was no way to conduct evaluations.

"I see, you did a good job, didn't you?" Emily answered, smiling, as she placed a lantern containing a spirit on a scale.

"Fifty goblins. Thanks for your hard work."

"Whoa, amazing! You defeated the equivalent of two hundred goblins."

Emily and the others calculated the lantern owners' battle results from the values displayed on the scale and issued certificates.

While the adventurers had been battling, the fire spirits appeared to only twinkle within the lanterns, but their tiny bodies purified just a little bit of the corruption released every time a creature was slain, and they grew as a result.

As the fire spirits got stronger, the offerings they required during their manifestation increased proportionally. Thus, weighing a spirit candle gave you a good idea of how many monsters had been defeated.

After hearing this explanation, an adventurer praised, "Man, you're really somethin'," and his tiny flame proudly replied, —Mm-hmm!—

After receiving the certificate of his battle results, the adventurer headed to the plaza in front of the Labyrinth.

This was the site of the closing party. Since anyone could participate for free, it only featured simple dishes and drinks, but the adventurers' objective was to meet the comrades they'd made acquaintance with during the battle.

Those who unluckily hadn't yet been able to meet also had a chance to do so here.

Today, only part of each adventurer's reward had been distributed to them, and the rest was given as a certificate they could redeem at a later date for meat or money after verification. This was so they didn't inadvertently spend it all in pampering women due to the lingering excitement of the battle. It was a considerate system. The crucial part of the festival started now, and even in the unlikely event they missed their chance today, many more stampedes would happen in the future.

There would be many more nights and festivals, and the possibilities spread limitlessly before them.

The festival was unofficially dubbed the Unlimited Meat Festival to celebrate the limitless potential in the Labyrinth City. As the revelry grew more and more lively, the one person who should have showed up as soon as she caught wind of a celebration was instead deep within the dark Fell Forest.

"Lyro, are you okay with this?" Freyja asked. She stood on the bank of the river that separated the Labyrinth City from the source of the stampede.

The stream, which normally had a calm current that allowed monsters to walk across it, now made a deep sound as its turbid waters churned. Many monsters stood at edge opposite Freyja, looking for a place to cross.

"It's fine, Frey. The corruption dwelling within those monsters was too strong, and they wouldn't have regained their sanity unless they were sent back to the ley line. A considerable amount of corruption was purified in this deluge, so this will last for a while. Those monsters on the other side of the river were lured and are agitated, but they'll calm down before long and go back into the woods."

Lyro Paja was a spirit who had long taken in corruption, like the many monsters of the Fell Forest. Even now, after separating from the ley line and completing their incarnation, they still supported the monsters, and they had no obligation to protect humans, let alone celebrate their victory. They hadn't flooded the river to guard the Labyrinth City from more monsters. It was to keep those with only a small amount of corruption from being killed.

Ever since Lyro Paja had decided to resign as the ley line's warden, they knew this would happen, and even if they'd continued to manage the ley line, the amount of corruption they could purify was limited. This was fated to happen sooner or later.

"Well, little stampedes now and then would be less harmful to the humans than a great big flood of monsters, but..." Freyja was being evasive.

Humans were the ones who'd created the corruption, that source of misfortune, but even if a stampede occurred, people were the only ones who survived. Considering how Lyro Paja felt, even Freyja, who had lived among humanity for a long time, thought it improper to express her relief that the Labyrinth City hadn't come to much harm.

"Corruption isn't the only thing humans bring into being. You know that more than anyone, don't you, Frey? Besides, look at your kin over there..."

Lyro Paja turned in the direction of the Labyrinth City. The spirit shouldn't have been able to see anything. Not only were the two deep in the Fell Forest, but it was nighttime. Yet it was clear that Lyro Paja was watching something.

His gaze was kind, and his eyes seemed to hold a small light, like the lights of the city reflecting off a liquid poured into a glass.

"Cheers!" said the young adventurer to his fire spirit.

"What's with you? You're drinking with a lantern even though there're so many cute girls here?" a friend ridiculed.

Few spirits remained in the lanterns. Those who had completed their duty moved to other flames or returned to the ley line. However, the one who had teamed up with this youth seemed quite taken with him and remained in the lantern, flickering happily.

"Well, you know, this one is surprisingly cute. Wonder if there's any way to keep it so it won't go out?"

"Ahh, there's a shop called…what was it, Sunlight's Canopy? Seems like they sell spirit candles."

"Oh yeah? Maybe I'll go buy one tomorrow."

After the end of the Meat Festival, many adventurers wanted to stay with their spirits, so the lanterns were relinquished to them.

Mariela was so thrilled that she sold spirit candles barely above cost to ensure every adventurer obtained votive offerings for their tiny fire spirit. However, fickle fire spirits couldn't stay in this world for long, so more than half of them disappeared within the day, and those who remained disappeared after a few more days.

A scant few got along well enough with their human companions to remain for even longer. Supposedly, those pairs enjoyed many experiences together. While it wasn't many, Mariela continued to sell spirit candles in the months following the stampede.

Freyja and Lyro Paja, who frequented Sunlight's Canopy, wore somewhat awkward expressions in response to the adventurers who sometimes brought spirits to the shop, and Mariela and Sieg marveled at the infinite potential of the Labyrinth City. Where else could they have seen such faces on a water or a fire spirit?

People, monsters, and spirits.

Both the worlds they lived in and their natural temperaments differed—all three groups should have been incompatible.

However, even if their steps didn't match, there were times when they could walk together.

That was almost certainly enough.

None among them could help but feel a world like that was more wonderful than anything.

Appendix

Guide Map of the World of Water

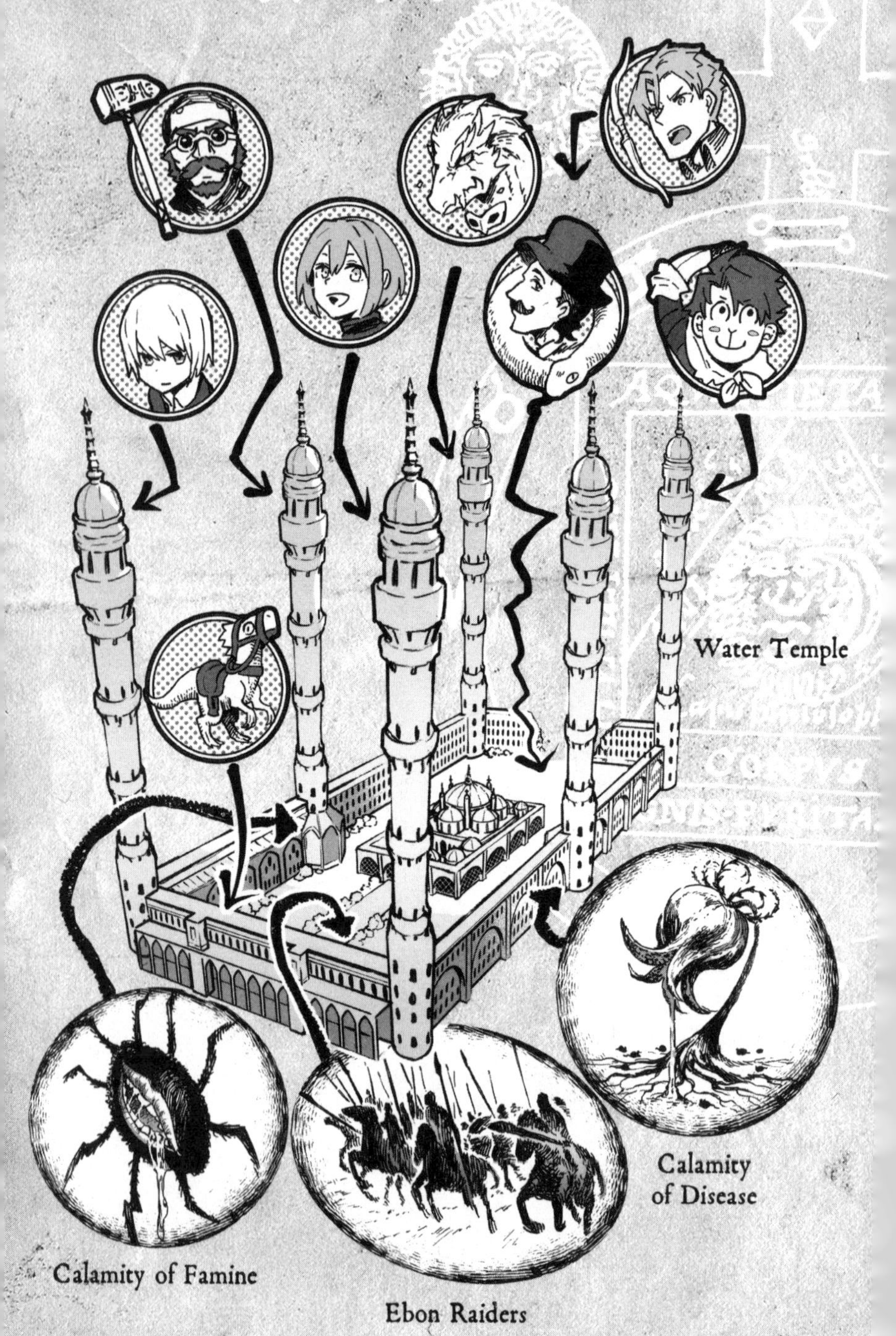

Southwest Tower

Southeast Tower

Fourth Floor

Third Floor

Second Floor

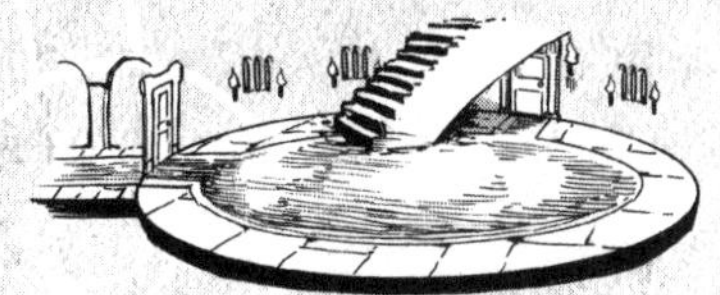

First Floor

Entrance

Alchemy Dictionary of the World of Water

Harnonius

An aquatic plant also referred to as the Guardian of Waterholes. It has tough and solid leaves, and its roots inhabit rocky areas and the like. Because it feeds off monsters' corrupted magical power, they keep away from it. This creates safe habitats for prawns and small fish.

Rarity: ★★

Recommended Use: easy monster-warding potions

Rope Ivy

An aquatic plant bearing cord-like ivy. Its fibers are supple and strong, and they're used to make rope or as a material for baskets. The leaves are fleshy, and if you dry them, they become sponge-like; in this form, they're used to absorb water or as kindling. It's a very useful plant.

Rarity: ★

Recommended Use: fire bottles, rope

Gepla Seeds

The seeds of this water plant contain a lot of oil. The small seeds look tasty because they grow in tufts, but they're not suitable as food due to their foul, fishy taste. They're highly nutritious, and frog monsters happily eat them. They swell up when they absorb magical power. Some subspecies produce an oil that can be used in cooking, although those don't grow in size.

Rarity: ★★

Recommended Use: fire bottles

Fire Bottle

An explosive made simply by filling a bottle with gepla seed oil and stopping the container with rope ivy leaves. Although it's easy to make, the oil foams up like beer froth when you put magical power into it, and this strengthens its firepower. It combusts easily, so a rope ivy fuse is required.

Rarity: ★

Recommended Use: Fire!

Mojolaus Meiyo Larvae

Enormous, hairy caterpillar monsters that attack with poisonous fibers. Their barbs are so thick that Necklaces apparently keep them as pets in place of a fur scarf. The ferocious bugs paralyze their prey and then eat it, and they also move quite fast. The body fluids they use as the base of their cocoons are one material for Potions of Binding.

Rarity: ★★★

Recommended Use: Potions of Binding

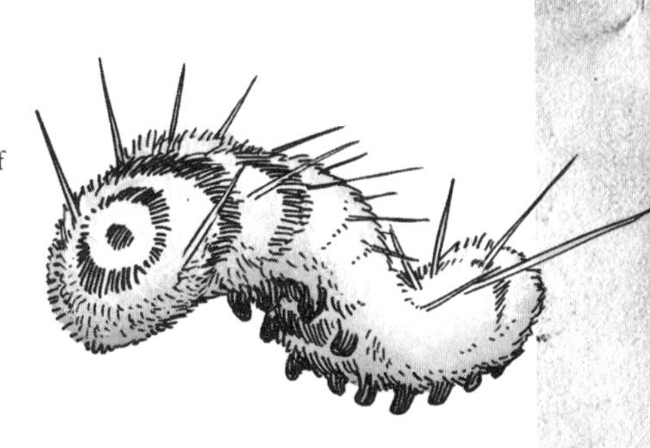

Bravado Frog

A frog monster with cheek pouches that can inflate to considerable size. It fully expands the sacs to deflect attacks and then blows out the air as it escapes. Even if the frog doesn't suck in air, the pouches will inflate if magical power is poured into them, so these cheek sacs were a vital part of old ventilators.

Rarity: ★★

Recommended Use: ventilation magical tools, Potions of Binding

Potion of Binding

A potion made by combining body fluids from hairy caterpillar monsters and the inflation property of bravado frogs. When thrown, it changes into tough thread and binds the target. Easy to use and effective against both people and monsters, but obtaining the hairy caterpillar body fluids is difficult, so they rarely appear on the market.

Rarity: ★★★★

Recommended Use: restraining/confining enemies

Necklace

A vain tree monster that decorates itself and ties its parasitic vines around its prey's necks. A truly tasteless creature, it even keeps hairy caterpillar monsters as pets. Although it isn't especially active, it can move, and its lumber is flexible and hard. Along with the monster's vines, its wood has many uses, and it's particularly prized as a material for weapons.

Rarity: ★★★★

Recommended Use: crossbows, bows, clubs, etc.

Gladere

A whale monster that feeds on magical power.
This demon of the sea attacks ships with its strong, multilayered jaws and swallows sailors whole with its mouth that can tear wood to shreds. It can use magical power to change its own density. This enables it to dive and ascend rapidly. Its oil is priceless.

Rarity: ★★★★★

Recommended Use: high-grade lamp oil

Lamia

A snake monster that has an upper body similar to a human female's. The one Grandel nurtured grew into an imposing, advanced type with six arms. Despite appearances, it's not a demi-human. It's a fiendish creature that doesn't speak. However, it knowingly petrified itself to protect Grandel from the ebon raiders.

Rarity: ★★★★★★★

Alchemy Dictionary of the World of Water

AFTERWORD

Thank you so much to everyone who picked up this book and read it.

In the afterword of Volume 5, I wrote about it being the conclusion and so forth, but I was able to take the side story posted on the Internet as "The Alchemist Who Survived and the Abyss in the Fell Forest," rewrite it, and publish it as Volume 6. I have no words to express my gratitude toward everyone who enabled me to put it in novel form and cheered me on to the very end. A big thanks to ox the illustrator, Shimizu, and everyone else at Kadokawa who worked to create this.

Volume 6 was conceived as a tale focusing on the identity and real goal of Freyja, Mariela's master, who remained a mystery even after she left following the Labyrinth's subjugation.

The opening scenes of being chased by black monsters while moving through locations resembling castle walls were inspired by a castle in India that's said to be haunted. I started writing it because I wanted to tell a story with a gloomy atmosphere about a powerless girl escaping from a scary place with some sort of frightening creature lurking about. Well, Mariela is a greenhorn in terms of fighting power, but she's strong in terms of personality. So, far from trying to flee, she ended up making fire bottles to go "Fire!"

After deciding on that sort of framework, I incorporated the

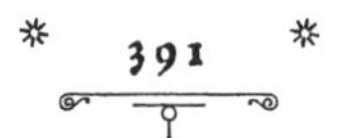

Black Iron Freight Corps members' backstories. They all had deep personalities but had hardly appeared in the main story. I wanted to give them more time to shine, since their pasts were too much to include in the first five volumes.

The Internet version of this story always got warm responses, and that was really encouraging. Using the feedback from a questionnaire I sent out partway through this novel's online edition, I decided on the best way to continue the story. When making something into a book, the complete version comes together by cutting out the redundant parts and adding the paths that weren't chosen before.

By the way, the true purpose of that questionnaire was to find a companion for the boyish girl, Yuric. The contenders were Franz, her foster parent, and Edgan, who's never treated seriously because of his personality. Unfortunately, Edgan's route ended up being completely, utterly ignored. I was really impressed at the magnificent swing and miss. That's our Edgan.

And the mermaid's tear from the bonus chapter "The Flickering Shadow" in Volume 2 was the perfect item for the ending in this volume, so I used it to make a happier ending. I hope you enjoyed it, along with the subsequent "Unlimited Meat Festival" that depicted the state of the Labyrinth City.

Now that I've plunged into my third year of novel writing, I think it has finally become part of my daily life. I had to update the Internet version and work on turning it into a physical book during my first two years, but from now on, I'd like to write at a balanced pace as part of my life's work.

I hope that someday, I can provide an exciting tale again.

Usata Nonohara

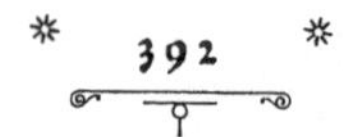

OOON (AWOOO)
GASA (RUSTLE)
BASA (FLAP)
BASA
BASA

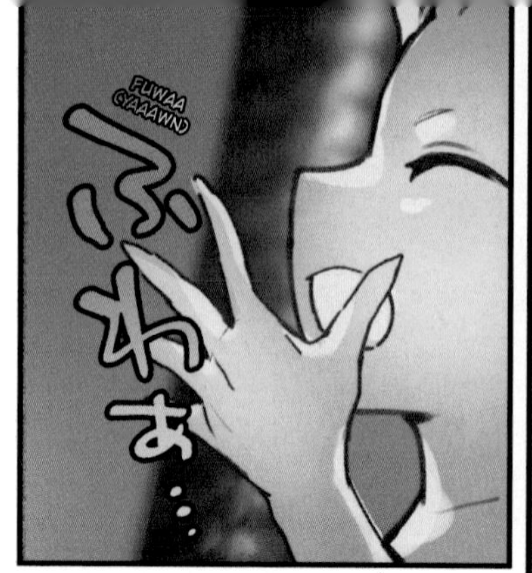
FUWAA (YAAAWN)
ふわぁ…

BOOORING. NOW I GET WHY THE OTHERS TOLD ME NOT TO DO THIS.

SHOO! SHOO!
GASASA (RUSTLE)
ガササッ

.....

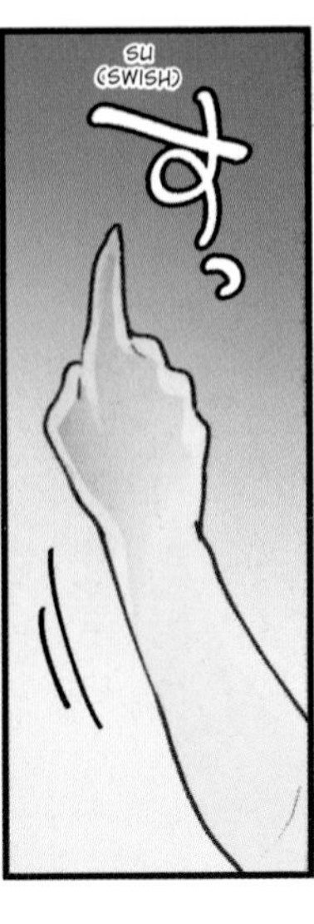
SU (SWISH)
すっ

BOU (WHOOSH)
ボウ…

WHOA... BEAUTIFUL.

コト
KOTO (CLINK)
ギシ
GISHI (CREAK)
カパ
KAPA (OPEN)

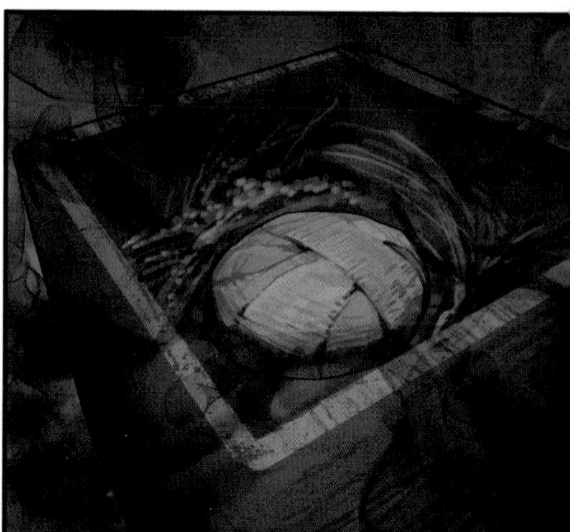

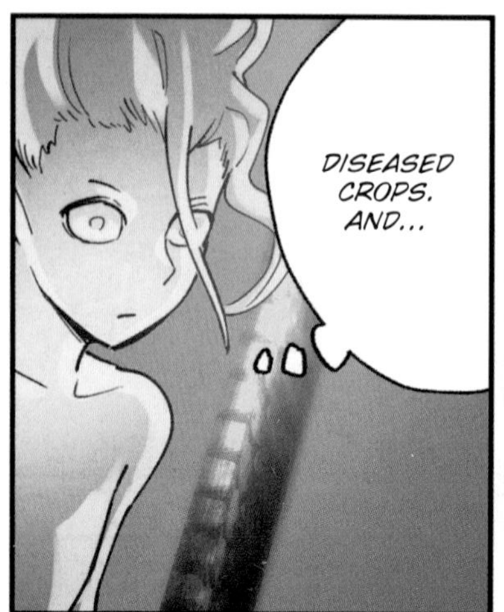
DISEASED CROPS. AND...

...GRY...

HU...Y...
ZAA (FWOOSH)
ザァ…

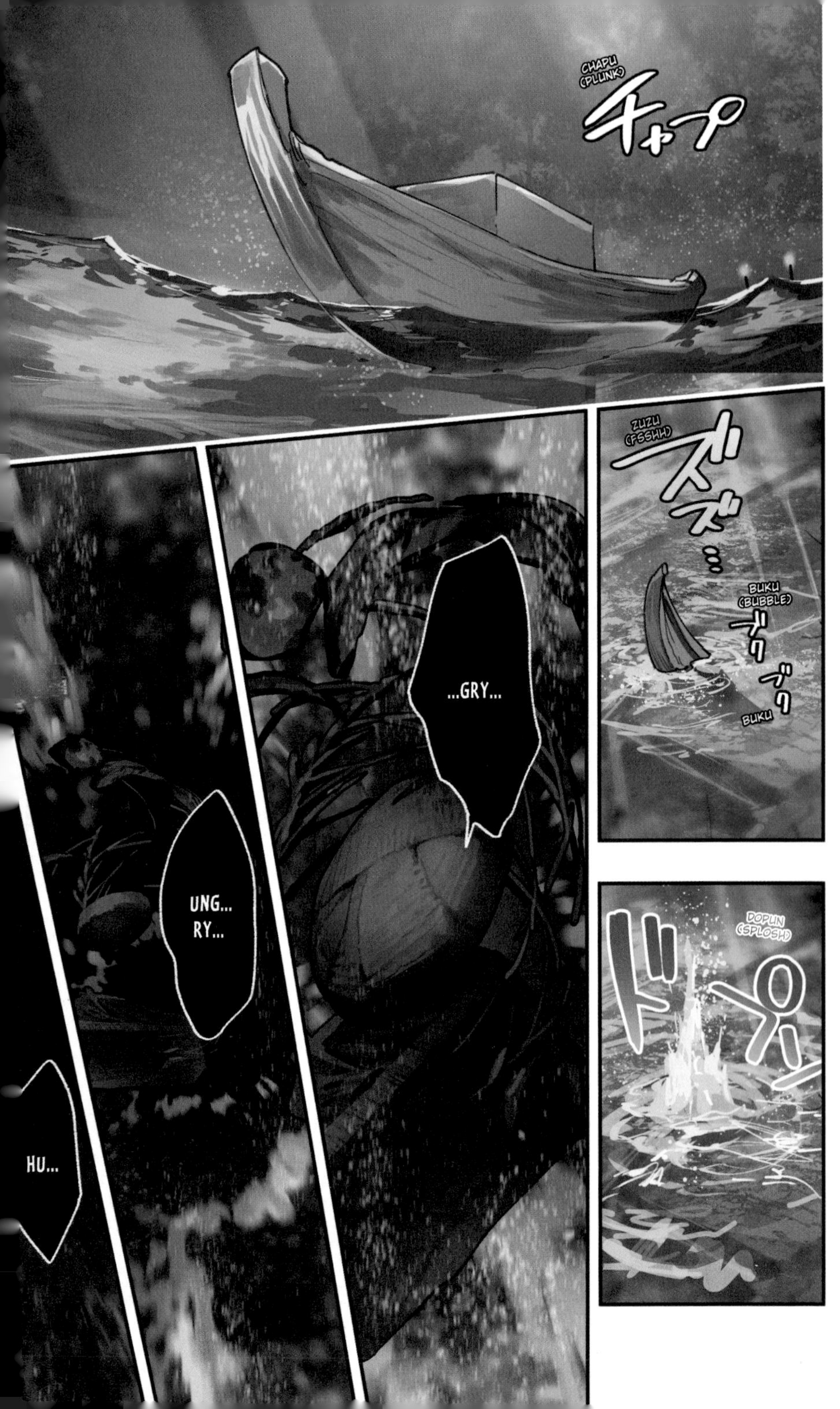

CHAPU (PLUNK)
チャプ
ZUZU (FSSHH)
ズズ…
BUKU (BUBBLE)
ブク ブク
BUKU
DOPUN (SPLOSH)
ドプン
...GRY...
UNG... RY...
HU...

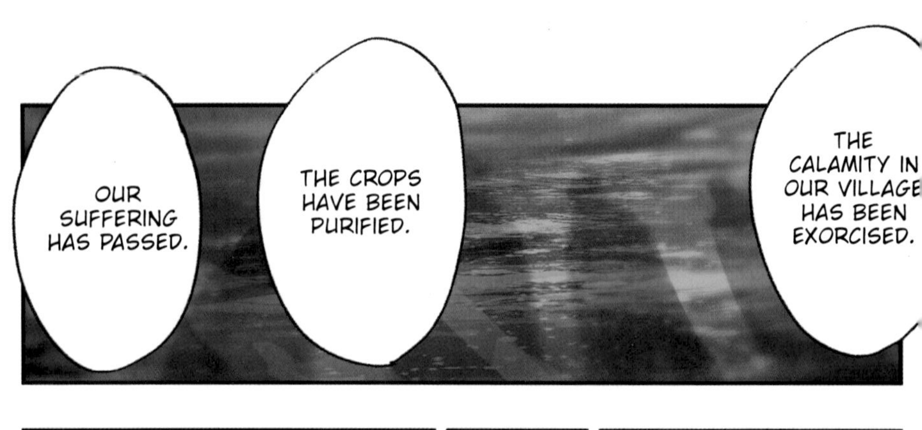
THE CALAMITY IN OUR VILLAGE HAS BEEN EXORCISED.
THE CROPS HAVE BEEN PURIFIED.
OUR SUFFERING HAS PASSED.

ZA (CRUNCH)
......
ZA
HEY...
...YOU OKAY?
NIKO (SMILE)